SHIELD AND SHATTERED CAGES

THE ENERGY OF MAGIC
BOOK ONE

J.E. NEAL

To Chuck — For teaching me how to believe in my own magic

CONTENTS

PROLOGUE

CROWN GOVERNOR JOSEPH LAWSON

"Finally!" Logan Haydenshire huffed as Joseph followed his son Rainer into the kitchen. Joe grinned as Rainer raced to his best friend. They were only two days apart in age and they were a matched set if there had ever been one. "Cal's gonna help us with the fort, and Will's gonna bring fireworks for after dinner." Logan's body couldn't contain his excitement. He was bouncing on his toes.

"Awesome!" Rainer sounded every bit as thrilled. Joseph tried not to feel the sting of regret that always came when he left Rainer with his dearest friends, the Haydenshires. It seemed they were raising his son far more than he was able.

The boys raced outside and were greeted by several of Logan's big brothers. Joe smiled, but the ache in his heart robbed him of breath.

Stephen, Logan's father, pretended not to notice. "Do you have time for a glass of lemonade before your flight?" He gestured to the large blue pottery pitcher on the island.

"Yeah, Rainer was eager to get over here so we left early."

Lillian, Stephen's wife, gave Joseph her kind, reassuring smile. "Here, let's have it on the deck. We'll keep an eye on them while they play."

Joseph assumed his longing to be with his son must've been

evident in his energy rhythms. Lillian could see the pain etch his face and his energy. He followed them out onto their deck and stared out over the vast property Stephen had purchased when they'd won their seats on the governing board.

"Hey, Governor Lawson," Will, the eldest Haydenshire son, approached carrying two large boxes of fireworks. He set them on the porch and offered Joseph his hand.

Joseph smiled. "How are you? Where's that lovely fiancée of yours?"

Will beamed. "I'm good. Brooke's mom is in town. They went to run a few errands, but she'll be here for dinner."

"Where's Garrett?" Lillian asked. "I thought he was riding over with you."

A cloud of concern dampened Will's features. "He uh…he went to check on Dan a while ago. Got another call he didn't like. But he'll be over here once he's sure Dan's all right."

"I wish Daniel would come with him," Lillian worried. "I haven't seen him in ages, not since the funeral I don't think."

"You know he won't."

Joseph and Stephen shared a troubled glance. Joe knew he was going to have to step in on Dan Vindico's account. He just hadn't quite figured out how. He added that to his lengthy list of things to discern.

Stephen settled into one of the deck chairs beside his wife. He wrapped his arm around her shoulders, and Joseph's heart began its familiar ache yet again.

He closed his eyes for an extended blink. His mind thrust him backwards in time against his permission. Maggie's red hair and that luscious, vexing smile formed in the composing imagery. He didn't have time to let his eyes travel down the rest of her gorgeous curves before Stephen interrupted the desperate fantasy. "Did you get that matter that came up Friday taken care of?"

Joe forced the pain away again by sheer strength of will. It had been nine years. How could it still sever his soul every second of every day? He drew an agonized breath and focused on the present, though the past held so much more appeal.

"I get multiple death threats every day. You know that. The only real difference was that this one was credible. Iodex located the guy. He's being detained in New Mexico. The Interfeci was behind this one as well, but you knew that too."

Lillian's relief that the man was in custody juxtaposed Stephen's deep concern that the threats were increasing. A few minutes later, Garrett, the second son in the lengthy line of Haydenshire boys, joined them on the deck.

"How's Daniel?" Lillian asked. Her face betrayed her deep concern.

Garrett shook his head. "I don't know any other way to put it so don't freak, but he's fucked up. Bad."

The fact that neither Lillian nor Stephen asked Garrett to watch his mouth around his younger siblings gave credence to the vow.

Joseph turned his gaze to Rainer. His thirteen-year-old son was carrying a load of scrap lumber that appeared to significantly outweigh him. The boys' mission that summer was to construct a fort in the back of the Haydenshires' property. So far, they'd managed to put together something that looked as if several large trees had been infected with a rampant scrap wood rash, and it had been treated with a heavy dose of rope. The tarp they'd managed to hang at an awkward angle between the trees had given them hope, and they'd continued on with the project.

"I want to help you build the fort," Stephen's only daughter, Emily, with all of her redheaded sass, had given her decree. Joseph chuckled under his breath.

"Go away, Emily!" Connor sneered. "We don't want your help."

"You're so annoying," Logan added in an obvious effort not to be lumped in with Emily by his big brothers.

Stephen scowled from the deck.

"She's fine," Lillian soothed with a slight chuckle at her husband's ever-overprotective treatment of his baby girl.

Emily narrowed those fierce emerald-green eyes. "I am not annoying, and your fort is stupid-looking! You need my help."

"Maybe she could just help us with the walls," Rainer urged.

Joe knew Rainer wasn't just playing peacekeeper. He wanted Emily to come along. He always did. Joseph stopped chuckling and watched Emily beam with pride. Rainer was visibly thrilled.

Joe studied his son's energy rhythms—evident as they developed just above his skin. He was a Shield just like Joseph, an Ioses Predilect, and Joseph couldn't have been more proud.

Construction on the fort ran dry quickly, and the kids returned to the deck for some of Lillian's famous chocolate chip cookies and lemonade. Joseph found himself wishing that life beyond the gates of Haydenshire Farm could be so idyllic for everyone. That's what he was working for. That's what was always out of reach. That's why he traveled more than he should.

"Come push me on the tire swing. We'll take turns." Emily grabbed Rainer's hand. The broad, delighted grin on his son's face as he glanced from their hands to Emily's face made Joseph's day.

"Okay." Rainer let Emily pull him back out onto the grass. Joseph was certain he would've followed her most anywhere. They took off for the swing set.

Lillian chuckled both at her husband's concerned glance and at Joseph's pride. "At least she didn't make him play wedding with her again," she teased Stephen. "Poor Rainer is so sweet to do that with her. I know the boys tease him."

Raw pain formed in Stephen's eyes as he stared after his baby girl.

Joseph shook his head at him. "She's been telling all of us since she was four that she was going to marry him. Take it from me, don't argue with a redhead. It won't get you anywhere."

Before Stephen could insist that his little girl wasn't old enough for love, Emily's terror-ridden screech reached them. Joseph took off toward Rainer. All of the Haydenshires followed in his wake.

He made it to them just as Rainer's shield, the fierce energy that would always protect, formed from his body. Still somewhat undeveloped and a little young for that, Rainer trembled as he pulled Emily back and put himself and his energy shield between Emily and a copperhead poised to strike.

"Shit," Garrett spat as he arrived with his father. Garrett threw his fully developed shield over the kids. At ten years Rainer's senior, he knew how to summon his energy shield from his body, knew how to cast it, and knew how to control it. Rainer did not. His timid shield whirred and trembled the longer he tried to hold it. There were still bands within the shield that weren't developed. They were open and wouldn't keep the snake away.

"Is there more than one?" Stephen demanded.

"Not that I see." Garrett cautiously walked around the large play area.

"Rainer, take Emily back up to the porch. Keep her safe." Joseph said the words he knew would define his son's entire life. It was both who he already was and who he would become.

Rainer scooted Emily back farther as the copperhead slithered closer. His shield continued to pulse in an effort to fully form around her, but it wasn't yet able. "Come on." He grasped her hand and eased her back toward the farmhouse, but they both continued to stare at the snake.

Joseph summoned. His own fierce green orb of protective energy pulsed in his hand. He casted and harnessed the snake's energy. He shared a quick ominous expression with Stephen. Just as they'd both suspected, this was no ordinary Northern Virginia snake.

Defeat tugged in Joseph's shield as he fought the energy from someone else's cast. Someone was controlling the snake.

Joseph flicked his wrist to the right. The snake moved with the motion but remained poised to strike.

Stephen stepped in to help. He summoned his fiercest bands, though he was not a Shield, and joined his cast with Joe's. Steadily, they harnessed and pulled the energy out of the snake. Inky bands of dark castings drained from its skin and fangs until it finally collapsed at Joseph's feet. He threw the energy off him and back out into the air. He didn't want to carry it.

Stephen located a shovel from one of the barns. He removed the head from the beast. "I don't think we should tell the kids," he insisted.

Joseph agreed. "I know, but I'm going to have to try to explain what Rainer just felt happen to him."

"I take it you're not going on your trip right now."

"No. Maybe I'll leave in the morning. I'm going to take him home so he can ask me all the things I'm sure he wants to know."

"You could talk with him here. We could go over it all together with Logan. He's going to want to know what happened with Rainer's shield as well. It won't be too much longer before it will happen to him."

As much as Joseph appreciated the offer, what had happened with Rainer's shield was only half of the conversation he wanted to have with his son. It wasn't only that Rainer was nearing the end of puberty and was going to have full access to his powers soon. It was who had been in danger that had summoned Rainer's shield. Stephen wouldn't likely want to delve into the details of that half of the story. "I think I'll take him on. I don't get to spend near enough time with him."

They headed into the house.

Will grimaced. "I take it we're not doing fireworks for the kids tonight."

Stephen shook his head. "Most definitely not. You're all staying inside this house."

Garrett ended a call on his cell phone. "Iodex is heading in, but you know he's not still out there." He gestured to the backyard. Garrett was already an Elite Iodex officer, a Gifted policeman on the highest skilled force in the Realm, but Joe knew he was right. The snake-caster would be long gone by now.

Joseph eased through Stephen and Lillian's large living room dominated by a sectional sofa that would hold all eight of their kids plus Rainer. "Do you mind if I go up and talk to him?" Joe asked Lillian as he pointed up the stairs to all of the many bedrooms. He knew where Rainer would be.

"Of course not."

Joseph paused to listen on the top step just outside Emily's bedroom.

"Are you sure you're okay?" Rainer's voice cracked in the middle of his question. He coughed in an effort to cover it.

"Yeah, I'm fine. Are you?" Emily's tone was laced with deep concern.

"I'm okay." This time Rainer's voice shook. Joseph knew he wasn't okay. He was likely terrified and fascinated in equal measure.

Simply unable to remain there while his son was afraid, Joseph crested the stairs. "Rainer." He smiled at him seated against the side of Emily's bed right beside her. They were holding hands.

The interlacing of their fingers spoke volumes that would never take on words. Part childhood adoration, part adult relationship, part destiny that could never be rewritten, all woven together within the fingers they both used to use to show off their age.

The tender, hesitant strands of energy developing under their skin were already trying to connect in their palms. Joseph tried to hide his grin. "I...uh...I decided just to fly out tomorrow morning instead of leaving tonight. Why don't we head on home? I'll bring you back in the morning in time for Lillian's blueberry muffins. I promise."

Rainer shifted his concerned eyes back to Emily.

"Can you have dinner with us first?" She trembled beside his son.

He didn't want to leave her, and she didn't want him to go.

Joe gave them both what he hoped was a reassuring smile. "Sure. We'll go after we eat. And hey, I'm really proud of the way you kept her safe." He gestured to Emily. They both beamed up at him.

Two hours later, Joe gave Lillian a quick apologetic glance as Rainer served himself a fourth helping of her lasagna. She chuckled under her breath. "I have seven boys. There's a reason I always make four." She gestured to the four casserole dishes lined up on the lengthy dining room table. They'd been full to bursting with meat sauce, six different kinds of cheese, and noodles. Now, three and a half of them were empty. The salad and bread had been met with almost as much exuberance. Lillian was an Occamy Predilect. She could create most anything, but her cooking was always her masterpiece.

Joe and Stephen did the dishes. They listened to Logan grill Rainer in the living room while they loaded both dishwashers.

"But what did it feel like?" Logan restated the same question he'd asked twice now.

"I don't know. Weird kinda." Rainer shrugged.

"Weird how?"

"I don't know."

"Was it like something inside of you wasn't in there anymore or like you were in two places at once?"

"Logan," they heard Cal say with a chuckle, "lay off him. It won't always feel weird. I promise. You'll get used to it. You're gonna be a mighty strong Shield to have done that at barely thirteen."

Joe was certain that assessment greatly pleased his son.

"When will I be able to do it?" Logan demanded.

Stephen and Joseph both chuckled under their breath.

"There's a reason he was able to do it today. You won't be far behind," Cal assured him.

"What was the reason?" Rainer suddenly sounded far more interested in the conversation.

"Ask your dad."

Joe put the handful of silverware he'd been rinsing into the dishwasher and dried his hands on a nearby towel. "With that, I think we'll head on."

Stephen offered him a wry grin. "I should've just recorded what Lill and I told the oldest four, so I could replay it for the rest," he teased.

Joseph knew Stephen relished every conversation he got to have with any of his kids, difficult or not.

"I guess I only get one shot to do this right. Good thing I work well under pressure."

"Good luck. We'll see you in the morning."

The air outside the farmhouse hung thick with the humidity of an incoming storm. The clouds rolled across the sky, and the air took on the customary sweet pungency of summer rain. Rainer halted just before they reached the '69 Vette that Joe and Rainer had restored recently. "Maybe we shouldn't go yet. Emily doesn't like storms."

Joe nodded his understanding. "Most Receivers don't like storms. We can talk about that too, but she'll be okay. Stephen's not going to let anything happen to his baby girl."

Rainer pulled open the door. "Yeah, but Emily usually wants me to sit in her room with her if it thunders." Joe joined his son in the car and waited on the statement he knew was coming. "I don't want her to be afraid."

"I know, son. But right now, we need to go home and have several long talks. You'll be back over here with Miss Emily tomorrow. Besides," he soothed, "this doesn't look like much more than a summer rain."

Rainer gave him a forced nod, but his jaw clenched and he glared at the clouds like they were his mortal enemy. Joe knew since the clouds were what would frighten Emily, they were.

He drove back through the Haydenshires' lion crest gates and turned onto the road. "Do you want to ask me all of the questions bouncing around in your head or do you want me to just talk and hopefully I'll get them all answered?"

"Can we get milkshakes?"

Joe chuckled. "I'll make you a deal. We'll go get shakes and take them home to drink if you'll ask me whatever you want to know." He pulled in another driveway and turned to go back the direction they'd come from. He headed to Mae's Milkshakes, both a Lawson and a Haydenshire favorite. "Deal?"

Rainer nodded and shot another threatening glare at the offending clouds overhead. "Does that mean I can do that all the time now like you and Garrett can?"

Determined to do this right, to answer each and every question without allowing any discomfort, Joe considered. "Yes and no. You probably won't be able to summon your shield into your hands whenever you want to like I can or like Garrett and Cal can, but if Emily was ever in danger again, you could do it."

Rainer considered as they joined the waiting drive-through line. "I kinda thought that's what Cal meant, but I didn't want to say it in front of Logan."

"Someday, Logan will fall just as in love with someone as you are with Emily, and that person will become the object of Logan's shield the way Emily is of yours."

"You mean...Emily controls my shield?" Rainer didn't sound certain he liked that.

"Not exactly and I'm sorry there aren't easy answers to these questions. We're just going to take them one at a time until you feel like you understand, okay?"

Joe handed Rainer his chocolate shake just as, "I kissed her...on the lips. More than once," spilled from his Rainer's mouth.

One of the greatest parts about Rainer and Emily being kismet almost from birth was that there were things Rainer probably would've told Logan, had he not been Emily's older brother, that he told his dad instead. Joe was tremendously thankful.

"Oh yeah? And how'd you two like that?"

"We liked it, but I'm not sure we did it right. And uh…it kinda made my shield sort of do what it did today only she wasn't scared so maybe I did something wrong."

Joe drew a long sip of his shake to keep from laughing. Once he'd swallowed down the icy confection, he nodded. "Kissing isn't one of those things you have to get just right the first several times you do it. You can keep practicing as long as that's what Emily wants to do as well. And your shield is doing exactly what it's supposed to do. You didn't do anything wrong."

Relief eased his son's tensed features. "Good."

"And I bet your shield didn't do exactly what it did today. I bet it felt a little different, right?" What Rainer had felt was an involuntary reaction from his soul and it had clearly thrown him.

Rainer refused to meet his eyes, but he did manage a quick nod.

"Do you want to talk about the kissing first, or the snake, or about why Emily is afraid of storms? We'll talk about anything you want to know." Joe was perfectly willing to talk about any and all of it. He'd do anything in his vast power to explain the world to his son, to let him know that he understood, and that he wanted to help.

"The kissing." Rainer still refused to meet Joe's eyes. He stared out the window at the onslaught of Virginia pines like they were the most interesting thing in his world.

"I had a feeling." He considered where to begin and wondered if he should pass a law to get children of the Gifted Realm into Gifted education academies at an earlier age. Currently, they all began their Gifted education their junior year of high school, but Joe worried about the kids who didn't have someone to explain it all to them.

He was the Crown Governor. Maybe it was time for a change. "You already know that Gifted people have storehouses of energy in our bodies. Different kinds of energy are housed in different parts. You and Emily both have a storehouse of…"—he really didn't think thirteen was old enough for the word erotic so he went with—"loving energy in your mouths. Emily will, uh, well, she'll have a few more storehouses than you will, but you'll learn all about those at the academy. For now, let's focus on the ones in your mouth. When you kiss, you engage that energy. But both your and Emily's energy strains aren't fully developed yet. So your shield is trying to make itself work, but it's not entirely sure how. Kind of like your old man in the mornings before I've had my coffee."

Rainer smiled at him as he nodded his understanding.

"But the most important thing for you to know is that because you love Emily, your Shielding energy and her Receiver energy will want to be joined. That's why you like kissing and why you like holding her hand. It gives a chance for your rhythms to almost be close enough to combine. But hear me out—don't do the things that cause your energy to fully join Emily's rhythms until you're much, much older. For me, wait, even though you won't want to. It's really intense and..." Joe considered. "It changes a lot of things."

"Like what?"

"Like the way you two interact, the way you share things not only with her but with other people in your life too. You asked me if Emily controls your shield. She doesn't and she does. She will always be the person your shield wants to make certain is the safest all the time. You are *her* Shield. And that means you'll want to keep her safe not only from snakes out to do her harm but also from doing things she's really not old enough to do yet. Things that you know would feel really good but that neither of you are quite old enough to understand. Sometimes you'll have to protect her from herself, and that's not always an easy thing to do when we love someone."

"I don't care. I'll do it," Rainer vowed. "I will want to. It won't be hard because...because I have to keep her safe."

"I know you will. I have no doubt. Just remember what I said. Sometimes keeping her safe and keeping your relationship safe is going to take a tremendous amount of patience and fortitude. Sometimes things might scare her or scare both of you, or there might be something neither of you is sure about, and your shield will want to join your rhythm bands with hers because it will believe that's a way to keep her safe. But it might not really be the best way to handle frightening things. You have to learn to determine when it is a good idea and when it isn't. But we'll keep talking about it all. You don't have to figure any of this out on your own."

The thankfulness in Rainer's eyes warmed Joe's heart. Maybe he was doing all right by his son. God knew he was trying.

"Governor Haydenshire says we aren't old enough to love each other yet, but Emily says he's wrong and I think she's right." There was a heavy note of defiance in the declaration. It pleased Joe. Rainer would need that.

"Don't ever tell Stephen I said this, but Emily is right. He doesn't know what you feel or what Emily feels. And because Emily will be an Empathic Receiver once her bands are fully formed, she can already feel your feelings too. There's no doubt in her mind that you love her. But it's hard on us dads to watch our kids grow up. Sometimes we want to hold on to the time when you were little, because we tell ourselves you're easier to protect when you're babies. That makes us feel better."

Rainer turned his soulful hazel eyes on Joe. "Was the snake after you or after Emily?"

He already knew. As hard as Stephen and Joe tried to protect their children from any knowledge that might frighten them, their kids were too damn smart.

Joe considered for a long moment. "There is a lot of fear in this world, and the thing about fear is that it can make people do terrible things. Other people will tell you it's greed, or pride, or envy that cause people to hurt other people, but fear is the root of all of those and several more. When Governor Haydenshire and I, and all of the governors you know, won our seats on the board, we changed a lot of things. We made the Realm better for so many people, but change is always scary. It can be especially frightening for people who were already letting their fear guide them."

Rainer's brow furrowed. "So, it was after you because you're Crown now?" His voice was choked with terror, and it killed Joe.

His jaw clenched, and he debated. He didn't want to tell Rainer the truth, but his agony betrayed him.

Rainer's chin trembled. His voice shook. "It was after Emily."

Joe managed a haggard nod. "Your shield wouldn't have reacted that way if it had been me."

"But I love you so much. You're my whole family."

"I know, son. And I love you more than life itself, but…your shield works on instinct. And your instincts are to protect Emily at all costs."

The entire American Realm knew that Stephen's pride and joy was his baby girl. If they wanted to punish Stephen, Emily was how they planned to do it. The Realm also knew Rainer and Emily had been bound at the hip since Emily's birth, and they knew Joe lived and breathed for his son. Emily was a high value target, and she wasn't quite twelve years old.

"I'll always keep her safe," Rainer stated with more force than Joe had ever heard him use.

"I know you will. There will always be fear in the world, and that means there will always be danger. There will always be snakes in the grass so to speak. Sometimes those snakes will be much closer than you're aware. Evil can take on many forms. Sometimes we're related to it."

He tried to delicately explain just how close the danger always was. Joseph's own brother was one of the most fearful men he knew.

Rainer nodded and didn't ask. Joe suspected he already knew that as well.

"You know, there are a lot of Gifted legends about Shields and Receivers."

"You said all the legends aren't true."

Joe hemmed. "The thing about legends is that we have to remember who wrote them before we decide that they're infallible. So, most of the legends aren't true because they were written by a Shield and we all tend to cast ourselves as the heroes in our own stories. We don't much care for being told that we aren't. But there is one legend in particular that we can learn from and it is the most important. We have to take everything with a grain of salt so to speak. Want to hear it?"

"Will it help me keep Emily safe?"

"It might help both of you do any number of things throughout your life."

Rainer nodded adamantly as they pulled in their garage.

"A long, long time ago…"

"Why do legends always start a long, long time ago?" Rainer interrupted.

Joe chuckled at him. "Legend status has to be earned, don't you think? Anything less than a hundred years old is just a story, not a legend. Now, can I go on?"

Rainer nodded and a slight heat settled in his cheeks.

"So, a long, long time ago there was an extremely powerful Receiver named Sentina. She was exceptionally Gifted. She could feel the emotional energy around her all the time, from everyone. She could feel the emotions of not only her people but those of neighboring lands and the energy in events that were to come. Just like you and Emily, she grew up with a Shield she loved very much. His name was Cuthwolf."

"Cool name," Rainer said.

Joe grinned. "He earned his name. His family's crest was the wolf, known for wisdom and the ability to hunt down their enemies and end them quickly as long as the pack worked together. Sentina's father was a highly skilled Occamist. He could grow most anything. He worked the king's land near the castle, and Cuthwolf's uncle was the king. He lived in the palace so they were together most every day.

"But they lived in a place where fear had taken hold. War had broken out, and there was constant fighting. That's what happens when we become so afraid of people who are different from us that we try to destroy them and their way of life instead of trying to understand them."

Rainer's brow furrowed. "But Cuthwolf was her Shield so he kept her from getting hurt in the wars, right?"

"He certainly tried," Joseph eased. "But remember I told you how powerful she was. She could feel the emotional energy around her from all over, not just from the people she was near."

"Is that the part that isn't true?"

"That part was true, but I don't personally know any Receivers who are that powerful anymore. There might be some though. Right after Sentina and Cuthwolf turned eighteen, another war broke out in a neighboring land, and the invading forces got closer and closer to Cuthwolf's uncle's kingdom. Sentina could feel them and sense their actions all around her. The closer they got the harder it was for her because she could feel all of their fear and the hatred that came from the fear.

"Meanwhile, Cuthwolf's uncle's armies prepared to fight. The only time Sentina couldn't feel the warring emotions was when she was in Cuthwolf's shield. That's the only time any Receiver can fully process the emotional energy they have to take on. It's the only place they don't have to feel anything but their own emotions and those of the Shield's that they're in."

Rainer drew a long sip of his milkshake. "So when I'm older and my shield works right, if Emily is sad or scared or has a bad day or something, I can put her in my shield and make her feel better?"

Joe nodded. "Yes, but remember that you can also talk to her about what she's feeling and believe her when she tells you something is going to happen. They know, but they get discounted all the time. Emotions rule the world, and they frighten people so they prefer to pretend that Receivers don't really know what they're talking about. That's what happened with Sentina and Cuthwolf.

"She woke him up terrified in the middle of the night and told him that if his uncle went to battle the next day, like he was planning to, that their kingdom would be lost. She could feel the devastation that was to come. She begged Cuthwolf to tell his uncle not to go, not to fight, because if they did they would lose."

"Did he tell his uncle?"

"He did. He was her Shield, true and good and loyal to her and her alone. He told his uncle what Sentina said would happen. But his uncle had seen Sentina crying and reacting to everything she was having to feel. He thought she was weak so he didn't listen. He was known as a skilled fighter and hunter, remember? He was a Vis Virres Predilect, an enforcer, so he didn't much care for listening to anyone other than himself. So, instead of listening to a Receiver, he listened to his own ego, and he lost almost seventy percent of his army that day and all of his land."

"Then what happened?"

"See, it's a pretty good story, right?" Joe winked at Rainer. "When the king came back to his palace and found it being overtaken by the bad guys, he was enraged, and he was afraid. Instead of admitting that he should've listened, he ordered Sentina to be executed."

Rainer's eyes goggled. "Why?!"

"Because his ego was running the show. He convinced himself that Sentina had cursed his armies and that it was her fault they'd lost."

"Did Cuthwolf save her?!"

"He did. He rushed to her as soon as he heard the decree, and he took her from her home and from her family and they ran away. But imagine how useful it would be to men out to do harm to have access to someone with Sentina's powers. As the king sent out his remaining men to find her, the legends of her powers grew even larger than they existed in reality. She became a very valuable prize. She was in constant danger, and Cuthwolf blamed himself. If he'd never told his uncle of her prediction, then his uncle wouldn't have known of her far-reaching powers. The farther they ran away and the harder he tried to keep her safe, the more relentless the people after her powers became."

"Did they catch her?"

"Eventually, yes. But before that they killed her family trying to get Cuthwolf to give her up."

"I don't like this story anymore."

Joe nodded. "I know, but listen anyway. Cuthwolf never left her side. He was her Shield, but he continued to blame himself for telling his uncle about her powers. He became so afraid for her that his shield overtook his mind."

Realization dawned on his son. "So, it was like you just said where he put her in his shield but he didn't talk to her about what was wrong."

Joe nodded. "Eventually, he convinced himself that she was better off without him. That he'd brought her so much pain he should leave so he couldn't cause her any more."

"But wouldn't that make her have even more pain?"

"Yes, but his shield had overtaken his brain, remember?"

"Then what happened?"

"One of the warring countries captured her, but they wanted her predictions so they didn't want to do her harm. But after Cuthwolf left, she no longer had a Shield to allow her to process all of the emotional energy she was having to take on, and her own devastation over him leaving affected her ability to make predictions. And Cuthwolf was no better. After he left her, he was no longer able to summon and cast his shield. He hunted day and night and slaughtered anyone who'd ever threatened her. Endlessly. He lived for the fight and nothing else. That's all that made sense to him. To end anything or anyone who might do her harm. He warred and ravaged for months until he made his way back to where they'd come from."

"He was gonna kill his uncle," Rainer knew.

"That was his plan. While he was out hunting down his uncle, Sentina made a prediction for her captors, but Cuthwolf was so far away from her by then that her prediction was wrong. She'd read the energy incorrectly because her Shield was gone, and she was so devastated she couldn't feel through her own pain. They executed her for being wrong, and Cuthwolf's uncle executed him for losing him his kingdom. Cuthwolf couldn't defend himself against his uncle because he could no longer cast a shield."

Rainer gave him a bewildered glare. "Why did you tell me that, and what does it have to do with me and Emily?"

"I know it's a terrible legend, but we can't change it so what can we learn from it?"

Rainer's brow furrowed. "Not to tell anyone about Emily's powers."

Joe shook his head. "Try again."

"To listen to her and not let my shield overtake my brain."

"There you go. That story is where the belief came from that there is one Receiver for every Shield and that if you separate them for any reason, they'll both perish. I don't believe that every Shield needs a Receiver or vice versa. The way the legends are always written is that Receivers need Shields to save them, and that isn't true either. If I'd been writing the legend, I would've changed a few things."

"I hope so," Rainer huffed.

"See, I bet Sentina could've cured Cuthwolf. She could have taken all of his guilt and his self-hatred over what had happened to her from his shield, but he clung to it. He shielded it inside of himself and wouldn't let her have it. If he'd allowed himself to be healed by her, they could have lived happily ever after in another kingdom. But he discounted her powers as well. He didn't really believe that she was the more powerful force because he didn't think she could possibly be stronger than his shield. And ultimately, that was both of their undoing. You and Emily can make entirely different choices."

CHAPTER 1

THE GIFTED REALM

RAINER LAWSON - AGE 20

"He's gonna kill us!" Logan Haydenshire panicked as both he and Rainer hit the thick blue mat of the Venton Gifted Academy Gym with a hard slap of their bodies under the intense shield cast. The stench of sweat and gym socks combined with the force of the hit threatened to make Rainer vomit.

He shook his head. "He's not allowed to kill us."

"Has anyone told him that?"

Rainer gritted his teeth. He had to get up. This was it. This was what he'd wanted since he was old enough to know what National Elite Iodex was. He and Logan had worked too hard, they'd studied too long, they'd worked their asses off for this day, and he wasn't going to let the opportunity slip through his aching hands.

"Come on, Lawson, if you want something fight for it," Dan Vindico, the Chief of Elite Iodex, urged them on despite the fact that for this duel he was their opponent.

Rainer dragged himself back up. Sweat poured down his face. Dammit, he was better than this. He was the Venton Academy Head of Ioses Order for his graduating class. He was Joseph Lawson's son. He could do this.

He summoned and cast his shield out at who he sincerely prayed after this match would become his and Logan's boss. The fact that

Vindico looked both amused and bored did nothing to bolster his badly bruised ego.

Logan joined his shield cast with Rainer's. Okay, this was good. Dan Vindico was an incredibly rare Double-Predilect of equal Gift. So, two on one seemed fair in this scenario.

The gym glowed in fierce green energy. Vindico chuckled. Rainer and Logan advanced and pushed their combined shields toward him. Suddenly, Vindico summoned his fierce shield with both hands and drew them apart. Crackles of protective energy sizzled between his hands.

"Oh shit," Logan whispered. "I've seen Garrett do that before."

Vindico projected and harnessed their combined shields. He siphoned the energy out of their casts. Once he'd pulled more than half of their combined energy into his own massive, muscle-bound body, he projected the cast back out, and once again Rainer and Logan hit the mat hard.

Dan Vindico

Dan tried to figure out if making Rainer and Logan endure this for twenty minutes was enough to sell them the story he was about to tell them. He didn't give a damn how well they fought. He didn't care that they were at the top of the graduating class. Didn't give a flying fuck whose kids they were or how strong they were in their Predilect.

They both had something he wanted desperately. Something no one could train into them, no one could purchase, and no birthright could guarantee. Their vengeance was all Dan needed.

He could turn them into warriors. It was their losses he sought, not their power. Logan's brother Cal had been murdered four years before and both of Rainer's parents had been killed prior to that. Governor Lawson had been assassinated when Rainer was only fourteen years old. All of the death that Logan and Rainer had endured had been executed under the orders of the man Dan wanted to crucify above all others. He'd watch Dominic

Wretchkinsides burn for what he'd stolen from Dan ten years before.

They both had scores to settle, and that was worth ten times more than every single dollar Rainer Lawson was set to inherit here in a few days' time. Besides, he owed Joseph Lawson his life, so making sure Rainer never had to live Dan's life-shattering regrets was how he would pay back his debt to Governor Lawson.

Dan dropped his cast, and they followed suit. They both looked crushed, and Dan grimaced. He let them go on too long. "You were both great," he immediately vowed. Truthfully, they weren't bad, just untrained.

Neither of them looked like they believed him for a second. "I'm serious. I've seen a lot of academy grads, and that's the best I've seen come out of here since Garrett graduated." If he wanted the vengeance, he had to access the ego. "I can't wait to get you on the Elite team. Congratulations!"

Their eyes goggled. "We made it?" Logan sounded like he was concerned he'd taken a hit to the head.

"Hell yeah. We'll get you trained. I'll teach you to siphon a shield. I'll teach you everything you need to know. You've got a ton of raw talent." That was true. The fact that Venton Academy had done a piss-poor job of teaching them to use it wasn't the point.

"Thank you, sir." Rainer's expression was still one of shocked excitement. But it fell a moment later. "But…" he choked.

"What?" Dan demanded.

"I just…" he hesitated.

"*We* just…" Logan corrected.

"You just what?"

Logan and Rainer shared a quick glance.

"We pretty much sucked, and we don't want spots on the team because of our dads," Logan explained.

"Your fathers have nothing to do with why I'm offering you spots on National Elite Iodex Squadron. I promise, but I appreciate you saying that. I get growing up in the shadow of a governor." Dan's father was a governor as well. "It'd piss me off to think your dad only made me Chief because of my old man." He gestured to Rainer. "You both earned this entirely of your own merit. Like I said, congrats. I can't wait to get you on the team. If you want to start before Service Day, let me know. I'll get you in." He sincerely hoped they'd take him up on the offer. As soon as Rainer accessed his inheritance, the price on Emily's head would go up exponentially. Rainer needed to know how to keep her safe.

He shook both of their hands and tried not to chuckle at their wide-eyed thrill. He'd make men out of them yet. He just needed a little time.

~

Rainer Lawson

When Rainer and Logan finally made their exit from the gym, Emily was standing right outside the doors. "You made it!" She threw her arms around Rainer and bounced up and down. He tried not to enjoy the way her breasts slid against him when she did that since her big brother was standing not two feet away.

"You could've let him tell you," Logan harassed.

But she didn't need Rainer to tell her. She could feel both of their glee.

"I'm so proud of you both!" She turned and threw her arms around Logan.

"Thanks."

"Tomorrow is our exit exam, and Friday we're graduating, and this is exactly the way we planned it." She was exuberant.

Logan chuckled at her. "I guess I'll let you congratulate him the way he wants you to. I'm going to go find Adeline. Don't get kicked out of here with one day left for feeling her up in the hallway," he goaded Rainer.

CHAPTER 2
EDUCATED MEMORIES

The next day Rainer deleted and corrected one line in his final essay on all the many ways the Gifted people had used their powers illegally over Non-Gifted people. He reread the second paragraph one final time. Then with a rock-like snare closing in his throat, he summoned the energy housed in his laptop, saved the file, and sent it to Mentor Durtrox's computer at the front of the room.

It was over. The words struck him. Six long years he'd been preparing for it to be over, and he'd just completed his *final*, final exam.

Graduation was Friday night, and the Haydenshires were throwing a big party after the ceremony. This had been the tradition whenever one of their children was graduating, which was most every year. This year would be no different.

In fact, Mrs. Haydenshire was going all out since Logan and Emily were graduating together. The Haydenshires always insisted that it was three of their children graduating that year, instead of just two. They always counted Rainer as their own. He'd never deserve them.

Emily and Logan sat a few desks ahead of him since they'd been arranged alphabetically. She was still working on her essay. Her lips were pursed, and she brushed a strand of her long auburn hair behind her right ear to cover the bright pink, heart-shaped birthmark there.

Rainer loved it, but she hated it. He'd taken to kissing it whenever he got the opportunity just to make her roll her eyes and grin at him.

Fergus Martin, a friend of Rainer and Logan's, popped Rainer on the back of the head. He turned to scowl at him. Fergus's slumped stature only added to his lack of height, and half of his face was his nose.

"Are you finished?" Fergus mouthed his concern.

Rainer nodded. If he didn't know all of the stuff his dad had accomplished well enough to put it in essay format, he certainly didn't deserve to be graduating top of the class at Venton that year.

Fergus rolled his eyes and shook his head, clearly not thinking Rainer was taking their exit exam seriously enough. But Rainer had far more important things on his mind. Besides, he'd just earned his spot on Elite Iodex. Everything else was a formality at this point.

Since he had a few minutes, he indulged himself in images of what was to come in the next few weeks. He tried only to think about how they were now officially adults and were going to have jobs and maybe get a place to live that wasn't at Emily's parents' house, but his mind was far more interested in her wishes that she expressed with more and more frequency as they neared graduation.

Being madly in love with the only girl in a family of twelve could be potentially hazardous to one's health. For instance, if one were to be found making out heatedly with said girl on the couch one evening. If, say, her bra happened to be lying on the floor, and her jeans happened to be unzipped, after everyone else had turned in. He'd found this out the hard way when the governor had appeared suddenly one evening a few months ago.

Rainer had insisted that they cool it off unless they were certain they were alone, but she'd propositioned him yet again. She wanted to take things further, and she wanted to do this on graduation night.

With another glance at the clock, Rainer allowed himself the last minute of his final class to panic over her plans. His father's words of warning from years before replayed in his mind so often he both wished they'd give him a break and hoped they'd remain. He tried desperately to remember every word his father had ever spoken to him before his assassination. Rainer clung to the memories since he could no longer cling to his father.

It would change things between them echoed against his skull. He didn't want anything to change. She was perfect. He was her Shield. What more could he ask for than that? Why did everything always have to change?

As much as he longed to be with her, to combine their energies together, he didn't want her to do something just because it would feel absolutely incredible. He had to make certain she was really ready. He knew if his father were still alive that's what he'd tell him to do, to make sure she was truly prepared for what she kept saying she wanted.

It didn't help that Logan was not only his very best friend in the world but was also the guy he normally talked over everything with. They had become blood brothers when they were six. This had happened by the sheer convenience of it all. They'd ridden their bikes into one another accidentally and had both been bleeding from the incident. Instead of returning to the Haydenshires' farmhouse to be cleaned up and healed, they'd simply used the blood for the purpose of cementing their friendship. It had seemed very logical at the time.

Being best friends and blood brothers with your girlfriend's extremely protective older brother made discussing plans to take things further with her rather uncomfortable.

For what must've been the millionth time in the last seven years, Rainer longed to talk with his dad. His father would know if they were really ready to do what she was damned and determined they were going to do Friday night. His father knew everything, and he always knew how to make Rainer understand. Now, he had no one to talk to about this.

The bell rang and effectively ended his panic and lamentations. Rainer reached instinctively and caught Fergus as his shoe got got hung on the leg of his desk and he almost fell on the floor. Rainer shook his head and gathered his things.

Emily scooted in front of him as he made his way to the door. He planted a kiss on the top of her head. She grinned up at him sweetly.

Mentor Durtrox glared at Rainer. "If you feel you could keep your lips off of Miss Haydenshire whilst in my classroom, the gesture would be most appreciated by myself and your classmates."

Rebellion flooded his energy. "How about I promise never to do it again?"

Logan and Emily laughed. Since this was the last time he'd ever be in her classroom, he didn't believe that would be a problem.

Mentor Durtrox didn't find his quip entertaining in the least, so he pulled Emily out the door before he risked his exam grade reflecting his retort.

CHAPTER 3

MANY PATHS TO BECOMING A MAN

They traipsed along the concrete paths that divided the many varied brick buildings and manicured lawns of Venton Academy. All children of Gifted families in Virginia began attending the academy their junior year of high school. It was the Realm's premier Gifted school. All of the children of the national governors attended there.

As it was fairly well-known amongst Gifted and Non-Gifted alike, Non-Gifted children often applied to the college, but they were always denied entrance. The explanations that the school had unheard-of qualifications and extremely rigorous classes were most often cited as the reasoning. This also provided a nice way for the Gifted graduates from the academy to find jobs in the Non-Gifted world.

It was the end of May, and the weather in Arlington couldn't have been more beautiful. It was quintessentially spring. Rainer would've much preferred taking Emily on a drive up the parkway with the top down instead of going to make certain his uncle actually had food and that rats hadn't taken over the apartment again. He wrapped his arm around Emily.

"Can you believe we're actually done?" she squealed. He kissed the side of her head as they walked.

"I can believe that I am actually done. I cannot believe *you* are actually done." She'd done it. She'd combined her sub-freshman and pre-freshman years' classes, worked her gorgeous ass off, and was graduating with him. He'd never deserve her, but my god, he'd never stop trying to.

She beamed as they approached his car in the parking lot off of the Humanities building. His father had written into the will that Rainer was to be given a portion of the estate upon turning sixteen for the purpose of purchasing a car. Rainer had taken to the task with great finesse. He and his father shared a deep, fanatical love of classic American automobiles. Some of their best conversations happened over the opened hoods of cars Joseph rebuilt with Rainer.

Although he loved his car, he wasn't terribly interested in acquiring the rest of his parents' estate in two days' time other than to pay back the Haydenshires for all they'd done for him his whole life. He saw his acquisition as a complication for the most part.

He held open the door of his 1964 and a half crimson Mustang convertible with Le Mans stripes.

He placed his hand on the curve of Emily's back and guided her into the seat. That touch alone had him reeling. He ached to run his hands over all of her luscious curves, but her proposition had him nervous again as he sank into the cushioned leather seat and turned the key. He revved the engine just to make her smile and slung his arm behind her seat to check behind him as he eased out of his parking space. He loved the way her eyes always lit when he did that.

Rainer chuckled as he took in Logan backing his girlfriend Adeline Parker up against the brick wall of the breezeway between the Humanities building and one of the Science buildings. He leaned, and she gave him a grin that unmistakably said, come get me. Emily giggled at her brother's moves.

Rainer took it slow through the winding lanes of the academy. He tried to get his mind off what he'd like to be doing with Emily. He reminded himself to take in the beautiful campus since it would be one of the last times he'd be making this drive as a student.

"I want to go with you," Emily started in as soon as they made their way onto Venton Drive.

"Em,"—he shot her a pleading gaze—"I'm just gonna go down there and make sure he hasn't imploded. I need to go today. I want to spend all day with you tomorrow, and I really don't want to see him Friday." She knew perfectly well why seeing his loafing uncle on his twenty-first birthday could be problematic to say the least.

"But none of that is a reason why I can't go with you now."

"You can't go with me now, Miss Haydenshire, because he is a vile, repulsive individual who I would never allow you to be within arm's length of and because he lives in the most dangerous part of Norfolk."

Emily gave her customary eye roll. "Says my boyfriend, head of Ioses Order."

"He's my uncle, my only living relative. I owe it to my dad to go check on him, but I don't care how well trained I am, or what Order I'm the head of. I'm not dragging the love of my life into god-only-knows-what I might find when I get there. I'm your shield. And trust me, based on my Elite tryouts, I still have a ton to learn."

Rainer tried not to pout. He'd love nothing more than to spend the six plus hours round trip in the car with her. Especially if along the route somewhere, they could stop and maybe do a little more than talk, but he wasn't giving in.

He'd walked in on too many extremely disturbing things on his biweekly trips to check on his uncle. He would never allow Emily to be near his Uncle Stan. She crossed her arms over her chest and stared out the open top of his convertible. She glared at the onslaught of pine trees like they'd greatly offended her.

"But you'll be gone all afternoon and half the night." She gestured at the clock on the dashboard. Well aware that she might smack his hand away, he moved his hand from the gear shift to her thigh.

"I know, baby," he soothed as he stroked her leg. "But just please let me go do this, and then tomorrow we'll do whatever you want to do, okay?"

"Whatever I want," she challenged.

"Em, come on." He willed calm into his tone as he turned onto the two-lane that lead to the Haydenshires' vast farm.

"We are going away this weekend."

"So I've been told."

"You know, I'm kind of starting to get a complex." He saw it as her eyes flashed and her jaw clenched. As many times as he'd tried to explain to her why he was nervous, she just kept settling on the preposterous idea that he didn't want her. He hit the brakes and made a turn down a dirt lane several miles from her parents' homestead.

"What are you doing?"

"We're going to talk." He took it slow over the bumpy lane. He pulled into a spot that overlooked a cluster of trees and turned off the car.

"Now, you want to tell me why you're so upset? I know that you know I have to go see my uncle. And you also know that there isn't anything I want more than you. So, what's going on?"

"I don't know," her voice caught, as she gazed at a blue bird building a nest in a tree nearby. Rainer put his arm around her and scooted her closer to him. It was moments like this when he wondered if he should have purchased an automatic since the gearshift was between them. He waited on her to continue. He knew there was more, and when you'd been with the same girl since you were four years old, you knew when to wait and when to talk.

"Everything is changing," finally spilled from her lips in a quivering gush. "You're going to go off and join Iodex, and I'm going to try desperately to play for the Angels, or go and work for Auxiliary Order, and what then?" She shrugged. "I didn't do all of this work to graduate with you to never get to see you." He held her and rubbed her back as he kissed her forehead.

Receivers like Emily felt every emotion of the Gifted people around them. It tended to make them extremely empathetic and also very emotional themselves. If Rainer was nervous or upset, Emily could feel it. If her parents or one of her brothers was having a difficult time with something, she felt that as well.

Because Receivers could feel emotions all around them, they tended to develop their own internal shields of sorts. But relationships between Receivers and Ioses Predilects Shields were extremely common, and they tended to last. Receivers needed Shields to protect them from the often exhaustive emotional lives they led. If a Receiver was inside an Ioses's shield, it would block out the emotions all around them. It gave them time and space to process all of the emotional energy they'd taken on.

Protectors needed Receivers to soften their view of the world. They usually needed help thinking with their hearts and not always with their logistical minds. Shields could make terrible decisions if they let their protective energy overtake every other thought. And Receivers were the only Predilect capable of pulling emotions out of a Shield.

"Baby, nothing, not one single thing, not Iodex, and not the Angels, or the Auxiliary, is as important to me as you are. I would give it all up in a second if I thought any of that was going to come between us. We'll do whatever you want to do." He tenderly wiped away her tears with his thumbs. "I don't know if you know this…" he teased. "But I happen to be coming into a fair amount of money here in a day or two. If you still want us to move in together, nothing would make me happier. I'm just a little worried your dad might shoot me." He'd finally made her giggle. Her smile faded fast though.

"So, you want to move in with me, you just won't sleep with me."

"Emily Anne Haydenshire, I feel very, very certain that I've said all of this before, but allow me to reiterate—our first time will not be in my car. It will be in a bed, and for you that bed should be in a palace."

She rolled her eyes at what she considered hyperbole, but he was quite serious.

He continued, "Your parents have given me everything good in my life, most importantly you. I want to be able to look your father in the eye when I sit down at his table and eat his food. That may not be a big deal to other people, but it's a huge deal to me. I love you. I want to spend the rest of my life with you. If you're ready for us to start sleeping together, then I want that as well, but it will be treated with the respect that it deserves and that you deserve." This finally seemed to elicit a genuine smile.

"I know, and I love that you feel that way, but I want to be with you like that. I want to join our energy streams. They've wanted that forever now. I want to move in with you, and marry you, and I want us to go off and celebrate being done with school. Just take a little time for us before we go about doing all of the things we've been training to do for the past six years." She used the full power of her emerald-green eyes to plead her case.

"You're sure?" He'd heard this often enough to know that she was.

"Yes," she urged.

"And you don't think it might irritate your father or any of your brothers that I'm taking you off to have my way with you?"

She laughed. "I might not phrase it that way. I know Henry and Keaton can be terrifying." He rolled his eyes. The toddlers weren't really who he was concerned about. "But, no, I don't think they'll mind. I'm almost twenty years old. Everyone thought we'd done that after we got back from London."

He glanced at the clock discreetly. He didn't want to rush her if she needed to talk, but he also didn't want to be driving back from Norfolk at midnight. He also didn't want to think about the two weeks he'd spent in London without her. That was the stupidest mistake he'd ever made. He'd left her trying to keep her safe, but all he'd succeeded in doing was destroying both of them.

"Okay, where do you want to go?" he asked.

"Let's go to the beach house." A delighted grin lit her face.

"It's still too cold to swim." He studied her.

"I don't want to swim." Her eyes darkened slightly, and the real estate in his jeans became nonexistent.

"You think your parents will be okay with that?" He'd been with the Haydenshires to their beach house for vacations most of his life. He'd even gone with his parents when they were alive. It had never entered his psyche that at some point he might be staying in one of the master bedrooms with the Haydenshires' only daughter.

"They'll be fine with it." She was growing annoyed with his constant concern over what her parents might think.

"Do you want me to ask them?" He was certain he should be the one doing the asking, but she shook her head.

"No, I'll talk to them tonight while you and Logan are gone." She smirked. She knew him too well. She'd known all along that he'd ask Logan to go to Norfolk with him, and that Logan would agree.

"I love you so much." He gazed into the depths of her eyes, the windows to her soul.

"I love you too." She leaned in as he placed his hand on her cheek and guided her lips to his.

As soon as he tasted her, he decided Norfolk and his uncle could wait. She was the sweetest candy he'd ever had in his mouth. He slipped his tongue between her lips and devoured the energy there as he held her face tenderly.

He let his other hand travel back to her thigh. She shifted, and his hand slipped under her skirt. With a hungry moan, he began to knead her silky skin.

Her hands brushed over him as she began to caress his zipper line. He needed to stop her, but he desperately wanted her to keep going. Unable to fight it, he traced his hands up her thigh and hesitantly caressed the scrap of damp satin between her legs. She panted and let her legs fall farther apart.

"That's it, baby," he coaxed. The wet heat urged him onward. He slipped his fingers under her thong.

"Yes." She panted.

He shook himself. "Not in my car," he vowed more to himself than to her. She nodded and let her eyes open hesitantly. She seemed to be willing composure as much as he was.

"Okay, but Friday night at the beach house."

Rainer swallowed hard as he nodded. He cranked the car and backed up enough to turn around. His mind was full of her, the sweet heavenly way she smelled, the way she tasted, the way her hands felt on his cock. And god, the way she felt in his hands. He wanted it all, and he wanted it now.

He forced himself from his reverie as he turned down the gravel lane that led to Haydenshire Farm. He proceeded through the massive wrought-iron gates that displayed the Haydenshire crest—the lion seated inside the widespread falcon wings. It was the perfect crest for the Haydenshires. The lion represented the strength of family and fierce protectors, and the falcon was the sign of all Gifted families within the American Realm. It stood for the understanding of the earth's energies.

The Lawsons' crest had a Phoenix splayed over the falcon wings. It stood for overcoming impossible odds and transformation. That was certainly what his father had done and what he'd expected of Rainer. As he forced that pressure from his mind, for the moment at least, he made the approach to the large barn where all of the Haydenshires parked their cars.

Logan's hand-me-down Accord was already there next to Mrs. Haydenshire's Suburban. The governor's minivan was missing, as was Patrick's recently acquired F-150 and Connor's Supra. They were all still at work in DC.

CHAPTER 4

THE FARMHOUSE

They took in the expansive farmland as they approached the house. Rainer opened the door and they entered the kitchen.

"Where'd you go?" Logan mumbled with a hunk of apple in his mouth that he'd just plucked from a bowl on the windowsill. Adeline giggled as she watched him and shook her head.

Rainer shrugged. "Just to hang out for a few before I head to Norfolk."

The twins raced into the kitchen with Mrs. Haydenshire following in their wake. Both boys were wearing nothing but diapers and wielding water guns. Rainer laughed as he and Emily each scooped up one of her little brothers.

"We only play with water guns out in the yard." Mrs. Haydenshire removed the weapons from the boys' grasp. She also used the opportunity she'd gotten with the twins unable to run away to slip T-shirts over their heads and shorts over their diapers. "Not in Mommy and Daddy's bedroom," she finished her scolding as everyone tried not to laugh.

Emily grinned. "Adeline, why don't you stay here with me since Rainer is just about to ask Logan to go with him to Norfolk?"

Logan nodded. "Actually, I was going to offer. We haven't hung out in forever, and I've been craving Griddle's."

Logan was well over six feet tall, just like his father and brothers. They were all tall and muscular, but Logan was also perpetually hungry. Griddle's was a diner in Norfolk, and its most-bragged-about dish was a seven egg omelet. It was Logan's favorite.

Since Rainer stood just slightly below six feet, he was thankful Emily had taken after her mother and was on the shorter side. He'd never understand Emily's concern that she was too short and too curvy, which she informed him of on a regular basis. To him, she was perfection. She was petite and had ample cleavage, which Rainer generally drooled over. It went right along with her equally luscious ass. She qualified herself as short and in need of losing weight, no matter how many times he'd adamantly disagreed.

Mrs. Haydenshire relieved Rainer of Keaton. "You can't save people who don't want to be saved," she reminded him. Her words shook Rainer from his reverie over Emily. Keaton placed his thumb in his mouth and laid his head on his mother's shoulder.

"I know." This was something she quoted to him whenever he insisted on checking on his uncle. "But I owe it to my dad to check on Stan occasionally."

Adeline looked concerned. "I probably shouldn't stay. I need to get home."

Logan clenched his jaw. Adeline's mother was a source of constant tension in their relationship. Logan had been begging her to come and live on the Haydenshires' farm for years now, but she'd adamantly refused to leave her mother to fend for herself. Adeline's mother, Candy Parker, was Non-Gifted. She was also perpetually abusive to Adeline and frequently banned her from their apartment when she was practicing her chosen profession of prostitution with drug-dealing as a side hustle.

Mrs. Haydenshire stepped in again. "We'd love you to stay for dinner even if you can't spend the night. I'm certain you and Emily have lots to talk about with graduation Friday."

Mrs. Haydenshire was always happy to celebrate any child's accomplishments, whether she'd given birth to them or not, but she'd been a bit melancholy over having Logan, Emily, and Rainer all graduating the same year.

Adeline's weight was another concern for both Logan and Mrs. Haydenshire. She was painfully thin. It was well-known that any money Adeline's mother received went to support her many varied habits and not to feed her daughter. To combat this, Mrs. Haydenshire plied her with food any time Adeline was at the farmhouse. Rainer was certain that was why she wanted her to at least stay for dinner.

There was already a cherry pie in a covered cake plate on the large island that ran through the center of the Haydenshires' kitchen that Adeline had been eyeing.

"Why don't you at least call and see if your mom would mind you staying here tonight with Emily though, and then Logan can take you home tomorrow?" Mrs. Haydenshire suggested. Relief played heavily in Adeline's eyes.

Rainer's heart pricked. He couldn't imagine what Logan went through as he watched the abuse Adeline suffered at the hands of her mother.

"Are you sure it wouldn't be any trouble?" Adeline asked.

"No sweetheart, we'd be thrilled to have you as long as you'd like to stay," she urged for what must have been the hundredth time in the almost five-year span that Logan and Adeline had been dating.

"I'll just call my mom."

Logan pulled his cell phone from his pocket and handed it to her. She smiled up at him, but he braced himself. He seemed to have a pretty good idea how her conversation was likely to go.

Everyone in the kitchen heard Adeline hesitantly explain her plans to her mother and then insist that she had no money. She promised she'd see if she could come up with some by the next day.

"I'll see you tomorrow." She shook her head. "No, Mother," she spat.

Everyone was aware that Candy had asked Adeline if Logan had any money, but no one commented. She handed Logan's phone back to him, though he insisted she keep it when she wasn't with him.

He shook his head. "Rainer has his. We probably won't be back until after you're asleep. Just call him if you need me."

"All right. It's nap time for my littlest ones." Mrs. Haydenshire hoisted Henry from Emily's arms and put him on her right hip.

Keaton was almost asleep on the other. "You two be careful, and don't be out too late, please."

"We're taking the Mustang, right?" Logan asked.

"Of course," Rainer assured him.

Logan pulled Adeline outside with him. Rainer made the same move with Emily. They all headed back to the barn.

Adeline gave one longing look back at the farmhouse kitchen, with its soothing colors of creams and blues. Shelves that contained Mrs. Haydenshire's cookbooks and sewing books, along with mixing bowls and the twins' latest finger paintings were all on display.

Glass canisters filled with many varied candies, homemade cookies, and snacks for anyone who might be hungry between meals were situated neatly around the large room. Adeline and Rainer's report cards were on the refrigerator amongst school schedules and crayon drawings. They'd both received straight As the first semester of the year. The homemade potholders, crafted by Will, Garrett, and Levi when they were in elementary school, were on the counter under a large pot of chili set to stay warm under Mrs. Haydenshire's cast. Her rocking chair, where all of her children and Rainer had been rocked to sleep or soothed throughout their life, was near the stone fireplace, with a quilt slung over its back.

Rainer knew how Adeline felt. It was what a home was supposed to feel like. It was peaceful, calming, and welcoming. He knew that both Emily and Logan adored their parents and their home, but they'd never fully appreciate what it meant to those who didn't have a soft place to land when the world outside took its toll.

"Will you come kiss me good night?" Emily teased as she walked Rainer to his car.

"That's my favorite part of the entire day."

Emily beamed as he brushed his finger across her cheekbone and watched her eyelashes lower delicately. She leaned up on her tiptoes to brush a kiss across his jaw.

"Please be careful."

"I thought it was okay because I'm the Head of Ioses." He winked at her.

"Yeah, well." She rolled her eyes as he chuckled. Rainer grabbed her hand as she started to walk away. He pulled her back for a long, drawn kiss.

Logan cleared his throat several times until he finally grabbed Emily around the waist and physically lifted her away from Rainer. "Thanks for that, but I'm feeling a little queasy now."

She stuck her tongue out at her big brother.

"Yeah, I'm sure he's got something he'll let you lick," he continued to harass though the joke appeared to make him cringe.

They waved to the girls as Rainer backed up and headed down the long driveway.

CHAPTER 5
THE TALK

"Do you mind if I put the top up?" Logan asked.

"Sure, go ahead." He wondered what Logan wanted to talk about. Rainer pulled into a gas station before getting on the interstate, and Logan raised the top.

They loaded up on Dr Pepper, Cheetos, honey-roasted peanuts, and various candies, none of which Mrs. Haydenshire would really want them to eat. Rainer grabbed a bag of cinnamon discs with the cinnamon syrup in the middle. They were Emily's favorite. He always kept them in his glovebox for her.

Logan rolled his eyes. "She's got you so wrapped it has to hurt, man."

"Trust me, she's worth it." They got back in the car and headed off. "Okay, spill it." Rainer threw several peanuts in his mouth and flew down the interstate.

"That obvious?" Logan looked annoyed.

"We've been friends since I was two days old—so I'm going to go with maybe not to anyone else, but yeah to me. Plus, you wanted to put the top up."

Logan popped open one of the Dr Peppers. It was the cola of choice for most Gifted people. The secret ingredient was an added neutron to the carbon atoms. This meant that the drink possessed potential energy, which could occasionally be felt by the Non-Gifted as well, but not often. For Gifted people, it upped the energy that existed in their bodies and made them able to do more things faster.

"I need to talk to you about this, but I need you to pretend you're dating someone besides my sister."

"I don't know how, but that seems like it could get me into trouble, so how about I won't say her name, and you can pretend whatever you want." He was now extremely curious to hear what Logan had to say.

"Okay, fine. Have you and Em…you know…slept together yet?" he hedged and stared out the window. He refused to look Rainer's direction.

Rainer debated between telling Logan it was none of his business and actually answering because he was desperate to talk with his best friend about this.

"No." He changed lanes just to have something to do.

Logan turned back and stared at Rainer in shock. "Really?"

"I just said no."

Relief etched Logan's face. "I believe you. I just thought…you know…when she stayed with you in London."

That's what everyone thought. For the most part, they'd let everyone go on believing they were sleeping together. Most of their friends had been having sex for some time.

"We didn't…I mean Cal had just been killed…she'd just gotten out of the hospital from the wreck." *That was entirely my fault.* He grimaced as he remembered her lying there with him unable to do anything except watch Gifted medios work over her.

"And I'd just made the biggest mistake of my life by leaving, so we talked all night, nothing more." Relief eased his shield to have cleared the air at least with Logan.

Logan, however, seemed to be rethinking his decision to talk.

"Is that all you wanted to know?"

"Man, you don't know what it's like, growing up with six older brothers, and the stories…most of which probably aren't true." Logan wolfed down a Reese's cup in one bite.

"Am I to take it that you and Adeline are thinking of taking things further?" Rainer didn't point out that he knew only too well. He'd also grown up with all of Logan's brothers, and he'd certainly heard *all* of the stories.

"She wants to, and I want to as well. I just..." He drew another deep breath. "I made a deal with her." Logan's face colored rapidly.

"What kind of deal?"

"She's been wanting to for a while, but...with the way her mom is and the way she grew up and everything, I wanted her to be sure, and then there's the whole other thing. So, I told her if she'd move in with us, either with us like at Mom and Dad's, or if we all want to get a place together or whatever," he hemmed. "I told her if she'd move out of her mom's apartment, then we would."

Rainer understood Logan's discomfort and the whole other thing only too well. Being Gifted meant that everything, including having sex, was somehow more than it was for those not Gifted with energy abilities.

To be able to see and understand the energy in the universe around you, to tap into and summon that energy, to have energy housed in your body affected each and every part of their lives.

Casting the energies in their bodies or using the energies of the earth was a life force that Non-Gifted scientists had no idea even existed. It also meant that to be with another Gifted person was to join their energy to yours. To make your rhythms join in one solid combined stream. It was felt by those with Gifted abilities just like gravity or magnetism was felt by the Non-Gifted. It was another level of sharing intimately, one that had the Gifted population waiting much longer to have sex than most Non-Gifted teenagers. It added an additional level of complication, and it required a deeper commitment to maintain.

It was beautiful and wonderful, so Rainer had been told in the numerous Amative Energies classes he'd been required to take at the academy, but you needed to know the person you were sharing energy with fairly well, or it could be quite disturbing.

This, of course, didn't matter if a Gifted person chose to be with a Non-Gifted individual.

Garrett often bragged about his escapades. 'That's just fun, no energy, no crap. Just get in, have a little fun, and get out.' Garrett's stories were certainly some of the ones Logan was referring to.

"Will kind of tried to tell me about it, I guess." Logan cringed. His face was now the color of Rainer's car.

"What did he say?" Rainer was suddenly much more interested in the conversation. Will was Logan's oldest brother, and the only Haydenshire thus far to get married, although Patrick and his girlfriend, Lucy, had been ring shopping recently.

"I don't know. I guess he figures with us graduating and all, and you and me talking about moving in with the Em and Adeline, that he'd offer me some advice."

"What was the advice?" He'd take as much advice as he could get between now and Friday night.

"He said..." Logan grimaced slightly before forcing himself to go on. "He said to be careful not to hurt her." He sounded like he'd been punched in the gut.

"Hurt her like breaking up with her after doing that, or hurt her, like injure her?" Rainer was slightly nauseated.

"Hurt her like...painful ouch, you're hurting me, hurting her."

Rainer opened another Dr Pepper and drew a long sip. He hoped the carbonation would calm his nerves and his stomach.

"I told him that I knew that, and that I had the basic mechanics down, and he laughed at me." Logan was clearly offended by Will's lack of finesse.

"We're not barbaric assholes." Rainer suddenly felt the need to defend himself and his best friend.

"Exactly." Logan joined in the nonexistent fight they were taking sides against. Silence filled the car for a few minutes. Rainer switched on the radio in an effort to drown the quiet.

"Ad's thinking about telling her mom that she's moving out after graduation," Logan added in a terrified whisper as he stared at the surrounding fields fading with the setting sun. "If her mother even shows at graduation, which I'm sure she won't."

Rainer offered him a sorrowful glance. "Yeah, but we'll all be there, and your folks, and she's coming to the party, right?"

Logan opened another bag of chips and threw a few in his mouth before answering. "Yeah, of course. Her mom just makes me crazy. I wish I could find her dad for her. He has to be out there somewhere. He has to come from some Gifted family somewhere. What if he doesn't even know what an amazing daughter he has?"

Rainer knew that Logan had dug deep to commit to a conversation of that magnitude, so he nodded.

"Maybe when we start at Iodex we'll be able to find him. I mean if anybody can find him, it's Iodex, right?"

"I'm hoping," Logan admitted.

Gifted DNA was always dominant. Since Candy wasn't Gifted that meant whoever Adeline's father was, he was Gifted.

"You're sure you're okay talking about this?" Rainer had to be certain. Any other time he'd brought up sleeping with Emily, Logan had balked.

"I'm the one that brought it up."

"I remember one time I was talking to my dad about it. Not the talk per se but just about the energy thing. He said it would change everything between me and Em. I just wish he'd explained how exactly."

Logan nodded. "It has to be in a good way, right? I mean,"—he cringed slightly—"surely my parents wouldn't have had ten kids if sex wasn't something they enjoyed." He gagged involuntarily, and Rainer laughed.

"Yeah, but my dad was kind of warning me off so I don't know. Maybe."

"How old were you?"

"It was like two weeks after our thirteenth birthdays."

"Okay, well, I'm sure that's why he was warning you off."

"Yeah, I know. Still wish I'd asked him for specifics on how it would change things."

They discussed graduation and Rainer's speech. Rainer broached the subject of taking Emily to the beach house, which had Logan laughing and wishing he was back at the farmhouse to see his father's reaction to Emily's plans.

Rainer rolled his eyes as he exited off of the interstate and headed down the streets of downtown Norfolk.

"Are you gonna keep coming here after Friday?" Logan asked as they turned into the derelict apartment complex that made Rainer's skin crawl every time he turned past the entrance sign. At one time, it had read Goddard Downs Apartments, but someone had removed most of the black stick-on letters from the cheaply made sign, so that it now read, *Go Down.*

"Maybe." Rainer considered. "I feel like I owe it to my dad to check up on him even if I do despise him." He pulled into a parking place and flung open his door in an effort to get the visit over with quickly.

Once Logan was out of the car, Rainer glanced around the abandoned parking garage. Logan checked the area as well and then nodded.

Rainer formed a cup with his right hand and scooped it upward. He concentrated until his hand held a green, glowing orb of shielding energy. He opened his fingers out wide and directed his palm toward his car.

He was an Ioses Predilect. His protective shield was the energy he could access and use with the most ease. It existed inside of his body. It was already exceptionally strong, but based on the duel he'd just been in with Dan Vindico, he knew he had a great deal left to learn. Dan was one of the most Gifted officers ever to hold the title of Chief, and he ran an extremely tight ship. Rainer couldn't wait to start his career.

Once the energy had been transferred to the Mustang, he shook free of its force. He followed Logan to the shabby, brown, hole-in-the-wall that his uncle called home.

CHAPTER 6

UNCLE STAN

"Do you ever think about some Non-Gifted prick actually trying to steal your car when we come here? That would scare the shit out of them once they touched it." Logan looked very intrigued.

Rainer laughed. "I'd prefer everyone just stay the hell away from my car."

Logan raised his fist to knock on the door. The number 139 was hanging precariously from ancient screws, making a valiant effort to adhere the numbers to the door. It was a battle they were clearly losing. When Logan banged on the door, the three tumbled to the ground with a metallic tink.

Logan cursed under his breath and retrieved the number. With a quick glance around, he made the same move Rainer had just made with his hand. He was more discreet than Rainer had been with the car. The magnetic cast for the number wouldn't require anywhere near the energy the cast on the car had needed.

As he placed his cupped hand over the three, he summoned and reapplied it to the door. The three glowed a faint yellow after Logan re-magnetized it. The magnetic energy faded as a gruff-looking guy with greased black hair, bulging muscles, and a hate-filled scowl flung the door open. Rainer and Logan stepped back automatically and shared a concerned glance.

"Move," the guy spat. He stomped out onto the stoop and shoved past Rainer.

They took a half step into the filthy apartment as they stared after the man. Rainer gagged. His uncle had food in his mustache and beard. He was wearing a wife-beater undershirt and boxers that didn't quite cover everything.

"Come to check on me?" Stan sneered.

"Who was that?" Rainer pointed to the man who was rushing across the parking lot. A slight shudder came over Stan as he narrowed his eyes. His reaction had Rainer all the more curious.

"You know, I don't need you any more than I needed that brother of mine. Look at what all of his good-for-nothing meddling with the Realm cost him," Stan huffed.

"Nice to see you too, Uncle Stan, and yes, we will come in. Thanks so much for inviting us." Rainer and Logan forced their way farther into the apartment.

Rainer's uncle was unlike his father in every possible way. He'd dropped out of the academy after only two years and had taken to performing magic shows at Non-Gifted children's birthday parties for a price. Since energy transformations were always called magic by the Non-Gifted, Rainer supposed Stan was decently paid for his lack of work.

There were loads of Gifted magicians who performed to the awe of the Non-Gifted. Most of them, having finished their education, were vastly better at what they did than his Uncle Stan. However, the Gifted Senate frowned on this practice, and the 'magicians' were watched closely. Anything that might make the Non-Gifted question the existence of those with powers could land a Gifted person in prison.

Magic by definition tended to be anything inexplicable, anything that couldn't be explained away with some loose grasp of accepted information. The Gifted people used that to their advantage. They hid in plain sight, scoffed over anything they were directly confronted about, and allowed the Non-Gifted to call energy magic. For them, Rainer supposed, it was one in the same.

The apartment wasn't in as bad a shape as they'd found it in before. That meant Stan had a woman he was interested in. He always attempted to look marginally human if there was a woman involved.

"Hey, you." Stan followed them to the kitchen to remove a boxed meal from the microwave. It was a task he could have performed all on his own without the use of a microwave if he'd stayed in the academy. "How old are you now?" he demanded of Rainer.

After sharing a knowing glance with Logan, Rainer shrugged. "Twenty."

"But they just said..." Stan gestured his thumb back toward the parking lot of the apartment. He changed course quickly. "Seems like you were twenty last year?"

With a smirk, Rainer shook his head. "Nope, last year I was nineteen."

Logan turned his chuckle into a cough. Stan took in Logan for a moment. He seemed to have just realized he was there.

"You still takin' up with his sister? Why don't you ever bring her by?"

Rainer clenched his jaw as, "I wonder," huffed from his lips.

"My brother's a real piece of work...not having his money released and will read 'til you turn twenty-one."

Though that was only partly true, Rainer didn't correct his uncle. The will had been read. The estate just hadn't been released.

Rainer glanced around the two-bedroom apartment. There wasn't much to it. Stan had filled one bedroom with magic tricks he used for the kids' parties. Most of them he still managed to bungle.

Stan had always fancied himself a regular playboy. The master bedroom sported a king-sized bed with cheap satin sheets and a red suede bedspread. The kitchen was tiny and filled with trash from every available take-out restaurant in a ten-mile radius.

Rainer decided to start there and spent several minutes locating trash bags. He began tossing out food wrappers from the past two weeks. Logan helped him as he gave Rainer a distinct eye roll and shook his head.

Stan reclined in a worn leatherette recliner and began inhaling his microwave meal. After the kitchen was once again inhabitable, Rainer took inventory of the rest of the small apartment.

The bathroom was disgusting. He cursed under his breath the entire time he scrubbed it by hand. By then, they were more than ready to leave.

With a slight shudder, Rainer moved in front of his uncle who'd slopped the tray that had contained his food onto the table beside him, while he clicked endlessly through the channels on his ancient box set television. He'd have to summon to get to the Gifted networks, and Rainer assumed he just didn't want to put forth that much effort.

"I'm going on vacation, so it'll be a few weeks before I can get back."

"What vacation? Where'd you get money to go somewhere? What about the academy?" Stan sneered the words *the academy*. Rainer decided to bend the truth just a little.

"It's summer. School gets out Friday. I'm going with the Haydenshires." Not mentioning that he was only going with one of the Haydenshires or that he was graduating seemed the best option.

Stan narrowed his eyes at Logan. "Don't your family ever get sick of him hanging around?"

Logan shook his head. "Rainer? Hell, no. We love this guy. Plus, there's so many of us, we can't really tell which are Haydenshires and which aren't anymore. He's family."

Rainer gave him an appreciative grin.

Stan rolled his eyes. "Whatever...have a nice time. Next time you come, bring that girl of yours. Be nice to have something pretty to look at while you're here." Logan scowled as Rainer clenched his jaw and his fists simultaneously.

"Bye, Stan." Rainer headed to the door. Stan didn't offer them any farewell gesture, so Rainer hastened their escape.

"Ugh, I always feel like I need a shower after I come here with you." Logan gagged.

"No joke."

Two of the three outdoor lights in the entire complex had been shattered, so they trekked carefully through the small parking deck. As they approached the Mustang, Rainer discreetly formed his hand into a cup again but rotated it the other way to release his shield.

He squealed the tires as he made his hasty retreat.

CHAPTER 7

THREE EGGS OVER EASY

"So, I take it you and Em *are* actually going to the beach house?" Logan had him cornered in his own car no less.

"I thought you didn't want to hear about it?"

"I don't, but as long as I only think about it as your best friend and not about what you're going to be doing to my baby sister, I'm better with it."

They both laughed at the cost of the truth that Logan had just uttered. Rainer took a left. They headed away from the interstate on-ramp and farther into downtown Norfolk.

"I don't guess I'll ask if Adeline and I can come with?" Logan smirked.

"You take that up with your sister."

"Trust me, as much as I don't want to be there for that, I really don't want to ask Emily about it. Don't tell her, but I am actually a little afraid of her."

Rainer laughed as he signaled and waited to turn into the parking lot of Griddle's. It was almost seven o'clock, but traffic was still heavy. He was thankful Logan knew that Emily was the one steering this ship and that he would never push anything on her.

"She can be quite fierce when she sets her mind on something."

"And what's her mind on now?"

53

Rainer knew he didn't actually want a response to that question. He raised one eyebrow as he shot Logan a cocky grin and watched him back down instantly.

He pulled the car into a spot near the entrance of the diner. Logan moved between Rainer and the large plate-glass windows that constructed most of the restaurant. Rainer set his hand on the hood of the car and tried to look nonchalant. He leaned down and pretended to check the tire as he summoned and then quickly dispersed his shield from his hand.

The Non-Gifted couldn't see the color change. They couldn't see the earth's energies all around them. So, as Rainer's Mustang tinged green, all they saw was a red convertible. Several of them shot him appreciative glances as he followed Logan into Griddle's.

They took a booth in one of the back corners. The smell of bacon grease and pancake syrup hung thickly in the air. The cook had been there for as long as either Logan or Rainer could remember. He always had a kind smile, and the food was phenomenal.

A waitress approached their table wearing an apron-dress that was a size too small. She looked pleased to have customers.

"What can I get you handsome fellas tonight?" she drawled in a thick Southern accent.

"I'll have one of Silas's specials with bacon and toast, and coffee with cream and sugar," Logan answered immediately.

The waitress scribbled on the short-order pad. Rainer was feeling a little queasy as he glanced over the menu he knew by heart. This was probably due to the fact that he'd never actually had lunch but had consumed three Dr Peppers and a tremendous amount of junk food over the past few hours, and visiting his uncle always nauseated him.

"I'll just have a Coke and three eggs over easy with toast." He handed the laminated menu, slick with grease, back to the waitress. She filled in his order before she returned behind the counter. After sliding their orders onto the metal clamp rings and spinning them back to the kitchen, she began preparing Logan's coffee.

Logan gave him the Haydenshire signature smirk. "So, I'm thinking your speech should go something like, 'I, Rainer Lawson, son of Joseph Lawson, decided to run for head of Ioses because I wanted to stick it to Mitchell O'Ryan, who is in fact a prick, and so that the guys would stop messing with Fergus, the bird-brained goober who hangs around with me and Logan Haydenshire, the coolest guy I know, and to whom I would like to dedicate this speech."

Rainer laughed. "All of that is actually true, except the part about you being the coolest guy I know."

Logan feigned insult. A few minutes later, the waitress returned with their food and drinks, and Logan dug in feverishly.

"Ah, Mitchell…" Rainer laughed. "I'm gonna miss him."

Logan nearly choked on his gargantuan omelet as he laughed. "He sure as hell won't be coming to work for the Senate. None of the O'Ryans have ever actually worked."

"Legally, you mean."

The O'Ryans were one of the Realm's elite families, at least in their own minds. They were extremely wealthy. It was all old money. Rainer hoped that at some point some of the original O'Ryans had actually put forth effort to acquire all of their vast funds. It was more likely that the O'Ryans had used their Gifted abilities to make most of their gains ill-gotten.

He shook his head as he thought about what a tremendous jerk Mitchell was. He plunged his fork into his eggs to break the yolks, and then scooped up the warm yellow liquid with his toast.

Mitchell had been named head of the Visvirees Order when they were sophomores, and he'd made everyone's life hellish as he wielded his power over those he hated.

The final straw had been when Mitchell keyed Emily's newly acquired Jeep. It was her sixteenth birthday present from her parents, after she'd been named one of the youngest heads ever of Auxiliary Order. She'd laughed in his face when Mitchell had asked her to go to the Spring Formal with him. Mitchell had asked her in an effort to get Rainer to lose his temper and get into trouble.

The following year, Rainer had won head of Ioses Order by a landslide. He'd held Mitchell by a string the entire year. He'd forced a confession out of him over Emily's car, with a plethora of witnesses, in front of the school governors, and Mitchell had been redacted as head of Visvirees.

Rainer smiled as he recalled the look on Mitchell's face as he'd given up his title. Not that it really mattered. Mitchell would fall into the long line of O'Ryans who contributed little to the world but still managed to escape any real consequences by sitting by idly.

They only made enough trouble to get what they wanted but usually not enough to call attention to themselves. Mitchell's father had recently been taken to a Gifted prison, however. He'd been charged with tax evasion, forgery, and ties to insurance fraud. So, at least one of them had actually been caught.

Logan inhaled his omelet and toast and waited while Rainer took the last few bites of his eggs. They both threw down enough cash to cover their meals with a generous tip, then sauntered out of the diner.

CHAPTER 8

TAKE IT SLOW AROUND THE CURVES

Rainer ran his hand over his car lovingly. Most Non-Gifted people would feel that Rainer was just proud of his automobile. They had no idea he had just released the protective cast.

They slid into their seats, and Rainer made his way back to the on-ramp. It was a quarter to eight, and the interstates were relatively empty since most everyone was home from work by now.

Logan grinned. "Wanna pick it up a little bit?"

"We nearly got caught by the police the last time we did that."

"If we get home soon, we can see the girls before they fall asleep."

The way it felt to have Emily tucked safely in his arms, the pure intoxication of her luscious curves wrapped around him formed its erotic poetry in Rainer's mind.

As much as he wanted to be with her, just to hold her while she slept was a pleasure like he'd never known. An image of that night in his tiny flat in London, with her deep auburn hair splayed across his bare chest and her hands on him as he cradled her in his embrace, pulled the air from his lungs.

He didn't need more provocation than that. He cupped his hand and harnessed the speed of the large engine under the hood of his car.

He gathered the energy from the air around him and pushed it from his hand into the engine. The car jolted and then shot forward.

A broad grin spread rapidly across Logan's face. His eyes twinkled as they watched interstate signs and billboards for everything from restaurants to strip clubs fly by them in a blur.

Logan summoned and cast the engine to keep it cool. Rainer concentrated. He probed the night for any sign of police or energy from other cars he may need to avoid.

After a little while, they edged closer to the exits for McLean. Rainer released the speed cast. Logan was fidgeting. "You know when I got thrown off the tractor and Adeline healed me?"

The Haydenshires always had a large garden on their property. It bordered the apple, peach, and cherry trees they grew. Mrs. Haydenshire's Predilection for Occamy made it an extremely fruitful garden, of course, but the boys usually worked the tractor for her.

Two years ago, Logan had been plowing and wasn't quite watching what he was doing. He'd been staring at Adeline lying out by the pool with Emily. Rainer knew this, but he'd never let on. Logan had been thrown off the tractor and injured his leg badly. Adeline had rushed to him and healed him before Mrs. Haydenshire had even realized what had happened.

Adeline's Valeduto Predilection for healing was rather extraordinary. This was another reason the entire Gifted Realm would love to know who her father was. Rainer nodded as he came back to the conversation.

"So, I've felt her, right? I've felt her energy or whatever? Our energy has already combined." His face colored again. Rainer considered, but he didn't actually have an answer for the inevitable question that was about to pour from Logan's mouth. "Do you think that's what it will be like when we sleep together?"

"I guess." He tried hard not to glance at Logan and further his embarrassment.

"It was kind of incredible after I could walk again. I've been healed loads of times by my parents and even the medios at the hospital. Remember when you and I decided to put our bikes on the trampoline?"

"We were idiots," Rainer declared as they cracked up. They both recalled the center of the Haydenshires' trampoline splitting open and them landing in a tangled heap with their bikes on the hardened ground. They'd both just turned ten and had received new Diamondback bikes for their birthdays. Logan had broken his wrist and was bruised head to toe. Rainer had shattered three ribs and his ankle.

"We really were," Logan agreed. "They worked on us for a while, until we were relatively healed up, but when Adeline fixed my leg, it was different." He stared steadfastly out the window up to the star-strewn sky. They could see the stars now that they were out of the city as they made their way to the Virginia farmland.

"Different how?" Rainer wasn't certain he should ask. Logan shrugged and seemed to clam up. It must have really been something.

He remembered sitting in the room he'd shared with Logan. He'd stayed with him to make certain he was all right. Logan had lost a fair amount of blood, and everyone was worried. Adeline had been in there as well. She'd sat on Logan's bed with him and kept him casted. After a few minutes, Rainer had left the room. The energy between the two of them after she'd healed him had made Rainer uncomfortable. He'd felt like he was viewing something so intimate it was voyeuristic.

Logan's parents had sensed it as well, and the governor had attempted to talk with Rainer and Logan about what had happened. At barely eighteen years old, they hadn't quite understood what he'd been trying to explain.

Adeline had been thoroughly confused as well. She was an excellent healer, but her abilities that day had been stronger than she'd ever felt them before. When it had been Logan on the ground bleeding, with his body contorted in pain, as he'd strained in an effort not to cry in front of her, she'd summoned a vast amount of energy to heal him. The bond between them had strengthened tremendously.

Rainer slowed the car as he turned down the two-lane road. "You feel it when you kiss her, right?"

"Yeah, of course."

Rainer's mind spun instantly back to Emily. The feeling of her energy as he dipped his tongue into her mouth was incredible. He couldn't imagine what actually joining their bodies would feel like.

"Is that what it felt like when she healed you?"

Logan smiled but never met Rainer's eyes. "Kind of…only it was so much more." The awe was evident in his tone.

"Then I guess that will be what it's like."

CHAPTER 9

CAN'T FIGHT THE FEELING

As he made the turn into the farm, Rainer waited for the gate to open. He eased the Mustang forward and carefully worked his way toward the barn.

A smile lit his face. Emily was lying on the porch swing on the side of the farmhouse. She'd been waiting for them to arrive home. He threw the car in park and rushed toward her. She sat up and grinned at Rainer as he neared.

"Hey there, beautiful."

Logan rolled his eyes. "Where's Adeline?"

Emily's smile faded. "Her mom called a few hours ago and made Adeline call the pizza place to see if she could get another shift. She did, and they told her she could work until midnight if she wanted. So, of course she had to. Mom and Dad dropped her off at work a while ago."

Logan ground his teeth. "I'll be back later."

"Here." Rainer threw him the keys to the Mustang. "You'll get there faster."

"Thanks." The pizza parlor was only about a ten-minute drive from the Haydenshires' farm, but Logan could make it in three if he played his cards right. "Why did Mom and Dad both go?" Logan turned back to face Emily. He walked backwards toward the barn.

Emily shot him a look that said if he thought about it, he could figure it out on his own.

"Geez, someone really needs to tell them ten is enough. What are they trying to do...replace us all as we move out?"

Rainer took the steps up to the porch two at a time. "I take it your parents aren't back yet?"

"No, I put the boys to bed a while ago. Patrick came home with Lucy. They've been up in his room this whole time, so I came out here to wait on you."

He sat on the swing beside her. She turned to lie in his lap. He pulled his fingers gently through her auburn tresses and smiled down at her.

She was wearing one of his Ioses T-shirts with a pair of extremely short knit shorts. The Auxiliary Order crest was on the bottom. He smiled. She'd always worn his Ioses shirts more than he had. That was the way it was done. The only guys who wore their own Predilect's T-shirts were the sub-freshman who hadn't quite gotten the nuances of the academy down yet. Well, them and Fergus.

Though he'd seen her in his shirts dozens of times before, the sight always took his breath away. She was his, and he longed to show her that. He might have been nervous about the way it would happen, but his longing far outweighed his nerves.

Desire swam in his energy, especially when she was lying in his lap, in the calm, cool evening air. When he soothed her with the rhythmic movement of the swing as she gazed up at him sweetly, the love between them became palpable in the air.

She pulled a quilt off of the side of the swing. It was one of many Mrs. Haydenshire kept there in case someone wanted a nap on the porch, or one of the twins wanted to snuggle underneath it. Rainer took it and draped it over her as she let him cradle her in his lap. She yawned, and her eyelids grew heavier.

"Want me to take you to bed, baby?"

"Is that an offer, Mr. Lawson?"

Every fiber of his being wanted to say yes. He longed to scoop her up and carry her to her room, a place she felt safe and comfortable. He could show her just how much he loved her, be with her, feel her around him and make her feel him.

He just chuckled and swallowed down his need for what felt like the millionth time. Her parents would be coming home soon as would Connor and Logan. He assumed at some point Patrick and Lucy would come up for air, and he would take her home. All of this would be a problem if someone should come looking for either of them.

"Friday night, sweetheart," he promised.

She trembled in his arms, and Rainer willed Friday night to come quickly.

"Mom said it was fine for us to stay at the beach house for a few days." His heart hammered as he nodded. As he smiled down at her, his body seized in anticipation. He slipped his hand under the quilt and caressed her side. He used his other hand to move her hair from her face.

She let her eyes close. He knew she could feel his rhythms in the air around her. A gentle breeze tempted Rainer with Emily's heavenly scent. She was visibly concentrating as his energy mingled with hers in the crisp night air. He pulled the T-shirt up to expose her midriff but kept her covered under the quilt.

He wanted to touch her skin and let the energy pass between them. As he wrapped his fingers around her waist, she smiled and opened her eyes as they darkened. He slid his hand higher. She panted as his fingers grazed her ribs.

She wasn't wearing a bra, and the strain in his jeans became readily apparent. Her breaths came faster. Rainer ached. She turned and slipped what he wanted into his hand, and a slight moan escaped him. He kneaded her breasts. Her nipples pebbled between his fingers. He drew slightly from that storehouse of erotic energy. She groaned from the draw.

She sat up but kept herself covered in the quilt as she let it drape over his lap. He used one hand to guide her mouth to his as he kept his other groping her, feeling her, as her energy began to fill him. It passed in tantric waves from her breasts into his hand.

As headlights came over the slight hill along the gravel path, she backed away. Rainer gasped as he tried to catch his breath. Emily rapidly folded the quilt and laid her head on Rainer's shoulder. He wrapped his arm around her and righted her shirt as they continued to swing.

The Haydenshires were giving each other longing glances. They were holding hands as they glided from the barn, up the stairs, to the porch.

"How was Norfolk?" Mrs. Haydenshire asked.

"Same as always." Rainer was rather impressed with how normal he sounded when his heart was still pounding and his jeans were still rather tight.

Governor Haydenshire smiled at Rainer and slapped him on the shoulder. "Your dad would be proud of you for looking after him. I know I am."

Rainer shrugged. He was fairly certain the governor wouldn't have been so proud of him if he'd known what he was just doing to his daughter.

"We're heading on to bed," Mrs. Haydenshire said. "Did Logan go after Adeline?"

Rainer and Emily both nodded.

"We're going to have to insist that she move in here," the governor dictated. This mandate seemed to delight his wife. "I cannot imagine treating your own child the way that woman treats Adeline."

"That would make Logan's whole year," Emily pointed out.

"Unfortunately, I don't quite have the pull over Candy Parker as I did over Stan Lawson." He winked at Rainer, who smiled his appreciation. "Son, are you certain you want me to come along with you Friday morning? I understand if you want to go alone or if you'd like Logan or Emily to go," Governor Haydenshire offered. He seemed truly worried he'd be intruding.

"If you wouldn't mind, I'd really like you to come. I think Logan was planning on going with us too."

"I'd be honored. I just don't want to intrude."

"No sir, I'd feel better if you were there." He wasn't certain he should have admitted that, but the Haydenshires gazed at him proudly.

"Then there's nowhere else I'd ever be."

"Don't stay up too late. You have graduation practice in the morning," Mrs. Haydenshire reminded as they headed into the farmhouse.

"Rainer?" Emily turned her pleading gaze on him as soon as the door closed.

"What, baby?"

"Will you come upstairs with me and stay in my room for just a little while, please?"

This had been happening with more frequency in the past few months. Turning her down on the swing on the side porch of her parents' home was nothing compared to the sheer amount of willpower it took to turn her down while lying beside her in bed.

The feeling, the all-encompassing magic, of holding her to him, of feeling her beside him, was irresistible. He leaned and kissed her forehead.

"Yeah, come on." After helping her up, he stood and took her hand.

They moved quietly up the stairs. She turned the pink glass knob on her bedroom door. Her mother had placed antique glass knobs on all of the many bedrooms in the farmhouse.

Rainer took in the room. The moon shone softly through the large bay window that sat in the center of the far wall, complete with a cushioned bench seat. The cherry wood double bed sat along the back wall on the rubbed oak floors. It had a warm duvet over a down comforter spread neatly across it. Several of Emily's favorite stuffed animals from her childhood or that Rainer had won for her on the boardwalk of Virginia Beach were on her bed.

Three large white bookshelves were along one wall and contained Emily's favorite books along with small mementos. There were several pictures of formals she and Rainer had attended and of the two of them at the beach. There were keepsakes of her charity work with Auxiliary Order. The purple AO flag hung over her headboard. There were numerous Arlington Angels posters of the team on the walls. Rainer was certain she was going to see her dream of challenging with the Angels come true at her tryouts in two weeks.

He smiled and let his hands drift over her curves and graze her backside as she walked away from him. The room was thoroughly her, and he loved to be there.

She spun and watched him as he began to pull off his shirt. He gazed at her hungrily as she slipped out of her knit shorts. His breath caught in his throat.

She moved to him then helped him finish removing his shirt. He realized he'd halted abruptly with his T-shirt up around his arms when she'd shimmied out of her shorts.

She slid her hands down his chest, and he shuddered in palpable need. He threw his shirt on the floor, and she took his hand and led him to her bed. He caught a glimpse of the slight, white, cotton thong she was wearing as she leaned to toss pillows and stuffed animals off of her bed. She crawled in.

"Just hold me, please. That's all I'm asking for." She seemed to know how hard this was for him. He slid into the bed beside her as he wrapped his arms around her and settled her on his chest.

"I want to do so much more than hold you. I want to feel you. I want to be with you."

Her stomach clenched against his side. Her heartbeat picked up pace in her rhythms. "Friday night," she whispered.

Yet another problem with Emily's room was that her parents' bedroom was right beside it. Emily frequently complained about noises she heard coming from her parents' room. They knew that meant that her parents could hear her as well.

Her bare legs tangled with his. He brushed a tender kiss across her lips, but that was all it took to catch the essence of her, and he wanted so much more.

Her hips gave a needy rise, and he moaned. He clenched his jaw to quell the noise. He devoured her mouth with his own to keep them both silent. He slid his hands up her shirt. It was much too large for her small frame.

Her breasts swelled in his hands as he pulsed against her crotch. He traced his right hand down her back, until he grasped her backside and massaged greedily.

She shuddered. Her breath came in quick gasping pants. He pulled her waist closer and let her feel how hard he was as he grinded his body against the damp cotton between her legs. He moved his hands to her inner thighs, and a moan escaped her.

"Are you needy, baby?" escaped his mouth in a whispered growl.

"God yes," she whimpered.

His fingers teased at her lips, swollen and wet with her need. Slowly, delicately, he slipped his fingers under the panties and pressed inside of her. She trembled. The liquid form of her erotic energy dripped down his fingers. He gave her the friction he knew she craved. Her energy pulsed in desperate arcs. She slipped her hand down his jeans and wrapped it over his strain. She drew his own erotic energy straight from its source. It was incredible.

If he didn't stop now, he wasn't going to be able to. He halted abruptly. "Baby," he panted. "I think I'd better go. If we keep going, I don't think I'll be able to stop," he forced the words out. She whimpered but then nodded.

Tears of frustration threatened her eyes, and his heart pricked as he held her. He wanted her so badly he could taste it.

"I'm so sorry, sweetheart," he tried to soothe her. "Believe me, getting out of this bed and walking to Logan's room will be one of the hardest things I've ever done."

She gave him a sweet smile. "I know. It's okay."

She nuzzled her head under his chin, and he held her until she fell asleep. He slipped from the bed and covered her tenderly. As he gazed down at her in the moonlight, he brushed another kiss across her cheek.

After summoning a faint orange glow, Rainer sealed heat in the fibers of the quilt. He grabbed the T-shirt he'd been wearing and tiptoed to the door. He eased it open and prayed Governor Haydenshire wouldn't suddenly decide to leave his room.

He headed to the bedroom on the opposite end of the hall. Logan was lying on his bed when Rainer entered. He looked furious.

"Do I even need to ask where you've been?" he huffed indignantly.

"Fight with Adeline?"

Logan nodded, then sank his fist into his pillow.

"She gave her mom all of her tips?" Rainer already knew the answer.

"Yes."

Rainer never knew what to say when Logan and Adeline had this same argument week after week.

He headed to the bathroom between Connor's room and the room he and Logan shared. He hoped he wouldn't wake Connor, if he was even home yet.

Showers had been Rainer's answer to lying in bed with Emily, half-naked and grinding against him. He closed and locked both doors then turned on the water. After shedding his clothes, he stepped into the water and let it rid him of the emotions of his day. The good, the bad, and the desperate desire that consumed him whenever he was in her presence washed down the drain.

Forty-eight hours from then, he'd be with her completely alone. If he didn't stop thinking like that, he was going to have to take another shower. He chastised himself as he turned off the faucet and grabbed a towel. He didn't bother to warm it first. His mind was too full of Emily.

He fell into his bed. Logan was whispering into his cell phone as he apologized to Adeline. Rainer shut his eyes and let his mind revel in Emily until he fell asleep.

CHAPTER 10
DECIDEDLY GUILTY

The next morning Rainer slid into his usual seat at the Haydenshires' large kitchen table. Mrs. Haydenshire plied everyone with heaps of scrambled eggs, cheesy grits, and French toast.

Logan had left early, before anyone else was up, and retrieved Adeline. She was devouring her breakfast.

Emily fell into Rainer's lap at the table. He beamed, but her father pointed to her own chair. She rolled her eyes as she seated herself. She ate her grits without much enthusiasm. Connor greeted everyone with a grin and then began loading his plate with eggs.

"You were home late last night." Mrs. Haydenshire raised her eyebrow as she tousled Connor's hair.

"Worked late and then went out for a little while," he informed his mother. Before either of his parents could ask who he'd been out with, Patrick came down the stairs. He looked decidedly guilty.

"Uh," he stammered. "So, everyone's up?"

Emily and Rainer shared a smirk. They'd already figured out what was going on. Emily giggled.

"Yes son, we all have somewhere to be in a little while." The governor studied Patrick. He was almost four years older than Logan.

"Right." Patrick nodded as he glanced around uncomfortably. He looked at his watch and grimaced.

"Why don't you just go get her, and she can have breakfast before you have to leave early to get you both to work?" Connor goaded. Logan and Emily cracked up while Rainer and Adeline tried very hard not to.

"Patrick!" Mrs. Haydenshire rolled her eyes. Although the Haydenshires were well aware that most of their children had sex, it wasn't something they wanted thrown in their faces. Rainer's stomach twisted uncomfortably as he thought of Friday night.

Patrick and Lucy had been dating for a couple of years, but they were both just beginning their careers. Patrick worked for an up-and-coming real estate investment firm, and Lucy was an aide to the Senteon. Neither had moved out of their parents' homes. They were both trying to save money. They'd done well at the academy. Lucy had been one of the heads of Adminis Order, and was climbing the ranks of the Gifted Senate quickly.

"Go get her!" Mrs. Haydenshire demanded.

"We fell asleep," Patrick pled, as he returned upstairs.

"Yes, well, we'll discuss that later," Mrs. Haydenshire huffed before she turned on Logan and Connor. "You will say nothing to her about this. Do you understand me?"

Logan and Connor shared a smirk and then nodded as they tried hard not to crack up once again. A large piece of scrambled egg landed in the governor's coffee mug. Keaton clapped. He was very pleased with himself.

"Okay, now I'm irritated with two of my sons, and it's not even eight in the morning." Mrs. Haydenshire sighed.

The governor scolded Keaton for throwing food. Keaton responded by shaking his head back and forth and spitting as his mother tried to wipe off his hands and mouth. She released him from his highchair while Governor Haydenshire fixed himself more coffee. He cupped his hand and moved it over the mug. The slight orange glow of the heat cast warmed what he'd poured. Everyone ate in uncomfortable silence as Lucy seated herself at the table. Her face was a solid shade of crimson throughout the entire meal.

"I guess we should go. Can I help you do the dishes?" Adeline offered in a barely audible whisper.

Mrs. Haydenshire shook her head. "No. You all go on. Have a wonderful day. Are you coming back here after practice?"

"Yeah, we're all going to Em's last challenge tonight," Logan reminded his mother. His phrasing clearly had her feeling nostalgic again. She gazed at Emily as she blinked back tears.

Adeline grimaced. "I…think Mom's busy tonight, so she said I could stay over with Emily if it's all right with you?"

The governor visibly held back his fury. Whenever Adeline's mother wanted her out of the house, it meant she was entertaining men for money, a practice Governor Haydenshire despised. His jaw clenched as he forced a smile and patted Adeline's hand.

"Sweetheart," he soothed. "Lillian and I would really like it if you would consider moving in here. You certainly don't need permission to stay over whenever you'd like."

"Thank you. It's just that I worry about my mom. She needs me. I make sure the bills get paid, and you know…clean up and stuff."

"I know," the governor huffed, "but your mother is a grown woman and needs to behave as such. She's not your responsibility. I know it's a lot to think about at twenty-one, but I would really like you to consider our offer."

Adeline nodded with a whispered, "Yes, sir," before she turned her pleading gaze on Logan.

As Governor Haydenshire was one of the Realm governors who worked closely with the Crown Governor, he certainly wasn't accustomed to being told no, and his irritation was evident.

"Dad," Logan demanded.

The governor shook his head as he moved from the table, kissed his wife, and waved to everyone before leaving for work.

～

Rainer held Emily's hand as they followed Logan and Adeline into the Summation arena in the back west corner of the academy grounds.

The Predilection Orders' flags were being unfurled around the stands as the seniors assembled in the middle of the field. They were lining up with each of their Orders to receive the appropriately colored cap and gown. Rainer walked Emily to her friends in Auxiliary Order. He waited as Logan escorted Adeline to Valeduto, and they proceeded on to Ioses.

Isaiah Donaldson and Akio Mori offered Logan and Rainer high fives as they entered the line. Everyone was thrilled to be where they were.

Sawyer Morris rumbled out the first notes of the Ioses' song, and was joined quickly by the other members of the Order. They chanted their song to all of the other students. Rainer saw Emily laugh as he winked at her while he drawled, *"We'll be your safe harbor, to fight the battle ever won, ever protect, ever respect, Ioses won't be outdone."*

Rainer's father had also been head of Ioses when he'd been in school. His mother and Mrs. Haydenshire were both in Occamy Order, and Governor Haydenshire was in Adminis. Mrs. Haydenshire was actually a Double-Predilect. She was not only an Occamist, but she also summoned for Auxiliary, which made her a Receiver, just like Emily. Only her empathic abilities weren't nearly as strong as her Occamist rhythms.

Rainer watched as Emily glowed when Mentor Sweden handed her the gold collar to add to her gown for being named head of Auxiliary Order. She was beautiful, and she was his. Rainer's breath caught. He was unable to believe his luck.

"Mr. Lawson," he heard from someone in front of him. He snapped his attention back to what he was supposed to be doing.

"Oh, uh, thanks," Rainer stammered as Mentor Sullivan handed him the hunter-green cap and gown and his own gold collar for being head of Ioses.

They spent the next several hours practicing marching, standing, and then stating, "To protect," after Chancellor Wilshire called out Ioses. Logan and Rainer rolled their eyes repeatedly and made fairly off-color jokes about the mentors while they were shouting instructions at them.

Mitchell O'Ryan glared as Logan and Rainer made their way past him.

"So, Lawson," Mitchell huffed, "is Miss Haydenshire gonna finally make you a man after you graduate? Let me know if you need any help."

Rainer's jaw clenched. He knew Mitchell had no idea that any of what he'd said was even remotely true, in the crudest sense, of course, but just hearing his voice made Rainer's skin crawl.

Logan scowled. "Yeah, Mitch, unfortunately for you, my sister's only into guys with something in their sac."

Mitchell laughed derisively. "And how would you know, Haydenshire? You hitting that on the side? Guess that's better than the gutter trash you're hooking. At least she has a last name."

Logan drew back his fist, but Rainer caught him quickly. He flipped Mitchell off as he shoved Logan back to the Ioses' seats.

"I'm going to pretend I didn't see that." Mentor Sullivan chuckled.

"Sorry, sir," Rainer offered with a grimace. Logan was still scowling in Mitchell's direction. Mentor Sullivan slapped Rainer on the shoulder and gave him a grin. The smile suddenly made his wise, aged face look several years younger.

"Don't let him get to you. He comes from a long line of extremely useless individuals."

Rainer nodded. He knew that, and today was not the day for them to get in yet another fight defending Adeline. As stupid and patriarchal as it was, the Realm was still hung up on Gifted last names and Gifted families. Cal, Patrick, Connor, Logan, and Rainer had all gotten in a fair share of skirmishes to shut pricks like Mitch up about Adeline's lack of a Gifted name and crest. Nobody took on the Haydenshire boys and walked away unscathed. But the day before graduation, all of the idiots they were graduating with weren't worth it. They were too close to having everything they'd been working toward. Getting in trouble with Vindico for fighting was not an option.

CHAPTER II
TANGLED COULOMB'S WEB

At one o'clock, the seniors were released, and Emily made her way to Rainer. "Let's go eat. I'm starved."

"And what would the lady like to eat?" Rainer reveled in her smile. Logan and Adeline meandered their way. Since they'd all ridden together, they began discussing where to get lunch.

Adeline grimaced. "I don't have any money."

"Baby, I think I can take you out to lunch. You're my girlfriend," Logan huffed.

"I know, but you always pay…"

"And I always will."

Emily gave Adeline a forced smile. "You know those Ioses boys… always so protective." She shot Logan a glare as she clenched her jaw and uttered, "Sometimes overly so."

Logan rolled his eyes, took Adeline's hand, and pulled her toward Rainer's car.

Garrett and Levi, the third in line of all of the Haydenshire boys, came by for some of Mrs. Haydenshire's spaghetti and meatballs before

Emily's final challenge of her academy career. It was Emily's favorite meal, and it was made in her honor.

Emily was the Lead Receiver for the Venton Vixens. They'd had a shaky season.

Mrs. Haydenshire wished Emily luck as she kissed everyone who was headed back to Venton goodbye. The governor was attending, but she was staying home with the twins.

"We haven't practiced all week because of exams," Emily fussed as Rainer drove them toward the interstate.

"You'll be great, baby. You always are."

"I should be sad that this is my last challenge for Venton, but I want to graduate and challenge for the Angels so bad. I'm kind of glad this is my last challenge," she admitted as she bit her lip.

"Yeah, I know. I'm ready to really start life too."

They returned to the stadium that evening to find it vastly different than it had looked that morning. The scoreboards were lit with Venton Vixens v. Venton Waves. Student-made banners were hung from the concrete walls around the stands. "Ioses for Vixens" was scrawled across a large white sheet that hung near the locker room entrance. "Rainer and Emily forever!" was on one made by Auxiliary Order. Rainer chuckled as he kissed Emily's cheek.

Mentors walked the track around the field to make certain no one brought libations to the academy stadium. Emily smiled at Mentor Bryant as she scooted by them and wished Emily good luck.

"Thanks!" Emily called. Her brow furrowed as Mentor Bryant passed.

"What?" Rainer quizzed.

Emily shrugged as she studied her Creative Writing Mentor. "Her energy is kind of weird."

Rainer knew there was more. This certainly wasn't the first conversation they'd had about what other people were feeling. He assumed it was standard protocol when you were madly in love with a Receiver.

"Weird, how?"

"Sort of happy and deceptive and kind of passionate, I guess."

Rainer glanced back around the stadium again. "There's her

husband and their kids. Maybe they made use of her office while her kids got popcorn or something?"

Emily giggled.

Rachel Carson, the Vixens' Junior Receiver, rushed to them. "I'm going to cry when this is over. You're leaving me."

Emily embraced Rachel. "Don't cry. After tomorrow, you're the Vixens' lead." Rachel was a sophomore and had been lamenting Emily's graduation for the entire last semester.

Rainer offered Emily another good-luck kiss and then headed to the stands to take the seat Logan had saved for him.

Connor scooted in just before the teams were called onto the field.

"Hey, man," he greeted a friend of his from Visium Order who'd graduated with him the year before. "Has Em been crying all day about this?" he quizzed Rainer with a slight smirk. Emily's brothers were rarely sympathetic to her occasionally emotional reactions.

"Nah." Rainer shook his head. "She's pretty jazzed about trying out for the Angels."

"You think she'll make it?"

"Yeah, definitely. She's amazing."

Connor rolled his eyes and turned his attention to the field. Rainer studied the field as well. He wondered what the course for today's challenge might be.

Summation had been played by Gifted people for generations. The first professional teams were begun in the early 1800s. Women weren't allowed to challenge until the Arlington Angels' inception in the 1920s.

The Angels had changed the face and fabric of Gifted Summation. They'd led the charge for teams to do service projects all over the world, in every available capacity. Emily was overjoyed to have been recruited to try out, and Rainer was certain with her exceptional skill, she'd see her dreams come true.

He gave a loud wolf whistle as the Vixens raced onto the field first.

The energy-field aegis was projected from the poles that had been raised. The aegis prevented energy from outside the field, or arena, to enter the challenge. The Vixens' joule meter armbands were filled until they all glowed orange and read full. The meters would monitor the players' energy levels. Once it reached zero, the player was out and had to move off of the playing field.

After taking their places on the left side of the field, the Vixens waved to their fans.

"Come on, Em, let's do this!" Garrett chanted as Emily waved to Rainer and her brothers. After the Waves' joule meters were full, they raced to the right side of the field to cheers and applause from their fans.

Chancellor Wilshire moved to the center of the field. He summoned an orb of sound energy to project his voice. "Welcome, students and faculty, to our last Summation challenge at Venton this year. We wish all of our challengers the best of luck. May the best team win."

He summoned again. Rainer watched as four additional metal poles rose from the ground on each side of the field.

"Oh, no," he sighed.

Logan's face fell. "Ah geez! Again?"

It was a Coulomb's web challenge course. They were fairly popular, especially in academy challenges. Professional challenges were much more complicated, with vastly more energy changes required from each professional team. Coulomb's webs were cheap to construct, difficult to execute, and Emily despised them.

Summation challenges could come in any shape or form. They generally required that energy be transformed or manipulated in a series of steps necessary to release an iode, a large glass tube containing potential energy.

Once it was released, the energy would shift and produce a reaction such as confetti spraying forth, a loud trumpeting noise, or a fireworks display, that announced the winner. As soon as one team's iode was released, the challenge was over, and the aegis would release from the field.

Emily looked morose. The Coulomb's web challenge was introduced into Summation decades ago. This particular challenge made use of the team as a whole, with every player on the field at once. The captain, always an Adminis Predilect, would arrange the players around the four magnetized energy poles based on what the

Duco Predilect challenger, the Gifted mathematicians and the Visium challenger, those able to predict patterns in energy, suggested.

The challenger would harness the magnetic energy and then pass it to their closest teammate. Emily and Rachel would be placed where they could not only receive the magnetic energy, but convert it to electricity as well. They would use the electricity to light the lantern that held the iode. Once the lantern contained enough electricity to light, the iode would be released.

Coulomb's law dealt with the energy levels contained between two sources and the rate of drop-off that occurred when the sources were farther from one another. The challengers would need to be positioned in a web-shaped pattern in order to pass all of the magnetic energy to one another without much drop-off. This way the last player, typically one of the team Receivers, could transform it into electricity and light the lantern.

A Shield was typically stationed directly beside the last Receiver. They would be able to surround the energy stream with their shield cast to make certain that as much energy as the Receiver could pass got to the lantern without a great deal of waste.

Two additional poles moved up from the field. They were energy drains. If a player or their cast got too close, the drain would syphon their energy and cause the joule meter to dip too quickly. In professional Summation challenges, there were typically four drains to accompany the four magnets.

"Come on, Em, you can do this!" Rainer called as he watched a grin form on Emily's sweet face. Governor Haydenshire chuckled and shook his head.

"Teams to your therms!" Chancellor Wilshire called. The Vixens and the Waves moved to their lines on the field.

"Summon!" Wilshire cried.

Latavia Cenders, the Vixens' captain, moved onto the field with Ina Judson, their Duco Predilect. Sarika Barnes, their Visium Predilect, studied the arrangement of the poles from the other side of the field. They quickly came up with how they wanted to position the players. With a nod, they began arranging the Vixens.

Latavia positioned Rachel in the center of the web to begin the conversion to electricity. Emily was placed nearest the iode beside Jada Pearson, so she could shield the energy she was provided until Emily released the iode. The other eight players were positioned around the magnetic poles.

Alicia Phelps moved up and down the sidelines. She was the Vixens' Valeduto Predilect, their healer.

Valeduto Predilects, like Adeline, were Gifted with copious amounts of extra energy. They were remarkably calm individuals. The extra energy was made to be given to others for the purposes of healing. Alicia could refill two of the Vixens' joule meters during the challenge.

If the Vixens chose to have a player refilled, a minute would be added to their time. There was a great deal of strategy involved.

Latavia nodded to Sophia Hebert, the Vixens' enforcer. She pulled a massive amount of magnetic energy from the first pole and then turned and sent it in a solid stream to Evelyn, who turned and moved it to the next Vixen. Unfortunately, Latavia had miscalculated slightly, and Evelyn wasn't able to keep the stream steady because of the rate of drop-off between her and Julieta Lopez.

Rainer's head shot to the right to watch the Waves. Andrew Westerfield, their captain, had positioned everyone equal distance apart. He wagered that all of his players were of equal ability and would be able to pass the stream. Rainer doubted that the Waves would be able to accomplish the web under that premise. He moved his intent gaze back to the Vixens.

Rachel had the stream. She closed her eyes in deep concentration as she made the first conversions to electricity.

The electricity was much easier to pass, but the loss of energy when passing electricity was greater.

Sophia's joule meter began to flash red, and Amanda ordered her meter filled. An additional minute was added to the Vixens' time. Rainer grimaced and clenched his teeth. Jada shot her shield over the electricity, and then Leah Morgan pushed the electricity to Emily.

"Come on, Em," Rainer joined in with Logan and Connor as they cheered their little sister on.

"Come on, baby girl! You've got this!" Governor Haydenshire

called. The stream was too weak. The loss between Evelyn and Hannah had been too significant.

"Come on, Emily. Rainer will fill your tank when you get home!" encouraged some rather crude Ioses juniors seated a few rows ahead of Rainer and Emily's family. The governor scowled, and Rainer pretended not to notice. Logan leaned forward and popped the offender on the back of the head. He turned to Logan, glared, and rubbed his head.

"That's my little sister, you creep." As Logan also held office in Ioses order, his reply was no more than an eye roll. Most of the school knew that Rainer and Emily were an item and lived together on Haydenshire Farm. Rainer doubted the quip about the energy exchange that happened when Gifted people had sex was meant to be derisive. He probably assumed that Rainer would, in fact, restore Emily's waning energies with his own after the challenge.

Rainer didn't want to give that too much thought, as he was currently seated near Governor Haydenshire, so he concentrated on Emily.

The Vixens' fans were going wild. As Emily gave everything she had, she leaned toward the iode and closed her eyes as she forced all of the remaining magnetic energy from the stream and converted it all to electricity. Her meter flashed red and showed only one bar.

Ben Cobson, the Junior Shield for the Waves, was casting the electricity, but their Receiver was struggling. All of the Haydenshires, Rainer, and most of Auxiliary Order were on their feet, screaming. Emily gave one final push with both of her hands joined. The waves of electricity lit the iode and it shattered.

Confetti showered over the Vixens as they all came together, screaming and jumping up and down on the field. The Waves had refilled two of their players' Joule meters and were already a full minute behind.

It was the first time the Vixens had won a Coulomb's Web Challenge that season. Emily was overjoyed. Rainer raced to meet her at the gates to the field. She flew into his arms, and he lifted her up in the exuberance of his embrace.

"You did it!" he gushed. She was surrounded by her cheering teammates.

The Vixens quickly decided to take Governor Haydenshire up on his offer to take them out for milkshakes.

~

A little while later, Rainer sat in a booth at Mae's with Emily leaned up against him as she talked with her friends. Graduation the next evening was discussed along with who the Vixens would be bringing as their dates to the party at the Haydenshires'. The girls all thanked Governor Haydenshire for taking them out after the challenge. Rainer noted the wistful, reminiscent expression on the governor's face as he congratulated the ladies on their victory.

Adeline was staying in Emily's room, which made it impossible for Rainer to hold her until she fell asleep. He lay awake in his room that night, staring out the window at the star-strewn Virginia sky and thinking about what the next day would hold. He would be twenty-one, and the full contents of his parents' trust and estate would be his. He planned on immediately writing the Haydenshires a check.

Then they would graduate, and then…his heart picked up pace. He and Emily were planning to leave the party around nine, which would put them in Virginia Beach before midnight if they didn't stop and he casted the engine on the straightaways.

He swallowed hard as excitement and terror swirled in a volatile cocktail in the pit of his stomach. He stared at the clock on the table between his and Logan's bed. It was almost one. Twenty-one doesn't feel any different than twenty, he thought wryly. After punching his pillow a few times, Rainer rolled his eyes at Logan who was snoring softly.

~

"Happy Birthday!" Emily lifted the quilts on his bed and scooted in beside him. He smiled before he opened his eyes.

"Hey there, baby." He wrapped his arm around her and pulled her back to his chest with his customary greeting.

After making certain Logan's bed was empty, Rainer shifted and eased Emily underneath him. He slid his hands to her waist and started to kiss her, but then remembered that he hadn't yet brushed his teeth. He grimaced as she giggled.

Emily shot him a smirk as she traced her hand over the slit in his boxers. He growled as his breath caught, and he shuddered from the heavenly sensation.

"What do you want for your birthday, Mr. Lawson?" she flirted and waggled her eyebrows at him as he throbbed in her hand.

"Mmmm…you, Miss Haydenshire."

She laughed. "That…has already been arranged."

"Has it?" He pulled her closer.

"It has…"

"Then this will be one hell of a birthday."

"I'd better go get ready. You need to leave soon." She scooted from his bed.

He sat up and ran his hands through his hair. After he raced through the shower and donned a suit and tie, he headed down the stairs.

"Happy Birthday!" rang from all of the available Haydenshires as Rainer blushed and thanked everyone. Mrs. Haydenshire had placed candles in his pancakes, his favorite breakfast.

"Thank you." He was truly touched by the effort. Mrs. Haydenshire had cooked his birthday breakfast every year since he'd turned fourteen, and Rainer was endlessly thankful for everything the Haydenshires did for him.

He pulled Emily in for a relatively long, drawn-out kiss. He figured Governor Haydenshire would let it slide for his birthday, which he did. After everyone ate, Logan, Rainer, and the governor piled into the minivan and left for the Senate in Arlington.

The Senate resided on the top floor of the Pentagon building. Very few Non-Gifted people knew what existed on the top floor, but those who did were watched closely to make certain their knowledge remained with them alone.

The pine trees and interstate signs blurred past the windows as Rainer contemplated how to get the governor to accept a check from him. He knew it wouldn't be easy. He was so caught up in the negotiations in his head he hardly noticed when they pulled into the parking deck.

"So, after we leave here, we can go buy me a new car, right?" Logan teased.

"Logan," Governor Haydenshire scolded.

"Kidding. I'm just kidding."

Logan and Rainer were quiet as they followed the governor through the many security checkpoints and up the elevator. They exited on the northwest side of the Pentagon, the wing that contained the governors' offices and Iodex. They heard someone shouting angrily as they moved down the corridor. The sign on the door read "Chief of Iodex."

"That's Vindico's office," Logan hissed. Rainer nodded and swallowed hard. From the sound of it, Vindico was reading the riot act to another Iodex officer who hadn't done something the way he'd wanted it done.

They moved on until they halted in front of the Crown Governor's office. Rainer and Logan had both been there before, of course, when Rainer's father was crown, but it had been several years. Every time Rainer was in the Gifted Senate for whatever reason, he always avoided the office. It just reminded him too much of his dad and how much he missed him.

Governor Haydenshire knocked, and the door was opened immediately by Crown Governor Carrington.

"Rainer," he drawled in his low, soothing intonation. His kind, dark face that matched his deep brown eyes was formed into a pride-filled smile. Rainer's shoulders lowered slightly. He pulled Rainer in for a hug.

"Come in, come in. Logan, I haven't seen you in ages, either." Logan shook his hand. Regis Carrington had been one of Rainer's father's dearest friends and his choice to succeed him as Crown Governor. He was kindhearted, thoughtful, and wise. He always made a person feel that he genuinely cared about what they had to say.

"I know you have a big day today." Governor Carrington grinned broadly. "And I also know that two strapping lads like yourselves would rather be spending time with the women who have you wrapped around their fingers than in here with me, no matter how much money I'm giving you. Isn't that right, Stephen?" He shared a chuckle with Governor Haydenshire.

"Oh, I'm certain." Governor Haydenshire sighed in agreement.

"As soon as Will gets here, we'll get down to business." Governor Carrington moved behind the large cherry wood desk in the center of the navy blue, plush, carpeted office.

Will Haydenshire was a powerful Duco Predilect. His ability to read and affect the energy of the economy had earned him his seat as one of the youngest Vice Presidents of the Senate Bank. A few months ago, Rainer had asked him if he'd handle the Lawson Family Estate for him.

Will rushed in the office a few minutes later. "I'm sorry," he offered everyone in the room. "Little distracted this morning. Brooke called me and then Warren had something to ask me before I headed down here. I have everything set for you though, Rainer." He handed Rainer several documents.

Governor handed Rainer an additional stack of papers. "This gives every penny in your parents' estate solely to you. If anyone should wish to make a claim against that, you come talk to either me or Will or Chief Vindico, who I understand will be your boss in a few weeks' time." Rainer's stomach clenched as he understood that even the Crown Governor was aware there could be trouble from his uncle.

Rainer tried to glance nonchalantly at the lengthy list of numbers on the documents Will handed him, but his eyes goggled. There were several more zeros after the number than he'd originally anticipated. He swallowed and directed his attention back to Governor Carrington.

"If you'll just sign here and here." Will pointed to two lines on longer piece of paper. "I thought it would be easier to just change the name on the accounts to your name, instead of going through all the trouble of setting you up new ones. But when you're ready to discuss how you want to invest it all, just come see me. For now, your dad has you well taken care of. The estate has earned quite a bit of interest since your father passed away."

"Thank you," Rainer choked.

"Now, if you still want to keep the account your monthly allowance has been deposited into for all these years, you can use that as your primary checking account. It's entirely up to you how we set this up."

Rainer nodded. "Let's just do that until 1 start working and then I just want to live off of my Iodex paychecks. I don't really want to touch the inheritance that much."

Will and his father shared a quick grin. "No problem," Will assured him.

"Here are the checkbooks and deposit slips for the various accounts, and here is a card to make withdrawals from the smallest, whenever the need should arise." Will handed everything to Rainer. "And if you need any help with the investments, Mr. Buffett said he'd be happy to help. I'm good, but I'm not that good," Will joked.

Everyone in the office chuckled.

"Now..." Governor Carrington's voice caught as Rainer looked up from the stack of papers. "Here is your father's safety deposit box. He wanted me to give this to you on your twenty-first birthday, but..." Governor Carrington held up his hand. "If I may suggest, why don't you wait until you're back on the farm to open this. Give yourself some time to go through it all." Rainer wondered what might be in the box.

"And one last thing..." the Crown Governor gave him another broad grin. "I wanted to give you something for your birthday." He handed Rainer a velvet box with a snap closure.

"Thank you, sir. You didn't have to do that." Rainer was shocked by the gesture.

"Your father was one of my closest friends. He left this to me in his will, but I want you to have it. It's the least I can do."

As he drew a steadying breath, Rainer popped open the box. Inside was a heavy silver watch. Tears immediately sprang to Rainer's eyes.

"Is this...?" The memories from the deepest trappings of his soul rushed to the forefront of his mind. It seemed too good to be true.

Governor Carrington nodded. "Your father's watch. It was one of his prized possessions. Look, the Ioses symbol is there in the center."

Rainer nodded. He was overwhelmed by the gift. He lifted the watch and flipped it over to read J.E.L., his father's initials carved into the back just over the Lawson crest, complete with the phoenix and the falcon.

Governor Haydenshire gave him a reassuring smile. "I don't recall Joe ever being without that watch, and he'd be thrilled that you have it now."

"Put it on," Governor Carrington urged. The heavy weight on his wrist was mirrored by the expectations on his shoulders. He couldn't ever recall his father being without the watch either. He couldn't believe it was now in his possession. He'd assumed it had been taken when his father had been murdered. He'd never thought to ask. He had no idea it had been willed to Governor Carrington. Everything around his father's assassination was a blur of crushing heartbreak.

"Maybe now you and Emily can make it in before curfew," Governor Haydenshire joked to ease the heavy emotions in the energy in the room.

After several additional documents had been signed, the Crown Governor escorted them out of the office.

They walked down the corridors until they stopped and smiled at Chief Vindico. Rainer wasn't certain how to behave since the guy had effectively crushed him and Logan in a duel a few days before and had then offered them a job.

He decided to keep quiet and let Governor Haydenshire carry the conversation. Chief Vindico appeared to be constructed entirely of chiseled muscle and raw nerve. His hair was dark brown and thick, fixed in a slightly messy cut around his face. His jaw was stubbled, and his eyes were bloodshot. He looked like he hadn't slept in several days. He wore a handgun in a shoulder holster that appeared to have been custom-made to fit over his bicep.

"How's it going, Governor Haydenshire?" His face was just as chiseled as the rest of his body.

"Good, Daniel. How are you?" The governor returned the kind smile.

"I'm all right." Vindico shrugged, but Rainer noted that he didn't meet Governor Haydenshire's eyes as he said this. He turned his attention to Logan and Rainer. "Can't wait to get you two trained and started."

"We're looking forward to it," Logan assured him.

"Enjoy graduation tonight and knock a few back for me. Then we'll bury you in work."

Rainer and Logan nodded, neither certain what an appropriate response might be. With a wave, they followed the governor out.

They entered the elevator once again, and Governor Haydenshire looked concerned. "Don't let Daniel scare you. He's just a little intense. He's...very driven." Rainer sensed there was more to the story, but he didn't ask. Neither Logan nor Rainer would ever have admitted that they were intimidated, so they simply nodded their understanding. Governor Haydenshire chuckled as they made their way back to the van before he checked his watch.

"I'd better get you both home so you can get ready for graduation. I don't want your mother to shoot me for leaving her with the twins all day while she's trying to get ready for the party."

In the end, everyone ended up helping prepare for the party until the moment they had to get ready to leave for the ceremony.

CHAPTER 12

THE END OF THE BEGINNING

Rainer reattached his father's watch around his wrist and donned the gold collar with the Ioses crest in the center. The pressure began to build.

Mrs. Haydenshire took endless photographs of the graduates, and then everyone loaded into the available cars and headed to the academy.

"So, we're not supposed to pick up Adeline?" Emily asked Logan for the third time.

"She swears either her mom is coming,"—he rolled his eyes at the preposterous notion—"or, she says she's going to let Adeline use her car."

Emily nodded, but she looked concerned as she turned back to face the windshield. "I have a bad feeling." Her voice was almost lost in the radio and the blow of the air conditioning.

Nervous energy rolled off her in waves. Rainer wasn't certain if it was graduation or Adeline that had her receptors pulsing tensely. Everyone was relieved to find Adeline waiting for them at the entrance gates to the stadium.

Logan's jaw clenched as he forced a smile. She was alone. "I'm not even going to ask."

Rainer slapped him on the back, and they made their way to Adeline.

Every Haydenshire son and their dates plus all of Emily's grandparents and her uncles were there to see Logan, Emily, and Rainer graduate. They took up almost an entire section of stands. The families that found the Haydenshires just a little bit too much looked on with disdain. Governor and Mrs. Haydenshire hugged all of their children, and then began trying to entertain the irrepressible twins.

"I guess this is it." Emily looked terrified.

"Are you okay?" They walked to the area where the graduates were to line up. Rainer concentrated and let soothing energy flow from his hand into Emily's. She nodded and gave him a sweet smile, but he saw the fear in her eyes. "Baby, if you're nervous about tonight," he whispered, "we don't have to do anything."

She rolled her eyes. "I'm nervous about my speech and about Adeline. I'm not nervous about tonight. That's the only thing I'm looking forward to, and I plan to think about that while I give this speech." She held up several notecards with her keynotes on them.

Rainer chuckled. "Just don't start telling the crowd what you're thinking about while you're giving your speech, please."

She laughed, and her eyes danced as she gazed at him. His heartbeat stuttered momentarily.

"I just have a weird feeling about Adeline," she explained. Rainer's eyes immediately sought Logan and Adeline. They were heading to the other side of the stadium.

"Weird how?"

"Like something bad is going to happen."

"Is there anything I can do?"

"I don't think so. It doesn't feel like the kind of thing that can be stopped. The energy around it is already in motion."

As they headed toward the appropriate Order lines, Rainer saw them. "Shit!" He slid in front of Emily. She sighed as cameras and microphones were thrust in front of him. He kept his hand shielding his face and used his body to shield Emily from the reporters. They'd been a constant source of pain in his life ever since his father's murder.

"What do you think your father would say if he could be here today?" a reporter drawled. *To get the hell out of my face and away from my girlfriend,* Rainer thought spitefully.

"Rainer, do you have aspirations to become Crown Governor after graduation?" another reporter called.

"NO!" The question was ridiculous.

"Any plans to get married soon, Miss Haydenshire?" a female reporter called to Emily.

"Miss Haydenshire and I are not answering any more questions. Please leave us alone."

He hesitated to leave Emily with the Auxiliary Predilects, but they needed to line up.

"Are you sure you're okay?" He stood between her and the numerous camera crews.

"I'll be fine. Watch this." With a smile, she scooted to the front of the line. She was the head of the Order, so she would march in first. It was extremely convenient that there were numerous other students, several of them rather large guys, now blocking her from the reporters. *That's my girl.* Rainer smiled as she grinned at him.

He winked then made the same move as he edged to the head of Ioses line with Logan right behind him. The reporters called out several other questions which everyone ignored. Security moved in and relocated the reporters back to the press box.

Music swelled from the casted speakers, and Rainer's heart raced. He checked his pocket to make certain he had his speech. When Mentor Sullivan nodded, he drew a deep breath and marched Ioses Order into the stadium. The thunderous applause reverberated in his soul.

The Predilects were seated in an oval pattern, all facing one another, flanking the center aisle. The chancellor stood at the large oak podium on a stage at the north end of the field. As each of the Predilect Orders filed into their specified seating area, banners with their large crest were unfurled behind them.

After the graduates were seated, Chancellor Wilshire welcomed the families and friends, along with the school governors, the attending Realm governors, and then the Crown Governor.

"And now we will welcome each of the Predilects represented here at the academy and at all Gifted academies throughout the world," Wilshire stated nobly. "Every Order is of equal importance to our people. For we must have a division of labor, work together, and use our Predilects for the goodness of the Realm as a whole if we are to succeed."

Rainer tried not to yawn as Logan chuckled.

"We'll begin with Adminis Order."

All of Adminis stood up, just as they'd been instructed. They vowed, "To govern," in unison.

"Auxiliary Order." Rainer smiled as Emily stood with her entire Order as they chanted, "To serve."

"And the Ioses Order Shields," the chancellor called. Rainer and Logan stood. "To protect," they vowed.

"Next we'll have Valeduto Order." Wilshire gestured toward the order seated to the right of Auxiliary.

Logan smiled at Adeline proudly as she stood with her classmates. "To heal."

"Occamy Order," was called next. "To create and provide," they chanted.

"And one of my favorites, as it is my Predilect," Chancellor Wilshire tried for a joke, but it fell flat, so he called, "Scholera Order."

Scholera stood and stated, "To teach."

Fergus Martin fell forward and almost took out a girl who was seated in front of him as Logan and Rainer shook their heads.

"Duco Order...." The Order stood and chanted, "To plan and calculate."

"And now, Visvirees Order..."

Rainer and Logan grimaced as O'Ryan stood with a smirk and pompously vowed, "To will."

"And last, but certainly not least," Wilshire assured, "Visium Order." The final order stood and chanted, "To observe, analyze, and understand."

Chancellor Wilshire seated the Orders and then droned on about what they'd learned at the academy. Rainer stopped himself from checking his watch, since he was on the front row and facing the assembled crowd.

With each passing moment, leashing his lust for Emily became more and more difficult. All day, he'd been losing the battle of trying to think about anything but her and the beach house. *Just make it through graduation and the party.* He slung the large sleeve of his gown aside and discreetly checked his watch.

Logan noticed and chuckled. "Eager to be somewhere else?"

"Shut it," Rainer demanded through his clenched teeth, which only succeeded in making Logan laugh harder.

The head of Adminis took the podium, and Rainer smiled at Emily. She was next. She bit her lip and pushed her hair behind her ear. He winked at her.

A few minutes later, Nigel Parmen seated himself. If he always kept his speeches that short, he'd be a shoo-in for Crown Governor.

Rainer smiled as Chancellor Wilshire said, "And next we'll hear from the head of Auxiliary House, Miss Emily Anne Haydenshire."

The crowd applauded as Rainer let out a loud wolf whistle, which made her giggle. Logan shook his head as he laughed at Rainer outright.

Rainer listened intently to Emily tell everyone about what Auxiliary Order had meant to her, what she hoped to accomplish after graduation, and how important Receivers were to the Realm as a whole even though their powers were often scoffed at.

Logan shot Rainer his customary smirk. "And right after graduation, I plan to take Rainer Lawson to our beach house and let him play hide the salami in my clam shack."

Rainer rolled his eyes as he elbowed Logan hard.

"Ouch." Logan rubbed his bicep and scowled.

A few minutes later, Emily looked relieved as she returned to her seat. Rainer tried not to focus on what she'd said she would be thinking about, since he now needed to be able to walk up to the podium.

"And our next speech is from a young man we're all so proud to call our own. We're so thankful to him. We share in his devastating losses, and will always be so grateful for all his parents meant to our Realm."

Heat scalded Rainer's face.

"I'd like to welcome the Head of Ioses Order, Mr. Rainer Emory Lawson!" Chancellor Wilshire called, and then began applauding as Rainer took the podium. He received a standing ovation.

I haven't done anything yet, Rainer wanted to scream. *It's my dad you're applauding, not me.* As he shook himself slightly, Rainer began his speech and steadfastly ignored the cameras that clicked feverishly from the other side of the field. He grimaced as he concluded his speech with a quote from his father. "With our gifts should come great generosity. We should expect greatness from those with much to give. We mustn't rest on our gifts, expecting them to serve us. We must serve them, and leave the world a better place than it was when we arrived here." He ended and glanced around at the crowds. People were wiping away tears as they stood again and offered him thunderous applause.

He clenched his jaw as he returned to his seat. He caught Emily's eye. She smiled at him sweetly. She knew him better than anyone else ever had. She knew how emotional and embarrassed he was by the display from the crowd.

Rainer did note that a small portion of Visvirees wasn't standing or applauding—all of Mitchell's friends. This brought about a genuine chuckle as he returned to his seat beside Logan.

The crowd settled, and the rest of the Heads of Orders gave speeches.

Finally, Crown Governor Carrington made his way to the stage. Chancellor Wilshire began calling names and handing out diplomas.

Emily's name was called and she blushed as she shook the Chancellor's and then the Crown Governor's hands, before she made her way back to her seat.

Rainer decided if he gave the press a little something now, they'd have a much easier time getting to the beach house without an entourage. He raised his eyebrow and gestured Emily to him. She beamed and rushed across the field. He wrapped her up in his arms and planted a long drawn-out kiss on her lips.

The crowd went wild. The cameras moved in. He released her, and she laughed and blew him another kiss as she returned to her seat.

The Haydenshires were laughing as well. The tension in Rainer's shoulders eased slightly as he waited to hear his name called. As Logan's name had been called right after Emily's, he'd missed most of the kiss, but he shook his head as he returned to his seat.

"Rainer Emory Lawson," rang from the Chancellor, and the crowd cheered again.

People Rainer had never even met felt they had some claim on his life because of what his parents had accomplished. Unable to discern how these people couldn't understand that he wasn't his dad, Rainer sighed. His father had been a great man. *I'm just me.*

He would never understand why they wanted to know his whereabouts or about his and Emily's relationship. People were perfectly willing to purchase papers and magazines and to give hard-earned money to get behind paywalls on news sites filled with more lies than truths just to feel a part of it.

The Chancellor moved through the names quickly, and all of a sudden caps were flying in the air, and they were graduates. Emily made her way to him.

"Is it bad that I'm really glad that's over?" She fell against his chest.

"I certainly am." He was still annoyed with the press and the crowds.

All he wanted was to be alone with her where no one would know where they were or what they were doing. He was sick of everyone intruding on their lives.

That night of all nights he just wanted everyone else to leave them the hell alone. In his mind, that night belonged to only him and Emily. But he knew, even if they got to the Haydenshires' beach house without the press finding out for a few days, it would make its way into the news eventually. It seemed inevitable.

He leaned in as he whispered how much he loved her and how proud he was of her. The Haydenshires made their way over to them. Friends from each of the different Predilects came by to shake their hands and tell them that they'd see them at the party.

"I can't believe we won't be back for a graduation or throw

another party until the twins are here." Mrs. Haydenshire was on the verge of tears again as she hoisted Henry up as her example.

"Honey, I'm certain we'll have much to celebrate over the next few years," Governor Haydenshire soothed.

"She'll be pregnant by morning," Emily whimpered. All of her brothers gave a dejected nod.

They all headed toward the parking lot to try to get back to the farm before the party guests arrived. Adeline looked extremely concerned. "I'm just going to go by and check on Mom. She said someone was going to drop her off here."

"Why don't I come with you?" Logan offered, but she shook her head.

"No, you go on. I'm sure your mom needs your help. I'll come over as soon as I make sure Mom's okay."

Logan handed her his cell phone. "Call me if you need me."

She kissed his cheek and headed to her mother's late-model Buick, with badly chipped paint and two spare tires.

"I'll catch a ride with Connor." Logan shot Rainer his signature smirk. "I'm sure you two have a lot to talk about." He shuddered slightly as he tried not to focus too much on Emily's evening plans.

Emily leaned up on her tiptoes, threw her arms around his neck, and kissed his jaw. "Thank you. You're the best big brother ever."

Logan chuckled. "And in *this* family, that's really saying something."

Rainer turned the key but skipped revving the engine since her father was standing near his car. "Are you ready?" His voice snagged on the lust gathered in his throat.

She smiled at him. She had his number. She always did. "Do you mean for the party or for the beach house?"

"Either." His pulse began to race.

"I'm ready."

He willed his heartbeat back to a normal rhythm. He drew steadying breaths as he drove the familiar route back to Haydenshire Farm.

"Are you all packed?" she offered him a slight subject change.

"Uh, yeah." His voice sounded distant even to himself. "I need to get gas before we head out, but I have everything else."

"I packed some stuff for us for breakfast, coffee and everything, but we can get more groceries once we get there." She gazed up at him. "I really can't wait to get there. I wish we could go now."

"Me too," he admitted in a choked whisper that made her smile. She slid her hand to his thigh. His breath caught sharply. His body willed her hand to slide higher. "Baby, how long do we have to stay at this party? I'm losing it."

She shivered. It made him ache. He longed to see her, all of her. Desperation to touch her, to feel her against him, to move her body with his own, coursed through him. His shield craved her rhythms. It pulsed in need acute to the point of pain.

To wrap her up in him, in his energy, to keep her safe, for her to surround him, consumed his every thought. He wanted to make love with her, and he wanted it now. He'd waited long enough.

"Just long enough to appease Mom and Dad." She looked as eager as he felt. He pulled his car onto the field and parked near the gate, so they could get out easily. Other party guests were arriving, and the fields were filling up.

"I'm gonna go get our bags and put them in the car." Rainer assumed she wouldn't want everyone at the party to know about their evening plans, and he would always be her Shield.

"That's a good idea." She didn't sound quite as sure of herself as she had a moment before.

Mrs. Haydenshire was already loading up trays with food. She cupped her hand and moved it over the platters as she casted everything to the perfect temperature, then took them out to the tables set up on the large back deck.

Rainer followed Emily to her room. She handed him her large, purple Auxiliary duffle bag that was full to bursting, and then several smaller bags. He grinned at her and tried not to chuckle. After retrieving his one loses duffle bag, he headed back to the car.

"That's all you packed?" She followed him back to the Mustang. He laughed, popped open the trunk, and then kissed her forehead.

"First, I'm a guy. Second, we're going to the beach." He winked at her. "And last, it was my understanding we wouldn't be needing much to wear."

She smirked. "But what will you do when we get there?" She gave him looks that threatened to make him spontaneously combust.

He shuddered and pulled her to him. He turned her and backed her up to the side of his car. He pushed his now-straining erection against her soft stomach. Her eyes goggled as she panted.

"You, baby." He let the lust that had been coursing through his veins leak into his tone just before he devoured her mouth.

She gasped for breath as he finally released her. "I want to go now. I don't want to wait anymore."

He closed his eyes and forced himself to breathe. He could feel her. Their energy danced around them desperate to be joined. He wanted to be a part of her, and he didn't think he could wait for another dose of her energy.

"Me either, sweetheart, but we have to stay for a little while." He prayed she wouldn't ask him again. He wasn't certain how many times he could put her off. Rainer had never wanted to leave Haydenshire Farm so badly in all of his life.

She moved away from him. She seemed to need a little space. He understood only too well. If they were going to have to spend the next couple of hours entertaining the crowd of people coming to her parents' home, then they were going to have to let the electricity between them die down a little.

CHAPTER 13

TO HEAL THE WOUNDED

An hour later, the party was in full swing as the sun sank low over the back fields. Rainer glanced at his watch again. He chuckled. If his father knew he was using his watch to count down the last hours of his virginity, he probably would have found that humorous.

A few people were singing with the karaoke machine and several others were dancing and applauding their efforts.

Logan was frantic. Adeline hadn't shown up yet. He'd called his own cell phone repeatedly, but there'd been no answer.

"Here." Rainer threw him his keys. Logan's Accord was locked in a sea of cars. "Go check on her."

"Thank you." Logan waved halfheartedly to Rainer and Emily as they danced to the loud music that played on the outdoor speakers.

The party was a huge success, just as it had been all the years before. Emily moved to the large metal tubs situated throughout the partygoers to retrieve a few Dr Peppers.

She was nervous about Adeline as well. Rainer could feel it as he swayed her in his arms. She was also distracted with thoughts about the beach house and worried that was affecting her reads. She hadn't wanted to mention her worries to Logan.

As soon as she'd moved away from Rainer, Will, Garrett, and Levi pounced. They looked like they were definitely up to no good.

"So, what's this I hear about you and Em going to the beach house for the week?" Garrett choked back laughter. Rainer glanced around to see where the governor was and how far away Emily had gotten.

"Uh, yeah." He nodded. He didn't want to appear intimidated or like he felt that they were doing anything wrong.

"You better take care of her," Will demanded, not joking in any way.

"Always, you know that." Rainer didn't bat an eye at that demand. Suddenly, they were all laughing.

"Hey, loosen up, man. Surely you know we're just teasing." Levi chuckled. "Have fun. We know you're a good guy. We raised you."

Rainer's chest released as he allowed himself to breathe. The sentiment certainly couldn't have been more truthful. What was wrong with him? He shook himself.

Emily returned and handed him a cold Dr Pepper. "And what are you three doing?"

"Making sure he takes care of our baby sister." Garrett tousled her hair. She rolled her eyes, but then a delighted mischievous gleam lit Garrett's face as he grabbed a Coke from a nearby tub and shook it violently.

He aimed it at Emily, but Rainer was faster. He cupped his hand and formed a green glow, and then he threw the shield in front of Emily and bounced the spewing cola back at Garrett. She laughed and threw her arms around Rainer who shot Garrett a cocky grin.

"Well played." He laughed as he cupped his own hand with a slightly heated orange glow and dried his clothes.

The good-natured joking ended suddenly when Logan returned. He wouldn't have even had time to make it to the end of the property to Rainer's car.

Adeline was in his arms, and she was sobbing. Concerned glances were shared by Emily and Rainer and then all of Emily's older brothers. Patrick and Connor joined the ranks quickly as Governor and Mrs. Haydenshire moved in.

"What's wrong?" the governor demanded. Adeline was cradled in

Logan's long, muscled arms. He was swaying her and soothing her. His shield was locked tightly over her. No one could get near her. He didn't answer his father's question. No one spoke. Other party guests moved away to give them some space. No one wanted to encounter Logan's shield cast.

"Adeline, are you alright?" Emily was on the verge of tears herself. Adeline turned from Logan's chest slightly. Her eye was swollen and purple. Her face was badly bruised. She was holding her arm oddly. It appeared to be broken.

Mrs. Haydenshire gasped. Emily's hand flew to her mouth.

"You are not going back to that apartment ever!" Logan commanded. "You are moving in here. I should never have let you go back alone. What was I thinking?"

This only served to make Adeline cry harder.

"Come here, sweetheart. Let's go inside," Mrs. Haydenshire soothed. "We'll get you all fixed up."

Adeline shook her head. "I can do it, Mrs. Haydenshire. I just can't get calmed down." She shuddered as renewed sobs stammered from her.

Mrs. Haydenshire continued to tenderly guide everyone into the kitchen.

"Do you know how that happened?" Governor Haydenshire demanded of Logan.

He nodded and looked like he might be sick.

"Her mother had a few *customers* when Adeline arrived. One guy thought he was getting a two-for-one deal. She held him off with a shield cast, but she's a healer, so she just barely escaped."

"Logan, you need to go be with her now, son," Governor Haydenshire ordered. "Don't yell at her. She needs you to listen to her. She knows she can't go back, but she doesn't need you to tell her that right now.

"William, call Dan. Have him take an Elite team to Candy Parker's apartment," the governor ordered.

"Garrett," the governor turned to his next son, but Garrett was already on the phone with the Non-Gifted police chief.

Garrett was a Gifted Police Officer, or an Iodex Officer as they were known in the Gifted Realm. He worked as a liaison at the Non-Gifted precinct. He handled situations like this one where the Realms collided. He handled plenty of Non-Gifted criminals as well, but this was his specialty.

Governor Haydenshire nodded. "Connor, you and Rainer stay here in case they followed her. Levi, Patrick, let's go." Emily laid her head on Rainer's chest and he held her, but there were no words to make what had happened to her best friend better.

"I want to go check on her," Emily pled. Rainer led her into the house.

Adeline was seated on the wide sectional sofa that took up a large portion of the Haydenshires' family room. She was still sobbing as Logan held her and wiped away her tears. Mrs. Haydenshire was working on her wrist, but Adeline was distraught. Mrs. Haydenshire had a difficult time harnessing Adeline's energy to guide her body to heal.

Logan stopped her efforts. "Let me do it, Mom." He cradled Adeline to him. Mrs. Haydenshire was crying as well. She nodded and backed away.

Rainer and Emily stood in the doorway. Logan was only an average healer. His Predilection was as a protector. His energy was to stop anything that tried to hurt others, to prevent terrible things from occurring. It wasn't to heal them once they'd already happened. Had Logan been with Adeline when she'd walked into the apartment, Rainer doubted whoever the sick bastards were would have survived Logan's shield cast.

"Look at me, sweetheart," Logan soothed.

She drew a shuddered breath, lifted her head off of his shoulder, and gazed into his eyes. Her tears continued to pour. Logan closed his eyes, and Rainer watched a powerful blue light glow from Logan's hand. His eyes opened, and he tenderly touched her wrist.

"Feel me, Ad," he urged. "Come on, baby, it's me, just let me in. Just let me heal you." Rainer and Emily watched as Adeline relaxed. Her body went limp as he healed her wrist.

To Rainer's shock, Logan didn't have to stop to summon in more energy as he moved to her face. The light in his hand seemed to somehow glow brighter.

Mrs. Haydenshire looked at her son adoringly as she wiped away tears. Emily began to cry in earnest as Rainer held her to him.

The swollen purple and green markings that had marred Adeline's delicate features begin to yellow and then disappear. When he'd finished, she collapsed against his chest.

"Take her upstairs, Logan," Mrs. Haydenshire directed. "Stay with her. Keep her in your shield."

Logan scooped Adeline into his arms as he moved her toward the stairs.

"She can stay in my room," Emily offered timidly as she swallowed down her tears.

"No." Logan carried her up to his room.

Mrs. Haydenshire shook her head. "I cannot believe this. That woman, who gave birth to one of the sweetest spirits I've ever been in the presence of"—she gestured her hand up toward Logan's room—"is actually mad at her after all of that, and that was the thing Adeline is most worried about."

"Dad told Will to call Dan Vindico." Emily tried to reassure her mother.

"Well, there's another spirit I'm not certain can ever be mended." Mrs. Haydenshire shook her head. Her statement thoroughly confused Rainer and Emily. "But good. Something needs to be done, and if you need something done, Dan is the Shield you want."

Will and Garrett had grown up with Vindico. They'd been the best of friends all through school. Garrett and Dan still worked together occasionally. Rainer wasn't certain why, but it seemed they didn't hang out much outside of work anymore. This didn't seem to be the time to ask questions though, so they followed Mrs. Haydenshire back into the kitchen.

"You two go on back outside. As soon as your father and brothers get back, you can head to the beach. I'm sure you're ready to start your vacation."

Emily glanced back up the stairs. She seemed uncertain whether they should leave after everything that had happened.

"Logan will take care of her," Mrs. Haydenshire reassured. "You two deserve a break."

She shooed them back to the party, and Connor cornered them. "Is she okay?" He looked just as disturbed as Rainer felt.

Emily shook her head. "Emotionally, no. Not at all. But physically, yes. Logan healed her. I've never seen anything like it. He just did it."

Connor smiled. "He loves her, and that's really something for her. She's never felt that before, so she's very responsive to him. She always will be."

Emily seemed to consider that. Rainer let it settle on him as well. His parents had loved him very much, and though he'd lost them when he was young, he'd never doubted that he was loved. All of the Haydenshires had loved him from birth as well. Adeline had never had that from anyone before she met Logan.

A half-hour later, Will navigated his Volvo SUV through the sea of cars in his parents' front pastures. His father's minivan was right behind him. Emily, Rainer, and Connor took off toward the cars.

Will and Dan Vindico spilled out of the Volvo along with two men Rainer didn't know. Governor Haydenshire and Emily's brothers leapt out of the minivan. Garrett had blood on his shirt.

"What happened?" Emily gasped. Her father pulled her to his chest and hugged her tight.

"Emily Anne, you know how much your mother and I love you, right?" She nodded but looked bewildered. "And all of your brothers, and you know how much Rainer loves you." She and Rainer both nodded adamantly.

"I know." Her tears returned. Whatever she felt in her father's energy seemed to devastate her.

"Good," he sighed. "Just never forget all of that, baby girl." Whatever they'd found at Ms. Parker's apartment had deeply disturbed the governor. "Let's go inside," he urged everyone forward.

They all spilled into the Haydenshires' kitchen. The party guests eyed them curiously. Mrs. Haydenshire rushed down the stairs. She reheated a plate full of her famous chocolate chip cookies and set them on the table in front of everyone.

"What happened?" she demanded when she noticed Garrett's shirt.

"I'm fine, Mom," Garrett assured though that didn't answer her question.

Governor Haydenshire drew a deep breath. "Lillian, you know Landon Portwood and Mike Ericcson. They're some of the top officers on Vindico's Elite Squadron," he explained as the two men offered kind smiles.

"Of course. I don't get up to the Senate that often, but I know we've met. Please make yourselves at home," Mrs. Haydenshire offered as she turned back to Garrett. "Now, tell me what happened."

"I need to talk to Adeline," Vindico edged. His demeanor was sorrowful, but his tone was gruff.

"No." Logan's voice came from behind the crowd assembled around the Haydenshires' kitchen table.

To Rainer's shock, Dan didn't look upset. He looked impressed.

"Why?" He studied Logan.

"She's been through enough. I finally got her to sleep. I just came down to grab something to eat. If I keep eating, then I can keep her casted all night. I'm going right back. She keeps waking up, and she's terrified. Dad, please." Logan turned to his father.

He wanted the governor to tell Vindico no. Though Dan was the Chief of Iodex, he still had to answer to the governors. Governor Haydenshire gave his son a sorrowful look. "They arrested her mother. It was much worse than I imagined," he tried to explain, but Dan stopped him.

"No, it's okay. Let her rest. You take care of her. She's been through hell."

"I will...always," Logan vowed.

Rainer watched, still stunned, as Vindico's chiseled face pulled into a genuine smile. He gave Logan a reassuring nod. "Go on...it's fine. I'll talk to her tomorrow."

"Garrett, tell me what happened to you right now," Mrs. Haydenshire demanded yet again.

"We stopped two men on the side of the road heading here," Vindico began the story. "They knew why we were after them, and one of them had a pistol. He fired at Garrett."

Mrs. Haydenshire's eyes closed as she visibly willed repose.

"I deflected the bullet. I don't miss, and I really don't like men who want to force themselves on young women. That really, really pisses me off," Vindico seethed.

Will and Garrett shared a knowing glance, but no one spoke. Dan had reflected the man's shot off of his shield cast. The bullet obviously hit the gunman, and his blood was on Garrett's shirt.

Dan continued, "We arrested Ms. Parker, who kept insisting I call her Candy." He rolled his eyes. "And we recovered enough drugs in that apartment to fund Iodex for two years."

"But Adeline's mother isn't Gifted." Mrs. Haydenshire seemed uncertain how this was going to proceed.

Vindico nodded, but Garrett explained, "We've been watching her for a while. We could've arrested her years ago, but we didn't want to take Adeline's mother away from her. She didn't seem like she wanted to move in here yet, so we let it be, but I took care of everything. Candy is going to be in for a while."

Vindico nodded. "I really just need to make certain Adeline wasn't hurt other than her wrist and the bruising on her face." No one wanted to think about other ways that she might've been hurt. "I, uh… have a kit in the car, and I can get a female Iodex officer out here if I need to."

"No," Mrs. Haydenshire assured him. "I would've sensed that in her rhythms."

"And I need to make certain she isn't using." He grimaced. Everyone immediately assured him that she was not.

"Good." He sighed in relief. "We arrested a guy in the apartment, but he's so high he's not really aware he's been arrested yet." Vindico shook his head in disbelief. "We also took in the man who didn't fire a weapon at one of my best friends."

There was no need to arrest the man who'd pulled the trigger. He was no longer alive.

"And you'll be taking care of her until her twenty-first birthday?" He seemed to know the answer already.

"We'll take care of her for as long as she'll let us, and I'm pretty sure Logan will take over after that," Governor Haydenshire assured him.

"Then despite the events of this evening, I'd say she's a lucky girl."

Mrs. Haydenshire threw her arms around Dan, who embraced her, though he looked quite stunned by the gesture.

"We miss seeing you. You're always welcome here just like you were growing up."

Vindico patted her back hesitantly. "Uh, thanks, Mrs. Haydenshire. I stay kind of busy."

"Ease up, Mom. He's a big boy," Garrett joked as everyone chuckled.

"You promise you'll come by for dinner one night soon?" Mrs. Haydenshire insisted.

"Yes, ma'am, of course." He seemed to turn into a younger version of himself before everyone's eyes. Mrs. Haydenshire released him, and he smiled.

"We'll let you get back to your party. Please tell Logan and Adeline how sorry I am. We should've stepped in sooner. I was trying to wait for her to say she wanted help. We couldn't force our way in. Like you just said, her mother isn't Gifted." He looked truly sorry.

"No, Dan, this was on me." Governor Haydenshire shook his head in defeat. "I've known about this for a while. I just never imagined Adeline would get caught up in her mother's twisted world. I should've come to you sooner. I don't ever want any of my children to feel like I'm forcing them to be here. I'd hoped she'd get fed up on her own and move in, but...."

Rainer smiled. The Haydenshires already thought of Adeline as their own, just like they did him, just like they apparently did with Dan Vindico. He'd never met two people with so much love who were so happy to give it away. He marveled at them.

"All right," Mrs. Haydenshire began to soothe her family.

"You, no more bullets," she ordered Garrett. "You two are welcome back on the farm anytime, but you have to bring him with you." She smiled kindly at Portwood and Ericcson and pointed to Vindico. They promised her they would take her up on the offer and thanked her for her generosity.

"And I know how well trained you are, Daniel, but you should really try to take on the twins. It's like nothing you've ever seen, trust me. And if I don't see more of you, son, I'm phoning your mother," she stated wryly as Vindico laughed.

"Please don't do that." He shuddered slightly. "I've never even seen the twins before, I don't think." He seemed shocked by that fact.

"We don't take them out much. Like Lillian said, we're frightened of them," Governor Haydenshire quipped.

"You should bring them by the office."

"He doesn't know what he's saying," Mrs. Haydenshire assured. "Since our family is throwing this party, some of us should be outside with the guests. And you two,"—she turned to Emily and Rainer with a smile—"you head on now. I don't want you on the roads late." She looked like she might tear up again as she gazed at them.

Emily gave her a reassuring smile as she reached for Rainer's hand.

Governor Haydenshire gave Rainer a look that said he knew precisely what was on his mind, and he wasn't particularly pleased. "You be careful." There was more than a trace of a threat wrapped in the command.

"Yes, sir."

"And you take good care of my baby girl."

Rainer nodded again, but Emily cut him off before he could speak again. She wrapped her arms around her father's neck. The gesture seemed to elicit tears from him though he fought the emotion. "He always does, Daddy."

Governor Haydenshire nodded, held Emily's face in his hands, and gazed into the depths of her eyes. Rainer knew he wasn't looking at her as the academy graduate that she was. He was gazing at his baby girl.

Rainer almost called the entire trip off right then and there. After a few minutes, Governor Haydenshire seemed to forcefully will his hands off of Emily.

"Uh, actually, before we leave..." Rainer's voice squeaked. He cleared his throat as he wondered what was wrong with him. Everyone but Governor and Mrs. Haydenshire meandered back out to the party. "I'd...really like you to have this." Rainer handed the governor an envelope he'd pulled from his back pocket. Governor Haydenshire shared a knowing grin with his wife.

"I have a feeling I know what this is, and you should already know we would never accept one penny from you, son."

Rainer shook his head. "Please, you've given me everything. I don't even want to think about where I would be without you. You're the most wonderful people in the world. This is the least I can do."

Mrs. Haydenshire placed her hand tenderly on the side of his face. "And the fact that you feel that way means more to me than you'll ever know, but we will not be accepting any money from you, sweetheart. What little we did to raise you was our pleasure. We'd do it all again in a heartbeat."

Governor Haydenshire smiled wryly. "I tell you what." He handed the envelope back. "You promise me that you'll always take care of my baby girl. Make certain she has everything she needs, not everything she wants..."—he winked at Emily, who rolled her eyes—"but everything she needs, and that's all the payback I'll ever need. Now, take this and tear it up, and you two go have fun at the beach. We'll get Adeline all taken care of while you're gone."

The urge for them to have fun seemed forced.

Rainer sighed, but knew he wasn't going to get anywhere, so he took the envelope back. "Please," he tried once more.

The Haydenshires chuckled. "No, Rainer," they said together.

Emily laughed at him outright. "I told you." She took his hand and pulled him toward the door.

But Rainer turned back before they exited. "I'll always take care of her, sir. Always."

Fear flashed in the governor's eyes. It wasn't an emotion Rainer had ever seen the governor exhibit.

"You'd better, son."

Shock tensed in Rainer's shield. The governor hadn't expected him to turn back around. He'd fought the fear and the fury while Rainer had stared into his eyes, but they'd surfaced immediately when he thought he was no longer looking.

They met Will and Vindico, along with Portwood and Ericcson, on their way to Rainer's car.

"Have fun, you two," Will goaded and gazed at Emily like he couldn't quite believe she was all grown up.

"Where you headed?" Dan asked with a kind smile.

"Our beach house," Emily explained.

A deep chuckle rumbled from Vindico's chest. He gave Rainer an impressed smile. "Taking Governor Haydenshire's baby girl to the beach house. I knew you had guts, Lawson."

Rainer shrugged. "I guess." He wasn't certain what else to say, but his voice caught again.

Vindico visibly held back more laughter. It seemed he knew why Rainer was so nervous. He slapped him on the back.

"Relax, you'll be fine. Just take everything nice and slow, *really* slow. The more confident you are the less nervous she'll be," he assured him quietly so no one else could hear him. Rainer was appreciative of the vote of confidence and the advice. "And have fun," he called before climbing back into Will's car. "Your life's not likely to get any easier."

"Thanks, we will." Emily tugged on Rainer's arm before he could ask Vindico what he meant by that.

"Not too much fun," Will demanded.

CHAPTER 14
THE BEACH HOUSE

They made their way to the Mustang. Rainer opened Emily's door for her and then edged around the car.

It's four hours from here to the beach house if I don't cast the engine. Don't freak out yet. He turned the key and propped his arm behind Emily to make certain he could back out safely. He tried to appreciate the sly grin on her features. It was sexy as hell, but the insistent hammer of his heart and the sweat dewing on his forehead distracted him.

With all that had happened to Adeline, they were actually leaving a little earlier than they'd planned. As eager as he'd been for this for the past two days, or hell, for the past several years, he was terrified as he drove to the gas station to fill up before leaving.

"Do you want anything to drink, baby?"

She popped open the glove box. Her cinnamon candies were in there. This seemed to delight her. "You're the best. Just a Dr Pepper, please."

As he pumped the gas, he stared at the rolling numbers hypnotically. He drew deep breaths and tried not to inhale the fumes from the gasoline.

This is Emily, he repeated in his head. *You and Emily. You've been together since you were toddlers. Nothing could be more natural than being with Emily.* He tried to convince himself, but other thoughts intruded in his mantra. His father's warnings about it being intense and changing things coupled with *What if I'm terrible at it? What if she hates it?* All of the blood in his body slithered to his feet. *What if I hurt her?* He shuddered from the thought alone. He was her Shield. He was incapable of hurting her.

But he didn't know how to do this. He walked into the gas station and picked up several Dr Peppers and a few snacks he knew she liked. He returned to the car and handed her the drinks.

"Thank you," she offered nervously as she unscrewed the cap. "Hungry?" she teased as she glanced in the bag of snacks.

"I don't know. I think I'm just used to making this trip with Logan."

"Are you okay?" she whispered.

He smiled as she took his hand and flooded his body with her intoxicating, soothing Receiver's cast. His shield responded readily as it drank in her rhythms. "Little nervous."

"Me too." She bit her lip.

"If you don't want to..."

"I definitely want to. I just don't want to disappoint you, and I'm not entirely certain what I'm doing." Her face colored as she stared out the windows. They sped onto the interstate.

"You could never disappoint me, ever. And we'll figure it all out together." He willed her to understand what she meant to him, what making love to her meant to him. "I think we'll just take things a little further than we ever have before, but we'll go slow, *really* slow." He echoed Dan's advice.

"I still can't believe what happened to Adeline." Her voice was rough and ragged. "I wish I'd told someone what I felt. I just wasn't sure. I couldn't stop thinking about this." A crimson fire burned in her cheeks. "Erotic energy is...uh...difficult to read through for me." She grimaced.

"You told me. I...guess I wasn't focused on it enough either. Do you want me to call Logan and check on her?" He wondered if they should have checked on her before they left.

"No, I kind of think she just needs Logan right now."

They continued to talk just like they always had all the way. She tensed slightly, and he drew a steadying breath as they pulled onto the bridge.

"Are you okay?" he repeated her question from several hours before.

She nodded but didn't say anything. The bridge, he remembered suddenly.

"I'm so sorry. I should've gone the other way." He was an idiot.

"No." She shook her head. "That's farther out of the way. This is fine." She clung tightly to his forearm. She drew strength and calm from him. The sensation was heavenly. Emily drawing from him had their evening plans flooding through his mind again.

But it wasn't fine. The afternoon her brother Cal had been killed working with Iodex in Moscow, Rainer had gone to Norfolk to check on his uncle.

She'd begged him not to go. She'd told him that something was wrong, that she could feel it. He'd stupidly assured her everything was fine. He should've listened to her. He should have done everything differently.

She'd had to experience all of the horrifying emotions that came from Cal's death, not only her own, but all of her family's as well. And she'd tried to process it all without her Shield.

It had overwhelmed her. She'd run out the door and into her brand-new Jeep. She'd been driving less than three weeks. Storms had ravaged Arlington that day. The press had chased her as she'd searched for him. They'd run her car off of a bridge. She'd nearly been killed. That was why he'd left for London. He was trying desperately to keep the press, who was always after him, away from her.

Coming back to the present, Rainer decided that talking to her would be the best way to distract her. He certainly couldn't turn around on the bridge.

"So, besides the obvious thing...what do you want to do this week?"

"Just relax." She forced a smile for his benefit he was sure. "I've been studying forever. I just want to hang out with you."

"That sounds perfect."

"Watch the road," she panicked as he glanced her way. Guilt took up ruthless residence in the pit of his stomach.

He edged the car to the center lane. "How about I get you off of the bridge a little faster?"

He cupped his hand, harnessed the engine and the energy in the air, and then threw the car forward with a jolt. She tensed, but they were off the bridge in less than a minute.

He slowed the car as they came back to flat land. A few minutes later, they were entering Virginia Beach. She grinned as they passed signs for the lighthouse. She loved the beach house.

Rainer smiled as he drove the two-lane roads that edged closer to Sandbridge and the Haydenshires' vacation home.

It was just after eleven when he pulled up to the house. It stood as it always had every time Rainer had ever been there. The dusky-blue clapboard home had screened porches and raised decks that faced the water on three sides. It wasn't overly fancy, and it was much smaller than the farmhouse.

Emily beamed as Rainer opened her door. The beach house was her favorite place to be. She loved the water and the sandy shores. She'd explained to him several years before that water helped Receivers wash away some of the emotional energy they had to take on every day. The ocean did it better than any other source.

She pulled the key from her purse and opened the back door. They stepped inside. A broad smile lit her beautiful face. She moved about the house, turned on the lamps, and uncovered the furniture, since they were the first visitors of the year. She threw back the curtains in the living room and slid open the glass doors, revealing the mighty Atlantic Ocean.

Rainer set their luggage in the hallway that led to the bedrooms and went to join her on the deck.

He wrapped his arms around her waist, held her to his chest, and cradled her tenderly while she enjoyed the moonlit ocean view. He inhaled the scent of her hair mixed with the salty air, and he swallowed hard. He wanted her more than he wanted to draw his next breath. Suddenly, she spun in his hands and laid her head against his chest.

"I love you so much." He kissed the top of her head.

"I love you too." Her heartbeat reverberated through him. "I guess we should figure out where to sleep."

"We'll do whatever you want, whenever you want."

"I'm ready." She sounded much more confident than he felt.

There were five bedrooms in the beach house. Two of them had king-size beds, each with its own bathroom. One room held two double beds. The other rooms, the only ones either of them had ever stayed in before, contained bunks and trundle beds for everyone to fit. The bedroom her parents normally stayed in also contained two cribs for the twins. The bottom floor, under the main decking, had a large game room with foosball and air hockey tables.

She grimaced slightly and pointed to the other large bedroom. Thankful that she didn't want to use the bed her parents normally slept in, Rainer carried their things into the room she'd chosen.

He set her cosmetics case in the en suite bathroom and grabbed his shaving kit from his duffle bag and placed it in there as well. She began putting clean sheets on the bed, and he moved to help her.

After she tucked the top sheet under the mattress, she shook her head and moved closer to him. "Stop worrying," she commanded. She'd always been able to read him like a book. "I'm tired of just dreaming about being with you like this, of you getting to hold me all night long. I want to feel it. I want to feel you." She let her gaze rise slowly to meet his.

He pulled her to him. He wanted to feel it as well, but his father's warnings that this would change things between them wouldn't give him peace.

"I can still hold you all night if that's all you want to do. I don't want you to do anything you're not sure about. I don't want to hurt you, and I know it's going to." He managed to get his full confession out quickly. He wasn't certain he'd be able to stop once they started this time. He didn't know if he had the strength.

"I've never wanted anything as much as I want you right now." Her voice was low and eager.

She pulled the light from the lamps she'd lit into her cupped hand

and darkened the room. Streams of moonlight spilled through the sliding glass doors and illuminated her.

Unable to stop himself, he lifted her chin with his fingers and brushed a kiss across her lips. She let her eyes close as he turned his head and kissed her again hesitantly. He added to the intensity until he was consuming her with greed. As he tasted her and felt her, he shuddered as her energy began to swirl around him.

He finally gave in to the passion that flowed so readily between them. "I want to see you, all of you. I want to feel you." He slid his hands down her back and then up her skirt as he began massaging her backside hungrily. "I want to be inside of you."

"Yes," she gasped. A tender tremble shook through her. She stepped away from him and held his gaze as she began unbuttoning her shirt.

She was exquisite. Her hair hung in loose waves over her pale shoulders. She shed her shirt, and his breath tangled in his throat.

Her breasts were swollen and spilling over the black satin bra she had them bound in. He panted for breath. "You're so damn beautiful."

He kissed her heatedly and slipped his hands to her back. He ached. His cock throbbed in desperation. God, he needed more, he needed her. His shield flared in craving desperation. The room shimmered in the light of their yearning rhythms.

As he popped the clasp of her bra, she moaned in abject need. He had to steel himself not to lose it as he dropped her bra on the floor. He took her breasts in his hands. Her nipples were already strained and pulled taut in throbbing beads. A deep groan escaped his throat. He moved his hands down her waist, unzipped her skirt, and slipped it down to her feet.

"The most beautiful thing I've ever seen." He ran his hands up and down her body. He consumed what she was giving up for him. Her body released her energy in heady waves. He could feel it as it flooded through him, like nothing he'd ever felt before. He'd never get enough. She fumbled with his belt, but he gently grabbed her hands.

"I've got it, baby." He kissed down her neck and across her collarbone as she panted. "Go get in the bed. I'll be right there."

She gave him a heavy nod. He watched her move. The hypnotic

sway of her hips made him throb. He stared unabashedly at her ass in black lace panties. His heart hammered. His breath came in quick gasping pants. He pulled off his shirt and stripped down to his boxers.

He slid hesitantly in beside her. Her breath stuttered in anticipation as the mattress lowered under his weight.

"Rainer," she whispered, and he stopped immediately. She sounded scared.

"What's wrong, baby?" He pulled her to him. "We don't have to do this if you don't want to." He wasn't pushing anything on her. If she wanted to stop, they would, even if he was concerned it might actually kill him.

She smiled but shook her head. "I just haven't set the cast yet."

"Okay, whenever you want to." He traced his hands down to her waist.

She was perfect. Her alabaster skin was satin under his touch. He'd never seen so much of her, and he longed to see it all.

"I kind of wanted you to do it."

He gave her a hesitant nod as he pulled his hand away. He tried to draw steadying breaths. The cast to keep her from getting pregnant could be performed by anyone. Normally, the Gifted woman performed it on herself. It lasted twenty-four hours.

To allow someone else to summon it for you, or with you, meant that the woman was allowing you to hold the essence of her quite literally in your hands.

He would have to harness her energy to close her womb, and it was a tremendous show of faith and trust for her to offer. As Rainer considered what she was asking, and what he was about to do to her, it seemed the two should go together.

To perform the cast would be to combine their energies before he ever entered her. He would put a part of his energy in her to help her body close itself off until they were ready for children.

Thoughts of her pregnant with his child reeled through his mind. For her to carry his child, that they'd made together, made his desire to be with her grow exponentially in a matter of seconds. Just envisioning her luscious body round with his baby was overwhelming. He couldn't believe he'd never thought of it before.

"Are you sure?" He studied her. She nodded as the gravity of what he was about to do settled around them in the bed.

He tried to concentrate. It was extremely difficult when he was staring at her like this. She let her eyes close. Rainer tried desperately to remember everything Garrett had instructed him on when casting a woman but found it hard to think of anything at all. It was easier after you had a little of their energy in your hands, but he hadn't fingered her yet and she seemed to want to be casted now.

He concentrated. "Lie back, baby."

She reclined on the bed. He kissed her and then summoned from the erotic energy as it spun in waves around them. When she was ready, he moved his cast to her mound. Rainer remembered at the last minute that he should flood in his own soothing, calming energies into her while he performed the cast. He corrected quickly before he pulled his hand away.

"Are you okay?" He watched over her obsessively.

"I'm perfect."

He slid beside her and let his hands travel over her body again. "I need to feel that again, baby. I need to feel all of you." She nodded as she gave him longing, desperate looks.

Just take it nice and slow. Vindico's words came back to him suddenly. He kissed her sweetly, tenderly. He wanted to enjoy each part of her and every part of making her his own. She ran her hands down his chest. The hesitant friction made him pulse and ache. Her hands dipped in his boxers, and she began tracing him so gently the feeling was ethereal.

"That's incredible, baby," he groaned. "Pull from me," escaped the trap of his mouth in a demanding growl.

She did as she was told. She drew the erotic energy straight from its source into her hand, into her body. He shuddered from the effect.

"Touch me," she begged.

He'd never been able to deny her anything at all, so he hooked his thumbs in her panties and slid them down her legs. She was exquisite. Her body was flushed, her lips kiss-swollen. The tender auburn curls between her legs were wet from her desire. It all made him moan as he glided his fingertips over her.

He traced her slit, and she writhed. The motion nearly drove him over the edge. He forced himself to concentrate. The air around them shimmered. Their energy spun together, frantic to be joined. It was unlike anything he'd ever seen or felt before.

"Please," she begged again. Her body gave needy writhes beside his. He took a moment to steel himself as he slipped two fingers deep inside of her. She cried out for him. He could feel her seep into his soul as he entered her body.

Though he'd certainly done this much before, he began to consider his next moves. She was so tight he had no idea how she was supposed to take him. He was going to hurt her. The thought terrified him.

He stroked slowly and relaxed a little as her body started to give way. She widened ever so slightly for him. Her energy flowed into his as he opened and ripened her rhythmically. He continued to work. He wasn't going to do anything else until she asked.

"Rainer, please," she begged again and threw her leg over his to push them together. She showed him what she wanted.

After slipping his boxers off, he moved back to her and watched her lips spread as she rubbed against him. He groaned from the utter ecstasy of seeing them together, of feeling her energy permeate him. He gently guided her body under his and positioned himself to take her.

"Are you sure you're ready?" The terror was evident in his tone.

"Yes," she urged. He let his energy soothe her as he separated her slightly. As he prayed that this wouldn't hurt her, his shield entered her as he pressed his cock in as gently as he was able.

Her muscles clenched around him. She bucked. She could feel him now. He wanted her to have all of him, to replace what she was filling him with.

Desperation to go slowly and with extreme tenderness was at an all-out war with the desire to have her wrapped tightly around him. He longed to be fully inside her, surrounded by her, and to make every inch of her belong to him. He pushed until she grimaced, but then she panted, "Please, Rainer, you have to."

"Em," he swallowed hard, "this is gonna hurt, baby." He tried to prepare her in a choked, desperate whisper.

"I know," she gasped, "just please."

He could feel her open, and he could feel her tremble. Her energy weakened. She shuddered. His shield panicked and pulled back.

"Don't stop," she begged.

He fought his own shield. It seared against his skin and pounded brutally against his muscles. He shuddered. He closed his eyes and pushed the terror in his heart away as he pressed until he could fill her with all of him.

He throbbed inside of her. Suddenly, his shield pulsed in elation as their rhythms filled the room. They joined readily. It was the most exquisite thing he'd ever felt. She was so tight it was like being drowned in silk. It drove him over almost instantly.

As he spilled himself inside of her, it was terror that stole his thoughts. His release was utter perfection. Their energy spun together. It encased both of them, none all his or all hers, just the two of them as one. The joined spirals shimmered in the air around them.

"Baby." He pulled away as gently as he was able and turned to cradle her on his chest. "How badly did I...?" He fought to steady his voice. "How badly are you hurt?"

"I'm okay." She seemed relaxed. His release was inside of her. He could feel her emotions, but he could also feel the raw, tender pain as she lay on him with nothing between them.

"Do you want me to?" He placed his hand on her mound over the approximate place where he'd just widened her.

"You can't heal me," she soothed. "If you did, it would just hurt like that every time."

He wasn't thinking clearly. "But it won't..." he hesitated.

"It won't ever hurt like that again."

"Can I do anything at all?"

"Just hold me." He wrapped her up in his arms and cradled her body to his.

"I love you," he whispered, "so much."

She smiled against his chest. "I love you too."

"I'll get better at it. I swear."

She laughed. "I think everybody's first time is a little quick."

"Yeah, but..." He wasn't certain what else to say, but he ordered himself to get better at it immediately. She certainly hadn't enjoyed that, and he was determined that the next time he had the extreme honor, she would.

She was tired. He could feel that as well. He could feel the very essence of her now after what they'd just shared. It was a gift he'd never take for granted.

"Go to sleep, baby. I've got you." He cast his shield over them and filled it with soothing energy. He tried to ease the pain. His protective bands filled the air she breathed.

She relaxed against him. Her breath steadied, and her eyes drifted closed.

He lay there awake in the peaceful silence. He cradled her while she slept and kept her protected as he tried to soothe the pain he'd caused. He watched over her constantly.

He'd never get enough. One lifetime with her like that would never be long enough. In that moment, he decided what his first significant purchase with the fortune he'd just inherited would be. He grinned as he fell asleep wrapped up in her.

CHAPTER 15

THANKS DAD

Rainer's eyes blinked open as Emily slid from the bed. Her hair tickled his chest. Not fully conscious yet, he was aware of the sunlight as it poured through the windows. She winced as she eased to the bathroom.

Concern tensed in his shield. The deep green bands sizzled as he leaned up on his elbows. "What's wrong?" She looked at him like he might've lost his mind. "Oh, right. Sorry." He grimaced.

"I'm fine. Go back to sleep. We're supposed to be on vacation." He stayed in his upright position until she came back to bed.

"Are you sure you're okay?"

"I'm much better than okay."

He pulled her back to him and decided he'd rather talk than sleep. "I'm gonna go out on a limb and guess that your dad isn't really going to want me holding you naked all night while we sleep, and I really don't ever want to sleep any other way." She laughed. The sound soothed his soul. "So, I was wondering if you'd maybe like to take a small part of what my parents left me and get a place for us to live, or maybe me and you and Logan and Adeline?"

"Really? You're sure?" A broad grin spread across her features.

"Well, I've been living with you for a while now, and you haven't kicked me out yet."

She giggled but then studied him. "Yeah, but what if I get on your nerves and then you don't want to marry me?"

"You would never get on my nerves, but we can get married first," he instantly offered, "if say, you want to do that this week."

"Slow down there." She made him chuckle. "I appreciate your enthusiasm, but I think we may need to see how Adeline is doing before we try to find a place. We have a few weeks before we start work."

That wasn't quite the response he'd wanted, but he did need to slow down. He just didn't want to think about sleeping in a room without her ever again. He didn't want to think about doing anything without her. He was so much more when he was with her, a better person, a better Shield.

He studied the clock on the bedside table. "Do you want some coffee, baby?" If she was wincing just going to the bathroom, staying in bed seemed like the best idea.

She grinned. "I'll get it." She started to scoot out of the bed again, but he pinned her down.

"You'll stay here. I'll make us coffee, and I think your mom packed us some donuts. So how about breakfast in bed?"

She beamed but then studied him as she read his energy. "I'm really fine." She'd clearly sensed his guilt and worry.

"That doesn't mean I can't get you coffee and donuts."

"If you really don't mind?"

"I really want to take care of you always."

"Thank you." She fell back on her pillow and hugged the one he'd slept on to her chest.

Rainer kissed her cheek as he pulled the covers back over her. After he tugged his boxers back on, he moved to the kitchen.

He filled the coffee pot with water and casted to turn it on. Then he went to the food baskets Emily and Mrs. Haydenshire had packed them. He dug out a box of glazed donuts, Emily's favorite. He set them on a plate he'd pulled from the cabinet and waved his hand over them. He heated them until the glaze was just starting to melt.

While he waited for the coffee to finish, he glanced back in the basket. His father's safety deposit box was in there. He'd thrown it in and hoped Emily might go through it with him.

He pulled it open. There were letters tied together with a ribbon. Underneath those, there were several bonds—many decades old. He had no idea how to calculate their worth, but he assumed he should put them back in the bank or get Will to tell him what to do with them. His eyes landed on a small black velvet box. He furrowed his brow, and his heart picked up pace as he lifted it.

After glancing down the hall to make certain Emily was still in their room, he drew a deep breath. The hinge gave a slight creak as he opened the box. A gold band fell into his hand, but as he looked at the notched slit in the box, there it sat—the enormous, diamond engagement ring that had been his mother's and his grandmother's before her.

His heart raced as he carefully removed it.

All my Gifts I give to you, was engraved on the delicate band, so small that he was barely able to read the words. The thicker gold band had both of his parents' initials and wedding date on it. Swallowing hard, he returned both bands and snapped the box shut. He clenched his jaw and looked out the window to the restless ocean… timeless and everlasting.

"Thanks, Dad," he whispered before pouring coffee and cooling it slightly with his hand. He added in cream and sugar and returned to Emily.

She was sitting up with her legs crossed and wearing another of his academy T-shirts. Disappointed that she'd put on clothes, he smiled at her and tried not to let on. He supposed she couldn't just walk around naked endlessly, as much as he'd like that. He set the two mugs he'd tediously balanced in his hands on the bedside table and handed her the plate of donuts.

"I hope these aren't all for me."

"I thought I might eat too." He winked at her and watched her cheeks color slightly. "What do you want to do today?" He inhaled half of a donut in one bite. He was starving.

She gave him a deliciously naughty grin and waggled her eyebrows.

"You cannot possibly want to do that again yet." He wasn't letting her downplay the pain.

"And how do you know what I want, Mr. Lawson?"

He shook his head. That was his Emily. People most certainly did not tell her what she wanted or when she wanted it. He'd always thought that though her hair was a deep auburn, almost brunette just like all of her brothers, somewhere deep in there it was fiery orange. He was usually the one person who could persuade her. Her parents even occasionally came to him to try to get her to see something a different way.

"Okay, how about this." He took a sip of coffee. "I cannot do that again until I know that it isn't going to make you hurt even worse."

She rolled her eyes. "I really am fine, much better than last night. And even though it was...you know...a little..." she paused as she searched for the appropriate word.

"Excruciatingly painful and over with ridiculously fast," he provided for her. He suddenly felt the threat of the donuts making a return visit.

"No!" She shook her head. "Tender," she amended. "It was the most amazing thing I've ever felt, and I want to feel it again...and forever," her voice trailed off with the last two words.

She stared at the sheets and blankets strewn around the bed. She appeared to be worried he felt different. Rainer was astonished. She'd been telling him they were going to get married since she was four. He'd never argued. He couldn't believe he was lucky enough to be the one she'd chosen. What the hell had happened?

He thought through the years of Amative Energy classes he'd sat through at the academy. Receivers could feel every emotion from their sexual partner because their release was inside of them. It would be the closest read she would ever have.

He considered. Somehow, she must've been reading his excitement and nerves about the ring over all that they'd done and his fear and guilt that he'd hurt her. The intensity of the combined emotions had confused her and left her feeling uncertain.

How could she be worried about that? It was utterly preposterous. His mind immediately went back to the ring in the deposit box. He would not ask her until he'd talked to her father. He couldn't. He respected Governor Haydenshire too much for that. He owed the Haydenshires too much, but he also would not allow her to sit beside him in bed, after what they'd shared the night before, and feel insecure. He weighed his options.

"Look at me," he soothed. She lifted her eyes to his. "I love you more than life itself. I wasn't kidding when I told you I'd marry you this week. I'd marry you today. But you deserve an engagement and a wedding just like you've always wanted." He smiled and recalled all of the times she'd forced him to play wedding with her when they were kids. She'd usually make Logan officiate.

He couldn't help but laugh as he recalled the time Logan tried to make her vow to eat worms from the garden. She furrowed her brow as she wondered what brought on his laughter.

"I was thinking maybe we'd get a real minister instead of Logan for our actual wedding."

She doubled over laughing, and he listened intently. It was one of the sweetest sounds in the world. She quieted and seemed to study him.

"Are you sure? I just…I didn't feel like you really liked last night all that much and…." she faltered.

He stared at her in shocked disbelief. "How could you think that?"

"I don't know." She shrugged, and he couldn't stand it. He couldn't let her sit there drowning in doubt. He pulled her to him as he shoved away the plate between them. "I could feel how scared you were." Her voice caught as she trembled in his arms.

"I was terrified." He'd gladly tell her exactly what he'd felt and explain what she'd felt from him. She was an extremely Gifted Receiver. She'd felt every confusing emotion that had coursed through him as he'd made her his own while it was happening. She'd been able to feel him long before his semen was inside of her.

"Sweetheart, last night was the most extraordinary night of my life. I was terrified to hurt you. I guess…I always knew that was how it had to work, but it nearly killed me. That's why I was so scared. I want to be with you like that forever. I want to feel you in every way I possibly can, but…" He wasn't certain how to put this in words. "You could feel that I was scared when I had my fingers in you, right?" She nodded, and he forced himself to continue. "Baby, I could feel that I was hurting you when I was inside of you. I'm your shield. I cannot hurt you. It almost ended me. I had to fight my own shield to do it."

Sudden realization wiped the confusion from her face. "I'm so sorry. I never thought about that." She shook her head. "That's what Garrett is always talking about." She was referring to Garrett's rather crude comments on being with Non-Gifted women, ones Rainer wasn't aware Emily had ever heard.

"I guess." He'd certainly never been with anyone but Emily, but he understood how it would lessen the level of commitment if you weren't able to feel what the other person was feeling when they were with you.

She was still speculative. "But I mean, you didn't hate it?"

"Baby." He shook his head. There were too many emotions to sort through. She'd felt his fear over anything else, and it had frightened her.

"I hate that I hurt you. I don't understand why it has to be that way, but to share that with you is the most amazing thing I've ever felt. I want to feel that for the rest of my life as often as you'll let me have the honor. I swear I won't go so fast the next time. I was overwhelmed by how freaking good it felt."

A small smile played across her lips, and she seemed to finally believe him. "You really want to be engaged and get married soon?" She tried to hide her excitement but failed miserably.

"I really want to be your husband, but I'll settle for being your fiancé for a little while."

"I don't know. I don't want you to get me a ring or whatever just because I freaked out. I want you to do it whenever you really want to," she whispered, "if you really want to?"

Whatever she'd felt from him the night before had done a real number on her, and he was determined to undo the damage. He drew a deep breath and considered for the length of a few heartbeats. "I have a ring."

Her mouth fell open, and her eyes goggled to the size of dinner plates.

"I haven't talked to your dad, and I will do that first." He wasn't letting her change his mind. To his relief, she nodded and looked delighted by his determination. "And when I ask you, I want it to be perfect. You deserve that. Please just let me get this all worked out. Let me ask your dad. Then, when I put that ring on your finger, I want you to know you've always been it for me. My whole world rises and sets with you. You're all that matters." He wrapped her up in his arms and wiped away the escaping tears.

"I just cannot believe how lucky I am."

He smiled and tried to hide his chuckle.

"And that's why you're crying?" he teased as he tried to earn her laughter instead of more tears.

"No, I'm crying because I am the happiest girl in the entire universe right now." They both laughed at the juxtaposition. "Can I see it?"

"No," he drawled.

She'd gotten him, and he hadn't even realized what he'd just admitted. "So, it is here then."

"Emily Anne..."

She grinned mischievously. "Okay, okay. When are you going to talk to Dad?"

Rainer tousled her hair, still tangled from sleeping, as he raised his eyebrow. "Wouldn't you like to know?"

"Yes!"

"You, Miss Haydenshire, will only be engaged once, so you should let your boyfriend really do this right."

She laid back against him. He could feel her happiness. He could feel the peace that his revelation had brought her, and it scothed his soul.

CHAPTER 16

THE TIES THAT BIND

She leaned up to study him. Debate swam in the depths of her eyes. Suddenly she leaned in and brushed her lips across his.

He tenderly held her face as he formed her lips around his own. She moved to lie down, and he moved with her. He continued to kiss her, to taste her. That was all he'd been able to feel from her for so long, and it was still just as breathtaking, even though now he knew there was so much more.

She was his, and the knowledge overwhelmed him. She slid her hands down his bare chest, kneaded his skin, and grasped his length in her hands. He groaned from the sensation.

"I want to feel you again. I need it. Please."

"Em," he pulled back. He couldn't hurt her again. That would end him, but she advanced.

"Just feel me," she urged and kissed him again heatedly. He allowed her in. He could feel the hunger and the yearning. The need swirled inside of her rhythms. He moved his hands to her thighs and groped her skin. He worked his hands under the T-shirt. She hadn't put anything else on. His mind waged war with his body.

"I need you," she begged.

It nearly broke him. The slow fire that churned in his groin ignited, as he felt her desire grow.

"You won't hurt me again. I feel so much better when I can feel you with me."

He couldn't fight any longer. He drowned in the futility of the war. It was a senseless endeavor. She was irresistible.

He lifted the shirt over her head and gazed at her. She was no longer obscured in the darkness. He could see all of her, what she offered so willingly to him. He groaned and moved over her. He wanted her all for himself. He wanted to own her in entirety, to own her gorgeous body and her beautiful soul.

He wanted to shield her body with his own. He longed to stand between her and the rest of the world. He concentrated. If he hurt her at all, he was going to stop.

He slipped his hands to her breasts. Her nipples pulled taut into puckered, pulsating beads against his palms. She swelled all for him, and he panted.

"My god, you are so damn beautiful." His vow made her writhe in his arms as she released more of herself, adding to the heady cocktail of them together.

"I want to touch you, baby. Are you sure it won't hurt? I swear I'll be so gentle." He slid his hands down her stomach as she gasped for breath.

"It will feel so much better," she begged in heated need. As he prayed that she was right, he traced his fingertips up her slit and grazed them over her mound.

The tender red curls, slightly darker than her hair, glistened in the sunlight as her body prepared her for him. She bucked under his touch. The arc of her body matched the arc of the need in her rhythms.

"Please," she begged.

He groaned and eased his fingers back inside her. He let everything she gave up wash over him. It was almost more than he could fathom, the need, the desire, mixed with his own deep yearnings as he stroked her.

The slick, wet, heavenly space was only slightly wider than he'd felt her the night before, but she felt no pain. Her energy never faltered. It was strong and intoxicating as it filled him.

Certain he hadn't done a great job the night before, he forced himself to concentrate. He noted the slight changes in her energy, according to where his fingers touched and caressed. He dragged his thumb through the liquid heat now seeping from her and stroked up over her clit. She called out his name. Her rhythms leapt wildly.

He continued to move over it, tenderly coaxing out what he wanted from her. She resisted slightly. Her rhythms pulled her back, but it wasn't fear of pain, it was fear of release.

"Come on, baby," he soothed in her ear as he kept up his deep, rhythmic strokes and continued to tease her clit with his thumb. "I'm right here. I'll always be right here. I want it. I want to watch you come undone for me. Let me have you." Her body shuddered. "That's it," he continued to coax. Her rhythms spiked harder when he spoke. "Show me how good it feels."

"Rainer," gasped from her. Her head shook on her pillow. Her rhythms arced in tighter pulses. He understood more.

"It's almost there, isn't it?"

Her body tensed and pulled his fingers deeper.

"That's it. Just let it go for me."

She gave way. She let him own her. She came undone for him.

It was exquisite to watch her body tense and contort. Her loud moans were a siren song. Her body released more of her physically. It was more than he ever thought possible, and her aura unbound for him. Her rhythms were frenzied in their need for his, and his shield gave desperate, craving pulses for her.

She groaned out his name and then, "Please, please, I need to feel all of you," spilled from her mouth.

He concentrated again as he moved back between her legs and made certain he wasn't going to add to her tenderness. He traced his hands over her inner thighs.

She was soaking wet, swollen, and ready. He could feel it now. He understood so much better this time. He moved up her body, caught her breast in his mouth, and sucked gently. She went wild. He smiled and reveled in the education. He pulled harder, and she cried out for him.

He slipped all of himself inside of her. As he pierced the very heart of her, a low growl echoed from his chest.

"You feel incredible," he groaned reverently. He was unable to believe the exquisite feeling of her as he thrust gently.

She couldn't take much, he knew, though he longed to pound into her and to pump her full of him. He forced himself to wait. She wasn't ready for that.

She met his timed thrusts and pulled him deeper. He shuddered and clenched his jaw as her body milked his cock. He wasn't going before her, but he had to fight with every fiber of his being to hold on until her energy spiked rapidly and her temperature climbed. He watched her body flush, and he knew her release was imminent.

"Give it to me, baby. Come around me. Let me feel it with you," he commanded, and he set her free.

Her body trembled around his throbbing strain. She clenched tight, and he lost it all. She collapsed underneath him. Her body wrapped his in all of her. He filled her full of everything inside of him.

He wanted her to have it all. He wanted her to own him. She took it all in as she convulsed and writhed. This one was much stronger than the last.

She hadn't felt this the night before, he knew, and he vowed to do everything in his power to make certain she felt this any time they were together. He held her to him and shielded her with his body as she quaked. She released in waves that matched the arc of her rhythms. They shattered through her and then she stilled.

"Uh, wow," she finally managed, and he tried not to laugh. "That was," she stammered with a sheepish giggle, "wow."

He couldn't halt his slight chuckle. He eased away from her and settled her on his chest.

Her cell phone rang in her purse. She sighed and then glanced up at him.

"I'm not hurting at all, but I don't think I can walk just yet."

Concern shimmered in his shield, but he sprang from the bed and retrieved her purse. He handed it to her before crawling back beside her. She answered on the fourth ring after glancing at the screen. "It's Mom." She held her finger to her lips. "Hello," she sang, but then tried to modulate her voice, since she sounded slightly drunk. He bit his lips together and tried hard not to crack up. "No, I'm fine, really. How's Adeline?" She didn't say anything for a while but looked concerned. He could hear traces of Mrs. Haydenshire's voice through the phone.

Emily nodded with a few "Uh-huhs" before, "Well, when is Chief Vindico coming back?" she quizzed. "No, we just got up a little while ago. We haven't really done anything yet."

Rainer smirked as he feigned confusion. She almost giggled but batted his hand away as he reached for her. After deciding he liked the game, he began kissing and nibbling along the delicate skin of her neck. She shook her head.

"Mom!" Suddenly her face was drawn in a horrified scowl.

Rainer pulled away and studied her.

"I'm really fine," she assured with a hint of disgust in her voice. "I really don't want to talk about this, okay?"

Rainer was insanely curious as he debated casting her phone so he could hear as well, but he didn't want to upset her.

"Okay, well, thank you for that." She cringed. "I will be fine. Yes, of course. I'm not telling you that!"

Rainer held his hands out and silently pleaded with her to tell him what was going on. She shook her head. Her face was a deep crimson, and she squeezed her eyes shut. "Because that is between me and Rainer."

He now had a pretty good idea of the kinds of things her mother must have asked. He gave her a sorrowful look, rubbed her leg, and tried to soothe her nerves. She calmed slightly.

"Yeah, we're gonna get some groceries and maybe lie out. It's still too cold to swim," she sounded more like herself. "No, it's fine, just like we left it after Labor Day." She sighed and began absentmindedly playing with the edge of the comforter. "Daddy gave me some money before we left," she commented, and shock shot through Rainer.

Governor Haydenshire had been sitting not two feet away from him the day before when he'd been handed the bank cards and numerous checkbooks to almost a billion dollars. Why on earth was he giving Emily money?

Rainer was offended. She furrowed her brow and studied him. His face had not only betrayed his shock, but his rhythms had as well. She could feel every single thing he felt.

"Tell Adeline we're thinking of her," she said sweetly. "Yes, I'll call you later if we need anything. I love you too. Bye." Emily tossed her phone gently on the mattress.

"Why did your dad give you money?"

She looked as surprised as he felt. "Of all the comments I thought that conversation would elicit,"—she pointed to her phone—"that isn't what I thought you would say."

"I want to know what else she said, but I mostly want to know why your dad is giving you money."

Her brow furrowed. "Because I'm his daughter, and I might need to buy something while I'm on vacation, and my invitation to try out for the Angels only becomes a massive paycheck if I actually become their Junior Receiver."

"Okay, but I'm here with you."

"I know that, but that doesn't mean I might not need to get something while we're here."

"I will get you anything you need, or hell, anything you want. Your dad was sitting right beside me when Governor Carrington handed me my parents' fortune. He doesn't need to give you money."

She gave him an exaggerated eye roll. "I won't point out how extremely chauvinistic that sounded."

He cocked his jaw to the side in irritation. "That isn't how I meant it and you know that."

"I know," she soothed. "But sweetheart, we aren't engaged. I don't have a ring yet, and that money is yours, not mine. You shouldn't spend it on me. You should keep it, or invest it, or get stuff you really want. It doesn't have anything to do with me."

He drew a deep breath. It never occurred to him that she wouldn't understand what he'd meant when he'd told her he had a ring, but it should have. Just like her parents, Emily was one of the most giving people he'd ever known. For the most part, he'd never really even discussed his inheritance with her because he didn't want to think about it.

"Em," he shook his head. "I want to be your husband. I want

everything I have to be yours. I would never keep all of that from you. It *is* yours! If there's something you want, let's go get it. Nothing would make me happier."

She looked extremely touched, but then she giggled. "I would kind of like a Dr Pepper."

He rolled his eyes. "Fine." He was irritated she wasn't taking him seriously. He returned to the kitchen, pulled a can from the Styrofoam cooler her mother had packed, and chill casted the drink. The cast her mother had done on the coolers had worn off in the middle of the night. He started back to their room, but she met him in the kitchen.

"I was kidding." She looked hurt. She reached for the drink. "Thank you,"—she popped the top—"for this, and for what you said. I just...I feel like I don't deserve you. I mean...all of the money just seems like only you should have that. I'll be working soon, and we can stay at Mom and Dad's until then." The pieces began to cement in his mind. He took her hand and pulled her onto one of the couches in the living room.

"Is that why you don't want to move in with me? Because you can't help pay rent yet?" She nodded hesitantly. "Baby, what do I have to say or do to make you understand how much I love you? How much you mean to me? Since the moment Governor Carrington handed me all of that, I only ever saw it as ours. I only ever see my life being wrapped up entirely in yours. That's the only way I ever want it to be. We've been talking about getting married since we were babies. I don't understand where this is coming from."

"Because it's all real now." She stared him down. "And...I just...it's a lot. It's a lot of money and pressure and the Angels and Elite Iodex... and everything is happening so fast. This isn't like when I used to make you play wedding with me. This is real."

He gave her a tender nod and drew her to his chest. "I know." As he considered her overwhelm, he understood that for so long they'd been living in the protective cocoon of Haydenshire Farm, safe and secure, and now...real life was right at their fingertips. "I know that it's a lot all at once, but every single thing that's about to change doesn't change the only thing that will ever really matter to me, and that's us. You and me together. That's all I want."

Tender tears pricked her eyes. "Really?"

He pulled her onto his chest. "Yes, really. I want everything I have to be yours. I want to do life with you and only you. Did you honestly think I would make you sign a prenup or something?" He tried not to be offended, but truthfully, he was.

"I just tried never to think about it at all. I'm…afraid," she choked. His shield leapt at that admission.

"Baby, what are you scared of?"

"That it'll get in the way of what we have." Her voice broke along with his heart. "And," she continued as he held her tighter, "you know all the press and everything."

"I will never allow anything to get in the way of you and me ever," he vowed adamantly. "And the papers and blogs can go straight to hell."

Whenever Rainer refused an interview or shunned a cameraman, there would be retribution in the form of a particularly nasty story about him, or Emily, or one of his friends.

As of late, the Gifted media would snap photos of Emily out near a shopping mall, or once in a grocery store of all places, and then claim that she was only dating him for his inheritance. She'd been called all of the particularly unsavory names associated with people who did that kind of thing. He knew, as furious as it made him, it wounded her deeply. He just didn't know how to stop it.

Terror filled his soul, but he forced himself to go on. "If you really want to marry me and be with me forever, I think the reporters and the cameras are always going to be there. Is that okay with you? I'll do my best to stop it and keep them away, but ever since my dad died they've been there constantly. I prayed they'd lay off after your wreck, but they haven't, not really." The memories of her accident sliced through him. "If you want to think about it…or walk away…." he choked out. He couldn't live without her. He didn't even want to. "I'll understand."

"I'm not going anywhere, and certainly not because of some stupid reporters. I love you, and when you said you had a ring, seriously, I have never been so happy."

He was able to breathe again. His heart flooded his body with blood in a heated wave. It made him dizzy. "After I give you the ring, will you let me get us a place to live?"

"I'll move in with you whenever you want. I just really don't want to read about how I'm mooching off you, or that I'm some kind of kept woman, or whatever it was they said last time."

"Yeah, I enjoyed that. How exactly are you a kept woman if I'm living in your parents' house?" He rolled his eyes as she laughed. He lay back on the couch, turned onto his side, and pulled her beside him. She snuggled into him as she nuzzled her face in his neck. Rainer kissed the top of her head.

"What else did your mom say?"

She shuddered. "This is what I'd thought you'd want to know."

"I do want to know."

She hid her face in his chest and mumbled something he had no hopes of making out.

He chuckled. "Sorry, I missed that."

She sat up and cringed. "She wanted to make sure I used the cast, and she said…" Emily's face turned purple in her embarrassment.

"You don't have to tell me." He tried to ease her humiliaticn.

"No, I'll talk about it with you. I just don't want to talk about it with her."

He gave her a sorrowful look and kept his hands on her. He tried to soothe her any way he was able.

She rolled her eyes. "I believe her exact words were, 'If anything feels tender or rubbed, then a bath might help.'"

Rainer fought the urge to cringe.

"Apparently," she fumed, "she texted me that information last night, but I didn't respond."

"So, there's no hoping they were just thinking we wanted to spend some time alone not doing that, then?"

"This is yet another problem with having seven older brothers. They have us all figured out," she lamented. "It was just…awful." She folded herself into him. "She was like, 'So did you use the cast? And did you do it, or did you let him do it?' I said I didn't want to talk about it. So, she was like, 'Oh that's good, you let him do it.'" She whimpered against his chest as she hid from the world or at least from her mother.

"I'm sorry, baby." He had no idea what else he could say.

"It's fine. She's always been like that. Remember when I started my period?" She groaned, and he tried not to laugh.

Her mother hadn't quite understood Emily's desperation that Rainer and all of her brothers not know about her particular life change.

Mrs. Haydenshire wanted Emily to be proud of being a woman and had decided to hold a special dinner in Emily's honor. Emily had been mortified.

Rainer had felt terrible for her, but her brothers had harassed her mercilessly. She'd refused to speak to anyone for two solid weeks until Rainer finally got her to talk to him.

He'd found her crying out by the lake on her parents' farm. He told her about a few particularly embarrassing things that went on when a guy goes through puberty.

"You were so sweet." She clearly remembered the same part of the story he recalled.

"I felt terrible for you, and after what Connor and Patrick did…." He left out Cal's name, not certain if she wanted to talk about him.

Connor, Cal, and Patrick had taken dozens upon dozens of tampons and put them all over the house. Then, whenever one of them found one, they'd hand it to her with a snide comment about leaving them everywhere.

If Rainer stumbled upon one in the bread box, in his dining room chair, between the cushions of the couch, or once stuck in his baseball mitt, she would run from the room crying.

The final blow had been when they'd tied dozens together, and placed them discreetly on top of the blades of the fan above her bed. When she'd turned on the fan, they'd scattered like some sort of bizarre projectile weapon.

That was when her father stepped in. The teasing had halted when the culprits had spent two weeks doing manual labor outside in Virginia in July.

She shook her head and then smiled. "Want to go get groceries, and then go hang out on the beach, or do you want to go to the boardwalk or something?"

"Whatever you want to do, baby. I just want to be with you."

Her entire body seemed to light as he stared at her. He was overwhelmed by her. "We should probably get dressed."

He pretended to pout and reveled in her giggle.

"Come on." She tugged on his hand. He followed her back to their room. She pulled on a navy blue, fairly skimpy bikini, a pair of denim cutoffs, and a white button-down shirt that she left unbuttoned. It was the uniform of Virginia Beach.

As much as he appreciated the sight of her in a bikini, a sudden sense of possessiveness like he'd never known before took over his shield. He clenched his jaw.

He would never tell her what to wear, but the thought of other men admiring her made him furious. He pulled on a pair of his own cutoffs and a T-shirt as she slipped on a pair of flip-flops.

"Where do you want to go?" He called himself a prick for even debating asking her to wear something else.

She shrugged. "Let's go get groceries, and then we can go wherever you want."

Rainer grabbed his wallet, keys, and phone and shoved them into his pockets as she started to walk past him into the hallway.

He caught the back belt loop of her shorts and pulled her back to him. He guided her beautiful face to his and devoured her mouth. When he lifted his head, he whispered how much he loved her. The need to claim her consumed his shield, and he began to understand what his father had meant about it being intense.

He began informing her just what he wanted to do to her when they got back. He whispered his wishes between the intense kisses, and made certain she felt the effect she had on him.

He let her heady energy flood through his body. She was panting when he finally pulled away. With a broad grin, she bit her lip.

"Okay, this side of you that I've somehow been missing for the past twenty years of my life is really hot!"

CHAPTER 17

THE LIFE INSIDE THE PICTURE

She halted abruptly, and Rainer almost walked into her as they approached the entryway.

"What's wrong?"

She pointed out the paneled windows that surrounded the front door. There were photographers positioned in the street awaiting their exit. The Haydenshires owned a fair amount of the oceanfront on the back side of the house, but their front yard was smaller. It was only big enough to park three or four cars, which meant that photographers could easily get shots and still not be on the Haydenshires' property.

He sighed and shook his head. They'd surely already taken pictures of his car, so they knew that only he and Emily were there.

"Do you want to stay here? I'll go to the store. Just tell me what you want." At least she wouldn't have to be photographed.

"No, let's just get this over with. They can't come out on the beach. That's ours."

"I hate that I do this to you."

She smiled and took his hand. "You didn't do this, and you're worth it." She flung the door open and then placed a kiss on his jaw as cameras clicked feverishly. She turned back, and he blocked her while she locked the door. He shielded her from the reporters as he rushed her to his car.

"Are you two here celebrating your inheritance?" called one reporter.

"What are your plans until you start work?" called another.

"How long will you and Miss Haydenshire be on vacation, Rainer?" taunted yet another, in a syrupy-sweet voice. She batted her eyelashes at him.

"Get the hell away from my car!" Rainer spat as a cameraman leaned across the passenger side door in an effort to get a shot of Emily's face. The photographer moved as the reporters scribbled furiously. Rainer was going to pay for that.

He opened Emily's door, moved to block her while she got in, and then slammed it shut.

"Would your father approve of your being here with your girlfriend unchaperoned?" sneered a reporter who Rainer recognized from a particularly conservative paper in the Realm.

"Does Governor Haydenshire know you have Emily here?"

Rainer sprinted to the driver's side, leapt into the seat, turned the key, and threw the Mustang in reverse. He watched as the photographers and reporters scattered. One even came down out of a cherry tree near her parents' property line.

He shifted and then took off down the road, but he knew they would follow.

"Why is our coming to the beach so freaking interesting to everyone?" he fumed.

Emily took his hand. Her soothing Receiver's cast moved up his arm. "Because it's just us, and because we just graduated, and because you got your inheritance yesterday." He shook his head and rolled his eyes in disgust. "I think everyone's expecting you to do something crazy now that we're out of school, and you have the money and everything."

He drew a deep breath. None of this was her fault, and he needed to calm down. "I'm sorry," he offered, but she furrowed her brow.

"For what?"

"I don't know…everything." He gestured his head back to the news van that had just pulled out from a side street behind them and was edging closer.

Her explanation settled in his mind. "Why do they think I'm gonna do something crazy?"

"I don't know. It's a lot of money. They're looking for a story. I guess I should have said, they're hoping you'll do something crazy."

He shook his head, turned abruptly down the next side street, and then doubled back. This wasn't the first time he'd lamented purchasing a fairly recognizable car.

He pulled to a stop and checked his side mirrors before proceeding. "I plan to get down on one knee, beg you to marry me, move out of your parents' home, move in with the love of my life, and hopefully let her plan the wedding of her dreams. Oh, and I thought I'd actually go to work, pay bills, eat, you know, crazy shit." He rolled his eyes. All he'd ever really wanted was a normal life with her. It just didn't feel like he was asking too much.

"I won't make you beg for too long," she teased.

He gave her a smirk. "I would if you wanted me to."

After making several unnecessary turns, he pulled into the parking lot of the Bottom Dollar market, where the Haydenshires always shopped when they were at the beach. In an effort to conceal the Mustang, Rainer edged it between two large trucks.

Relief washed over him when no one shoved a camera in his face as he exited his car. He opened Emily's door for her and breathed a prayer of thanks that she was willing to put up with all of the press for him.

They proceeded down the aisles. Emily would halt every few feet, pick up an item to consider, and then either place it in the cart he was pushing or back on the shelf.

As they frequently did the shopping for Mrs. Haydenshire, this was something Rainer was quite accustomed to. This market was much smaller than the one Mrs. Haydenshire preferred back in McLean, so it didn't take them long.

They edged to a checkout with the light off and no attendant around. Emily picked up a copy of *The Times*, *The Post*, and the *Daily Press*, then grabbed *The Enquirer*, and *US weekly*.

One of the things they'd decided back in his tiny dorm in London, during their talk when they'd reunited, was that if they chose to read what was being printed about them in the papers and tabloids, they sure as hell weren't paying for them. The papers and Gifted news networks were all making a killing selling them out already.

Rainer glanced around to make certain no one was paying them any attention. They backed toward the nearest corner. He spotted the security cameras, cupped his hand, and harnessed the potential energy in the swiveling mount. He edged it the opposite direction.

This was their small and fruitless rebellion against something that seemed like it would all spin wildly out of control. Emily glanced around and then cupped her hand. It took less than a moment for her to harness the heat from the laser printing on the page. Rainer braced himself as *The Enquirer* turned into *The Illusionist*, and the print changed to the stories of The Gifted Realm.

They always started with that one because it was always the worst. They studied the headline.

"Is Lawson looking to trade up after being awarded his father's estate?"

"I'm not trading in my car," he huffed.

Emily clenched her jaw as fury permeated her energy.

"They're not talking about your car!" she spat.

He studied the pictures and then his mouth dropped open in shock. They'd gotten a shot of him winking and beckoning Emily to him the previous night at graduation. In the next picture, they showed a different Venton student, a girl from Adminis who Rainer remembered seeing around campus, but he didn't recall her name. They'd made it appear that Rainer was winking at her. He shook his head in disgust.

"That's Samantha Peterson," Emily seethed. "She's Governor Peterson's daughter."

The Petersons were an extremely wealthy family in the Realm. They were fully of the opinion that they were better than everyone else. Governor Peterson was jockeying to replace Governor

Carrington as Crown Governor. He'd been elected to the seat Governor Carrington occupied before he'd become Crown.

The Realm had been reeling from Rainer's father's assassination, and Peterson had taken advantage of the collective hysteria. He'd said and done all the right things, and no one had listened to the Receivers who'd all tried to tell everyone he was lying.

Emily rolled her eyes and moved on to the next paper. Rainer watched *The Times* turn into *The Realm Times*. This had pictures of him giving his speech and of him and Emily kissing. There was one of him seated beside Logan as he'd stared at the Chancellor at the podium. The caption read, *"Rainer Lawson contemplating the future of the Realm as it rests on his shoulders."*

"Yeah see, they're all full of crap. I was thinking when the hell can I leave? I'm bored to death."

Emily shook her head at him as they made the same move with the other papers. Most of them were reporting on graduation. One of them listed options of what would be the smartest investments for Rainer to make with his inheritance.

She took the *US Weekly* and pretended to glance through the Non-Gifted stories as a store manager passed. When he'd moved on, she waved her hand over it again and then gasped in horror.

The full-cover spread was in two blocked pictures, one of Rainer, Logan, and Governor Haydenshire entering the Pentagon the day before. Rainer hadn't even noticed a photographer, but from the looks of the photo, they'd used a long-range lens. The bottom photo was one of Emily, with several of her friends from Auxiliary Order in a department store near Venton. They were all carrying shopping bags.

"Emily Haydenshire and her closest friends celebrating boyfriend Rainer Lawson's inheritance birthday in style,"

read the caption under the photo. The photograph of Emily was at least a year old, and Rainer sighed. "Please don't let them get to you."

She shook her head. Defeat settled on her features.

They returned the papers to the stands and got in line to purchase the groceries. *It could have been worse.*

He recalled the time when Emily had been photographed cradling newborn Keaton, and the papers had declared that she'd secretly birthed Rainer's child at barely eighteen years of age.

They were loading the groceries into the trunk when the press caught up with them again, but they made it inside the car before the cameras started clicking.

CHAPTER 18

INTRUSIONS

Rainer's phone rang on the way back to the beach house. He hit the speaker button. He knew better than to be photographed talking on the phone with Emily in the car. He'd done this a few months after her wreck. The papers had called him out for being careless with Emily so soon after her near-death experience…that they'd caused.

"Hey, Logan, you're on speaker."

Logan laughed. "Ah, they trying to get your mug shot again?"

"Something like that."

"Hey, Em…I heard Mom talking to you earlier. Wow, that was not something I wanted to hear or think about."

Emily's head fell into her hands. "Please tell me no one else heard all of that?"

"Just the twins," Logan teased, "and Dad."

Her face turned the color of her hair as Logan cracked up. "Just kidding. Only the twins and I were blessed enough to have to hear that."

She looked slightly mollified then shook her head. "How's Adeline?"

Logan stopped laughing abruptly. "She's okay. That's what I wanted to talk to Rainer about actually."

If Logan needed him, the press could stick it. Rainer picked up the phone and turned off speaker. "Okay, it's me." He glanced in his rearview mirror. "It's okay with me. I'll talk to Em," he agreed after Logan's rather lengthy request. "Yeah, okay, I'll call you back." After ending the call, Rainer pulled back into the beach house driveway.

"What did Logan want?" Emily asked. He glanced around to make certain no one was in the trees and then he hoisted the bags of groceries out of the trunk.

He decided it would be better to discuss his and Logan's conversation inside the house, so he didn't respond. She seemed to understand.

They began unloading the groceries. "Logan thinks it might be good for Adeline to get away from Arlington for a few days. We apparently missed the stories about her mom's arrest." Emily looked crestfallen as he mentioned this. "He wanted to know if we'd mind them joining us here, but he didn't want to interrupt anything."

"Of course they can come. She does need a break, and that would be fun. I mean, we can still,"—she gestured toward the bedrooms,— "right?"

Rainer laughed. He was extremely pleased that she seemed just as thrilled with the next level of their relationship as he was. "I don't think they want to bunk with us, baby. They just want to come hang out. We just might have to be a little quieter." He waggled his eyebrows as she laughed.

"Have they ever…?" she asked hesitantly.

Rainer shook his head. He hoped Logan wouldn't mind him sharing that.

"And they want us here for that?"

"I don't know if they're going to be doing that, sweetheart." He didn't really want to explain the other part of his and Logan's conversation.

"Oh right. I shouldn't have assumed."

"I think Logan's a little hesitant to do that after what happened. He wants to make sure she's really okay."

"Adeline has wanted to do that for a while now. We talk about it all the time." She grinned mischievously. "I keep telling her Logan's such a good guy he doesn't want her to do that until he's sure she's ready, but I think he's starting to hurt her feelings."

Rainer nodded. Logan knew that as well. He just didn't know what to do about it. "It'll be good for them to come down here if the photographers will stay the hell away."

Emily glanced out the window automatically and then relaxed. A broad grin spread across her face. She seemed to revel in the fact that they were completely alone.

She hopped up on the kitchen counter and began swinging her legs as Rainer put the last few things in the refrigerator. He moved to her with a hungry smirk. He edged her thighs apart, and she slid forward until she could wrap her legs around his waist. He moaned as she positioned herself very suggestively over him. He grabbed her ass and massaged it as he leaned in to kiss her.

"You should call Logan back." She arched her back and thrust her breasts in his face. With another moan, he slipped his hands from her backside to what she clearly wanted him to caress.

"In a minute." He popped the clasp of the top of her bikini. He pulled it away from her and spun his thumbs over her nipples as she began to pant. The sound drove him wild. He kissed down her neck and quickly made his way to what he wanted.

Suddenly, a flash went off in his face.

"Shit!" He jerked her to him and wrapped his arms around her in a tight hug to block her from view. She trembled.

The windows in the kitchen were uncovered so everyone could see the shoreline. A photographer dressed in black was sprinting toward the front of the house.

Emily's back was to the windows. The most the picture would show would be him kissing her neck or collarbone. He was immensely thankful he'd left her shirt on. No one else would have known her bathing suit top was off. He allowed himself to breathe.

Fury lit through Emily like a fuse soaked in gasoline. "Oh, I don't think so!" She buttoned her shirt enough to cover anything she wouldn't want photographed and leapt off of the counter. She was talking to her father two seconds later. Unable to believe the audacity, Rainer was still reeling from what had happened.

"Yes, in the backyard, right at the back windows in the kitchen!" she shrieked. "And they were right at the property line when we left to get groceries. There was one in the Willards' cherry tree." A gotcha grin spread across her face. "Yes, they followed us."

Photographers and reporters following her after what happened with her wreck infuriated her father. He generally went into orbit when it happened.

As one of the Realm Governors, he had more power to stop the photos from being sold and printed than Rainer ever had, but even he couldn't stop them all.

"If we came home, they'd just follow us there. That's the last thing Adeline needs or Mom and the twins," she huffed, though Rainer knew there were other reasons she didn't want to leave. "I know." She nodded, and Rainer continued to listen to half of the conversation.

Suddenly her mouth fell open in shock. "What?" she gasped. "What did you do?"

"What?" Rainer mouthed.

"You had him arrested?"

"Who?" Rainer whispered.

She mouthed the words, "Your uncle." Rainer reeled as he continued to stare at her.

"Do you mean arrested like he's going to Coriolis or you're just scaring him arrested?"

Rainer gripped the countertop and tried to steady himself. Emily was nodding and looked slightly relieved. She gave Rainer a sweet smile and shook her head.

"He's at the Senate," she mouthed, and Rainer nodded.

Coriolis Prison was one of the many Gifted reformatories. It was the closest Gifted prison to Arlington, and it was where many war criminals were held. The most heinous of criminals, the ones who felt mind-casting, kidnapping, rape, and murder—generally by summoning the life force out of someone—were customs that the Gifted should use at their whim, ended up in Coriolis.

His father's murderer had been held there before his execution. Nausea always washed over him whenever he thought about the man who had taken everything from him. He tried never to think of him.

Each Gifted prison was located at a different level under the earth's outer crust. The depth of the prison went along with the crime committed.

At its deepest point, Coriolis was precisely 11.8 miles under the earth's crust. This was the depth at which the earth's gravity and the geothermal energies became so erratic that the Gifted were prevented from being able to summon and harness any energy at all. It rendered their Gifts useless.

The magnetism and the heat that caused the energy drain was excruciating for Gifted people. That was why Coriolis was reserved for those who committed a heinous crime.

"Okay," Emily sighed. "I appreciate it." She smiled. "I love you."

"I love you too, baby girl." Rainer heard Governor Haydenshire's parting line.

"My uncle was arrested?"

Emily wrapped her arms around his waist, and he held her tight. She slipped her hands up the back of his shirt. She was calming him. He could feel it instantly. She could do it without even thinking about it now.

He held her, closed his eyes, and let her energy wash through his soul as she restored him.

The night of his father's murder he'd clung to her. Barely fourteen years old, terrified, not capable of doing anything else, he'd lain on a quilt in the Haydenshires' back pasture while the Realm unraveled all around him. While every adult he knew came unglued, he'd held on to her, and she'd soothed him.

He'd always known that if holding on to her was all he accomplished in this life, that would be enough for him.

"Garrett arrested your uncle."

"What did he do?"

She pulled away slightly but held his hand. She knew he needed to feel her.

"He read the papers this morning."

Rainer's head fell in defeat. "My inheritance."

"He was looking for you, so he came to the house. He and Dad had several words," she stated hesitantly, and Rainer found himself chuckling.

Governor Haydenshire's viciously sharp tongue when someone did something he found appalling was lethal. Emily's father's lectures for his children were often harrowing, but Governor Haydenshire could be downright terrifying when it came to protecting his family.

"Apparently, the yelling woke up the twins and that irritated Mom. So, she called Garrett, and he arrested your uncle." Her face pulled into a delighted grin. "Actually, my mother called your uncle a disgusting baboon and threatened him with a wooden spoon just prior to calling my brother."

They both cracked up. Mrs. Haydenshire was also extremely protective of her children but not quite as terrifying as her husband. She certainly got the job done though.

"So anyway..." Emily shook her head. "Daddy's taking care of the photographers. I don't think anything taken on our property will be making it to the papers unless our personal photographer would like a one-way ticket to Felsink."

Felsink Prison was another Gifted prison. Not nearly as deep as Coriolis, it was reserved for lesser crimes but was deep enough that the earth's energy would prevent a person from summoning and escaping. The painfully penetrating energy of the sheer amount of iron ore that surrounded Felsink was enough to make most Gifted criminals not want to make a return trip.

"So let's just try not to think about that." She gestured to the window. Rainer was in awe of her fortitude. He was still dismayed from being photographed while taking off her bikini top.

CHAPTER 19

REASSURANCES

"I noticed you didn't tell your dad what I was doing when they snapped the photo."

"It doesn't matter what we were doing. We could've been buck naked going at it on the countertop. This is our property. They cannot be here taking photos."

He shook his head and tried to forcibly remove that image from his brain but found the task impossible. The idea of taking her on a countertop was extremely appealing, but the thought of a photographer snapping photos of such a thing made him simultaneously sick.

"We were not doing anything wrong. The fact that someone photographed that is disgusting. And what's worse is that if it somehow made it to the papers, just a photo of you kissing my neck," —she'd clearly done the calculations as well—"would make some idiot millions." Defeat settled on him in a crushing blow.

"Dan Vindico showed up at our house with Garrett." Her delighted smile returned. "And he said he'd take care of your uncle after he talked with Adeline."

A broad grin spread across Rainer's face. Picturing his uncle in a room with Chief Vindico, one of the most intimidating men Rainer had ever met, had him unable to hold in his laughter.

Emily joined in. "Yeah, what I would give to see that."

It was nearly one o'clock by this point.

"Why don't I call Logan back, and then we'll go out and get some lunch?" Rainer assumed doing something so mundane might be a pleasant change from the past few hours.

"Dad said for us to go get some blinds."

"I'm not blocking the view because of some dumbass photographer." He gestured to the idyllic picture of the sand and the surf with a few groupings of tall sea grass set on the dunes just outside the massive windows.

Emily giggled and bit her lip. "I think Dad was thinking he'd rather not see the views than to have to see photos of us laid out on the kitchen table."

He shook his head and pulled her back close to him. "I'm going to need you to stop saying things like that. I'm kind of new to all of this, and the images you're putting in my head are driving me wild. If you don't stop, I am actually going to lay you out on your parents' kitchen table. I won't be able to help myself."

Excitement lit in her eyes. Her intrigue made him ache. He clenched his jaw. "I'm serious. You're killing me."

"Aww, poor baby." She giggled. "Okay, how about this? Let's go get some lunch, pose for some photos, and then later, when we come back here…" she suggested flirtatiously, "I want to make use of somewhere we won't be able to use once Logan and Adeline arrive."

He groaned as his heart began to hammer. He gave her a look that said he'd very much like to take a bite. "Yeah, because I'll be able to eat when all I can think about is that." His abs clenched in anticipation.

She grabbed her bikini top from the floor of the kitchen and pulled him into the living room. After pushing him down on the couch, she turned to make certain the curtains in the living room were still drawn. She unbuttoned the few buttons on her shirt that she'd closed and flung it off.

Rainer growled in heated need. She gave him a deliciously naughty grin, then crawled in his lap, straddled him, and thrust her breasts in his face.

"I thought you wanted lunch." He wrapped his hands around her waist and guided her body upward. He caught her breast in his mouth, and she trembled.

"I do, but I really wanted you to finish what you were doing in the kitchen. That feels amazing."

"You like that, baby?" He knew she did. He could feel it. He began laving her nipple with his tongue, and her eyes flashed. Her breath caught in a sharp inhale as he took her right nipple into his mouth. Her energy flowed through him as he sucked fervently from the storehouse in her breast.

She writhed and ground against his strain. He wound his fingers around her backside. He guided her body in rhythmic circles over his erection.

"Do you feel that, baby? That's what you do to me. That's all you." He wanted her to know the sheer power she held. A low, loud whimper shuddered from her.

"I want you so bad, but I think we should wait a little while."

He drew a deep breath and shut his eyes as he forced himself to stop. He knew she didn't want to tell him that she was afraid that doing it again so soon might make her hurt. He'd picked up on the fear when he kissed her.

"Let's go get lunch." He patted her backside and willed away his erection. He repeated his vow from the night before. "We'll do whatever you want, whenever you want."

She gave a hesitant nod as regret colored her eyes.

"We have the rest of our lives," he said, just as much for himself as her. "Let me call Logan back, and then we'll go eat." He willed the images of her naked and riding him in his lap on her parents' sofa from his mind.

She pulled her bikini top back on before she shrugged into the white shirt and tied the open sides up at her waist.

He assured Logan that he and Emily would love for them to come to the beach house.

Logan told him how kind Vindico had been with Adeline. Rainer could tell he was impressed. There certainly seemed to be many sides to Dan Vindico. Rainer smiled. He was still appreciative of his advice the night before.

"Hey, do you think Em will talk to Adeline? She doesn't believe that we won't be intruding."

"Yeah, sure." Rainer handed the phone to Emily. "Logan wants you to tell Adeline we don't mind if they come."

She smiled. "Hey Adeline. Of course, I want you to come. It'll be fun. We can all play dodge the photographer together."

Rainer chuckled, but he was still in shock over what had happened.

"Yes…" Emily blushed as a broad grin spread over her lips.

Rainer didn't have to ask what Adeline wanted to know.

"Yes!" Emily giggled, and blood pooled rapidly in Rainer's cheeks.

"Uh, yes." She was still giggling. "Just come here and then we can talk about it." There was a brief pause and then Emily huffed, "Tell him I said to shut it!"

Rainer assumed either Logan or Connor had made a comment for Emily's benefit.

"Okay, yeah, sure." Emily nodded. She picked up Rainer's wrist and checked his watch. "If you get here in time, we can all go eat at Buoy's."

Eating at Buoy's was a Haydenshire family tradition. They ate there repeatedly on their many trips to Virginia Beach between Memorial Day and Labor Day.

The past few times the Haydenshires had made the trip, Logan had refused to go unless Adeline came along. His parents certainly never minded, but Adeline always felt she was imposing. When she'd eventually relent, she always had a good time. Buoy's was her favorite place to eat.

The seafood was outstanding. The low, smooth, sultry tones of the island band, along with the seating on the expansive decks overlooking the beach and the tiki bars down on the shoreline made it the perfect place to cut loose and have some fun.

Rainer let his favorite night at Buoy's from several years before replay slowly in his mind. He and Emily had managed to get away from her family. They'd found a secluded dune near the base of the pier. He'd backed her up to the round fixing that held the pier in the sand.

His heart still hammered every time he remembered that night. If he allowed himself, he could still smell the salty air, the scent of the red cedar deck, mixed in with the heady scent of her, and of sex, as it hung in the humid night air.

His breath caught as he recalled her lit by the moonlight and the strung lights off of the pier. He'd caressed her face and kissed her slowly and intensely as he pushed himself against her abdomen. She'd slipped her hand into his swim trunks for the first time. The feeling had been exquisite.

"Touch me, Rainer," she'd whispered in his ear as she'd wrapped her hand around his length.

No one had been nearby. No one was looking for either of them. Everyone else was off having fun. It didn't matter. He didn't care. In that moment, the world had existed for the two of them alone.

He'd slipped his hand down her cutoffs and traced his fingers into the crotch of her bikini. She'd panted. It was the first time he'd touched her there. The first time he'd felt the wet heat her body emanated for him. He'd been just about to slip his fingers deep inside of her when he'd heard Logan calling him.

"Don't stop, please," she'd whimpered.

"Logan's coming," he'd explained in a regret-filled whisper as he pulled his hand away. She'd clung to him as their energy sizzled from the disconnection.

He'd wrapped his arm over her shoulders, and they'd walked to meet Logan and Adeline. Everyone had been ready to go back to the beach house.

He'd let the feeling of her swollen and wet for him hold him until he could feel it again. All the way back to the house, he'd fantasized. How that would feel pressed in around his aching cock had made him frantic and desperate.

That night he'd lain quietly in one of the bunks in a room with most of her brothers and thought about her. The way she'd felt in his hands. The way her eyes darkened. The way her lips swelled when he kissed her. The way her energy arced in craving need for his shield. His heart had raced, and he'd ached for her.

Unable to sleep, he'd snuck to the living room. Emily met him there. She'd sensed his craving need. She'd tiptoed out to the deck off of the living room. She'd been wearing one of his Ioses T-shirts and a pair of white cotton panties with innocent lace edgings. He'd never forget.

"I didn't get to finish what I started on the beach," he'd whispered.

She'd trembled as she nodded. "Will you now?"

"I'm so, so sorry." Emily's distress shook him from his reverie. "Just grab whatever you want from my closet. I brought all of my bikinis. You can wear one when you get here. Just grab a bunch of Logan's T-shirts." She smiled sweetly.

"No, please don't feel bad. I'm sure Mom is delighted." Emily nodded. "Okay, go shopping, and then come here. Why don't you and Logan meet us at Buoy's at eight?" Another broad smile lit her face.

"I can't wait. I was just gonna ask Rainer if we could go to the boardwalk for a little while. Then we can shop for some stuff for you tomorrow." Emily rolled her eyes. "Adeline, you're starting at the hospital soon. You can pay me back later. Don't worry about it." Emily shook her head. "Okay, see you tonight." She handed the phone back to Rainer. "Wanna go to Dough Boy's and get a few slices of pizza? Then we can eat at Buoy's tonight with Logan and Adeline."

"Sure." It sounded like the perfect afternoon at the beach.

Astonished by how quickly Governor Haydenshire had worked, Rainer noted two Virginia Beach Iodex officers make a second loop near the house. He'd clearly called in the infantry.

CHAPTER 20
ADELINE

"Is everything okay with Adeline?" Rainer reveled in the fact that they could proceed peacefully to his car.

"No," Emily lamented.

"What else happened?"

"Her mom freaked when Adeline threw that shield last night, and then..." she shuddered.

His stomach twisted uncomfortably. He could feel her disgust. "What happened, baby?"

"Her mom got mad because when the...guys," she stumbled on the last word.

"Let's go with sick bastards," Rainer offered, and Emily nodded her agreement.

"When they ran after her, I guess they never paid or whatever. Logan took Patrick and Connor back to the apartment this morning to get all of Adeline's stuff, but her mom threw all of her clothes and everything she owned in the incinerator before she got arrested. So she has nothing. No clothes, none of the stuff Logan's ever given her, nothing." Tears tracked down Emily's face. Rainer's heart ached. "Even all of her books."

There were only a handful of times Rainer had ever seen Adeline without a book. She read avidly. It was her escape.

When Logan was trying to ease Adeline into being more comfortable with him buying things for her, he would frequently give her secondhand books. He took them to her almost every time they went out, like some guys give their girlfriends flowers.

She was more comfortable with him giving her used books than buying her new ones. She treasured each and every one like he'd given her gold. Eventually Logan had purchased newer editions of a few of her favorites. He'd even taken her to book signings of her favorite authors.

"That's awful." He couldn't bear to think of Adeline's most treasured gifts from Logan in an incinerator.

Emily's chin trembled and then she began to cry in earnest. He rubbed her leg and willed calm into her.

"Adeline said Logan put her in one of his shirts when he took her to bed last night. He stayed up and casted her all night in his shield so she could sleep." She shuddered out the words. "So, Mom's taking her shopping before they leave for here, but you know she won't let Mom get her much."

"Why don't I just give you one of the bank cards, and you take her shopping tomorrow."

"That's so sweet of you."

"No, that's what's right," he insisted.

That's what his father would have done. That's what he wanted to do with all of the money. He wanted to help people and maybe spoil Emily when she'd let him. He could feel his dad there with him in that moment, and he knew he would be proud.

CHAPTER 21

ON THE BOARDWALK

Rainer pulled into one of the parking lots off of the boardwalk and helped Emily out of the car. She seemed to float beside him. She held his hand as they proceeded down the well-worn planks that made up the vast Virginia Beach Boardwalk.

It was idyllic. Carts with ice cream, pretzels, and cotton candy were being pedaled along the oceanfront. Children scrambled for balloon animals from a clown. The salty ocean air permeated the space around them.

It was soothing. Peace settled on him and flowed from Emily as well. He'd been to the boardwalk with her dozens of times, and she was always so happy here.

After Cal had been killed and she'd gotten out of the hospital, she'd begged him to bring her to the beach, but he'd left her instead. The sharp, stabbing regret seared through him again.

They made their way to Dough Boy's and took a booth near the back. Rainer ordered them a large pepperoni, sausage, onion, and bell pepper pizza. It was Emily's favorite. She beamed at him and scooted closer in the booth.

An idea came to him suddenly. It would be nearly impossible, and he'd need a lot of help. His mind flew. Their pizza arrived, and she dug in. Her eyes rolled dramatically as she took her first bite. Rainer chuckled at her exuberance.

"This is delicious! Seriously, Dough Boy's is the best."

As he consumed five pieces quickly, Rainer realized he'd been starving.

Emily giggled as he picked up another. "It's like coming here with Logan."

When the pan was empty, Rainer paid the bill, and they proceeded back to the boardwalk. After the massive intake of calories, he could think a little clearer. His idea began to take shape. If he could get all the pieces to fall into place, this would be perfect.

He slowed his pace near Indigo's, an accessory store off of the boardwalk, and tried to hide his excited grin over his plan. It was Emily's favorite shop. She loved the eclectic one-of-a-kind pieces.

Since most everything in the store was under thirty dollars, her father would generally let her get whatever she wanted when they visited. She was eyeing an emerald-green-and-navy-blue scarf on one of the racks. He winked at her and handed her one of the bank cards he'd received the day before.

"Go get it and whatever else you want. I'm gonna run to the restroom. Will you be okay for a minute?" He glanced around and made sure there were no photographers ready to pounce.

She leaned up to kiss his jaw. "I promise I really only want the scarf."

He shook his head and tenderly cupped his hand under her chin. "Get whatever you want…please."

He caught the eye of one of the Iodex officers who'd been following them discreetly. Rainer knew he would step in if anyone else got too close to her. Rainer gestured his head to a store down the boardwalk a few yards away that had a public restroom.

The officer nodded and followed Emily into the store. As soon as he was certain she was distracted, Rainer pulled his cell phone from his pocket and sprinted into the surfboard souvenir shop. Excitement and nerves coursed through him as he made the first call.

She was waiting on him outside the shop when he returned. "What took you so long?"

"Uh," he paused, "Logan called. They're about to leave."

"Good, but you know the great thing about cell phones is that you can walk and talk."

"Right, got distracted in the surf shop, I guess," he lied. His heart was hammering from his phone call. She studied him. Lying caused a specific distortion of emotional energy rhythms, and it was almost always apparent to Receivers. But his emotions were likely concealed within his nervousness so she wasn't getting a clear read.

Keeping anything from Emily, even for a few hours, was nearly impossible. He moved her farther down the walk and prayed she wouldn't ask. They came in sight of the amusement park and her face lit in delight.

"Can we ride the Ferris wheel tonight?"

He hid his smirk. "Of course. Don't we always?"

A broad, delighted grin formed on her features. Her eyes twinkled. He was overwhelmed. The little things always made her the happiest. Emily loved the boardwalk Ferris wheel. They had a whole routine whenever they rode. Though Logan and Connor harassed him about it mercilessly, Rainer loved it just as much as she did.

"Did you get the scarf?" He took the Indigo's bag from her hand.

"Oh gosh, I didn't give you back the card," she panicked.

"You keep it."

"I don't want to." She shook her head.

"Baby." He pulled her toward one of the large statues on the boardwalk with umbrella-covered picnic tables surrounding it. They grabbed an empty table. "Listen just a minute. Yesterday, Will helped me understand all of the accounts and where he thinks we should keep some of it invested. It's not all tied to that one card. Honestly, there are more accounts than I can count, and I want you to think of it all as ours."

She bristled suddenly and reached for his hand. She was scared.

He panicked as he looked up and down the boardwalk trying to find what frightened her. His shield flared around them. "What's wrong?"

A man with bulging biceps covered in snake tattoos from his wrists to his neck walked past their table. Emily's face tinged green.

"Rainer," her voice trembled. Her hands flew to her forehead as she tried to block out the terror. Rainer held her to his chest and pushed his shield out over her. He wasn't certain what else to do. Part of her abilities, part of what made her so empathetic, so good at helping and serving others, also made her aware of the darker side of Gifted people.

Rainer gestured his head slightly toward the man who was now making his way to one of the parking lots. She gave a slight nod.

He was never sure how to help her when she felt this. It happened so rarely.

If a Gifted person had ever used black energy, had ever summoned the life-giving energy out of another Gifted person, she could feel it. With each draw of dark energy, the soul blackened. The more often a Gifted person summoned black, the stronger the effect was felt by Receivers.

Judging by her reaction when the man had been more than ten feet away from her, he belonged in Coriolis for the rest of his life.

Emily had never gotten sick from being near a person who had summoned black energy, but Rainer knew it could be a common side effect of having a Receiver too close to the level of hate-filled evil it would take to siphon the life energy out of a Gifted person.

"Let's get out of here," he urged.

She clung to him as they walked farther down the boardwalk. All talk of bank accounts and money was quickly forgotten.

They walked up and down the boardwalk hand in hand until Emily was back to her cheerful self. She'd drawn his soothing strength and protection into her rhythms from their interlocked hands. He'd fought not to go slack-jawed and beg her to go back to the house so he could more effectively get his energy into her.

She'd stopped by a swimsuit shop, and she'd picked out a few bikinis for Adeline.

At seven, Rainer's phone rang. He uttered a quick prayer and then answered.

"Hey." He smiled at Emily. "Thank you." She furrowed her brow, but he pretended not to notice. "We'll head over there now and get a table. See you in a few."

"Are they almost here?" Emily trilled. Rainer nodded as excitement began to bubble in his stomach. He owed Logan big time. He must've flown. He was immensely thankful that the extra police Governor Haydenshire had called in hadn't caught Logan.

CHAPTER 22
NEGOTIATIONS

At seven thirty, Logan and Adeline sauntered onto one of the decks of Buoy's. They joined Rainer and Emily at the table.

"Adeline!" Emily leapt to her feet and wrapped her arms around Adeline who beamed at her. Logan and Rainer shared a quick glance as Logan slipped something into Rainer's hand while Emily was distracted.

"I got you swimsuits," Emily announced.

Discomfort formed on Adeline's features. "You didn't have to do that."

"I don't think you're allowed to skinny-dip here, so it's probably good that I did."

Adeline giggled, and the sound seemed to elate Logan.

"Rough day?" Rainer asked as the girls chatted.

"You could say that." Logan ordered himself a beer when the waiter returned to the table.

"Is my uncle still at the Senate?"

Logan cracked up. "Wow, was he pissed!" He shook his head with a smirk. Rainer rolled his eyes. He wasn't surprised. "Dad and Vindico were going to keep him in a holding cell until he piped down. So, he may be there 'til next spring."

The waiter returned with Logan's beer and Adeline's water. Logan ground his teeth. He must've missed Adeline's order while he was chatting with Rainer. "Would you please bring her a Dr Pepper?"

Adeline started to protest, but Logan gave her a look that had her backing down. He ordered two large platters of appetizers, daring anyone to object, and after the waiter had returned to the kitchen he started in, "Adeline, please…please, for me, just for the next few days, let me buy you stuff. It would make me feel so much better. I don't want to fight with you about this anymore. You're my girlfriend. I love you. Let me take care of you."

Emily and Rainer looked out over the ocean and watched the sun set. Rainer wondered if they should leave and give them some privacy.

Adeline's cheeks burned crimson as she blinked back tears. Logan stood and took her hand. He guided her away from the crowd of tables so they could talk.

The waiter returned, and Rainer informed him they wouldn't be ordering for a while. Several minutes later, Adeline and Logan returned and appeared to have reached some kind of conclusion. Adeline looked more at peace than Rainer had ever seen her, but Logan looked quite terrified.

He seemed to physically shake himself from his torment and began consuming the appetizers like he hadn't eaten in a week. After making his sixth trip back to their table, the waiter was pleased they were finally ready to order.

Logan gave Adeline a challenging, almost defiant look. She drew a deep breath and ordered more than a side salad. She ordered one of the most expensive pasta dishes loaded with seafood that Emily had been urging her to try. Logan looked like she'd just made his entire year.

She stared at him like she couldn't quite understand the depths of his love for her. It was a distinctly intimate confusion. Rainer glanced away. He winked at Emily as she offered him a quick grin. He wondered what she was feeling from both Logan and Adeline.

It was almost nine when they left Buoy's and headed back down the boardwalk.

"Let's go ride the Ferris wheel," Emily chanted. Logan and Rainer exchanged a quick glance.

Rainer was astonished at how one meal seemed to have soothed Adeline. She'd inhaled the large platter of pasta, and she already looked better. Her face held a healthy glow, and her eyes lit more readily when Logan took her hand.

"Let's get ice cream first," Logan urged.

They headed to a nearby ice cream cart and each ordered a small cone. Rainer added sprinkles to Emily's, because she loved them, and then he paid before anyone else could offer. Emily licked the vanilla ice cream, and Rainer was enthralled.

They proceeded toward the amusement park. Logan slowed up and let the girls get a little ahead of them. "I'm trying not to freak."

Rainer slowed his gait again. The girls were chatting happily and didn't seem to notice.

"What's wrong?"

Logan looked pale. The girls stopped outside of a women's clothing shop.

"Do you care if we go in for a few minutes?" Emily quizzed. Logan and Rainer insisted they go. They seated themselves on the bench along the boardwalk just outside the store.

"You're not upset about...?" Rainer stammered.

"Huh?" Logan's brow furrowed, and Rainer slapped his hand on his pocket. "Oh no. Why would that upset me?" He looked distracted and panicked.

"Okay, then what is it?"

"Will you tell me what happened last night? Please, I'm begging you. I don't know how to do this." He shook his head. "I'm sorry," he offered before Rainer could respond. "I know it's none of my business, and I swear I really don't want to know about you and Em, but I'm gonna screw this up. I don't know what I'm doing, and this is what she wants. This is why she's in there letting my sister buy her clothes, and that's how I got her to actually eat something that cost more than five bucks."

"Okay, calm down," was Rainer's first instruction, but it appeared to fall on deaf ears.

"Look at her." Logan gestured to the store. The girls were flipping through a rack of sundresses near the front. "She's so beautiful, and sweet, and perfect. Why does she want to do this now? Last night, she almost got..." He halted abruptly and looked like he was going to be sick.

"Logan," Rainer spoke firmly. "Deep breath."

Logan nodded, but panic pulsed in his shield. A million thoughts raced through Rainer's head. He didn't know where to begin so he decided to wing it. "She wants to do that because she loves you." He willed Logan to believe him. "I think she wants to be with you because she wants you to have that, and she wants you to give her that." He sincerely hoped this wasn't too much for Logan right then.

"I want all of that too." He laid it all out in his terror. "But that doesn't mean that I know what the hell I'm doing. What if I do it wrong?"

Everything that had happened in the past twenty-four hours coupled with the fact that Logan hadn't slept at all had nearly driven him right over the edge.

Rainer wasn't going to let him down just because he was embarrassed. He tried to remember everything he'd wished someone had told him the night before.

"Okay." He drew a deep breath. "Uh, the first time is a little rough, but it will be way better the next time."

Logan nodded and looked deeply appreciative of the advice. "Rough, how?"

Rainer grimaced. He closed his eyes and willed away the repulsion that always washed over him when he thought about this particular part of it. "It's...gonna hurt her, a little." He shuddered. "And your shield is going to react to her pain."

To his shock, Logan didn't look quite as appalled as Rainer had expected.

He nodded. "Right, because of the..." He couldn't say the word hymen, but he gestured to his own abdomen for a split second. Rainer nodded, and Logan shuddered slightly.

"Yeah, and you're...uh...gonna have to fight your own shield which also hurts you, but that hurt isn't nearly as overwhelming as how good the rest of it feels so…it's complicated."

Logan managed a haggard nod. "I heard Mom tell Em about the bath thing. Did that work?"

"I don't know. We didn't know that until this morning." He considered the gravity of this night for both of them. "Do you want me and Em to stay somewhere else?"

"No, then she'll know I told you."

"Yeah." Rainer finally met Logan's eyes. "Well, she's in there talking to Emily about it right now, so…."

"Still, though." Logan shook his head. "I don't want her to freak about anything else. The whole thing with her mom, and I still don't know how to do this!"

"Well, yeah, you do." Rainer didn't really want to tell Logan anything else. "Just do whatever she asks. It'll work itself out, but you have to chill."

"Whatever she asks?!" Logan rolled his eyes. "You've been my best friend since I was born. I've been dating her for almost five years. When exactly has Adeline Parker ever asked for anything? She's perfectly happy with nothing at all. I've never seen anything like it. Emily might tell you what she wants,"—Logan scowled momentarily —"but Adeline isn't going to!"

"Then ask her."

"What do you mean?" He suddenly looked less frightened.

Rainer forced himself to go on. "You'll be able to tell what she likes based on when her rhythms pick up pace once you stop freaking out, but if you can't the first time, then ask her." He shut his eyes to finish the command. "Ask her if it feels good. If she seems like it does, keep going. If not, change it up. Pay attention to her rhythms."

A long haggard breath slipped from Logan's lungs. "Do you think that will really work?"

Rainer nodded. "She may not say what she wants out loud, but her energy isn't going to lie. It can't."

"Okay." Logan finally managed to breathe. His face was crimson, but Rainer was certain his was as well.

The girls made their way out of the store. Logan seemed thrilled they were both carrying bags.

"Good luck," Rainer whispered as they stood and took the bags from the girls.

"Thanks," Logan mumbled. He still looked rather frightened as they continued on toward the amusement park.

CHAPTER 23

THE RIDE OF YOUR LIFE

Emily and Adeline were thick as thieves as they traipsed along the boardwalk. Emily was beaming as they walked. Rainer knew why, but he didn't call her on it. He didn't want to embarrass Adeline.

They made their way to the ticket booths. Logan and Rainer bought enough tickets for them all to ride several rides.

Rainer's heart picked up pace, and his palms began to sweat. He told himself he was being stupid. He kept his hand on Emily's back as they got in line for the Ferris wheel. Her excitement tensed in elated bands in her rhythms.

"Good luck," he repeated Rainer's wish back to him as Emily took her seat.

"Thanks," Rainer breathed as he seated himself.

"Are you okay?" Emily quizzed as she studied him.

How does anyone surprise a Receiver?

"I'm fine." He gave her a forced smile.

She knew he was lying. "Are you sure?"

He managed a haggard nod.

The ride began with several metallic clicks of the motor, and Rainer's heart stuttered as the wheel lurched and began its rhythmic spin.

A broad grin lit Emily's face as she stared out over the boardwalk and then turned to see the ocean as it kissed the shore below them. He let the wheel circle a few times until she gave him a goading grin, and he winked at her.

Harnessing the energy from a lift motor that spins a Ferris wheel was one of the first things they'd learned at the academy. The energy was fairly simple to lock on to, and Governor Haydenshire had taught Rainer and Logan how to do it before they'd even started at the academy.

Rainer chuckled as he thought about the fact that most often when a Ferris wheel stops, it's because some Gifted sub-freshman is trying to impress his date.

He drew a deep breath and cupped his hand. It wouldn't take much to stop it. He did it every time they came to the beach.

He waited until they were at the very top, closed his fingers, and halted the ride. She beamed and then giggled. After giving him an adorable, mischievous grin, she began the script. "Hey, Rainer," she sassed. Her eyes sparkled in the moonlight as he gazed into their emerald depths.

"Yeah, Emily?" Her eyes closed in a slow blink as she continued. Delight and love rolled in her rhythms. Rainer could feel them as they filled the air around him. It took his breath away.

"Betcha won't kiss me," she taunted, just like she'd done when she was seven years old. He laughed and shook his head at her.

"That got me in a whole lotta trouble the last time I took that bet."

He leaned in suddenly and brushed a tender kiss across her lips. He edged closer and added to the pressure and the intensity. He groaned as she responded.

He pulled away after a few minutes and tried to catch his breath.

"Look, there's a shooting star." He pointed out the open window behind her. She spun, and he pulled it from his pocket.

"Hey, Em," he choked and swallowed down the emotion that settled thickly in his throat.

"Hmm?" she spun back. Her eyes goggled.

"Betcha won't marry me."

Her mouth fell open. "Yes I will! Watch me!!" she gasped just before tears consumed her. He lifted her hand and slid his mother's engagement ring on her finger. Emily threw her arms around him, and he held her tight. Everything in his world settled into perfect accord in that one unbelievable moment.

"It's so beautiful." She tried to swallow down her tears. "Is this...?" She held her right hand over her mouth as she stared at her left.

"It was my mom's." He swallowed down the rock-like enclosure of emotion that clogged his throat. "But, if you want something different, I'll get you whatever you want." He was suddenly worried she might want something her uncle had designed.

"No." She shook her head. "This is amazing!" She seemed unable to take her eyes off her own hand. "Thank you, I mean...are you sure you want me to have this?"

He nodded but was unable to believe the depth of love he held for her. "I want you to have everything. This is just the very beginning, okay?" He wiped the tears off her face. People began calling to the man running the Ferris wheel, and Rainer chuckled.

"Whoops." He released the Ferris wheel from his cast and allowed it to spin again. She laughed and laid her head on his shoulder.

"Got a little distracted," he admitted sheepishly.

"When did you ask Daddy?" She studied the large princess-cut diamond on her hand.

"I called him this afternoon when I went in the surf shop. That's what took me so long. Logan and Adeline went by the beach house and brought me the ring at dinner. I'm surprised you didn't hear your mom squealing from McLean. We have to be back by Saturday, because she's throwing an engagement dinner for us." They laughed together as she blinked back another round of tears.

"I love you so much." Her words filled his soul.

"I love you too."

The ride halted again after a few more turns, and the patrons were getting disgruntled.

"Logan!" Rainer chastised. He heard laughter from the boxed seat behind them.

The Ferris wheel began again, and after a few more turns, they exited.

To Rainer's shock, Governor and Mrs. Haydenshire were standing at the entrance. The governor gave Rainer a wry smile, and Mrs. Haydenshire was crying. All of Emily's brothers were there as well. Logan and Adeline exited right after Rainer and Emily.

"What are you doing here?" Emily gasped as Governor Haydenshire lifted her off the ground in the exuberance of his embrace.

He chuckled. "I figured my baby girl getting engaged was worthy of booking one of the jets."

Logan held up his cell phone and revealed the text he'd sent that let his family know that Rainer and Emily had entered the ride.

"We don't want to intrude on your evening. We just wanted to be here," Mrs. Haydenshire assured Rainer as she gave him a fierce hug. He was elated they were there.

"Thank you for everything," Rainer vowed, "especially for her." He stared at Emily as she shook her head and hugged him again. Governor Haydenshire slapped Rainer on the back. "My pleasure, son, but she's still my baby girl."

"Well, let me see it." Mrs. Haydenshire took Emily's hand and rolled her eyes at her husband. "Oh, honey, it's beautiful." Mrs. Haydenshire patted Rainer's face sweetly. "I'm so happy for both of you."

Keaton wiggled down from Connor's arms. "To ride, EE!" he demanded of Emily. Everyone laughed as they began exploring the amusement park. They guided Henry and Keaton to their favorite rides which delighted the twins.

Rainer clung to Emily. He wanted to savor every moment of the delighted smile that lit her face for the entire evening.

"Well played." Garrett gestured back to the Ferris wheel, but he wore a deeply concerned expression.

Rainer nodded. "Yeah, I figured she wouldn't turn me down on the Ferris wheel here."

"It was perfect!" She beamed.

Henry toddled over to her and lifted his arms. She smiled, and Rainer released her as she scooped him up. He laid his head on her shoulder and began to suck his thumb. It was getting late.

Rainer stared at them and allowed himself to imagine her holding their son. Right then and there, he knew he wanted it all. He wanted the whole deal, but most of all he wanted her.

He longed to be with her again, to feel her around him, and to feel her body's responses to his. He wanted to feel the wet heat. He wanted to hear the sweet sounds she made for him.

He let his mind travel back to that night by the pier at Buoy's. He wanted to take her and make her all his own. Desperate longing to fill her with his energy, and with him, overtook him. He wanted to explode inside of her, and he wanted it now.

He forced himself to be patient. Her family was surrounding her. She was cradling her little brother as he drifted off to sleep. Rainer knew why Keaton and Henry always wanted her. She calmed them and soothed them. She quelled their fears and relaxed them. He knew, because he felt it when he held her. Mrs. Haydenshire beamed at Henry snuggled on Emily's shoulder.

"We'd better get back." She lifted Henry and laid him on her own shoulder. He stirred momentarily but then was out once more.

"You all have a good week," she wished Logan and Rainer. "For me, try to get Adeline to relax and have a little fun."

Rainer tried hard not to chuckle over Logan's pallor.

They spent the next ten minutes in the middle of the amusement park being hugged and congratulated. The Haydenshires finally climbed into several rented cars and headed back to the airport, just a few miles from the boardwalk, where one of the enhanced Senate jets for the governors awaited them. They'd be back in Arlington in fifteen minutes.

"Ready to go?" Rainer waved to her family and watched the cars drive away.

Emily nodded, but Logan shook his head. "Don't you want to ride the Tilt-A-Whirl, Em?" he pled.

She gave him a concerned glance but didn't give in to his wishes. "No, I want to go back to the house now."

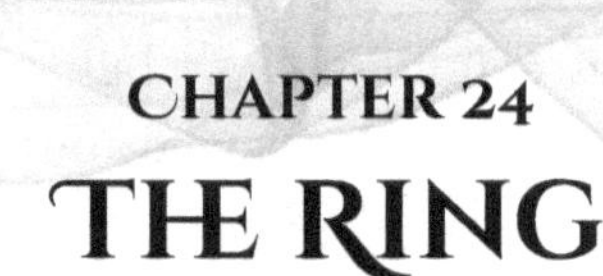

Adeline didn't look much more confident than Logan, but Rainer knew there wasn't really anything else he could do to help.

"Okay," Logan choked as they walked slowly toward the gates. Rainer released Emily's hands and gestured for her to try to talk to Adeline. She scooted her brother out of the way. Logan backed up to walk with Rainer.

"Relax. You'll be fine," Rainer vowed. "Vindico told me last night just to take it really slow, and that if I was more confident she wouldn't be so nervous. That was really good advice."

Logan looked stunned. "You told our boss that you were gonna fuck my sister?"

"No!" Rainer scowled. "He just sort of knew why I was so nervous, I guess."

"Yeah, the Double-Predilect thing." He seemed thankful to talk about something besides his and Adeline's plans for the evening.

Having Double-Predilected energy bands wasn't the norm, but it wasn't that rare. But to have equal gift, like Vindico, equal storehouses of two kinds of energy inside your body was almost unheard of.

"Dad said that Venton let him choose since he was of equal gift. He chose Ioses instead of Visium," Logan elaborated.

"He must've seen himself as more of a Shield."

"I keep thinking that's probably why he's so intense."

"Probably."

They caught back up with the girls, and Rainer took Emily's hand as they exited.

"Dammit," he spat as a million flash bulbs went off in his face. They must've very conveniently stayed out of sight while the governor was there.

"Why was the governor here, Miss Haydenshire? Is that an engagement ring?" called a reporter from the Realm Times.

"Is that your mother's ring, Rainer?"

"When's the wedding?" demanded a gruff voice from behind Rainer.

He and Logan formed their usual stance to try to block the girls from the cameras as they rushed down the boardwalk.

"Did the governor try to get you to come home, Miss Haydenshire?" called a reporter Rainer loathed from *The Illusionist*.

Iodex moved in but couldn't do much to help on public property. They tried to block the reporters, but there were just too many. Emily's father must've booked the jet right after Rainer called him, and the press had been on high alert for hours.

"Will you and Rainer be moving off of your parents' farm, Emily?" called another reporter Rainer didn't recognize.

"Logan! Logan! Logan!" rang from several at once.

"Can we get a picture of you and your sister?"

"Yeah, I'll give you a picture," Logan snarled, but Rainer grabbed his hand before he could flip them off.

"Don't! It'll only make it worse."

"Emily, did he ask you at dinner or at the park? Rainer, are you going back to the Haydenshires' beach house for the night?"

"Emily, can we see the ring? Can we see the ring?" It echoed from all around them.

"Is that the Lawson family ring, Rainer? Was that your mother's ring?" That question rang from every reporter surrounding them.

Rainer cursed the fact that she was now wearing the Lawson ring. Photos of her hand just went up exponentially in value.

By the time they reached the cars, Iodex had called for reinforcements, and the press had been halted at the pier.

"Guess what the headline of tomorrow's paper will be?" Logan opened Adeline's door for her. Rainer shook his head after putting Emily in his Mustang. He took off before the cameras could dodge the Iodex blockade.

"I should have gotten you a different ring," Rainer lamented as soon as he slammed his door shut.

"Why?" Emily's brow furrowed

"I just made your hand the most valuable hand in the entire Realm." He was furious. She couldn't even have the ring without all hell breaking loose.

"I don't care. They can take pictures of my hand. The fact that you wanted me to have your mother's ring means the world to me. Please, please, don't let this ruin tonight."

He gazed at her tenderly as they drove toward the beach house. He took random turns, well out of their way, to make certain they weren't being followed. Emily still looked elated, much to his relief.

"So, I guess Logan's gonna have a good birthday, as well." She giggled. That finally elicited a laugh from Rainer.

"Yeah, if he doesn't puke."

"Poor guy." She shook her head. "He doesn't have to be a porn star. She really just wants him."

"I kind of tried to tell him that. Not in those words, per se."

They pulled into the Haydenshires' driveway. He was thankful no one fell out of a tree as they made their way to the porch. It seemed like Governor Haydenshire's warning had been heeded at least when it came to their private property.

Dan Vindico

Every curse word Dan could come up with flew out of his mouth as he watched the television screen's live feed of his two newest officers leaving the Virginia Beach boardwalk. What the fuck was Lawson thinking?

At that moment, the Haydenshires headed through the Iodex office to return to their cars after their impromptu trip to celebrate the blessed engagement. Dan ground his teeth. He marched out of his office and cornered Garrett. They shared a knowing look as Dan pointed him into this office and slammed the door behind him. "He gave her the fucking Lawson ring?!" he seethed. "Is he just damned and determined to live his old man's life? Is he trying to get her killed?"

Garrett narrowed his eyes and took several breaths. His shield reverberated like he'd been hit. "He doesn't know any of that. My dad, your dad, the whole fucking governing board has kept him locked up tight on the farm with my baby sister after Governor Lawson's assassination. No one ever told him anything. He knows nothing about why his mother was killed. He doesn't even know the circumstances of his father's death. They shielded the shield, and now we're here. But what else could they do? He was a kid."

"Yeah, well, I think it's high time somebody shatters Rainer's gilded cage before he gets to live my hell."

"I don't disagree, but all of the legends are shit. None of it's true."

"Nic Wretchkinsides doesn't believe the legends are fake, and that is the only thing that matters." Dan could not believe he was going to have to do what he was about to do. He rubbed his temples and pulled out an arrest warrant. Before he filled it out, he stared Garrett down. "You're telling me he knows nothing. At all."

Garrett nodded. "They didn't even tell them about the snake. Unless Governor Lawson explained it to him, Rainer has no idea that snake was casted. If they didn't even tell him that, he knows nothing. And that was all my father's doing."

"I think it's high time our illustrious governing board stops trying to pretend that Rainer gets to live in their pipe dreams for this Realm. Somebody's got to fucking talk to that kid."

"I know, but he's been through hell already. He's a fucking orphan. He's got no one but Emily and us."

"Yeah, I know," Dan seethed. "I'm trying to keep him from being a widower as well."

Garrett swallowed down raw fear for his sister. "I'll talk to him."

"No." Dan forced himself to breathe and to think. "I'm going down there. He just gave her the ring. Let him have his fucking fantasy for one more night at least. I'll watch the house. And I'm putting out a warrant for Pendergrath."

"Do you have anything to hold Pendergrath on?"

"Not for any length of time, but I know where he'll be tomorrow night. I can force him back to Russia, and for the time being that works."

"I'm really sorry," Garrett offered sincerely.

"Yeah, me too."

"Don't say anything to him until I talk to my dad. He needs to be trained before you scare the piss out of him, or he's gonna go to complete shit. His shield will take over again. He was so convinced her wreck was his fault he left her and flew to London. He's a brilliant kid but he loses all rational thought when it comes to my sister. He almost destroyed them both."

"But all of the legends are shit, right?" Dan threw his words back in his face.

Garrett's neck contracted with a harsh swallow. "Okay, fine. But the legend of the ring is shit. I'll come up with some reason to get them back to the farm sooner than later." He considered for a long moment. "I'll tell Dad I want to use the beach house. I'll get Chloe to go with me."

"I'm heading down there now. When I need to leave, I'll have an Elite team keep an eye on them."

"Dad let on that there are officers following them because of the press. I'd just leave it at that."

Dan rolled his eyes. "You let me know when the governors decide that Lawson gets to live here in the real world with us. If it isn't soon, he's gonna die in the one they've created for him."

CHAPTER 25

WHERE THE PAST MEETS ITS FUTURE

LOGAN HAYDENSHIRE

After deciding that he didn't mind driving around Virginia Beach for a while, Logan made a sudden left and lost one of the news vans following them.

"Are you okay?" He glanced at Adeline uncomfortably. She was gazing out the window at the star-strewn sky. She gave him her sweet, unassuming smile.

"That was so sweet. Emily's so excited. It was the perfect way for him to ask her." She looked thrilled for their best friends.

Logan laced his fingers through hers. "Rainer's had her number since she dared him to kiss her when she was seven, so…"

He halted as the customary sadness permeated her energy. He knew she wished that she could have lived the life that he and Emily and all of his brothers had lived. Emotion strangled him as he squeezed her hand before making another hard left.

The black SUV tailing them aggressively swerved and hit a fire hydrant. Logan laughed. Adeline bit her lip and tried to hide her grin.

"I'm sorry, but that's just funny," he said as she covered her mouth to quell her giggle.

She grew quiet again. He was certain she was thinking about what she'd asked him to do that evening. Logan was happy for Rainer and

Emily. But for him, the night held nervous tension and plaguing thoughts. He worried that he shouldn't have given in just to get her to eat or to let him replace the things her mother had destroyed.

He shuddered as the memory he wanted so desperately to keep and so desperately to go and give him peace began replaying. The last conversation pulsed through his mind.

He could still hear the gravel crunching under his boots as he strolled around the lake. He could feel the chilling cold move through him.

"Her mom tried to hit her?" Cal quizzed. He sounded as horrified as Logan felt. Logan nodded as he blinked back burning tears of defeat.

"Lo, come on. It's me. Talk to me. I have to go back to Moscow in the morning, and I know there's more to this." Cal walked steadfastly beside Logan just as he always had. "You haven't even talked to Rainer. You won't eat. I know you're worried about her."

"Yeah, well, I just took her back to that hellhole she lives in."

Cal nodded. "You can't hold her prisoner here. She told Mom and Dad she doesn't want to move out here, so..."

Emotion drowned Logan. He couldn't fight the riptide of terror. He wasn't strong enough to outswim it.

"Before I took her home," he finally choked. Cal looked devastated over whatever Logan was about to share with him. "I went up to Emily's room to get her stuff for her." The relief from just talking to his big brother about what had happened calmed his shield. "She was terrified. She'd been crying." Logan shuddered.

"Because she was going back home?"

"No," Logan choked. "That would have been so much better." He pulled his coat tight around him. He tried to ward off the autumn winds and the chilling dread that had taken up residence in his soul.

"Why then?"

Logan swallowed down the bile that rose violently in his throat. "She, uh...she thought that since I stopped her mom from hitting her Friday, let her spend the weekend here, and sleep in an actual bed, and Mom fed her and everything..." He stumbled over the words.

Cal waited patiently while Logan gathered courage.

"She thought I expected her to sleep with me," he finally forced the horrifying words from his mouth. "She was taking her clothes off and crying when I went into Emily's room. She was petrified." He squeezed his eyes shut. He didn't need to see to make the trek around the lake. He could make the walk from the feel of his boots on the graveled shore, and the sound of the lapping water alone.

"Oh my god!" Cal gasped.

"Yeah." Logan allowed himself to breathe after relieving a portion of his burden.

"I'm so sorry, man."

Logan nodded and waged war against emotion. It seemed to be a losing battle. "How could she think that? I'm crazy about her. I really, really think I could love her." He didn't just think it. He knew it. "I would never have done that this weekend as bad as I might want to. And, make her do that? That's what she thinks of me?" He laid it all out for Cal and knew that he could make it all make some kind of sense.

"No," Cal soothed. "No, that's what she thinks of men because that's all she's ever known. She never had a dad, and her mom sure as hell doesn't love her. So, all of the men she's had any dealings with have been her mother's dealers and her Johns. That's how her world works," he gained fervor as he continued. "So if you love her, and I know you do..."

Logan was shocked he didn't seem to have any issue with that fact.

"Then you'll be the first person in her entire life who has. And as much as this might suck, you're going to have to teach her that she's worth being loved. You're going to have to make her believe in you, and that means you can't jump into bed with her until you're damn sure she feels love from you. Doing that too soon might just screw her up more. Take it slow, painfully slow. Don't let Garrett and his shit stories get to you. Half of the stuff he swears he's done isn't true, and even if it is, that's not you, and it's not what you want. Don't let the idiots you go to school with harass you. You know you're doing right by her, and that's what matters. Don't let her or anyone else talk you into doing anything until you know the time is right. Be her Shield before you're her lover. Protect her and love her and make sure she feels that from you before you take her to bed."

"How do I know that she knows that?" The plea spilled frantically from Logan's mouth.

"You'll feel it. Don't let her down. Don't be like everyone else."

Logan nodded and let Cal's wisdom wash through his soul. She was worth fighting for and worth saving. He wanted to be the one to catch her when she finally let go of her mother and of her past.

"Does she know anything about her father?"

"No." Logan shook his head.

"Do you want me to see what I can find out. Iodex has records on every Gifted family from all around the world."

"Maybe," Logan hemmed. "I don't want her hurt anymore, but... I think it would go a long way to have one parent who even kind of liked her."

"Let me see what I can find out and then you can go from there."

"Thank you."

His big brother slapped him on the back. "You can do this. You can make this work, but you're gonna have to go at her pace and make her believe in you, and then in herself. It won't be easy."

"I don't care. I'll do it."

Cal gave him the customary Haydenshire smirk. "Good for you, and she's great."

"She is," Logan agreed.

Cal was killed two weeks later.

"Logan?" Adeline whispered.

"Yeah, baby." His breath caught from the haunting memory.

"If you don't want to..." she choked.

Logan glanced at her, and then drew from her as he tried to read her energy. "Baby, I want to more than you know." He decided to go with the truth. "What I don't want is for you to do this because you think you have to for me to stick around or because Rainer and Emily did. I will be perfectly happy to lie in bed with you and hold you all night long just like I did last night."

"I don't think I've ever felt so safe when I slept even after everything that happened." Her voice broke and terror flooded her rhythms. She blinked back tears. "And I felt that way because I knew you were there."

Logan's heart ached as he lifted her hand to his lips and kissed it tenderly. "I will always be there. Always. I will always keep you safe. I love you so much." He turned down the side street and finally arrived at the beach house.

"I know you do. That's why I want to do this."

CHAPTER 26

NIGHTLY ENGAGEMENTS

RAINER LAWSON

Logan pulled in behind them. They'd learned a long time ago to split up when the press was involved.

Rainer helped him unload the Accord. Mrs. Haydenshire had packed loads of food in an effort to put some weight on Adeline.

After they unpacked, they all fell onto the sofas in the living room. Emily laid in Rainer's lap, and he wished Logan would get on with his evening plans. He desperately wanted to take Emily to their room and wrap her up in him.

"Hey, Rainer, would you help me a sec?" Logan pled as he stood and scooted away from Adeline.

"Sure." Rainer followed Logan down the hallway.

They moved into the room Emily's parents usually used.

Logan huffed, "I cannot do it in a room with two cribs in it. Seriously, I just can't."

Rainer chuckled. He helped Logan pull the mattresses from the baby beds and fold them up before storing them in the closet.

Logan stared at the bed. He shuddered slightly as he made his return to the living room.

Rainer couldn't wait any longer. He gazed at Emily reclined on the couch and wearing the ring. Her skin was flushed from her excitement. Her eyes gazed at him longingly. He swallowed and then faked a yawn.

"I'm kind of tired," he hinted.

"Yeah, me too." She was careful not to meet her brother's eyes.

Logan grimaced. Rainer wasn't certain if he didn't want to think about what they were going to go do, or if he was terrified of what he was about to do.

Adeline nodded as she studied Logan carefully. "Yeah, we'll probably head to bed soon." Desperate hope perforated her tone.

Rainer clenched his jaw. He couldn't watch her sit there convinced that Logan didn't want this.

He narrowed his eyes. "Hey Lo, I just remembered there's something in my car I need. Would you help me a sec?"

"Oh, sure." Logan whisked to the front door that Rainer was holding open.

He slammed the door and turned on Logan. "You've got to get it together. You're hurting her feelings."

"I know," Logan lamented. "I will. I swear…I just…" He shook his head. "Don't you think growing up like she did…with her mother… that she might have all of this a little messed up? I don't want her to do this because she thinks she has to for me to stick around," he confessed the final piece of the puzzle. Rainer had already assumed that's what he was afraid of.

"I think in spite of all that, she knows what it means, and she wants to share that with you. I really, really think that. I'd tell you if I didn't."

"I sure as hell hope you're right." Logan marched back into the house. "You sleepy, sweetheart?" He suddenly sounded much more confident. Adeline nodded and gave him a hopeful smile. "Come on, let's go on to bed."

She drew a deep breath and took his hand. "Good night," she called to Emily and Rainer. She sounded simultaneously terrified and thrilled.

"'Night," they replied and returned to the sofa. They seemed to decide at the same moment to give Logan and Adeline a few minutes before they retired to the bedroom right next door. Rainer reclined on the couch, and she lay back beside him.

"I can't believe I'm actually your fiancée!"

"I'm the luckiest guy around."

She wriggled in her excitement beside him. "I can't wait to tell Samantha Peterson."

"You know I didn't even know her name." He knew that the sheer number of girls the papers reported that he cheated on Emily with, she needed to be reassured of his undying devotion often.

They were quiet for a few minutes. He eased to the side until they were face to face. Then, in a quick move, he pulled her underneath him. "I want another kiss."

He brushed her lips with his own. Emily's hands slipped down his back and then to his ass. He thrust against her and tempted her lips with his tongue until she parted them. She was the sweetest confection he'd ever tasted. "I want to take you to bed, baby."

Her heartbeats quickened in her rhythms. Her breath panted in desire. Her eyes turned dark, and hunger swirled in their depths.

"You are so beautiful." He brushed an errant hair behind her ear. "And when I'm with you like that, it's like nothing I've ever even imagined." She trembled in his arms. "The sounds you make for me, the way you feel, baby. You drive me wild." He throbbed against her.

She gasped his name. It seared through him as a low guttural groan escaped his throat. She attempted to get up, and he shifted to help her. She took his hand and pulled him toward their room.

She slipped away from him as soon as they entered the bedroom and grabbed one of her bags off the floor. She closed and locked the bathroom door.

He was panting and staring after her. He cupped his hand and lit a few candles in the room.

He hesitated to open the sliding glass doors. He knew the Haydenshires often slept with them open. It allowed everyone to hear the steady thrumming ocean throughout the night. With the day they'd had, he decided to leave them closed.

He let his mind race back to their time together that morning. He'd rather hear her sweet cries and feel the waves she made anyway.

He pulled off his T-shirt and wondered what she was doing. As he stared at the door, he ordered himself to wait. He wanted desperately to push it open, to take her wherever she was, to be a part of her, and make her a part of him.

He spun when he heard the knob on the door turn. She emerged wearing a pale pink see-through nightie with black lace trim. The pink was the exact color of her flushed skin. It just barely covered her nipples. The gown was just long enough to skim her backside.

"You are so fucking gorgeous." His breath caught as he stared at her. She gave him another sultry smile and spun for him. The gown was cut low on her back, and she was in a matching G-string that covered nothing at all.

He made his way to her in a second flat. He crushed her mouth to his and ran his hands over her body. He could never touch enough of her to satisfy himself. He forced himself to pause as he held her to him. His heart pounded. Need quaked in his rhythms as they spun around her in a haze of erotic energy.

"Do you want me to cast you, baby?" He didn't want to get ahead of himself.

"I didn't know if you'd want to. You seemed kind of worried last night."

"I want to. I want to be a part of every single thing you do, especially that." She looked like that meant a great deal to her as she nodded. "Go lie down."

She lay back on several pillows. He allowed himself one long moment to take her in. Her lips were kiss-swollen, her body flushed, and her eyes slightly darkened. The slight fabric of the panties was already wet. He shuddered in longing. He moved to her and seated himself beside her on the bed.

He edged the flowing fabric of the gown aside. It fell away and revealed her to him. He let his hands trace over her tenderly. The satin of the panties rubbed against her mound and made her moan.

Rainer closed his eyes and cupped his hand as he summoned the erotic energy seeping from her pores. It was much easier to summon from her after a little bit of foreplay, but Rainer wanted her too badly to wait.

He paused and held the orb of her energy as she hesitated, but then her mind relaxed and she allowed him in. He could feel her heartbeat, her body heating for him, the need and the yearning desire that coursed through her blood.

He gathered her energy slowly, as he reveled in her. He added his own calming energies to the cast and placed his hand over her mound. After sealing her off, he soothed her before he pulled his hand away.

She trembled slightly as, "Please," whispered from her lips. He traced over her again. Suddenly he wanted more, he wanted to taste her, but he didn't want to do anything that she didn't want.

"I want to see you, baby." He edged the nightgown up until he pulled it off of her. "You are the most beautiful thing I've ever laid eyes on." He slipped the panties down her legs.

She writhed and panted as he removed them altogether. Starting with her neck, he kissed and licked his way down her body. She panted as her energy climbed rapidly. He felt her pulse race as he neared her breasts. He spun his tongue over her nipples swollen cherry-red for him.

With a loud groan, he caught one in his mouth and began sucking gently. Her energy become frantic as it poured into his mouth. He took them with more force. She quaked and called out for him. It drove him wild.

"Shh, baby, it's not just us tonight."

She nodded, but her body was still thrumming all for him. He trailed his kisses lower, nibbled down her stomach, and felt her abdomen clench in heady anticipation. He traced his thumbs over her, and she bucked. Her energy soared. She wanted it, as well. He strained in desire as he brushed his tongue over her hesitantly.

"Yes," she gasped.

He smiled and groaned his appreciation. To pull the erotic energy from its main storehouse into his mouth would be exquisite.

"I want to taste you, baby. I want you in my mouth."

He delved between her folds, and she went wild. Her rhythms soared. He could feel it all as he licked and sucked. Loud, longing moans spilled from her lips.

He wanted more. He wanted to taste her release. He moved his tongue to where she was most sensitive and studied her. He lapped at her clit, and she writhed, unable to hold her body still. The energy inside of her was too strong.

He kept his tongue moving in steady, swirling rhythms. She clung to the sheets as he began to suck her. She was fighting it again. He could feel her resist. She was afraid to give in to it. He moved his mouth away and replaced his tongue with his fingers.

"Come on, baby, let me taste it. Give it to me. Just let it go for me." Her rhythms tensed when he spoke.

She spiraled over.

He replaced his fingers with his tongue once again as he sucked and tasted her. The energy was incredible as it flowed into his mouth. Heaven couldn't taste better than the essence of her.

Her eyes were wide, her body contorted, as she grabbed his biceps and pulled him toward her. The air around her was so thick with her need it seemed to vibrate. He could feel the sharp jagged rhythms as they pulsed from her, and he wanted to soothe them. "Please," she panted.

He separated her slightly. She was swollen and fevered as he pressed inside of her. He opened her as tenderly as he was able. He stretched her and formed her around his length. She wanted more. She was ready now, and he pushed harder as her moans gasped from her in heavy, panted waves.

He hesitated for a moment before thrusting deeper. He made certain he didn't hurt her. Her muscles clenched tightly around him. She pulled him deeper still, and he groaned. He pounded into her, grinding against her, and she met his every thrust. Their energies began to pass in perfect accord.

"Yes," gasped from her as she arched her back. The arc matched that of the energy that thrummed out of her and into him.

He replaced everything she gave up until they were moving as one. Their energy passed to each other in perfect rhythm. This, he finally fully understood, was how it was supposed to work.

She dug her fingers into him as it took hold of her. He pushed hard once more, and she broke. The waves shattered through her as she shook from the force.

He filled her with all of him and gave her everything. He buried himself deep inside of her perfection as she gasped for breath. She clung to him as he eased out of her and held her.

He shifted slightly to hold her on his chest and covered her with the sheets and quilts.

"I love you," he whispered, and she smiled against his chest.

"I love you too, and now I know I'm the luckiest girl in the world." Her whispered vow thoroughly delighted him. She was wearing nothing but the ring, and the sight of her naked, save for that, filled his entire being.

"Rainer," she whispered as he pulled the fire away from the candles.

"What, baby?" He used the residual heat, in his hand from the fire, to massage over her. She relaxed in the warmth.

"Even after we get married, will you still hold me all night? I don't ever want you to stop that."

He kissed her forehead. "I don't ever want to stop that, sweetheart. I don't know how I'm supposed to sleep without you there now."

"Yeah, I guess we should find a place for us soon because this is the happiest I've ever been."

"Me too."

"I hope Adeline and Logan are as happy as we are someday."

"I think they will be. I really do."

She smiled and yawned. He tucked himself around her.

"Go to sleep. I've got you." He watched as her body relaxed beside his. They both fell into a deep sleep.

CHAPTER 27

HAPPY BIRTHDAY, LOGAN!

The sunrise was reflecting off the water. Rainer let one eye open hesitantly. A broad grin spread across his face.

Emily was on his chest. Her breaths came in a smooth, shallow rhythm. He brushed a kiss across her head and glanced down her body.

She was wearing the ring. It hadn't all been just a fantastic dream. She was really his.

With all of the strife and turmoil that had been his life for so many years, she was the one thing he knew he couldn't survive without. And somehow, she was there, laid out on him naked, with his ring on her finger. He let the contentment wash over him again.

She was sound asleep and still full of his release. He read her with ease. Her rhythms were steadily flowing, relaxed, and peaceful. He smiled and held her to him as she slept. As he lay there in utter bliss, he wondered how Logan's night had gone. Rainer hoped they'd worked through everything. *It's so much better on this side.* He was certain Logan and Adeline would get there as well.

Streams of consciousness washed through him. He thought it odd that they'd not been out on the beach yet.

He wondered if Emily would want to lie out today. It would be nice just to relax and not have to see the papers. He wondered how their engagement would be misconstrued. The press had a way of always doing that, no matter the story. They'd make up whatever bullshit they thought would sell.

Someone moved in the hallway, and he made sure Emily was fully covered. It sounded like Logan's heavy footfalls.

The man who'd frightened Emily on the boardwalk flitted through his mind. He wanted to protect her. The need to know she was safe permeated every fiber of his being. His father had been right. He always was. Sleeping with Emily had intensified his shield. He was almost obsessed with her safety now.

He wondered what the man on the boardwalk had done in the past to have drawn such a strong reaction from her. He wondered if he'd ever served time in Coriolis or if he was wanted.

Emily stirred slightly, and he forced himself to stop thinking about the man they'd seen. She was likely picking up his worried rhythms.

He moved on to how perfect it was that her family was able to be there. Even if he'd planned it for weeks, he knew it couldn't have been better for her. He hoped his parents had seen it as well. He fell back asleep somewhere in his reverie and awoke again an hour later as she wiggled beside him.

"Hey there," he drawled.

"I didn't mean to wake you."

"S'okay, I woke up earlier."

She nodded and bit her lip. "I really want some coffee, but I don't know what to say to Logan and Adeline. It's going to be awkward."

"How?"

"I'll be able to feel whatever they're feeling and…it's intense. I mean it was for us anyway. What if I get really uncomfortable and laugh or some other weird thing?"

Rainer pulled her to him. "We'll go in together, and if you start laughing, I'll just kiss you really quickly."

"Sounds like a plan."

"I thought so." He grabbed her and hoisted her in the air over him then pinned her down and began tickling her. She shrieked, kicked her legs, and squirmed, but he didn't let her get away. He stopped and gave her a momentary reprieve as he kissed her and then started back again.

"Stop it!" she squealed as she squirmed away from him. He laughed as she made a frantic retreat from the bed.

She cocked her jaw to the side and sassed. "Daddy said you weren't allowed to tickle me." She bit her lip to halt her laughter.

"Uh-huh, that's because when he walked in and I had you on the couch, I wasn't tickling you. That was just what you told him." She doubled over and giggled hysterically.

"It kind of worked."

"I think the ring means all bets are off," he informed her.

"Is that what you think?"

"I do."

"You have to say that to the minister, sweetheart," she sassed.

"Shall I go get Logan? I'll see if he'll make you vow to eat sea slugs or something?"

She continued to laugh as she put her hands on her hips and shook them for him with a sassy smirk. He waggled his eyebrows.

"Come back over here and do that." He gestured to his crotch.

"Uh, no, Mr. Lawson, we're going to get dressed and then having coffee."

He leaned on his hands and knees and pulled her back to him, kissed her, and then crawled out of bed.

She pulled on her favorite of his Ioses T-shirts. It was the one she'd been sleeping in for so many years the printing was starting to fade.

"I really like what you wore for me last night."

She looked extremely pleased. "I'm glad, but that's really only for you."

"And I am a lucky, lucky man." He watched her dig out a pair of knit shorts with the Venton logo on them.

It wasn't lost on him that she'd put on nothing underneath. He slipped his hands to her backside.

"I like this," he commented as she laid her head on his chest.

"Good."

∼

Logan and Adeline were seated at the table drinking coffee and staring at one another in rapt adoration. They seemed completely unaware that Rainer and Emily had even entered the room.

Rainer cleared his throat and then poured coffee for himself and Emily. He caught Emily's eye. She was about to lose it. She bit her lips together to keep from laughing. He chuckled and then thumped Logan on the back of the head as he took the seat beside him.

"Hey!" Logan scowled as he shook himself from his distraction.

"Happy Birthday. Nice of you to notice our existence."

Logan rubbed the back of his head. Adeline grinned and then stood to pour more coffee for herself. As she brushed by Logan, she touched his head. She tried to be discreet, but Rainer saw the pale blue light orb emit from her hand.

"Seriously, Miss Adeline?" Rainer quipped as everyone laughed. He couldn't believe she'd healed that.

"Ha." Logan's hand brushed over Adeline's backside as she returned with the coffee pot.

"What do you want to do today?" Rainer asked as Emily echoed his birthday wish.

"We're definitely going shopping," Emily defied Adeline to challenge her.

Adeline bit her lip. "I really would like a hair dryer...maybe we could..."

Logan raised his eyebrows in challenge. "If you're about to say something about a secondhand store or some sort of lay-away program for a hair dryer, I will scream."

Everyone cracked up.

"No." Her face tinged pink. "I don't know what my mother was thinking. We only had the one hair dryer."

No one chuckled, though that had been her goal. The desperation and the fear in her tone robbed the room of any joy.

Emily forced a smile. "You can borrow mine this morning, and then we'll pick one up while we're out today."

"Thank you. My hair's all frizzy from my bath last night." She ran her fingers through her long black hair.

Rainer stared steadfastly at the table. Emily and Logan grimaced.

Adeline hadn't heard Mrs. Haydenshire's phone call to Emily the morning before and didn't know what she'd just confirmed.

"Hey, Mom packed cinnamon rolls!" Logan remembered suddenly. Emily shot him a thankful smile.

"I'll get them." She leapt from the table.

"I'll help." Logan beat her to the counter as they began unloading the food that hadn't been put away the evening before.

Emily pulled two aluminum pans of Mrs. Haydenshire's cinnamon rolls from the refrigerator. She cupped her hand and moved the orange glow over the rolls. When the icing had just begun to melt, Emily scooped up the pans and set them on the table.

"Thanks, baby."

Logan rolled his eyes as was the customary procedure in the Haydenshire household if Rainer called Emily a pet name. He handed out the plates and sat down.

"What, I don't get a thanks, baby?" he cooed sarcastically. He mimicked Rainer's voice, only many octaves higher and gestured to the plate he'd just given Rainer

"No, you get a thanks, smart-ass.'" Rainer was pleased to see that Adeline helped herself to several rolls. Whatever deal she'd struck with Logan, it was clearly good for her.

Logan's phone rang. He furrowed his brow as he fished it from his pocket.

"You better hope that's not Mom." Emily shuddered.

Logan laughed and shook his head. "She's already called." He cringed as Emily and Rainer cracked up. "Fergus," Logan informed them as he rolled his eyes and glanced at his watch. "It's barely nine o'clock, and it's summer."

"What's up, Ferg?" Logan began stuffing cinnamon rolls in his mouth. "Um hmm," he attempted to talk with his mouth full of food. Adeline and Emily shook their heads.

A mocking grin spread across Logan's face as he swallowed. "A party, huh?"

Rainer rolled his eyes and shook his head. "No," he insisted.

"Uh, that's not just a no that's a hell no!" Logan said in response to some request of Fergus's.

Fergus was constantly attempting to throw parties. He'd done it all six years they'd been at the academy together. He'd started out with video game parties, but his extremely overbearing mother wouldn't allow him to invite girls. The lack of women meant that very few guys wanted to attend.

Logan and Rainer would end up spending the evening at Fergus's parents' home, playing Xbox and PlayStation and sincerely wishing they were anywhere else doing anything else with Emily and Adeline.

Their junior and senior years Fergus finally convinced his mother to let him invite girls. This, however, proved worse. Either only Logan and Rainer would show up with Emily and Adeline to hang out with a disappointed Fergus, or the party would turn into a massive rave. Hundreds of uninvited guests and their dates would storm Fergus's house to use it for purposes other than hanging out with Fergus. That left the five of them to clean up the mess before his parents returned home.

Logan shook his head. "Yeah, I know, but we graduated. Em and Rainer got engaged last night. I think we're too old for parties." He looked thoroughly nonplussed. "No!" Logan nearly shouted. "How long have you been friends with Rainer?" Logan gave Fergus a half second to answer. "So when are you going to learn that you can't believe any of the shit they write in the papers?"

Rainer wondered what it was this time. Emily squeezed his hand as Adeline offered him a sorrowful look.

"No, that isn't true either." Logan scoffed and then shouted, "Because she's my sister and he's my best friend, so I would know!"

Rainer and Emily shared a confused glance. Suddenly, Logan was rolling his eyes. "Yes, Fergus, you're my best friend too," he placated as Rainer and Emily cracked up. Even Adeline joined in.

"Okay, okay, I'll ask them, but I'm pretty sure we all have plans tonight."

"I definitely have plans," Rainer announced loudly.

Logan sighed in defeat. "Okay, I'll call you back later."

"What did he say?" Adeline soothed. She looked upset that Logan was irritated.

"He's here, and he saw that we were here this morning in the paper."

Rainer waited on the rest of the tale to unravel.

"Oh and just FYI, *The Illusionist* is reporting that you gave her the ring because they outed you and Samantha, and you were trying to mend the relationship. *Kinetix* is reporting that you knocked her up." He grimaced as Rainer rolled his eyes. He knew at least one blog or newspaper would declare that and they'd get rich from the headline. "Anyway, Fergus wants to throw a beach party."

"How the hell is he gonna have a beach party? His parents' house isn't on the water," Rainer pointed out.

"Yeah, Fergus says that's what makes it ironic," Logan choked out before he laughed with everyone else at the table.

"He needs to stop throwing parties. What did he say when you told him we were too old to party anymore?" Rainer asked.

"He said we're only as old as we feel."

"Yeah, well...I'm feeling about ninety, so I think I'll just skip Fergus's tea party and take my hot young fiancée, who's clearly marrying me for my money, to bed at about seven. After I have my way with her, I'll try not to drown her in my drool as I sleep."

Emily and Adeline roared with laughter, but Logan gagged.

"Okay...no, no, no!" He shook his head. "I've been really okay with everything. I came and got the ring for you, but no, I can't take that." He shuddered and gagged again.

"Sorry, couldn't resist."

Emily continued to laugh. The sound made it worth it in Rainer's book.

"So, Fergus wants to have a non-beach beach party with just us?" Adeline sounded hopeful.

"No, that would be much better. First, he wanted to throw the party here. To which I told him not no, but hell no. Then he told me that he was going to throw this shindig at his parents' house and invite people he met around town today."

Emily looked horrified. "Just invite him over here. He can hang out with us. No parties!"

"Yeah, I wish, but he's pretty insistent."

Emily wriggled. Rainer thought she was actually going to stomp her feet. He bit his lips together to keep from laughing at her outright.

"Noooo!" she whined and shook her head. "No. I'm engaged! I'm at the beach with my fiancé. I want to shop. I want to lay out." She smirked at Rainer. "I want to do other things." She waggled her eyebrows as Logan pretended to gag again. "I do not want to go clean up after another one of Fergus's unintentional orgies."

"I don't think they're quite that bad." Logan rolled his eyes. "But I'll call him back and tell him we aren't coming. Then he'll just move the party to another night because, let's face it, he doesn't really have a lot of friends willing to attend yet another of his lame-ass parties and then clean up after them."

"All right, how about this?" Rainer negotiated. "Call him, and tell him to have it later in the week. That way we have a couple of days to hang out and relax."

Emily nodded. "That's a good idea. And tell him that more people from school will be coming down this week, so it would be better to wait."

Adeline looked thoughtful. "Maybe you could say something about this being the last one. You know, we graduated, and this is a farewell party because we're all starting work soon, so no more after this."

Logan grinned at her as he chuckled. Adeline was most definitely not a party girl. Considering the way she'd grown up, Rainer thought she did amazingly well. Patrick, Connor, Logan, Emily, and Rainer—though he'd never put himself in the popular category—did seem to be invited to most parties. She got dragged along with Logan a fair amount. Rainer had seen Adeline sitting and reading while a party went on around her on more than one occasion.

"Unless you want Fergus to throw your birthday party." Rainer goaded.

"Uh, no thanks."

"Aww, Lo, we do need to do something special for your birthday. What would you like?" Emily grinned at her big brother.

He glanced at Adeline, and Rainer tried to hide his chuckle. He knew perfectly well what Logan really wanted for his birthday.

"Or..." Rainer offered as he gave Logan a grin. "Em and I could go out tonight, and you could take Adeline out for your birthday just the two of you."

Logan grinned at Adeline, but she shook her head.

"No, I'm sure you want to spend your birthday dinner with Emily and Rainer. I feel terrible you're missing it with your parents."

"I was there for his original birthday. We shared a crib. I'm pretty sure he'd rather be with you," Rainer assured her as Logan nodded.

Adeline giggled but then looked upset again. "I don't even have a way to get you a gift."

"We're gonna go get ready." Emily pulled Rainer from the table. They scooted away quickly but not fast enough.

Logan started talking before they'd made their escape. "Baby, you are everything to me, and you gave me you. There is nothing else that will ever mean as much as that does, okay?"

Rainer and Emily missed the rest of the diatribe.

BIRTHDAY SHOPPING

"She doesn't know how to let him love her because she's never been loved." Emily sank onto the bed.

"Logan's pretty stubborn." Rainer kissed her forehead. "He won't give up on her, and I still want you to take her shopping. Get her whatever she wants. Get Logan a birthday present from her."

She grinned up at him. "You're just amazing."

He shook his head in disagreement. He glanced back down at the ring and then out the windows of their room and onto the beach.

"I think I'd better come with you, but I'll try not to get in your and Adeline's way."

"Worried I'll get smothered by photographers?" She stood and wrapped her arms around his waist.

"I'm your Shield. I worry." He couldn't quite name the specific fear that continued to taunt his shield. He just knew he couldn't let Emily out of his sight.

"I know and I love that." Emily's tone turned flirtatious suddenly. "I need a shower."

Rainer shot her a cocky grin. "Do you?"

She nodded against him.

"And would you need any help in the shower, baby?"

"What kind of help?"

"I don't know…" He traced his fingers down her spine. "If you need anything washed, or kissed, or licked, or touched…" She shivered deliciously. "I could take care of that for you."

"What if I need something else?" she breathed the words in his face. He pulsed. She could feel it.

"I can do that too, baby."

She whisked toward the bathroom, but she halted at the dresser in the room.

He followed after her. Edging her T-shirt up, he began to rub his hands over her soft skin and up her back as she melted into his body. He lavished her mouth with gentle, tempting kisses.

"I'm scared to wear the ring in the shower." She gazed at her ring as he pulled away slightly.

"I think we'll still be engaged if you take it off long enough to shower. I will be attached to you the entire time you're in there, so…" Rainer grabbed her backside as he pulled her against him forcefully.

A hesitant knock sounded at their door. "Emily?" Adeline sounded terrified.

Rainer clenched his jaw and tried to will away his now-straining erection.

"I'll, uh…" He gestured to the bathroom.

She managed a nod, but her face was flushed and her lips slightly swollen. This did nothing to help his current problem.

Rainer closed the door and began shaving. Emily entered a few minutes later wearing nothing at all.

"Adeline needed a bra. She didn't want to buy that with Mom yesterday."

Rainer couldn't take his eyes off of her luscious curves. He didn't pay much attention to what she was saying. He was thankful he'd been shaving long enough that he could do it mindlessly because his cock had taken over all rational thought.

She leaned to turn on the shower water, and he groaned as she reached out her hand and led him in.

As they were getting ready a little while later, what she'd commented on before their shower filtered back through his mind now that he could think at all.

"Hey, Em, I swear I'm only asking this because I'm a guy and don't fully understand how this works. And believe me I've never noticed, but do you and Adeline wear the same size…undergarments?"

Emily laughed at him, but he really hadn't noticed Adeline, at least not in any other way than that she existed and was Logan's girlfriend. He knew Logan thought she was a knockout, but Emily was it for Rainer.

Everything about her had always driven him wild. He remembered the changes in her from about the age of eleven until she was around fifteen. His father had been killed just after his fourteenth birthday. He'd always felt extremely guilty that the feeling of her developing curves against him distracted him from the pain temporarily. But Emily was deliciously curvy, and the only word he would use for Adeline would be thin. So, he thought the question was fair. Emily, however, was still giggling.

"Well, no," she shook her head. "But, I guess it'll do in a pinch. I imagine a lingerie shop will be our first stop."

Rainer tried to determine how he and Logan could hang around enough to make sure Emily wasn't bombarded by press wanting pictures of the ring and not bring Adeline to tears from embarrassment.

They ended up at Lynnhaven mall. It was Emily and Mrs. Haydenshire's favorite. Adeline had never been before, so Emily was excited to show her all that it had to offer.

Logan seemed happier to be shopping than Rainer had ever seen him before. He supposed love could do that to a guy. Emily, Logan, and Rainer had sat Adeline down before they left to plead with her to get things she needed and wanted and not just the least expensive thing.

Rainer insisted on Emily using his card to pay. He'd vowed that his father would've wanted him to do this. After almost an hour of rather forceful begging, mostly from Logan, they'd finally gotten Adeline to relent.

Logan and Rainer sat on a bench outside one of Emily's favorite lingerie shops. They were dipping gigantic pretzels, oozing with butter, into a container of melted cheese, and sucking down Dr Pepper from the pretzel shop.

Rainer had noticed several photographers gathering. He was braced to spring, but there were several Iodex officers there as well. He wasn't sure how it would play out. He also wasn't certain what Governor Haydenshire had done to get Iodex out in force, but he was thankful for whatever it was.

Emily was determined and didn't seem to care what pictures ended up in the papers. She was going to help her friend.

"So, did everything go all right last night?"

Logan nodded with his mouth full of pretzel. He took a long sip of Dr Pepper before answering.

"Uh, yeah, better this morning. You were right about that." He refused to meet Rainer's gaze.

"Damn. You move fast. We got up at nine."

Logan glowed crimson as Rainer laughed.

"I'm not dignifying that with a response."

"I was really hoping you wouldn't."

"Hey, do you think Adeline would freak if I took her to Mick's tonight?" He was clearly ready for a subject change.

Mick's was a five-star restaurant on the bay that was phenomenal. Rainer still remembered eating there with his dad the last time they'd visited the beach before he'd been killed. The average plate cost around a hundred dollars, but it was worth every penny.

"I thought that was part of your deal? You know, you did that, and she lets you spoil her a little, which now that I think about it, is kind of a win-win for you."

Logan laughed and nodded his agreement. "Yeah, but I don't want to push her too far. She still freaks over every price tag. Mom bought her a hairbrush yesterday, and she fussed that it cost too much. It was like five bucks."

A moment later, a guy about Logan and Rainer's age took post on the bench, while his significant other proceeded into the lingerie shop. Logan was wearing his customary Venton sweatshirt and a pair of khaki shorts that he sported whenever they were at the beach in the early summer.

The guy smiled at Logan. "Hey, do you go to Venton?"

Logan nodded as he continued sucking down his gigantic drink. "Yeah…we both did…just graduated." He was staring at Adeline who was looking at panties on a table near the front of the store. To Rainer's shock, her hands were already full of bras, panties, and nightgowns.

"I had a 4.0, valedictorian of my class, perfect SAT and ACT scores, everything, but Venton turned me down. It must be some school."

Rainer and Logan nodded. They were never certain what to say.

"What did you major in?" he asked.

They shared an uncomfortable glance and then gave their usual answer. "Government and Law."

The guy glanced at his girlfriend. She was near the front of the store admiring a nightie. "Guess you have to know somebody to get in or something. I got in everywhere else I applied. I'm a senior at Yale."

Logan nodded. "That must be it," he offered with a slight smirk. To their relief, the guy's girlfriend returned, and they left.

Emily sauntered out a few minutes later. Determination etched every inch of her features. She pushed her hair behind her right ear and Rainer knew, whatever was coming, she wasn't taking no for an answer.

"Logan, Adeline wants your opinion," she stated with hesitant force.

Logan choked on the hunk of pretzel he'd just thrown in his mouth. Rainer slapped him on the back and tried not to laugh, while simultaneously trying to keep his best friend from needing the Heimlich maneuver. Logan finally managed to swallow.

"On something in there?" He pointed to the store.

Emily furrowed her brow and pursed her lips. "Yes!" She seemed to will Logan to show a little bit more maturity. Rainer found this all hysterical right up until the moment Emily challenged, "And I want you to help me pick out a few things as well, Mr. Lawson."

He glanced around nervously. "Do you know what kinds of things will be in the paper if I go in there with you?" He hoped against hope that this would get him out of it. But he knew once Emily decided something, that was the way it was going to be.

She shot him an incredulous look and rolled her eyes. "That Rainer Lawson's fiancée wears underwear and nightgowns."

"You know perfectly well there will be a whole lot more to it than that."

"Not so funny now, is it?" Logan huffed.

Emily's hands went to her hips as she cocked her jaw to the side.

"Would you two please both grow a pair and come on?"

Rainer and Logan stood and shared an ominous expression before they followed her back into the store.

To Rainer's chagrin, they were photographed exiting the store, but there were only two photographers available to capture the shot.

The things Emily had purchased had his mind reeling with vastly more interesting things than being chased by the press.

Emily was in heaven. She led Adeline around to store after store. After a while, even Adeline seemed to be having fun, but Rainer noted she kept close to Logan. He didn't seem to mind at all. He kept a hand on her anytime they were close enough to be in contact.

Adeline insisted that she didn't need more swimsuits. The two Emily had picked for her the day before were all she needed. Meanwhile, Logan insisted that she eat several times throughout the day. He was her Shield in every possible way.

They returned to the beach house loaded down with bags. Emily was buzzing. Adeline looked exhausted.

"Let's go play in the sand, and then we can get ready for Logan's birthday dinner tonight." Emily's eyes danced. She was almost as thrilled as Logan that Adeline had agreed to going to Mick's.

"I'm still a little worried about that," Adeline fussed.

"That's where I want to eat for my birthday. It's phenomenal."

"I know, but if we have to get all dressed up, then it must be really expensive."

Logan had been trying to be patient with her. "It is expensive," he soothed, "but I'm not asking you to eat there every day, okay? Just this once, for my birthday, please."

She smiled up at him and nodded, but she looked deeply

concerned. Both girls donned rather skimpy bikinis, and Logan and Rainer pulled on swim trunks.

They grabbed the volleyball from the garage. The game fell flat when both girls flipped over on their stomachs and undid the tops of their swimsuits to avoid tan lines on their backs.

Rainer's stomach clenched as he watched Emily lift her head and flip it the other direction. After deciding that volleyball could wait, Logan and Rainer moved to the towels to help the girls apply sunscreen and to lie on either side of them. They staked their claim for the benefit of the admiring men on the beach.

As the afternoon wore on, they returned inside and began getting ready for dinner.

Rainer was barred from the room he was sharing with Emily as she and Adeline applied makeup and dressed together. An hour later, Logan and Rainer were in the living room throwing popcorn at one another and attempting to catch it in their mouths as they waited for the girls.

"What could they possibly be doing in there?" Logan huffed. Rainer laughed and shrugged. Growing up in a house full of men made Logan edgy when it came to things like waiting for Adeline to try on fifteen outfits before going back to the original one she'd picked.

Emily emerged, wearing a short black skirt with a low-cut, gathered, hunter-green top that displayed her cleavage quite nicely. Rainer was mesmerized. A low whistle slid between his teeth and made her beam.

"Logan, wait 'til you see her!" Emily trilled. She suddenly looked like she might tear up as they turned to stare down the hallway. Rainer couldn't quite take his eyes off of Emily.

Adeline peeked out from around the door.

Logan chuckled. "Well, can I see you?"

She walked down the hallway with a smile that Rainer didn't think he'd ever seen her use before. Logan's mouth dropped as his eyes goggled.

"Damn!" he gasped reverently.

"Too much?" Adeline quizzed. She wrinkled her nose, but Logan shook his head.

She was wearing a skintight, one-shoulder dress, with cutouts discreetly placed that showed off small sections of her back and sides.

"Wow," Logan stammered again. Adeline glowed over Logan's inability to close his mouth or form coherent sentences.

"I'm glad you like it." She sounded more confident than any of them had ever heard her.

Logan was enthralled.

Both of the girls had pulled their hair up off their shoulders. Emily had wispy auburn curls that cascaded down around her face. Rainer brushed one to the side as he leaned in to whisper in her ear. "You look stunning, and I can't wait to get you back here and take all of this off of you."

CHAPTER 29

THE DOUBLE CLUTCH DINNER

Rainer entered the line for the valet parking and grimaced. Emily giggled. She knew his usual routine for this sort of thing. The valet, who appeared to be approximately twelve years old, leaned in eagerly.

"Ever driven a stick?" Rainer asked. He tried hard not to sound like a prick, but he knew he was failing miserably.

"Of course!" the guy scoffed.

Rainer nodded. "Know how to double clutch shift?"

The valet's brow furrowed, and Rainer offered him what he hoped was an understanding smile.

"I'm just gonna let them off here, and I'll park it. It's no problem."

The guy looked crestfallen. With a hearty laugh, Logan exited and then offered Emily and Adeline each an arm as he escorted them into the restaurant.

If it didn't pain him so much to hear someone peal out in his car, then stall it ten times in a matter of moving a hundred feet, he wouldn't do that. But it killed him, and it happened almost every time.

He scooted into the restaurant just in time to join Emily as she followed Logan and Adeline to their reserved table. "I'm sorry," he offered.

She laughed and kissed his cheek. "It's fine. I totally understand."

Her reply made his heart swell, but suddenly, she bristled. They edged to their table in the back of the restaurant with a view of the ships coming in off the bay.

"What's wrong?"

She glanced around the restaurant. Her eyes landed on a nearby table with what appeared to be a father and son. There was a woman seated across from the man with hair dyed peroxide blonde. She was flaunting her cleavage in her extremely low-cut halter top every chance she got. She giggled ostentatiously at something the man, who was at least twice her age, had said. The dark energies rolling in the man's rhythms were so palpable even Rainer picked up on them. He couldn't imagine how strongly Emily must've felt them.

"I know that kid," she whispered. "He's transferring to the academy in the fall. I showed him around campus a few weeks ago. I guess that's his father. He came alone though."

"Are you okay?" Rainer kept his eyes on the man in question. She nodded as she studied the boy's father as well. "Do you want a different table?"

Emily glanced at Logan who hadn't noticed her preoccupation. He was still drooling over Adeline's dress.

"No, it's fine. Maybe he's reformed or something."

Rainer knew she was lying. She was pale and timid. She was frightened over the energy pulsing from the boy's father. She clung to Rainer as he seated her and then pulled his chair close to hers. She made constant draws of his energy in an effort to soothe herself.

Adeline's eyes goggled as she took in the menu.

"Ad," Logan sighed. "Get whatever you want. This is my birthday present from Mom and Dad, okay?"

She managed a nod, but that information only seemed to make her more uncomfortable. Logan took it upon himself to order for Adeline. This made her extremely anxious until the appetizers arrived, and she finally admitted that it was the best food she'd ever eaten. Emily stood after the soup course.

"I need to use the restroom." She looked terrified. Adeline stood to go with her, but Rainer understood more.

"I'll walk you both." He took her arm. Emily clasped his hand with her own and drew from him. The sensation was heavenly, and Rainer had to force himself to remember where they were and that she needed to use the restroom.

"Thank you," she whispered in relief as Rainer's energy soothed her own. His shield sought her in earnest. It attempted to cast her without having to be summoned. He longed to take her from the restaurant, tuck her in his arms, and keep her safe.

The man's eyes tracked their every move. Rainer waited outside the door. He took the opportunity to study the restaurant and the man.

He stood suddenly and slithered toward Rainer. He braced and glanced back to make certain the girls weren't coming out of the restroom yet. To his chagrin, Emily and Adeline appeared at the same moment the stranger made his way to them.

Emily trembled. She was less than two feet away from him. Rainer stood steadfast between the man and Emily. His shield flared viciously.

"Excuse us," Rainer sneered. He stared the man down in defiant challenge.

"That's a lovely ring, miss," the man drawled in a distinctly Russian accent. He grabbed Emily's hand, and she cringed.

Rainer jerked her hand out of the man's grasp. "If you'd just keep your hands the hell off my fiancée, I would certainly appreciate it."

The man gave a foreboding chuckle as he rolled his eyes and entered the men's restroom.

Rainer reseated Emily as Logan stood to do the same for Adeline.

"Are you okay?" Rainer was certain they should leave. Something was off. Why had that guy complimented her ring? She nodded and seemed to will courage from the air around her.

Logan wanted dessert, of course, so Rainer kept close watch on the man and on Emily.

He kept Emily's hand in his own to allow her steady draws from him whenever she needed his soothing strength.

As their tiramisu arrived, Logan's eyes widened. He gaped toward the front door. Rainer turned, and his mouth hung open. Several uniformed officers surrounded the man's table, and then Portwood and Ericcson followed Vindico in.

Dan glanced at Rainer and shook his head slightly. He didn't want them to act like they knew him, but he looked furious.

"Candor Pendergrath, you're under arrest for defrauding the Russian government. You're being extradited tonight. Let's go," he demanded with an expectant growl.

Emily's mouth fell open as they watched the man get handcuffed. Vindico touched the handcuffs. His shield cast formed around the them. They glowed a brilliant green.

The entire restaurant stared in shocked silence. They seemed dumbfounded by the scene. The blonde woman cried obnoxiously, but the man's son looked truly devastated as Vindico yanked his father from the restaurant.

"Can we just go, please?" Emily clung to Rainer's arm. Logan and Rainer both nodded. The dessert was forgotten as Logan handed his credit card to the waiter and asked him to hurry. As soon as he'd signed the ticket, they left.

Rainer debated. He wasn't sure if he should leave Emily with Logan and go get the car or take her with him. She was visibly frightened, but she was strengthening her resolve as she drew from his hand again.

"Stay with Logan. I'll get the car and be right back."

Logan gave her a reassuring nod.

"No!"

"Okay, I've got you." He led her to where he'd parked the Mustang. He saw several black SUVs with interior flashing blue lights pull away from the restaurant. He seated her and tried to give her soothing smiles as he closed her door and whisked to the other side of the car.

"Are you okay, Emily?" Adeline patted her shoulder as Rainer started the car.

"I don't understand. I've never felt that here before and now, that's twice in two days' time." She shook her head.

Logan bristled. "You saw that guy yesterday?"

"Different guy, when we were at the boardwalk yesterday," Rainer explained.

"Whatever he did, Vindico seemed to be on top of it. It didn't sound like he'll even be in the country much longer."

This did seem to bring Emily some peace, but she still looked worn. Rainer pulled into the driveway and waited as Logan and Adeline exited the car before he made his offer.

"Do you want to go home, baby?"

She shook her head and drew a deep breath. They headed inside.

The beach house seemed to steady her. Rainer made her a cup of tea, the kind her mother usually made for her when life seemed to be a bit too much to handle.

She smiled as he settled on the couch beside her. She clung to him as she sipped.

Logan and Adeline decided to walk on the beach for a little while.

"Come on," Rainer soothed after Logan pulled the sliding glass doors shut. "Talk to me."

She set the tea on the table beside her and curled herself up in his lap. He pulled the quilt that stayed on the back of the couch over her and held her tight.

"It was awful," her voice trembled.

He nestled her head under his chin. "What was awful?"

"I've never felt that from someone and then had them touch me. I thought I was going to throw up or pass out. It was terrifying."

Pain seared through him. Her fear cut him to the quick. She was normally so brave. Nothing ever got to her.

Growing up as the only sister of seven older brothers made her tough, but he didn't want her to have to feign bravery with him. He wanted her to tell him when she was afraid, and he wanted to vanquish anything that ever scared her. He was her Shield.

"I'm so sorry, baby. I will never let anything hurt you."

She gave him a sweet smile. He held her tight and felt her usual contentment begin to slowly seep back into her soul. She was drawing it from him.

Rainer panted and his eyes rolled back in his head again. It was almost as incredible as being deep inside of her. He was elated to give her that. He brushed his hands over her skin anywhere it was exposed, and she reveled in his touch.

Then he closed his eyes and concentrated. His shield spun from his pores. It encased her in his ultimate safety and in his undying love. It permeated the very air she breathed as he flooded the space around them with his protective energies.

"Everything just feels…different lately," she admitted.

"Different how?"

"Not bad different. Well sometimes I do feel like something bad is coming, but your shield feels so much stronger than it used to as well. I don't know. I'm probably going crazy or something."

"You're not crazy. My shield feels different to me too. It's more intense, more attuned to you."

"Yeah. I guess that's what all of those amative energy classes were really about. I didn't get it then."

"Me either."

His cell phone rang. It wasn't a number stored in his phone, but he recognized that it was from the Senate office. He furrowed his brow

"Hello?"

"Lawson," came a deep, gruff voice.

"Yeah?" Rainer stated hesitantly.

"It's Dan Vindico."

"Oh."

"I'm uh…guess I'm sorry I interrupted your dinner there." He sounded far more annoyed than sorry.

"It's fine. That's what Iodex does, right?" He massaged his hands down Emily's arms.

"Sometimes," he sighed. "Listen, I know Emily is a pretty strong Receiver. Governor Haydenshire told us all at least ten times when she was named head of Auxiliary and about her Angels recruitment." Rainer was certain his boss wasn't exaggerating. "I saw the look on her face when we entered. I'm assuming the guy we just arrested scared her," he probed for information.

Rainer was impressed that Vindico wasn't one of the Gifted who scoffed at the abilities of Receivers. Many of them did.

"She picked up on that guy as soon as we arrived. She showed his kid around the academy a few weeks ago."

"What?! Did he request her?" Vindico's tone bordered on fury.

"Uh…she was one of the Venton guides last year and I guess he got assigned to her when he visited the school. I…have no idea if he requested her." He had the distinct impression he wasn't giving his boss the answers he wanted to hear. Vindico was silent, so he continued. "The guy you arrested grabbed her hand when she left the restroom. She was pretty freaked out by the time you showed."

"What?" Vindico demanded again.

"Uh…" Rainer wasn't certain which part he was supposed to repeat this time either.

"Were you there when he touched her?"

"Yeah, of course. She was scared. I walked her to the bathroom and waited for her. He walked by and complimented her ring. I told him to keep his hands off my fiancée, and then he walked away. That was it." He was unable to determine if he'd done something wrong, but it probably wasn't a good thing to piss off your future boss before you'd even begun working.

"I need you to let me know if Emily picks up on anything else while you're there."

"Actually, we were at the boardwalk yesterday, and she homed in on a guy walking by. He was several feet away from her, but it was pretty strong."

"What did he look like?"

Rainer tried to think of how a real Iodex officer would give a description. "Little taller than me, muscular, dark hair, olive complexion, angry scowl. Oh, he had snakes tattooed all the way up, sleeves, covering both arms from his wrists to his neck." He hoped he sounded remotely competent.

Vindico was silent. Rainer wondered if he'd somehow lost the connection.

"Where were you when you saw him?" Utter hatred perforated every word that spewed from his boss's mouth.

Rainer wasn't quite able to believe that Dan Vindico could be just as intimidating over the phone as he was in person. "We were by the statue of the soldier on horseback, at the picnic tables, by the Lucky Oyster. He came by and went to the parking lot behind the restaurant. He didn't seem to notice us."

"He noticed you," was Vindico's ominous reply. "Lawson, listen to me, if you ever, ever see that guy again, you get Emily and get the hell away from wherever you are. Do you understand me? In fact…"

"What?" Rainer demanded.

"Nothing. Just don't let her out of your sight."

"Yeah, of course. You mean you know that guy?"

"We've met. I need you to be extremely careful. The entire Realm knows where you are thanks to the press. I'm going to try to put a stop to all of that before you start working. I'm not having one of my guys photographed every time he takes a piss. It's ridiculous."

Rainer tried not to laugh. He'd finally met someone who understood what he'd been trying to say all these years. "Hey, anything we can do to stop them sounds perfect to me."

"Yeah, well, I'll work on it. I can't wait to get you and Logan started. I think you're going to make a great addition. Whenever you're ready to start working, let me know." There was an urgency to his plea that Rainer didn't understand.

Emily stood and whisked off to the bedroom.

"Thanks. I can't wait to start either."

"No problem. And I'm serious. Please, for me," Vindico's voice sounded pleading for a moment. "Don't let Emily out of your sight."

"Yes, sir." He stood and followed the path to the bedroom she'd just made. She was changing clothes. He willed his heart back into rhythm.

"Be careful, Lawson," was Vindico's parting line before the phone went dead.

"Who was that?" Emily quizzed.

"Vindico." Rainer helped her unzip the skirt she was wearing.

She hesitated for a moment. "Would it be alright if we didn't…?" She gestured to the bed as she pulled on one of his T-shirts. The pained expression on her face had him reeling. "I just feel really weak. I'm still dizzy, and I'm still sick to my stomach. My receptors are still pulsing weirdly like something bad is going to happen."

He couldn't believe she thought she had to ask something like that. "Baby, I only ever want to do that if it's what you want as well, okay? I would never force you to do anything you didn't want to do."

"I know that. I just didn't want you to be disappointed."

"Hey." He pulled her to him. "If I get to lie with you in that bed, hold you tight, and make you feel better, there's nothing more I would ever want. You could never disappoint me."

She turned down the covers on the bed that she'd made earlier. He pulled off his shirt and tie, then shed his trousers. As he settled Emily beside him, he covered her in the sheet and quilts.

He could feel her rhythms soothing as he traced his hands over her body. He concentrated. They would spike suddenly whenever she recalled their dinner or the man grabbing her hand.

His shield spilled from his pores. He held her in his ultimate love and protection. "It's okay, baby. I've got you." She finally relented and let him soothe her to sleep.

∿

Dan Vindico

Utter hatred filled Dan's shield. It always did. Portwood and Ericsson eyed him speculatively from their SUV parked less than a block from the Haydenshires' beach house. Dan decided to make the best use of his time by informing everyone at once. He hit Garrett's name on his cell and casted the phone so everyone could hear.

"Rapid flight jet is touching down now," was Garrett's greeting.

"We have bigger problems," Dan huffed.

"I'm sure I do not want to know whatever it is you're about to tell me."

"Cascavel is here."

"What?!"

"Yeah, apparently he followed Rainer and your sister to the boardwalk yesterday."

"Jesus fuck," Garrett spat.

"You get your father on the fucking phone and you tell him that if he wants to keep his baby girl alive and with us that he needs to have a long talk with Lawson. And then you get your ass on a jet with my

Elite team and you all get down here and help me find him before he finds her."

"I'm on my way."

As soon as Portwood heard the name of who was in town, he'd begun typing on his Iodex laptop. "Ramier's pulling rental car info for his aliases. He'll have it to us in just a second."

"Good."

"We all get why you want Rainer to know the truth about everything, but he really is still a kid," Portwood pled.

Dan ground his teeth. "I'm not trying to take anything away from him. I admire the hell out of him. But he doesn't get to decide when his childhood is over, and neither does Governor Haydenshire. Life decides that. He either needs to understand what he's up against so that he can keep her safe, or the world is going to grow him up in an instant. Trust me, if I grow him up, it'll be a whole hell of a lot more pleasant than if we let the world do it."

Portwood gave him a begrudging nod. "Ramier says he rented a black Hyundai Accent under the name of Terrance Tavo, one of his more common aliases. Shit, he arrived the same night they did."

"Nic knew Rainer would bring her here after graduation."

Ericsson studied the information on Portwood's screen. "I'm sure he casted and shut down the tracker on the car, but I'm putting out a BOLO for it now."

"I'm sure he pulled the plate as well." Dan could not fucking believe any of this. If it were any other kidnapper, he'd leave one of his guys at the beach house to make sure Rainer and Emily were safe while he went after the guy, but not Cascavel. One did not go after the snake charmer without backup and live to tell about it. He wasn't dooming his officers.

In all likelihood, if they stayed right where they were, the cobra would come to them, and Dan would finally get his say.

He thirsted for it for ten long years. Maybe tonight was the night.

Twenty minutes later, Dan's cell rang again.

"We're here. I brought a Non-Elite team with me and I've got the choppers headed there. Ramier just found the car on a streetcam," Garrett said.

"Where?"

"First Landing. Parked outside a cabin near the swamps."

Dan rolled his eyes. "Should've figured that."

"We'll meet you there."

"No. You and the Non-Elite team come keep your sister safe. Portwood and Ericcson are staying as well. The rest of Elite is going after Cascavel."

~

Rainer Lawson

Rainer's shield tensed in his sleep. He gasped and sat up in the bed. What the hell? That had never happened to him before. Gently, he touched Emily's back. She was sound asleep, but her rhythms were troubled as well.

Rainer rubbed his eyes. He studied their bedroom and the oceanfront beyond. A shadow moved in the moonlight. His heart seized.

He leapt from the bed and threw his shield over Emily. The whir of helicopter blades beat the air over the house. He kept a constant scan on the darkened beach. He no longer saw the shadow, but the choppers seemed to be moving closer.

A million thoughts vied for his attention. Was the press that desperate for a picture of the ring? Was it Iodex? If the guy from Mick's had escaped custody, wouldn't Iodex scramble the choppers? He knew that was protocol.

Panic flared constantly in his rhythms. Emily eased up on her elbows. "What is that noise? Why am I in your shield?" Her voice trembled.

"I saw someone outside, and those are helicopters."

"What?!" She scrambled from the bed and made it to the windows in a few quick steps. They searched together but saw nothing. "I'm gonna call Garrett."

~

"Fuck, they saw me." Garrett held up his phone to show Ericcson who was calling.

"I told you not to get too close to the house. Lawson may be untrained, but he's gonna be one hell of a Shield. You better play it cool if you still don't want her to know anything."

"I can't play it cool. She'll know if I'm lying." He answered the call. "Is there some reason you're calling me at three in the morning, baby sis?" He prayed she was too tired to pick up on his deception over the phone.

"We can hear helicopters everywhere, and Rainer saw a shadow on the beach." She sounded terrified, and it sliced Garrett to shreds. "Maybe we should come home. All this weird stuff keeps happening. I have a weird feeling."

That would be ideal if they could have Elite escort them home, but since Garrett and his father were still at odds as to when to explain all of this to Rainer, that wasn't likely to happen. Rainer driving her home in the middle of the night unprotected was like sending Cascavel an engraved invitation to destroy them.

"Hey, you're okay," Garrett soothed. That, at least, was true for the moment. "I'm sure the choppers are either the press or some pilots coming in for the airshow." That was not true, but it sounded like Emily was struggling to read him through her fear so he went on with his lies but decided to sandwich it between two truths. "Rainer's got you. He'll keep you safe."

"I know," she spoke in barely a whisper.

"Do you want me to come down there?"

"No, it's okay." He could tell she did want that but didn't think she should want that, and she didn't want to hurt Rainer's feelings. God, they had to get the kid trained.

Garrett's eyes closed in defeat. "I don't mind," he offered again.

"Thank you, but you don't have to do that. Should we call Iodex about the guy Rainer saw?"

"Walking on the beach even in the middle of the night isn't against the law, Em. Go on back to bed. Tell Rainer to cast you."

"He already is."

"Good."

⌀

Dan Vindico

A twig snapped under Dan's boot and a whispered curse left his lips as he eased closer to the shore of the Rainbow Swamp. The Non-Gifted believed some bullshit story about the swamps at First Landing containing chemicals from the leaves that fell in the water that their park rangers told them created the striped prism effect in the water.

The Gifted knew the swamps at First Landing Park contained so much of the earth's energies that the water glowed with the Predilect colors constantly. The Non-Gifted could only see the rainbow effect when the conditions were just right and the sun was overhead. The Gifted could see them always. The stories about the swamps were legendary. Several different swamps that contained the earth's energy existed all over the world. It was said that one could draw power from the swamps until they ran dry.

"Watch the fuck out for snakes," Dan spat under his breath.

Tuttle and Ramier both nodded and shuddered simultaneously. Taking on Cascavel when he had access to the storehouses of energy in the swamps and all of the snakes that lived within the energized waters was damn near suicidal. But Dan was determined. He wouldn't get away again.

Dan halted when his eyes landed on a slight ripple in the water. His cell phone buzzed ominously in his pocket. Another ripple moved to his left.

Without taking his eyes off the water, he pulled both his pistol and phone.

"Shit!" Tuttle spat and summoned as three more ripples shook the prismed water near them.

Garrett's text had the blood surging through Dan freezing in his veins. *He's here.*

"Now," Dan growled. They all summoned from the shielding

energy held in the water. It shook and rolled from the draw. Ripples surrounded them now. One brushed against Dan's boot.

"Cast!" he commanded. They turned their hands outward and flooded the swamp with energy both protective and destructive. Two water moccasins near Tuttle undulated in the air as he threw them against low lying trees.

Dan pulled two apart and drove their lifeless corpses deep into the water, a warning to the others that wouldn't be heeded.

Ramier threw his right arm to the side and four moved in synchronization with the motion as he twisted his hands together and knotted the snakes before severing their heads.

"They're just going to keep coming," he panicked.

"Cascavel's at the beach house," Dan explained. "Draw more energy from the water, keep yourselves shielded, and run like hell."

Garrett Haydenshire

Another bullet ricocheted off of Garrett's shield. He'd have to drop it to fire back, and that wasn't going to be happening. Portwood stood behind him and fired around him.

They heard the whispered curse and a groan.

"You hit him," Garrett urged.

"It was only a graze," Ericcson lamented. He was deep inside his own shield but had the binoculars. "Fire again. Same spot!"

Portwood shot, but Cascavel must've ducked away.

A cast shot straight upwards from Cascavel's somewhat concealed location.

"What the hell is he doing?" Ericcson gasped.

They all watched astonished as the snake charmer himself locked onto one of the Iodex helicopters.

"Holy fucking fuck." Garrett sprinted toward him. Portwood and Ericcson were hot on his tail.

Garrett eased his shield back just enough to fire but he missed. The helicopter tilted. The blades came dangerously to the tops of the trees. It tilted back the other way under Cascavel's cast. He leveled it and brought it closer to the ground.

"There are two officers and a pilot in there!" Portwood sounded devastated.

"He doesn't want to crash it," Garrett reassured him.

"Then what the hell is he doing?" Ericcson demanded.

"Escaping." He brought his enhanced radio to his mouth. "Chopper IH58A can you hear me?"

"Little busy right now," the pilot huffed.

"Yeah, I see that. Bail out now. And when you land, run as far away from where you hit as you can. Now!"

"Sir!" They all saw three men roll out of the chopper. They cast shields in an arc above them and one against the gravitational pull to slow their descent to the ground.

Breath returned to Garrett lungs, but the chopper hit the ground and then a moment later took back off.

He'd slithered away again.

CHAPTER 30

MEMORIES

RAINER LAWSON

Rainer watched over Emily obsessively, but he wasn't certain what he was supposed to be protecting her from. Vindico's warning had him unnerved. His shield would flex around her constantly.

Emily had most definitely picked up on his apprehension, but she'd not felt anything unsavory from anyone they'd been around.

As they got ready for Fergus's non-beach, beach party Friday night, she spoke up. "I was thinking I might go to the bathroom alone, if that's okay with you."

"I'm sorry," Rainer offered again. "Vindico freaked me out with the press and your ring. Then the guy you saw. I'm just being a little overprotective. I love you. I can't make it without you."

She melted. "I know, and I love that you're overprotective. You're a Shield. You don't know any other way to be, but maybe we could dial it down just a little. Nothing weird has happened since he arrested that guy at Mick's, and it's like Garrett said—it's not illegal to walk on the beach even late at night."

Rainer nodded and forced a smile. "You sure you wanna go to this thing tonight?"

She glanced out the window and gnawed on her lip. Rainer's shield sizzled in his hands in an effort to cast her. "Em? What is it?"

"I don't know…exactly."

"What do you feel?" His heart slammed against his rib cage. Unable to keep his shield at bay anymore, he allowed it to form around her.

"Something bad is going to happen or is in the process of happening and…"

"Where?" Rainer kept her cradled in his arms and in his fierce shield.

"Fergus's party. It feels like if we go it will be bad, but it will also be bad if we don't. I can't get a clear reading. Maybe whoever is doing this hasn't made their decision yet so the energy isn't set."

"Let's go back to the farm tonight. I have to know you're safe."

"We're going back in the morning anyway. Garrett will be here, remember? Whatever this is, I think we're supposed to be here to deal with it."

Rainer debated but she seemed quite adamant that they were to stay there. "Let me go tell Logan we're not going. I'll be right back."

"I'll be in there in just a second."

He stopped short of telling her to be careful in the bathroom.

He almost ran into Logan in the hall. "We're not going," they both spoke simultaneously. Their brows furrowed.

"How did you know what I was coming to tell you?" Rainer asked.

"I was coming to tell you that."

"Emily has a bad feeling."

"Adeline *asked* for us to stay here. She *asked* me that." He sounded both delighted and astonished.

That brought a slight grin to Rainer's face. "Seems like maybe you finally convinced her that the things she wants are valid."

"I'm in shock, but apparently I should've slept with her years ago."

Rainer laughed. "I'm kinda betting the timing had a lot to do with it."

"Wait, what did Em say?"

"That something bad was going to happen, and that we needed to stay here."

"Can we stop it?"

"She says the energy isn't fully set yet, so she doesn't know."

"Is Fergus gonna be okay?"

"I don't know that either."

Logan grimaced. "I'm sure I'm not gonna get anywhere, but I think I need to see if Fergus will shut down this ridiculous party now." He lifted his cell from his pocket.

Rainer listened to him explain Emily's concerns.

Logan rolled his eyes. "Because that's what Receivers do. They can feel everything." He shook his head. "Okay, fine. Just take care of yourself, man, because we're not coming."

Fergus's voice rose several octaves. Logan grimaced. "I'm sorry," he offered humbly. "Em is never wrong."

Logan's head drooped. He held up the phone. "He hung up on me."

"I know he's pissed but…"

"We're grown." Logan knew what he was going to say.

"Yeah, and we have to be their Shields before we're anything else, including Fergus's friend."

Logan nodded. "I just hope he's okay. Who knew when we stopped that brat from sticking Fergus's head in the toilet in elementary school we'd end up babysitting him for the rest of our lives?"

Adeline and Emily joined them in the hallway in time to catch the end of Logan's lamentations. Adeline smiled as Logan laced his fingers through hers. "You stopped someone from putting Fergus in a toilet?" She was trying not to giggle.

"I've told you this story, haven't I?"

She shook her head, and Logan began the tale. "Well, you know, a lot of us went to school together before the academy."

Adeline nodded again. Rainer knew that she was already aware of that, but Logan always worried that she felt left out when they talked about growing up together.

Adeline's mother had no idea she was Gifted when she was born. Although she'd repeatedly told Adeline that if she could find her father, he could have her, she'd never made any attempt. Everyone assumed someone on staff at the birthing clinic where Adeline was born must've tried to tell her mother about her energy gifts, but she swore she didn't know.

When Adeline was four years old, she'd eased away from her mother to admire a doll in a drug store. This irritated her mother, and she'd grabbed Adeline's hand and jerked her back with entirely too much force. Her shoulder and elbow had been wrenched out of socket. Because Adeline immediately began to cry and there were so many witnesses, she was taken to the hospital to be checked.

There were numerous hospitals throughout the United States that employed Gifted healers, or medios. Johns Hopkins, the Mayo Clinic, Mt. Sinai, Vanderbilt, Duke, Emory, Cedars-Sinai, and Georgetown, the place where Adeline had accepted a job, just to name a few.

Since Adeline was so young, and several pharmacists witnessed what happened, she was sent to the National Medical Children's Center in Washington, DC, one of the country's premier hospitals for pediatrics. The doctor who tended to Adeline was Gifted and picked up on her energy.

She performed a thermographic scan. This was the only way, known to date, to be able to show the Gifted energies to the Non-Gifted. The medio had shown Adeline's mother the scans and instantly let the Gifted Senate and the academy know about Adeline.

As Adeline hadn't gone through puberty yet, she was unaware of her own energy. She certainly hadn't learned to suppress it or use it in any way.

"So..." Logan drawled, and Rainer came back to the present. "Fergus's mother always made him wear bow ties and sweater-vest things. He was forever getting picked on, and this huge kid had him by the neck headed to the toilet. Rainer tripped the kid, and then Connor and I sort of waylaid him while Rainer got Fergus out of the kid's grasp. I guess the rest is history."

Adeline smiled. "That's so sweet."

"Yeah well, remind me later and I'll tell you about the time when Em was four and decided she wanted to help Rainer use the bathroom." He laughed hysterically as Rainer and Emily both glared. "So, really," Logan continued to taunt, "Em saw Rainer naked a long time ago. Mom walked in right about the time she informed Rainer that she wanted to touch it."

Logan cracked up as Emily glowed crimson, and Adeline tried hard not to double over laughing.

238

Rainer cocked his jaw to the side and narrowed his eyes. "Shall I tell her about when you learned to go potty standing up?"

Logan roared with laughter. "Okay, okay, no more stories."

"Now I want to know." Adeline giggled.

Logan squeezed his eyes shut. "I was a little confused about which kind of bathroom experience boys can do standing up and, uh, I tried to do both."

A few minutes later they were all laughing.

∾

Logan Haydenshire

Logan grinned as Adeline spun more of her Pad Thai on her fork. She'd never had it before, and he loved that she was getting to experience new things. That she trusted his recommendations and ate until she was full.

They'd Grubhubbed from Thai Arroy, and it was delicious, but Logan was filled with far more than Thai Dumplings and rice noodles. Accomplishment and contentment and an almost urgent need to protect her constantly settled on him.

All he'd wanted since they'd started dating was to take care of her, to convince her that he loved her more than life itself. All he'd wanted was to be her Shield, and finally, finally he'd done it.

He glanced out at the darkening sky over the ocean that had raised them, and hoped his big brother would be proud of him.

He wondered how bad Rainer would harass him if he tried to take her to bed now. It was just a little after eight, but god he wanted her. He needed her. It was their last night at the beach house, and he wanted to savor every moment.

Logan wished Emily would stop biting on her lip. He was trying not to think about Fergus and what shit he might stumble into now. They had to grow up, but he couldn't help feeling like they'd abandoned their friend.

Adeline placed her empty plate on the coffee table and laced her fingers through his. "That was delicious."

"I'm glad you liked it, baby."

"Thank you for everything you've done for me this week." He also wished she'd quit thanking him.

"I love you," he reminded her.

She gave him a timid nod. "I know...I love you too," she squeaked out so low Rainer and Emily didn't even hear her from the other side of the room.

Logan's heart stalled and then raced back to life. That was the first time she'd ever said that to him. He pulled her into his embrace and squeezed her tight.

"I have for a long time. It's just...hard to say," she admitted in a choked whisper.

"You don't ever have to say it."

"I want to because I feel it all the time. It's just different...."

"What's different?"

"Your parents say it all the time, and I'd never even heard someone say those words until I came to your house."

Logan nodded. "I think my parents have always been of the opinion that it's better to say them too often than not enough."

She gave him her beautiful beaming grin. "Then I love you again."

He chuckled. "Do you want to go walk on the beach?" He just wanted to be alone with her somewhere, anywhere.

To his delight, she shook her head. Her onyx eyes were timid as she stared up at him.

"What do you want to do, baby?"

She couldn't seem to verbalize what she wanted this time, but she glanced down the hallway toward the room they'd been staying in. His cock took immediate notice. He stood and took her hand. "We're going to watch a movie in our room."

Rainer laughed at him outright. "There's not a TV in that bedroom, but sure, we'll go with that."

Logan flipped him off as he guided Adeline down the hall. He roared with laughter.

Logan sealed the door shut and pulled Adeline into his arms. "I really love this you telling me what you want thing."

She managed an adorable grin. "Can I ask you something?"

"Anything."

"Will you tell me the truth?"

"I've never lied to you, and I won't ever lie to you."

She managed a nod but refused to look him in the eye.

"What's wrong?"

"Nothing. I just wondered…"

"What?"

"Is…uh…well, in all of my classes where I learned about being an obstetrics medio they said that communication was key in a sexual relationship."

He loved how quickly her confidence always grew when she discussed her career. "Okay," he urged her on.

"So…I guess…I was wondering…if I…" She stopped again.

"If you what?" He caressed her face, unable to keep his hands from her.

"Do everything you like in bed," came out in rapid-fire succession.

He let his eyes close for the length of one heartbeat and grinned.

"Baby…you are everything I have ever wanted. You are sweet, and kind, and smart, and beautiful," he vowed adamantly. Then he paused, closed his eyes, and thought of her naked and vulnerable only to him, with him over her, protecting her, soothing her, being with her.

"When I'm with you like that, it is beyond anything I could ever have imagined or fantasized in my wildest dreams. When we make love, it is the most incredible experience of my life. Every night that I get to spend wrapped up inside of you is the most amazing night of my life. You are everything to me because I love you, and when I'm with you, I can feel it. When I'm inside of you, you feel loved. You allow yourself just a moment to let it wash through you and that is the most amazing thing I've ever felt."

"You can feel that?"

He smiled. "I can feel that, and what's more amazing is that I can feel how much you love me too."

She nodded and laid her head back on his chest.

He lifted her chin again and kissed her sweetly. She was tender and hesitant. She was rarely confident enough to ask for what she wanted or to believe in the power she held over him.

He planned to change that as soon as possible. She relaxed slightly in his powerful embrace.

He pulled her closer and wrapped his hands around her backside. He began guiding her hips in circles around him. She moaned, but she still didn't quite understand the point.

He began kissing her again heatedly. She responded with equal force, but she was still tentative and curious. He grabbed her hand. He brushed a kiss across her wrist as he lifted it to his mouth. Her pulse raced as he guided her hand down and pressed it over his crotch.

"Do you feel that?" Her hand on him drove him wild. He shuddered from the sensation. "That's what you do to me when you kiss me, when you smile at me. If you walk by me, and I catch the scent of you or just the thought of you being with me—that's what happens to me instantly. I ache for you."

He willed her to understand, and her eyes darkened as she panted and then she began to knead her hand over him. She grasped him and dragged her fingers from his hilt to his head, and he almost lost it.

A low guttural growl echoed from his chest. He ran his fingers through her silky hair and devoured her mouth. He slid his hands to her stomach and eased her out of the tank top she was wearing. He hoisted it over her head.

"Did you set the cast, baby?" He trailed his kisses down her neck. She nodded as he unhooked the delicate pink bra he'd pointed out earlier in the week when he'd finally gotten over himself and actually showed her some things he knew she'd be beautiful in.

Her nipples were swollen and flushed the exact shade of pink as the bra. It was the reason he'd picked it out, that beautiful shade of a blushing rose. He shuddered as he slid his hands to them and began kneading them softly.

She let her head fall back as he massaged. A slight moan escaped her as she began to let the rest of the world go. He popped the snap of her denim shorts and pushed his hand to the matching pink, lace panties she was wearing, but her anxiety came back full force in a moment's notice.

"You don't wish I was wilder, or more experienced, or bigger?" She gestured to her breasts.

After giving her a lust-filled, needy gaze, he shook his head. He knew she was insecure about that, but he couldn't determine why.

From the first time he'd brushed his hands by them years before, he'd felt it from her—the insecurity of not thinking she was enough for him. He also knew that borrowing Emily's bra a few days before had done nothing to strengthen her self-image.

To him, she was perfection. He pulled her shorts down, and she stepped away from them. Then he slid the scrap of lace between her legs aside and gently eased his fingers inside her. She needed to feel him.

"I wouldn't change one single thing about you." He stroked and felt her quake from his touch. His shield spilled around her. "You are the most beautiful woman in the world to me," he urged. "You're in my shield. You're in my rhythms. You know I'm telling you the truth."

He eased his fingers away, scooped her into his arms, and laid her on the bed. He moved beside her quickly and returned his fingers to her. He used his other hand to caress her breasts. They swelled under his touch, and he groaned.

"You are perfect." With a hungry grin, he massaged her, and she writhed. "Perfect handful." He cupped them and massaged with slightly more force as she cried out for him. "Perfect mouth full," he groaned as he took one in his mouth. He pulled and teased as her moans grew louder and more desperate. He gave the other equal attention until she bucked and her energy spiked wildly.

With a sultry smile, he moved down her body. He kissed and licked across her stomach. He edged lower as he bathed her body with his tongue. He concentrated, read her, and made certain he wasn't pushing her to do something she didn't want.

But he wanted it. He wanted it badly. He longed to feel the storehouse of her energy flow into his mouth. He spread her legs and massaged her thighs and then spread them farther.

"What are you doing?" she panicked.

"Baby, I love each and every single thing about you. You drive me wild from wanting you so badly. And right now, I want to touch and taste every single part of you. I want to feel you in my mouth. I want to drink you. You're so damn sweet. I can't imagine what that must be like. But I want to know. Let me have you. I'll never let you down, and I think you just might enjoy this."

Her body was at war with her mind. He could feel the ardent opposition. The fear swirled violently within the deep desire of her rhythms.

Logan decided to reinforce his plea and push her body to win out over her mind, just this once. He held her legs apart and dragged his tongue along her slit, hesitantly, and he had her.

"I want you to feel it, baby. I want you to let everything else go but you and me. Just be right here with me. Relax and let me give you this."

Her breath came in gasping pants as she spread her legs farther for him and made him smile.

"That's it," he encouraged as he licked again, and she called out his name. It drove him wild.

He delved deeper, plunged her depths, and swirled his tongue inside of her. He edged closer to the part of her that made her energy spike to its highest tilt before she fell.

Her moans began to echo around him. Her energy seared through him. Her body contorted in ecstasy as the slick, wet heat she made for him began to fill his mouth. He moaned against her. She tasted like the sweetest honey he'd ever had. Her energy was exquisite. It must've come from heaven.

But she was still frightened. It tensed constantly in her bands and he concentrated and tried to read her. She didn't seem to be frightened of him, or of what he was doing, but that he wouldn't like it, that she'd somehow disappoint him. He showed her with his body what she wouldn't believe with his words. He dragged his tongue up over her clit. He lapped at it constantly, then added to the friction until she laid her fears aside and reveled in the pleasure of what he was doing to her.

"Does that feel good, baby?" he asked as he blew hot air over her, and she bucked frantically. She didn't respond. She was too hesitant. That was fine. He knew she liked it. Her energy came in frantic, hungry pulses as he returned to his work and a quaking moan escaped her. She couldn't hold it back.

He waited until her energy peaked again. He concentrated on her needy rhythms. He sucked her and then she broke. He owned her. She couldn't fight it. The sensations overwhelmed her. She cried out for him and screamed out his name. She flooded his mouth with her energy, and he groaned as he drank her in.

She laced her fingers through his hair and pushed him in deeper. It drove him wild. It shattered through her. Everything pent-up inside of her released in heated waves of ecstasy.

He moved up her body and replaced his tongue with his fingers, but he moved slowly, letting it rock through her before he built her again. He quickly removed his clothes, and then he kissed her tenderly. He returned his fingers and pressed into the slick perfection of her. He added to the pressure. She writhed, and he was desperate to hear her.

"Tell me, baby," he urged. "Tell me if you like it. Do you want more?" he asked, though he didn't think she could take more than two fingers. He was still in awe of how she took him.

"It feels so good," she urged. "Please don't stop." Her timid plea seared through him.

"Oh baby, I'm not going to stop until I'm spent."

The wet heat she made for him began to flow around his fingers. He shuddered. Her body's responses were overwhelming. Her moans became frantic. Her body bucked under his touch. The energy was drawn too tightly. She needed to let go again.

"I'm right here," he soothed. "Just let it go. Let me make it feel better." She lost control. She let him have another one. The sensation of watching what he'd done to her almost sent him over the edge. He pulled his fingers back as she ebbed. His body bucked against the bed. If he didn't take her now, he swore he was going to fuck his way through the mattress.

"Do you want to take a break, sweetheart?" He forced himself to ask.

She closed her eyes as, "No" whispered from her in a needy plea. "Please, Logan." She could hardly bear to make the simple request.

He fought not to spread her legs and pound into her, to give her what she wanted forcefully, but he'd never do that unless he was convinced that's what she wanted as well.

She was too timid, too hesitant now, but as far as he was concerned they had the rest of their lives for her to make demands he'd gladly fulfill.

He moved over her carefully and kept his weight off of her. She spread her legs for him and framed his body. The movement alone drove him wild. He kissed her heatedly and prodded her as he tried to prepare her to take him. With a loud groan, she began to give way as he urged her open.

She gradually separated for him as he pushed inside of her. The feeling was exquisite. He could never have imagined anything so incredible. He formed her to his length as he delved deeper, unable to stop himself. The need to fill her with all of him, to make every inch of her belong to him, was too powerful.

She cried out for him and met his thrusts. She swelled around him and drowned him in all of her. Her name spilled from his lips in a reverent groan.

"Feel it, baby. Take it all," he begged. He drove her harder, and she spiraled over the edge as he took her with more force.

"Yes, yes," she gasped.

"I'm gonna lose it," he warned just as he filled her with everything inside of him.

He wanted her to have it all. Their energy joined in heated, spiraling waves. The air around them was thick with the essence of them together. He withdrew as gently as he was able and held her to him. This was when the doubt came back. This was when she was her most vulnerable.

"I love you," he whispered, and she clung to him. "You are amazing, the way you are with me, the sounds you make. You're just incredible. You're perfection."

She smiled against his chest. "I love you too." She nuzzled against him. "Are you too tired to talk?"

"Baby, it's not even nine. Talk to me."

"I know, but orgasms make men tired," she quoted yet another medical textbook.

He smirked. "Maybe some guys, but I am Gifted."

She laughed. It was the sweetest sound in the world. But then she gave him a slightly devious smirk. "I know."

They talked about what they thought life would be like once they got back home and where they could live. He finally confessed to her how intimidated he was about his new appointment to Elite Iodex. She soothed his worries and told him how amazing he was. It restored his ego. They talked until they were yawning more than chatting.

"Do you want one of my T-shirts to sleep in or can I keep you like this?"

"I might get cold." She giggled at her own attempt at flirting. God, he could never love anything more.

"I'll keep you warm, honey."

Suddenly, she pulled away from him with a horrified look. "Please never call me that."

He managed a nod, but his shield was frantic to have her back in his arms. "I'm sorry. My dad calls my mom that, and it just came out."

She scowled. "I know, but that's what they all call her and I just..." She shuddered and all but gagged. "Honey, or sugar, or ugh..."

"Hey." He sat up and took her hands. "I won't ever call you that again, and you are not her."

"I know. I just..."

"What?"

She gave him a sweet grin. "I love being your baby," she whispered and eased back beside him.

"You are always my baby, and thank you for telling me that you don't like when I call you other things."

"I'm getting better at it."

He grinned. "You're perfect."

Logan tried to understand the noise he was hearing. Some very large insect was buzzing in his ear. He sat up and glared at the offending creature, only it wasn't a bug. It was his phone buzzing. He picked it up and stared at the screen like it had mortally wounded him.

Who the hell was calling him at 1:15 in the morning? He'd been in the middle of the best sleep of his life with his girlfriend naked in his arms.

He managed to answer before it went to voice mail.

He almost hung up when he heard a recording telling him that he was being connected to the Virginia Beach Iodex Precinct, but then he remembered that he was about to become an Iodex officer and hanging up might not have been the best idea.

Of all of the outlandish scenarios his mind conjured as to why the local Iodex precinct might be calling him, none of them were as insane as who was actually calling.

He listened to Fergus tell him that he'd been arrested after Iodex had invaded his party and found drugs at the house. "What the hell?" Logan finally managed.

"They weren't mine obviously. There were a bunch of people there I don't know." Logan fought not to whimper. "Can you and Rainer please come get me out of here?"

"Yeah, okay, let me get him up. We'll be there in a few."

Garrett Haydenshire

"What are they doing?" Garrett stared through the binoculars at the beach house as Logan and Rainer stumbled out the front door.

Portwood's brow furrowed. "Where are they going?"

Garrett watched as Rainer turned at his car, cupped his hand, and then projected a shield cast out over the entire house. At least he'd done that.

Ericsson grimaced. "Do you know how fast I could siphon that shield?"

"I know. We've got to get them trained now."

"At least Cascavel is in Tijuana," Portwood reminded hopefully. Mexican Iodex had ID'd him entering one of the Interfeci safehouses. Garrett took some solace in that.

An hour later his cell rang. He held it up to show Logan's name.

248

"What the hell?" This time he had no trouble letting his irritation leak into his tone. The fact that he was irritated for something other than being awoken in the middle of the night was irrelevant.

"I'm sorry," Logan said. "Fergus got arrested on a trumped-up charge for a party he threw. Rainer's trying to bail him out, but they won't let him. What time are you going to be down here?"

"I'll leave in a few hours. Where are Emily and Adeline?" Maybe he could get them to think without actually having to explain the sheer amount of danger surrounding them until they got home.

"They're back at the house asleep."

"So, Rainer just left Emily at the house unprotected?"

"What the hell's gonna happen to her at the beach house?" Logan sounded like Garrett might've lost his mind. "He casted the house. What's wrong with you?"

"Nothing. I'll call the precinct and get them to release him to you, and I'll be down there soon."

"Thanks."

"It's fine, but Lo, listen to me…" He grimaced. "Just…be careful." He ended the call and shook his head. "A friend of theirs got arrested last night. They're trying to get him out."

Portwood cringed. "Dan's gonna love that."

Garrett's head dropped in defeat as he thought about his kid brothers being chewed out by Dan. He'd always been brutal, but now he was vicious.

Garrett looked up the Virginia Beach Iodex Precinct and tried to think if he knew anyone on the force there.

Ericcson tapped him on the shoulder. "See if Isaac Barnes is on duty tonight. We went out a few times before he moved down here. Great guy."

Garrett nodded his thanks and did as he was instructed. When Barnes came to the phone, Garrett explained who he was and how he'd known to ask for him.

"Tell Mike I asked how it's going," Barnes urged.

"Will do. Listen, my kid brother and his best friend are down there trying to get a friend of theirs out of lockup. Can you tell me what's going on?"

"Oh, the Sherman kid?"

"Yeah, that's him."

Barnes sighed. "I feel bad for the guy. He knows nothing. Johanas brought him in. They used the public disturbance call to get in the house and found the coke. All way too convenient on our part to me. Plus I'd bet my badge that the stash is up from our good friends in Brazil."

Garrett's heart lurched. "You're telling me somebody went to this friend of my brother's party and planted coke from Nic?"

"The Sherman kid literally knew nothing. He's a disaster. And Johanas is on his way out. Chief thinks he's two-timing us."

"Interesting. Uh, can you do anything to get Sherman out?"

"Does your brother have bail money?"

"Not likely, but his best friend does."

"Let me go talk to the chief. Is Mike out here with you?"

"Yeah, he's sitting right behind me."

"Okay, I'll call him back in a few."

"Thanks. I appreciate all of your help." Garrett ended the call and tried to force the only available conclusions outside of his shield.

"What'd he say?" Ericcson asked.

"He's gonna call you back in a few minutes." Garrett explained the rest of the phone call.

Portwood looked as sick as Garrett felt. "A big party would be a great distraction for one of Nic's snatch and grab teams."

"Yeah, and I'd bet my next paycheck that my baby sister told Rainer and Logan not to go tonight, and that's why they stayed here. And wouldn't it be just like Nic's boys to be pissed she wasn't there, plant some evidence, and call in a dirty cop."

"If only everyone would listen to Receivers," Ericcson sighed.

"Rainer learned his lesson on that the hard way." As Garrett began to really consider everything Rainer was up against, everything that stood to hurt his little sister, everything his family had already been through, and what being trained by Dan Vindico was really like, he called his father despite the late hour. He couldn't lose another brother. His very survival depended on theirs.

CHAPTER 31

STEADFAST

GOVERNOR STEPHEN HAYDENSHIRE

A knock finally sounded on the office door. Stephen stopped pacing and opened it. He didn't have to ask who was there.

Dan Vindico's face held every ounce of fury he was trying and failing to keep in his shield. He followed his father, Arthur, and Mason Willow into Stephen's office.

Mason was the governor over all of Iodex. Stephen assumed Arthur was there to try to broker peace between Stephen and Dan.

Garrett's pleading phone call in the middle of the night weighed heavy in Stephen's mind.

"Logan and Rainer decided to leave Emily and Adeline at your beach house alone last night while they went and got a friend of theirs out of jail," Dan informed him unnecessarily.

"I know that. Garrett called me last night. I'm going to talk to Rainer as soon as they get home."

"'Bout damn time," Dan huffed under his breath.

"What was that?"

"Nothing…*sir*," he begrudged the formality as per usual.

"No, you said something."

"Rainer needs to be told the truth and he needs to be trained. Your insistence that he be kept in the dark about just how much danger Emily is in because of him is going to get them both killed."

Stephen shook his head. "What Rainer needed seven years ago is the same thing he needs now—a family. A soft place to fall when the world is too much. Somewhere he knows he belongs and will always be wanted."

Arthur stepped in between them. "You're both right. Rainer did and he does need everything Stephen just said, son,"—he turned on Stephen—"but now he also needs to be told the truth and to be trained."

Stephen nodded. "I will tell him as much as he can handle today, and you can begin his training but not one day before he's set to begin work. They deserve the last few moments of their childhood. Rainer has already had most of his stolen away either by Wretchkinsides or by this Realm."

Dan threw his arms out. "You won't even sign the paperwork for him and Logan to join the Elite Squadron." He laid the documents on the desk.

Stephen's heart seized as he recalled the last underage document he'd signed for one of his children, the one they visited on a regular basis at the cemetery. Officers had to be twenty-five to join Elite unless their parents signed the waiver.

There was a reason he hadn't signed them the last four times they'd come across his desk. He didn't want to put his name, his signature, on another death warrant at the hands of Dominic Wretchkinsides.

Stephen's mind raced as he stared Dan down. He wondered where the years had gone. Dan used to hang out at the farmhouse with Will and Garrett constantly. He was a pompous but polite kid. He loved Lillian's cooking. He'd certainly walked through hell with all that he'd lost, but Stephen barely recognized the man who sat before him.

With defeat crushing in on him, he took a pen from the desk drawer and signed his name to the end of both Logan and Rainer's childhoods. It wouldn't have hurt any worse if he'd slit his own hand and signed them in blood.

Garrett's plea from the night before pushed its way through the terror in his mind. "Then Garrett comes back on the Elite Squadron and the task force," Stephen commanded.

Dan looked surprised but not disapproving. "If you can talk him into it, I'll take all the help I can get."

"I don't have to talk him into it. I do not order my children to different positions within this Realm. He asked me."

Dan turned to Governor Willow since he would have to approve the addition. "It's fine with me. You have budgeted money in ample supply." Concern formed on his features as he studied Dan. The entire governing board had worried about Joe's insistence that Dan be named Chief of Iodex, but none of them had turned him down.

"And if you send out Rainer and Logan, you send Garrett with them every single time," Stephen continued his orders.

"Fine," Dan agreed.

"Garrett is in charge of their training. Not you."

"No," he defied.

Stephen knew Dan wanted Logan and Rainer desperately, but not really for their skill and certainly not for their names. Between Cal and Rainer's parents, he seemed certain he could light the fire in them to go after and take down Dominic Wretchkinsides and his entire criminal organization.

Rainer and Logan had talked of nothing else but joining the National Elite Iodex Squadron since they'd been kids. The reality was like watching two full-steam locomotives collide on a one-way track in very slow motion.

"Garrett can help me train them, but he isn't in charge of their training."

Stephen nodded his defeat.

"They're coming home today, aren't they?" Mason soothed.

"They should be on their way soon." Stephen was desperate to have them back home safely on the farm. He hadn't slept well since he'd watched his baby girl walk out the door on Rainer's arm after graduation. That was at least partially because he knew what Rainer Lawson was planning on doing to his baby girl once he got her off the farm. Stephen shuddered slightly and turned back to Dan. He narrowed his eyes.

"Do you plan on telling them about Amelia when they start?" He never knew how Dan might react when Amelia's name was brought up.

"They don't know?"

"Rainer and Logan were eleven when that happened. It wasn't something we talked about over dinner. Joe didn't want Rainer to know that the men who killed Maggie were still at large and gaining power."

"Then yes, I'm going to tell them at least some of it." Dan leveled another cold glare at Stephen. "They're not kids anymore."

"Just how much danger is my little girl in?" Stephen demanded suddenly. Nervous glances shot around the room. Dan drew a deep breath and hemmed.

"Rainer just became a billionaire, and the press does a hell of a job of letting everyone know where he is at any given moment. It's obvious to everyone just how much he adores her. The entire Realm knows that you also have a very close relationship with Emily. So, we need to make it abundantly apparent to Rainer, and Logan as well, that she is to be watched closely and constantly. I won't let Rainer live with all of the shit I've lived."

Dan grimaced as he handed Stephen a copy of a gossip magazine. "I'm only giving you this because you asked me to tell you everything I knew about their trip. This is being widely circulated. They've gone back for a second printing."

Stephen's eyes goggled. Nausea roiled in his gut. There was a shot of Rainer and Emily as they exited a lingerie shop.

Then, to ice the incensed poison that had been surging through his veins since they'd left the farm, there were pictures of all of the nighties and rather skimpy panties that Rainer had purchased for Emily while they'd been in the store.

Stephen tried to rid his mind of a three-year-old Emily, with her hair up in curled pigtails, climbing up in his lap after dinner and laying her head on his shoulder.

She couldn't buy panties like that. She was barely out of diapers.

CHAPTER 32
A NEW DAY
RAINER LAWSON

Rainer hadn't really slept since they'd taken Fergus home last night. Everything about the arrest didn't sit well with his shield. He held Emily tenderly in his arms. He didn't want to go back to the farm. He didn't want to sleep in his and Logan's room. He didn't know what he wanted exactly, but he knew what he didn't.

Emily's eyes blinked open and she gave him a tender grin.

"Hey there," he whispered.

She squeezed him tight. "It's going to be okay." She could feel his trepidation.

He nodded. "Garrett will be here soon. We should probably get packed."

They spent the next hour stripping the beds and packing their bags. Logan looked every bit as morose as Rainer felt.

At nine sharp, Garrett walked in with none other than the captain of the Arlington Angels, Chloe Sawyer, on his arm. Emily's mouth hung open in shock. Garrett looked absolutely exhausted, and Rainer felt bad for wishing that he'd not asked to use the beach house for a long weekend. He definitely needed some rest. Rainer wondered what he'd been doing.

"Uh…hey, Chloe," Emily stammered.

"Hey," Chloe offered sweetly. "I can't wait to see you try out next weekend."

"Oh." Emily flushed and seemed to have lost her breath. "I'm really excited…and really nervous."

"Don't be nervous. You'll be great. You were our top pick out of the academy this year."

Delight lit Emily's eyes as she nodded and she squeezed Rainer's hand.

"If my baby brother and sister would get outta here, we could start our weekend," Garrett ordered.

Chloe hit his chest playfully. "Be nice."

Emily was still staring up at Chloe like she'd never seen anything quite so amazing.

"Yeah, yeah," Logan huffed. "We'll get out."

A little while later, Rainer and Logan had loaded the cars, and everyone was waving goodbye to Garrett and Chloe.

"Oh my gosh! My brother is dating Chloe Sawyer. What if he breaks her heart, and then she doesn't want me on the team because she's so mad at him?" She wrung her hands as Rainer proceeded down the road.

"Em, baby, she seemed fairly taken with you, with or without Garrett."

Garrett did have quite the reputation of being a heartbreaker. He refused to settle down, despite his mother's pleadings. He changed women like most guys change pants.

"She said I was the top pick!" Emily squealed a moment later.

"I'm telling you, you're going to make it on the team." He rubbed his eyes as a deep yawn overtook him. His exhaustion from their harrowing night settled on him in full force. "Would you mind if I stop for some coffee?"

"Of course not." Emily looked concerned. "Do you want me to drive?"

"No, I'm fine." He knew she didn't want to drive and was just being kind.

"Just call Logan for me, and tell him I'm gonna go to the Waffle House at the next exit, get some coffee, and maybe something else to eat. The eggs I ate a few hours ago aren't cutting it."

After they'd eaten, and Rainer had consumed several mugs of coffee and ordered a Dr Pepper to go, they started back on their journey.

"Do you want me to go around the bridge?" Rainer offered as he studied Emily's reaction.

"No, that'll take longer. We need to get you home and into bed."

"You're sure?"

"I'm sure. I know you'll keep me safe. You always do."

CHAPTER 33

WELCOME TO THE WORLD, RAINER

A few hours later, they pulled up to the Haydenshires' farm. Rainer was suddenly struck by how much had changed since the last time he'd driven the gravel path to the barn, just over a week ago.

"Rainer," Emily's voice quaked.

"What's wrong?"

She shook her head as she bit her lip. "Nothing really."

"Then why do you look like you're going to cry?"

She smiled through the tears that escaped her eyes. "I don't know."

As he studied her, Rainer racked his brain, unable to come up with why she was suddenly so emotional.

She drew a deep breath as she studied her surroundings—the expansive fields set off in the noonday sun, the barns, the lake, the serenity of it all, and suddenly Rainer knew why she was crying.

"Em, we don't have to move until you're ready. I love it here too. This is where I grew up, as well."

She fought the tears but didn't quite seem up to the task of halting their downpour.

"Baby." Rainer pulled the car into the barn and reached to hold her. She shook her head and looked embarrassed by her sudden emotion.

"I want to move in with you and plan our wedding and everything. I'm just overwhelmed."

"A whole lot has changed in the past week. I get it."

This seemed to bring on more tears. "I know. You're the sweetest guy ever. And I just don't feel like I deserve you, and we're engaged!" She stared down at her ring in disbelief. " I feel like I'm in some kind of fantastic dream, and I'm terrified to wake up."

He rubbed her back and tried to soothe her. "Listen to me. We've been through enough horrible things. The past few years haven't been the easiest. So, let's just try to make the rest the best we possibly can. We can take it slow. We don't have to move out tomorrow and get married the next day. I want you to plan the wedding of your dreams. Anything you want. And we'll start working, and we can look for a place to live whenever you're ready."

"But I can't sleep with you here."

He smiled and kissed the top of her head. "Probably not, especially if your parents are home."

"Then I want to move out soon."

"Okay, but not today. So, why don't we go inside and let everything that's happened in the past week settle in?"

After he'd pulled their bags from the trunk, they walked to the house quickly. A storm was gathering in the distance.

"You're here!" Mrs. Haydenshire pulled them into her forceful embrace. When she finally released them, Governor Haydenshire was chuckling.

"How's my baby girl?" He gazed at Emily and swallowed down visible emotion as she threw her arms around her father.

"I'm good, Daddy, perfect really." She took Rainer's hand with a smile.

"Are you hungry?" Mrs. Haydenshire asked as Keaton and Henry rushed to Emily. She grinned and leaned down to hug them both.

Rainer shook his head. "No, ma'am, we stopped on the way back. I'm just tired," he commented through a deep yawn.

Governor Haydenshire nodded and gave Rainer the smile he usually reserved for when he had to tell someone something they didn't want to hear.

"I know you had a rough night, but could we talk before you hit the sack, son?" It bordered on a command.

"Of course." Rainer's heart picked up pace. "Just let me put these upstairs." He rushed the bags up the stairs and placed all of Emily's in her room. After tossing his duffle into the room he shared with Logan, he returned to the kitchen.

Rainer thought the governor probably wanted to talk about his uncle. His stomach churned as he wondered what Stan had done now.

"I…uh…guess I'll go unpack." Emily shot Rainer a look that meant he was to tell her everything her father wanted to talk about as soon as possible.

Rainer gave her a slight nod. The look on Governor Haydenshire's face had the large amount of coffee and pancakes he'd consumed twisting uncomfortably in his stomach.

The governor started toward the back door, and Rainer began to sweat. Walks around the lake with Governor Haydenshire generally meant something was wrong. There'd been a walk when Governor Haydenshire had found Rainer on the couch with Emily with his hands up her shirt. There'd been walks around the lake for most of Rainer's life. The governor had walked Rainer and Logan around the lake after Logan had recovered from the accident on the tractor. He'd tried to explain what had happened between Logan and Adeline. Discussions about his father's death and funeral, his inheritance, his appointment to Iodex all began replaying in Rainer's mind. The setting was always the same for every discussion.

The governor was silent as they trekked toward the lake. Rainer's heart raced, but Emily's father seemed at peace for the most part. He offered Rainer a reassuring smile and commented on the garden. Rainer nodded, but wasn't entirely certain what he'd said. He hoped he hadn't asked a question.

Thunder echoed in the distance, and Rainer glanced back at the house. Emily hated storms. Almost all Receivers did. There was a tremendous amount of violent energy in storms, and Receivers could feel it all. It affected their reads and made them nervous.

It had been pouring when they'd found out Cal had been killed, and the rain was relentless when her car had been edged off of the bridge. He wanted to be with her and to hold her. If something frightened her, he wanted to make it better. He was her Shield. These thoughts distracted him slightly from the governor's impending lecture.

"Guess we better make this a quick jaunt." The governor glared at the darkening clouds in the distance.

"Did I do something wrong, sir?" Rainer finally asked as they took the well-worn path around the water. Governor Haydenshire studied him and then gave him a wry smile.

"S'pose that depends on whom you're asking," he allowed. "But I'd probably go with—not intentionally."

Rainer continued to rack his brain. Her parents knew what had happened between him and Emily at the beach house. Her mother had made that abundantly clear with her phone call the morning after.

Governor Haydenshire had seemed pleased when Rainer had called to ask for Emily's hand. He tried to reason as he walked beside his future father-in-law.

After drawing a steadying breath, Governor Haydenshire leaned over and scooped up a flat rock on the shore of the lake. He skipped it out across the water as Rainer waited impatiently.

"I couldn't be more proud of you. I'm thrilled that you and my baby girl are getting married, and you know how high my standards are." He smiled kindly as Rainer nodded.

"Thank you, sir." Rainer tried not to sound as nervous as he felt. "Is this about my uncle?" His desperation to know what he'd done was getting the better of him.

Confusion colored Governor Haydenshire's expression before he remembered what Rainer was referring to. He chuckled and shook his head. "No, Dan released him the next morning, but honestly, I cannot fathom how he's related to your father or to you."

The governor seemed to pick up on Rainer's nerves, and he began his talk. "I know your friend put you in a terrible position last night."

The pent-up air released from his lungs, and Rainer listened intently.

"I also know that over the past week you've grown up rather quickly." Governor Haydenshire looked momentarily nostalgic.

Heated blood rushed to Rainer's cheeks. He drew another deep breath as they continued walking. The governor halted abruptly.

"I don't know how to say this as gently as I'd like to be able to, so please just hear me out. Know that I couldn't be more proud of you and that I don't want you to feel guilty in any way."

Rainer wished he'd just get on with it.

"With the sheer amount of your inheritance, coupled with who your father was to the Gifted people, and frankly, who I am, you know that you and Emily are a source of constant intrigue for the Realm."

Rainer nodded.

"I just need you to always be the Shield you were born to be, always be overly cautious. You're a very wealthy young man now. The ring on my little girl's finger alone is worth tens of thousands of dollars. That makes her a very appealing target for people looking to make a great deal of money quickly, at her expense and at yours." It sounded like the words threatened to make him gag.

Rainer stopped walking and tried to determine exactly what he was being told.

"You mean…like someone would take her? Or…hurt her because of my inheritance?" All of the blood in his body froze. Waves of nausea washed over him in icy cold shards and unbearable heat.

"It's a definite possibility."

"I never wanted the money. I don't care about it. I just want her. I don't ever want her to be in danger." Vile revulsion threaten to overwhelm him.

"I know, son." Governor Haydenshire laid his hand on Rainer's shoulder to steady him. "And I want you and Emily to go on and live the life you've both worked so hard for, and that your parents died for, but you are going to have to be careful. You need to watch your surroundings, and she'll need to be with you or another Shield unless she's at work or here at the farm. You two are always safest here."

Rainer nodded as his breath came in panting gasps.

"I'll just give it all away." That seemed to be the only viable option. "I don't want it. I just want her to be safe. I didn't even earn it." He stated the thing about the inheritance that always bothered him most.

"I didn't want to scare you," Governor Haydenshire soothed. "Your family worked too hard for all that you have for you to do that just because you're frightened. There is always evil in the world, and there always will be. But if we let it rule our lives and our decisions, we're letting it win. Your ancestors earned that money. We've talked about this. You'll be adding to it, but it is yours, and you should use it as you see fit."

Rainer was still unable to draw a full breath. A jagged noose of terror had slipped around his neck. "That's what Vindico was talking about," he realized suddenly.

"When did you talk to Dan?"

"He called me after he arrested that guy… Oh my god. The guy at the restaurant."

The governor gave a morose nod and continued, "Like I said, I know your friend put you in a terrible position last night, and I appreciate your willingness to help him. You're a good man. You're not a boy anymore, and your father would be very proud of you."

Rainer let his eyes close.

"But…" The governor looked pained as Rainer refocused on him. "You shouldn't have left Emily at the beach house without a Shield."

"We casted the house before we left," he offered, though failure threatened to drown him.

Governor Haydenshire nodded. "I know, but that might not cut it anymore. I'm certain you'll learn as you begin training with Iodex, but for now, just please always make certain Emily is your first priority. Last night, you should have called Mr. Sherman's parents to come get him out of jail, and you should have stayed with Emily."

Rainer nodded before he began making his promises. "She's always my top priority, always, sir. Please believe me. I would give up anything for her."

"I know you would. That's why I let you put that ring on her finger." He chuckled softly. Thunder rent the sky once more. "Just be careful. Always. That's all I'm asking. Have you talked to Emily about getting a new car?"

"No, sir."

"She's going to need one if she's going to challenge for the Angels, and you're going to be at the Pentagon every day."

Rainer had been thinking about that for a while, but he was hesitant to bring it up with Emily. "I don't mind taking her to practice, before I go to work, but I'll buy her whatever she wants."

"I don't think she wants anything. I think she's still afraid and that you and I have catered to that fear for a bit too long."

Terror stole Rainer's thoughts. "Sir, how do I keep her safe, if she's at work and I'm at work and not with her?"

"We have to have faith that she'll be okay, that she can defend herself. She might not be a Shield, but she can certainly feel when anyone near her might want to do her harm. She'll be with her teammates when she's practicing. Angels Arena has an excellent security staff, and you'll be learning a lot of defensive techniques once you start your training. I'm certain you could teach her a little self-defense to go with her emotional gifts.

"Now, before it starts pouring, could I ask you one more favor?" Governor Haydenshire's face now held a mix of disgust and embarrassment.

"Of course." Rainer wondered what had elicited the sudden change of expression.

As he stared down at the bank of the lake, the governor seemed to will repose. "I know that you and Emily are all grown-up. And I'm not even all that upset about what I'm well aware happened between you and Emily at the beach." His voice was strained from the effort. "I suppose I knew that was inevitable. It was bound to happen sometime."

Rainer cringed.

Governor Haydenshire narrowed his eyes. "But you understand that's my little girl, my precious baby girl, who you had in bed with you." He pointed toward Emily's bedroom window.

Rainer gave a slight nod. The thunder of his heart was louder than the incoming storm.

"And that you took something from her she can't ever have back. And you understand what a tremendous gift that was, and that she is."

"Yes, sir." Rainer forced his head to nod.

"Good," Governor Haydenshire commented. "Now you just stood there and promised me that you'd always take care of Emily. I don't just want your promise that you'll take care of her if she were ever to be in danger. I expect you to take care of her in every single thing you do."

"Yes, sir, of course, always," Rainer rushed to get the vow from his lips. Governor Haydenshire nodded and finally held Rainer's gaze.

"Just a few more things…" He turned and headed back toward the house as the gathering clouds darkened to reflect what Rainer had just been told.

He could barely breathe as he paced beside the governor.

"First, I would appreciate it if you and Emily could make certain that I don't have to see the items that my baby girl wore just prior to you being with her like that ever again."

"What?!"

"The store you were in at the mall published the items you bought for Emily. Like I said, this Realm is endlessly fascinated with the two of you. I know that isn't fair, but it is the reality of the situation."

"Oh my god." Rainer let his head fall. His entire being was torn between mortification and terror. "I'm so sorry, sir. We had no idea that would happen." He was woefully unable to look Emily's father in the eye as he thought about just some of the lingerie they'd picked out.

"I assumed so," Governor Haydenshire huffed. "And second, a warning to you," he continued his commands. Rainer waited as he drowned in an abyss of embarrassment and terrorizing fear that he'd not only infuriated but also disappointed the man he admired most in the world. "For a while, it seemed every time I glanced Lillian's way, we were having another baby. Now, I'm thrilled you and Emily Anne are getting married, but I'd really appreciate it if she wasn't expecting when I get to walk my only daughter down the aisle. Don't get caught up in the moment and forget that it takes a split second to change the course of your lives forever. Please also remember that she cannot be pregnant and challenge for the Angels under the field aegis. It would take one split second for her to lose out on her dreams."

"Yes, sir, I know."

"Good. Don't ever forget that. It's good advice for myriad situations, but it's especially applicable here."

Rainer didn't want to apologize for what he and Emily had shared because that would be the biggest lie he'd ever told, but he felt he should say something.

"Uh…" Rainer stammered. "Sir, you said that you were upset about what happened?"

Governor Haydenshire offered him a wry grin. "I said I wasn't all that upset. And I appreciate that you're not apologizing, because I know you're not sorry." His statement left no room for debate. "But she's my baby girl, and the way I feel about that I can't truly explain to you until you and Emily have a little girl of your own. But once you hold your own daughter in your arms, you'll understand."

"Yes, sir." Rainer was still reeling from everything he'd heard in the past few minutes.

"Good man." Governor Haydenshire slapped Rainer on the back. "Now, I know and you know that Emily is sitting up on her window seat, watching us and wondering what I'm telling you. So go on up and tell her. And when you leave Emily's room, I would appreciate it if she was still wearing all of the clothes she's wearing right now."

"Yes, sir." Rainer gave up on ever getting his face to return to its normal color, as he followed the governor back up the porch steps and into the kitchen.

Logan and Adeline had arrived, and Logan was smirking. As soon as his father was out of earshot, he leapt. "Walk around the lake, huh? How bad was it?"

Rainer shook his head. He was unable to process the many varied things Governor Haydenshire had gone over with him.

"I need to talk to Emily."

Logan laughed. "I swear Dad will eventually forgive you for popping his baby girl's cherry."

"Logan," Adeline scolded as Rainer raced up the stairs, two at a time.

CHAPTER 34

A MAN AND HIS WORD

Emily met him at her door. "I saw you come in. What was that all about? You were as white as a ghost for a while, and now you're the color of the Mustang."

Rainer followed Emily into her room. He closed the door and sank onto her bed. Governor Haydenshire didn't have to worry. He couldn't have done anything right then if he'd wanted to.

"What did he say?" Emily shuddered as thunder shook her windowpanes.

"Uh." Rainer pushed his hands through his hair. He tried to calm down so he could calm her, but it was a futile effort. "That you could be in danger because of my inheritance, and that I shouldn't have left you at the beach house last night, and that guy at the restaurant may've been after you, and one of the gossip rags ran an article on the stuff you got at the lingerie store." Rainer cringed involuntarily. "And he wanted to remind me, basically, that he'd kill me if I get you pregnant before the wedding."

"What?!" Emily gasped. She looked just as overwhelmed as Rainer felt.

"Yeah." Rainer took her hand. He needed to feel her. She closed her eyes and willed her calming Receiver's cast into him. "I think we really just need to lay low, stay right here on the farm for a while. It's safe here."

"Okay. How exactly am I in danger?" Terror strangled the question.

"Because, I guess someone might try to take you so I'd pay the ransom or something." He shut his eyes tightly. The images were too horrifying.

"Okay, so we'll just be really careful, and Chief Vindico arrested that guy so he's not here anymore." He suspected she was saying that more for him than for herself.

"Please, please, just let me watch you like a hawk. At least until the press settles down about the money. Please."

She gave him her sweet reassuring smile. "I like it when you watch me like a hawk."

He kissed the side of her head and offered a fervent prayer that she would always be safe.

"What did he say about the lingerie?"

"That he'd really like never to see anything like that ever again." Her head fell into her hands.

"Yeah, well, I'd really like for no one ever to see my lingerie again, except for you."

"I'm so sorry."

"Stop." She put her finger over his lips. "This is not your fault."

He kissed her finger before she pulled it away from his mouth. She grinned and then she leaned in. Rainer kept the promise he'd just made to her father firmly planted in his mind as he kissed her. He needed her. He needed to get lost in her. The world was too heavy. It was too much. He wanted her and her alone and for everything and everyone else to leave them alone in blissful solitude.

He traced her face tenderly with his fingertips as he lavished her mouth a drawing kiss. She moved closer, and he slid his hands to her neck and shoulders. Her hand slipped over him through his shorts, and he groaned as she massaged him.

"I want you." Her hot breath caressed his hungry lips.

"No." He pulled away. He wiped the taste of her from his mouth with the back of his hand. He wasn't certain he'd be able to stop if he could still taste her rhythms. Sex couldn't always be the answer when things were going wrong.

"No?"

"I just promised your dad that we wouldn't, not right now, and we can't just do that because shit is going on." He understood his own father's explanation about Shields and Receivers more in that moment than he ever had before.

"Why did you tell Dad that?"

"What was I supposed to say?"

She rolled her eyes and pushed her hair behind her ear. "All right, all right, but don't promise him that anymore."

Rainer decided to forge ahead about the other thing her father had pointed out to him rather than make a promise he wasn't sure he could keep. "Your dad also thinks we should get you a new car," he stated hesitantly and watched her reaction.

She gazed up at him. Terror swirled in her eyes.

"Baby,"—he pulled her closer—"I don't ever want you to do anything you don't want to do." He cradled her head against his chest.

"But I have to drive," she concluded for him.

"I'll get you anything you want, whatever you feel safe in."

She leaned away from him and drew a steadying breath. "I don't feel safe driving. It doesn't matter which vehicle it is."

He knew that as well. "I can teach you to set a cast on the car that you're in. I will keep you safe. I swear."

"I know I have to. It's just going to take some time for me to feel comfortable again." She stared down at her duvet and began running her hands over the ring pattern.

He tried to come up with a way to help her. He kept his hands on her. He might not be able to take her clothes off, but he wanted to touch as much of her as he was able.

The rain began to pour with ferocity, and she shuddered against him as thunder echoed and lightning shattered the sky. His shield spilled out over her as he cradled her in the safety of his embrace. An idea came to him as he held her, but he decided to make the phone call later. "Do you want to go downstairs? I'll make you some tea." He kissed her cheek sweetly.

"No, I want to stay up here with you. Only I want you to hold me in the bed, preferably naked."

"You're not going to make this easy, are you?" He began envisioning what she wanted. He could get her mind off the storm, and they could make a storm of their own. The real estate in his shorts became nonexistent. She noticed, and her breathing quickened.

"What are you thinking about?"

The tension and stress that had swirled in her eyes a moment before was now replaced with a growing fire. Rainer shuddered as longing took its fierce hold.

"Em…" He shook his head.

"Tell me." The fire in her eyes beckoned him. He couldn't deny her, not with that look in her eye and the storm clouds darkening the room. "Please." She slid her hand back to him and grasped him through his shorts. He throbbed fiercely.

"I want you, baby. I want you so damn bad. I want to lay you out, spread your legs, and take you right here in this bed. I've dreamed about it so many times," he confessed just one of the many fantasies he'd kept running in his mind since he was about fourteen years old. "Make you scream, make you take it until I fill you full, and then watch it drip back out of you," he rasped. His voice was deep and fervent with his need. "But I'm not," he vowed to himself and to her. "I just told your dad we wouldn't do that, and I'm not breaking my word." The longer he spoke the more determined he became.

"I know." She pulled farther away from him. Their energy mingled too easily since they'd begun sleeping together. "But I don't want to wait much longer."

Rainer wondered how he was going to fulfill that particular wish.

"How about a nap? I know you're exhausted." She always tried to take care of him.

"Do you think that would bother your parents?"

"I'll open the door, and we'll use this." She pulled a loosely woven knit blanket off of the window bench.

So they wouldn't be in her bed and under the covers, he assumed. He hoped Governor Haydenshire wouldn't think he was being defiant as she opened her door slightly and then moved back to him.

He lay on his side and pulled her to his chest, then covered them in the blanket. He allowed himself a moment to run his hands over her breasts and then down to massage her backside. She gave him a sweet giggle.

"I left your clothes on," he pointed out, which made her laugh harder. Thunder assaulted the air again, and she tucked herself deeply into his protective embrace. All traces of laughter were gone. He kissed her cheek.

"I'm right here. You're safe. I've got you."

She nodded as he continued to let his hands explore her curves.

Then, with a deep yawn, Rainer relaxed beside her and listened to the rain falling steadily on the roof above them as he drifted off to sleep.

It was still oddly dark out when Rainer awoke. He blinked several times and made certain Emily was still safe in his arms. He smiled as he watched her sleep peacefully beside him.

He edged his left arm out from under her and glanced at his watch. It was just after five. Time seemed oddly variable. Rainer couldn't seem to get his mind and body in sync with the clock.

Governor Haydenshire's lecture seared through his mind again. He brushed a tender kiss across Emily's cheek. "It's almost time for dinner, baby. Are you ready to get up?"

She offered him a grunt and a whimper. He chuckled.

"Grandpa Haydenshire's coming over and Paps and Nana, to see the ring," she explained through a deep yawn, but she refused to open her eyes.

"So, we should probably get up, because I'm pretty sure Grandpa Haydenshire would kick my ass just for lying in bed with you."

Governor Haydenshire's mother had passed away when Emily was a baby, but his father was still going quite strong. He'd served as a captain in the Gifted branch of the army, two generations ago. Grandpa Haydenshire was not only a large man, but he was still rather abrupt and gruff. These were two qualities Mrs. Haydenshire didn't particularly care for, as his stories were often gory, and he cursed like a sailor.

"What time will they be here?" Rainer yawned.

"We're supposed to eat at 6:30."

"I'm gonna take a quick shower so your grandparents find me moderately acceptable as the guy who wants to marry you." He patted her backside as she begrudgingly crawled from the bed.

"Paps may not. I'm pretty sure he thinks you're my brother. He's kind of been confused lately."

"I obviously love your family, but I am really glad we aren't related yet." He winked at her. She leaned down and planted a kiss on his lips.

"You go shower, and I'll try to wake up and help Mom with dinner."

Rainer stretched as he stood. Nervous energy flowed through him. She picked up on it. Her hands grasped his, and she flooded her calming, soothing energy through him. Rainer stopped short of moaning. The feeling was exquisite.

He'd known Emily's grandparents since he was born, and they'd always been kind and caring. But for some reason, them coming to celebrate his and Emily's engagement, along with the talk he'd had with Governor Haydenshire, had him on edge.

With another quick yawn, he leaned over and kissed Emily's forehead. He squeezed her backside again while he was at it. She giggled and gave him a delighted mischievous grin, the one that always made his heart stutter momentarily.

"So," he drawled, "you sure you want to become Mrs. Lawson?" He let the idea of Mrs. Emily Lawson fill his heart and then his shield. Her grin somehow grew even larger as she nodded.

"I can't wait."

"Me, either."

CHAPTER 35

SAM

A few minutes later, Rainer was standing in his and Logan's room, checking to make certain everyone else was downstairs. He pulled the phone from his pocket and scrolled down the contact list. He smiled automatically when he found the number.

"Hey, Sam, it's Rainer Lawson. How are you?" Sam was one of his favorite people and one he hadn't talked to in a while.

"Well, as I live and breathe, if it's not the stud himself," Sam drawled with his signature chuckle. Rainer laughed and felt his nerves ease instantly. "And to what does Sam owe the honor and privilege of getting to speak to none other than the man?"

"Are you kidding me? The honor is all mine."

Sam gave his smooth, heart-filled, rumbling laugh again. "Ah, wait just a minute," he sighed, and Rainer fell silent for a moment.

"Uh, uh, uh, uh, uh…" Sam fussed as he came back to the phone. "My daughter's just gotten me one of these new phones, and I can't tell the heads from the tails, boy. What do I do when the screen looks like it split in half, and it's giving me stock reports that you know sure as hell don't mean a thing to me?"

"Touch the part of the screen that's black."

"There, thank you. This thing's crazy. To me, a phone should still be square, have a cord, and a spin dial like my record player."

Rainer laughed. "You gotta come into this century, Sam. That's old school."

"S'pose that's better than being an old fool, which is what I've been feeling since she gave me this thing and then moved all of my shop calls to it."

"Yeah, but I can show you how to store my number in it, and then when I call, it'll tell you that it's me."

"Or, I could pick up the phone and say hello, then say, 'hell's bells, Rainer Lawson's calling his dear old friend Sam,'" he chirped, making both of them laugh.

"I need a favor." Rainer checked down the hallway again to make sure Emily wasn't looking for him.

"Doesn't everyone?" Sam quipped. "What is it that Mr. Lawson, owner of the slickest '65 Mustang in town, might need from me?"

"I want to get Emily a car."

"Yeah, I saw that you asked your redheaded sizzle pop to save your sorry soul from bachelorhood. Is she gonna keep your dinner and your bed warm?"

"That's the plan."

"Well, then, let's get the girl the car of her dreams."

"Thank you for your help. I want her in something really safe, but sporty, you know? Like maybe an Audi or an E-class, or I don't know, maybe a Hummer."

"Now are you her fiancé or her sugar daddy?"

"Hey," Rainer drawled with a smile. "For her, I'd gladly be both."

A low, slow whistle slid from between Sam's teeth into the phone. "Boy, you better not let her hear you say that. All right, I'll see what I can find you. Bring Miss Emily over to the shop later in the week and we'll talk."

"That'd be great. I really appreciate it."

"Hey, for you, anything."

"Do you still have your GTO?" Rainer quizzed.

"Baby boy!" Sam grunted. "You better bury me in that car, or I will haunt you from the grave."

"It's a sweet, sweet car."

"You know it, and you know you should've gotten yourself one when you came to me whining about a '65 Mustang with a pop top and an engine so fast you can fly."

"Hey, lay off my 'Stang. You know you're jealous, old man."

"Jealous? Boy, I was here when they rolled your car off the line, and I said to myself then…Sam, *that* is a sissy white-boy car."

Rainer doubled over laughing. "I better go. Call me when you find something, and I'll bring Em over later this week."

"Now just hold on there, slick, and tell me, do you want her in something safe, and she wants to be in something flashy, or you two are in agreement with me building her a tank, as long as it has a fancy emblem on the hood?"

"I think she agrees, but if you come across something too good to pass up, we'll look at that too."

"Mmmm, smart man," Sam quipped. "All right, I'll call around and see what I can come up with."

"Thank you! I owe you."

"Don't they all, and don't you know nobody ever pays up."

Sam was an academy dropout. He quit in his junior year, but he had an astounding ability to harness and use mechanical energy. Rainer was perpetually amazed by his skills. He'd been friends with Governor Lawson since long before Rainer was born. His father had always said that if the Realm really wanted the wisest man to be Crown, they would've elected Sam. He was good friends with the Haydenshires as well.

Rainer and Sam had become close when Rainer was looking for a car to rebuild after his father's death. Sam had talked him through the worst of the loss. He'd been there and listened when ever Rainer hadn't understood what he was feeling. There were very few people Rainer admired more, and there was no one else he trusted to find Emily the car of her dreams.

Sam's specialty was finding the perfect car for the person making the request and then helping the customer make the car all they wanted it to be.

He'd helped Rainer install the screaming V-8 in his Mustang and rebuild almost everything under the hood. They'd also replaced the worn leather seats and dash panel and turned the fold-down rear seat into a permanent one. Sam had done a phenomenal job, and he'd taught Rainer a tremendous amount in the process.

His shop on the outskirts of Alexandria wasn't fancy, but it housed Sam's original turquoise '67 Pontiac GTO Lemans convertible and any other cars he was working on at the time.

It was one of Rainer's favorite places to be, and he couldn't wait to take Emily out to see it all.

CHAPTER 36

BUTTER-CHURNING BATTLE PLANS

Rainer found Emily and her mother sitting at the island whispering and giggling in the kitchen. The room was filled with delicious smells. Adeline was with them. She was at the kitchen table, smiling serenely.

The rain had subsided as evening had come. He whisked by Emily and planted a kiss on top of her head. Mrs. Haydenshire beamed.

"Where's Logan?" Rainer pulled a few grapes out of a bowl on the counter and threw them in his mouth.

"I sent him for more rolls, but I made Adeline stay with us so we could have some girl talk," Mrs. Haydenshire explained as she opened one of the oven doors and checked the food.

"Oh, sorry. I'll go back upstairs."

"No," Emily countered, "you'll come back here and let me sit in your lap."

"Is that okay?"

Mrs. Haydenshire rolled her eyes. "Don't let Stephen get to you, sweetie. He will eventually realize that Emily isn't seven years old anymore. It might just take him a little while. I'll see if I can't move the process along though." She winked at him.

Rainer spun Emily into his lap with a grin. She didn't remain there for long though. A minute later, Will and Brooke arrived, followed by

Levi and his girlfriend, Sarah. Patrick was eating at Lucy's parents' home, so he and Garrett wouldn't be attending the gathering. Connor emerged from the backyard carrying Keaton, who was screaming and kicking his legs with ferocity.

"What happened?" Mrs. Haydenshire fussed as she took Keaton from Connor.

"I brought him inside." Connor rolled his eyes. Mrs. Haydenshire chuckled and handed Keaton an animal cracker which quieted him down.

Emily's Nana and Paps, the Andersons, arrived next. They hugged Emily and shook Rainer's hand.

"Now that you're getting married, I can tell you the three things you can do for him to get him to do anything you want, my sweet Emily," her Nana teased.

"Nana." Emily blushed, and Rainer chuckled.

Logan returned carrying Henry and a grocery sack full of rolls.

Mrs. Haydenshire was very adamant that all of her children bond with one another, and she often sent one twin off with any of their older siblings for one-on-one time. Henry was sucking a cherry lollypop delightedly. Mrs. Haydenshire raised an irritated eyebrow at Logan.

"He wouldn't shut up." Logan handed her the rolls.

With that, everyone began helping to set the vast table in the dining room. Just before everyone was seated, the doorbell rang one last time. Levi pulled open the oak front door and offered Grandpa Haydenshire a forced smile.

"Levi," he grumped. "You and Emily sharing barbers now, son?"

"No, Grandpa." Levi stepped back and let his grandfather enter. Levi's hair was much longer than most of the other Haydenshire men's hair. It suited him.

Grandpa Haydenshire was of the opinion that a buzz cut was the only suitable haircut for a man and felt fully at liberty to remind all of his grandsons of this on a regular basis.

Dinner began, and everyone dug in. Mrs. Haydenshire had prepared three platters of beef medallions with mushrooms, potatoes, creamy spinach, and yeast rolls.

"This is delicious," Rainer complimented. Mrs. Haydenshire grinned at him.

"So," Grandpa Haydenshire leaned across the table, narrowed his eyes, and directed his fork at Rainer. He was still chewing a piece of beef that he swallowed before he continued. "You thought about the logistics of marriage, son?"

Rainer swallowed a sip of iced tea. "The logistics, sir?"

Mrs. Haydenshire and Emily rolled their eyes simultaneously.

"Yes, logistics. I thought you were an academy grad. Head of Ioses Order? You understand logistics, do you not?"

"Uh, yes, sir,"—Rainer suddenly felt that the collar on his shirt was a little too tight—"just not as it applies to marriage."

"A battle plan!" Grandpa Haydenshire roared. "You won't make it very long in this life without a battle plan."

All of Emily's brothers were fighting to hold back laughter as they watched Rainer shrink under their grandfather's derisive glare.

"Uh, well, I guess…I'll just do whatever I can to make sure Emily is safe and happy and has everything she needs. Always be there for her."

"That's a big bowl full of chocolate swirled shit with a cherry on top," Grandpa Haydenshire grumped.

Logan and Connor lost it. They doubled over as Governor Haydenshire and Emily said, "Dad," and "Grandpa," simultaneously.

"You listen up, boy." Grandpa Haydenshire ignored his son and granddaughter completely. "You gotta be ready to get up every day, work your ass off at the office, make enough money to keep her happy, buy her something pretty once in a while, pick up a gallon of milk, loaf of bread, whatever she forgot at the grocery that day, six pack for yourself, come home, tell her dinner's delicious, and that she's the prettiest damn thing you've ever seen, then get into bed and make her eyes roll back in her head several times, before you get back up and do it all over again the next day."

Rainer covered his mouth as the tea he'd just sipped came back out forcefully. Emily's eyes goggled as she promptly turned the color of her hair.

Every male in the Haydenshire household guffawed as Mrs. Haydenshire glared furiously at her husband.

The governor shook his weary head. "Dad, if I didn't think Rainer could handle it, I wouldn't have agreed when he asked me for her hand," he reminded before scooping up another fork full of mashed potatoes and trying not to meet Mrs. Haydenshire's glare.

"Now, Bill." Emily's Nana patted Grandpa Haydenshire on the arm. "I'm sure Rainer will keep Emily just as happy as Stephen keeps Lillian." She winked at Rainer who was still choking on his tea.

"As far as I can tell, for most of their marriage he just kept her knocked up." Grandpa Haydenshire speared another beef medallion with vengeance.

After Mrs. Haydenshire's orange-glazed pound cake with vanilla ice cream was served and devoured, the men and women separated. The governor handed out bottles of beer to his sons, Rainer, his father, and his father-in-law. They retired to the back deck as Adeline, Brooke, Sarah, and Emily stayed in the kitchen with Mrs. Haydenshire and her mother. They sipped tea and looked thick as thieves.

"Where's Garrett?" Grandpa Haydenshire demanded, as soon as he'd popped the top of his beer on the bottle opener that was affixed to the wooden decking. Garrett was Grandpa Haydenshire's favorite grandchild by a long shot. It was no secret.

"He's at the beach house for the weekend. He'll be back for work Monday," Governor Haydenshire explained.

"Gotta girl with him?" he goaded with a heavy smirk.

"I have no doubt." Governor Haydenshire didn't look pleased despite his father's obvious approval.

"That's my boy."

"Hey, yeah, how long has Garrett been dating Chloe Sawyer?" Logan asked Will discreetly.

Will and Garrett were barely eleven months apart and were best friends, so he was the obvious person to ask.

Will shrugged. "More than a decade."

"What?" Logan gasped.

As far as they knew, the longest relationship Garrett had ever been in was three months.

"Yeah, Chloe and Garrett dated off and on for years at the

academy. They tend to hook back up whenever one of them is feeling both amorous and nostalgic."

"Logan?" Grandpa Haydenshire inquired gruffly.

"Oh no," Logan whimpered just before he replied. "Uh, yes, sir?"

"You churning the butter of that hot mess in there that kept making eyes at you at dinner?"

Logan blushed violently as Will and Connor began laughing.

"Dad, please," Governor Haydenshire scolded.

"You listen to me," Grandpa Haydenshire commanded. "She's a mess of gorgeous chaos, son, and she'll either keep your fire lit forever, or she'll burn your house to the ground and smoke the ashes. So you just watch how you play your hand."

Logan nodded confusedly but seemed unable to speak.

When everyone finally left, it was well after ten. Rainer was on edge after spending several hours being picked out randomly to have advice from Emily's grandfather forced down his throat, which always resulted in mortal embarrassment.

"Good grief." Mrs. Haydenshire sighed as she shot the governor a glare.

"Here, I'll do the dishes, sweetheart. You go on to bed. I know my father's exhausting." Governor Haydenshire sighed as he made the offer.

"We can do them," Rainer leapt.

"No, no, you two head on to bed. You had a rough night last night. I'll help you, Stephen," Mrs. Haydenshire said. Everyone in her general vicinity knew better than to argue.

Emily nodded and kissed Rainer's jaw. "Good night."

"Night, baby." He grabbed her and brushed a kiss across her lips. Surely he could kiss his fiancée good night without offending her father.

She smiled at him sweetly with a mischievous glint in her eye and then trailed up the stairs. Adeline and Logan engaged in a longer kiss before parting ways.

∽

After brushing his teeth with Logan, Rainer spit out the toothpaste in his mouth and then dragged a towel across his face. "That was some dinner."

Logan chuckled as he performed the same move. "I'm still not entirely sure what churning her butter actually means."

Rainer laughed. He wasn't really tired after his long nap and from being in a state of nervous embarrassment for so long. He sighed as he fell into his bed.

Logan switched on the TV, and Rainer's cell phone chirped. He grabbed it from the bedside table.

> Meet me in my hayloft at midnight! Love, the future Mrs. Lawson.

CHAPTER 37
THE HAYLOFT

A broad grin spread across Rainer's face as he glanced at the clock. A quarter to eleven. He considered his options. He knew Logan probably wouldn't have too much to say about his sneaking out with Emily, but Rainer wanted to be all alone with her. He didn't want anyone else to know where they were. He wanted the world to exist for the two of them alone for a little while.

He glanced at Logan discreetly, and smiled as Logan yawned.

"I'm kind of tired," Rainer commented.

"Really?" Logan quizzed. "You and Em were asleep forever. Mom thought it was sweet. Dad said he could live without seeing her asleep wrapped up in you."

"We didn't do anything." He sincerely hoped Governor Haydenshire knew he'd kept his word.

"I know. Dad'll get over it eventually. You know how he is about Emily. He loves you and all, but he was better with everything before you started churning her butter."

They both cracked up. Rainer settled down on his pillow and hoped Logan would follow suit. To Rainer's delight, Logan flipped through the channels with the remote instead of summoning any of the Gifted networks. He gave up and turned off the TV. He scooted down in the bed with another yawn.

"So, when do you want to move out?" he asked.

Rainer faked a yawn himself. "Don't know. Whenever Em wants to, I guess."

Logan sank his fist into his pillow before settling in. "And that will be soon?"

"I take it you're missing Adeline."

"Well, I've been meaning to talk to you about this," he drawled as a grin spread across Rainer's face. "The past twenty years or so have been great, but I think we should start sleeping with other people."

Rainer clutched his chest and feigned heartbreak as he tried hard to stop laughing.

"I can't believe you're breaking up with me. I thought we were forever."

"Yeah, well, I mean, it's not me, it's you."

"Naturally." Rainer hurled an extra pillow from the floor at Logan. He caught it and then fluffed it dramatically. "If you're about to pretend that pillow is Adeline, I'm leaving."

Another hearty round of laughter played out before they settled down once again.

He decided silence was probably the best way to get Logan to sleep, so he refrained from any further comments. As he watched the minutes tick by slowly, he allowed himself to fantasize.

By 11:50, he'd filled his head so full of Emily that his entire body ached with a pain only she could heal. He'd been picturing her in the pale pink, see-through gown, with the black G-string, and then letting the way her skin felt as he'd pulled the silky gown off of her sear through his mind.

The way she tasted, the way she moaned and called his name as he pushed her over the edge. The heady scent of her, and the way her body felt when he pushed inside her. Her sweet gasping groan as he took her. His heart hammered. His muscles pulled taut in desire and expectation as he slid the covers off.

He studied Logan as he moved silently toward the door. He prayed he was really asleep and pulled on the shorts he'd had on earlier in the day. After grabbing his flip-flops, he decided not to put them on until he was on the porch.

"Have fun," Logan mumbled. He turned over and repositioned himself as Rainer reached the door. Before Rainer could ask, Logan yawned. "Saw Em sneaking a few quilts out there earlier."

"Plan to." Rainer pulled the door closed.

He eased across the wooden slat floor and took small, light steps as he neared the stairs and the Haydenshires' bedroom. He prayed they would remain asleep as he tiptoed down the steps.

With a sigh of relief, he edged across the entryway and around the pile of the twins' toys in the living room. He cursed under his breath as he stepped on one that squeaked. Someone chuckled, and he spun toward the kitchen. His eyes goggled, and his heart pounded.

"She's waiting for you." Patrick gestured his head toward the barn in the Haydenshires' backyard as he slid by Rainer with equal effort to remain silent. He was late for his new curfew, the one he'd been assigned for a few weeks after Lucy had been caught spending the night in his room. He slapped Rainer on the back. "I'm going to try really hard not to think about what you're going to be doing to my little sister, but from one guy to another—I hope you have fun." He shook his head slightly.

Rainer allowed himself an embarrassed chuckle as relief flooded through him. "Thanks for not saying anything."

"I'm no snitch. You don't grow up in a family with ten kids and survive if you tattle."

Rainer waved to Patrick as he eased the Dutch door open. He pulled it closed silently, slipped on his flip-flops, and tried not to run to the small barn behind the Haydenshires' home.

The larger barn sat on the gravel driveway across from the house. It had been converted to hold all of the cars owned by the different members of the family.

Another barn, this one much smaller, sat behind the house. It held Christmas decorations, old furniture, school projects, and other things with either very little usefulness or that were only needed a few times a year.

The hayloft had always been Emily's hideout. When her brothers got to be more than she could handle, or when she wanted to play dolls or some other decidedly girly game that the boys would tease her for, or when she wanted to think or just be alone to process the sheer amount of emotional energy she had to take on each day, she could usually be found in her loft.

She and Rainer had made out in it numerous times, but he'd never snuck out of the house to meet her in it in the middle of the night. Since all of Emily's family knew that's where she liked to go, it didn't offer a great deal of privacy.

Rainer's heart raced as he reached the barn door. He could see the flickering candlelight from the doorway. He forced himself to calm and not sprint up the ladder.

He made himself feel the soft well-worn rungs and inhale the scent of the red wood barn mixed with pine from the Christmas décor. Then he caught it—the soft floral scent of Emily's perfume along with the delicious, heady scent of her.

"Hey there." He crested the top rung and climbed up into the loft. He had to lean forward to walk up there.

She grinned at him coyly. Her hair hung in soft auburn waves. Her face had been scrubbed clean of all her makeup. She was wearing his navy blue Ioses T-shirt and was seated cross-legged as she gazed up at him. He could see the hem of a pair of his boxers peeking out from under the shirt.

He chuckled and slid beside her on the quilt she'd spread over the worn wooden flooring.

"Those look familiar." He tugged on the hem of the boxers. She giggled and gave him a look that threatened to set him on fire.

"You can have them back if you take them off of me." A storm of passion and desire swirled rapidly in her eyes.

He groaned and turned his head. He cradled her face in his hands as he devoured her mouth.

"Is that what you want, baby?" he asked between his hungry kisses. She gave a heavy nod as her breath came in quick, stuttered pants of expectation.

He devoured her mouth, too consumed with need to work slowly, as he slid her bottom lip between his teeth and felt it swell in his mouth. He gazed at her as she gasped for breath. He wanted her so badly he could taste it.

Her lips were ripe for his kiss, her eyes dark and eager with curiosity lit in their depths. She was flushed and couldn't quite catch her breath. As he watched her sit there in the candlelight of her childhood playroom, wanting him, it threatened to drive him right over the edge. He slid his thumb over her lips tenderly and caressed her face.

"I just want you." She let her eyes close as he brushed a kiss across her forehead. "I want to feel you. I don't want anything else. I just want to be with you," she pled, and he groaned in reverent need.

"Where do you want to feel me, baby?" He wanted to hear her tell him.

She didn't answer audibly. She did something much better. With a wickedly virtuous grin, she grabbed his hand and pulled it to the slit in the boxers she was wearing as a ravenous growl echoed from him. His eyes flashed as he stared at her with a look that said he'd drink every last drop of her gorgeous body if he were able.

"Lay back, baby." He moved another of the quilts she'd brought behind her back. "I want to touch you. I want to taste you. I want to suck those sweet lips until you let me drink you." His tone bordered on a command, but he couldn't help it.

The pent-up desire swirling in his body had him bound. She didn't seem to mind. His orders seemed to ignite a fire deep within her as she slid down the quilt. Her eyes were begging and needy as she reclined on the folded quilt he'd placed behind her. He kept up the mildly dirty talk as he tried to discern what she wanted. He concentrated to both feel and see when her energy spiked.

"I'm gonna take these off. Let me see you and give you what you want." He traced over her. "I want to hear how good I make it feel."

She moaned as her abdomen clenched under his touch and her energy gave a tantric pulse. He smiled and let it wash through him as he slid the boxers down her legs.

His orders and his promises had the soft red curls between her legs already glistening in the candlelight, and he moaned as he traced his fingers over them.

He separated her but didn't enter her yet. The humid air caressed her folds. He concentrated as she spiked violently, just like she did just before he sent her over. Her body writhed from the anticipation alone, and he reveled in everything he learned. He decided to continue to test her. He blew hot breath over her as he pulled her apart tenderly. Her body bucked wildly. She was unable to lie down. The sensation pulled her tight.

"Rainer, please," she whimpered, and he throbbed as he listened to her ask for it. With a moan, he lavished his tongue over her inner lips. She writhed and fell back as she hoisted her hips up to push him in deeper.

"Does that feel good, baby?"

She panted and groaned in ecstasy. Determined to find out just how dirty she might like it, he continued to concentrate on her body's rhythms and how they dipped and spiked according to what he did and what he said.

"I'm gonna do it again, baby. I'm gonna lick your clit and suck you until you let it go. Until I can taste you. I want you in my mouth."

"Oh, god yes," gasped from her.

He dragged his tongue back over her and began alternating his fingers and his tongue and then he delved between her folds. He sucked her lips and moved to suck her clit gently with his mouth. She came undone instantly as she cried out for him.

He pulled off the shorts and boxers he was wearing and grabbed her backside. He began grinding into her and letting her feel him throb against her.

The desperate, fiery need that seared through his entire body from deep within his groin drove everything he did. He grabbed her hand. Beyond the ability to use the head above his waist, he wrapped her hand around his length, but again she delighted him by panting out a needy, "Yes!" Her eyes flashed in excitement and she stroked him.

His body seized as she pulled him and spun her thumb over his head, then she went lower, cupped him, and watched his reactions as well. She moved her thumb back up him, spreading the pearly liquid that leaked from him. She wrapped her hand around him and pulled his erotic energy straight from its source. A low raspy growl echoed from him. He grasped her waist and dragged her to him.

Rainer kept his kisses deep and constant. He consumed her mouth with his own. She worked him over, tracing him with her fingers, and then added to the pressure as she grasped him in her hand. She was exquisite. Every touch threatened to end him.

He pulled her shirt over her head. He wanted to see all of her and to feel her in his mouth. Her nipples were straining and taut from her heated desire.

Her energy was swirling rapidly all around him. He wanted to drown in it. He moved his mouth to her breasts as her head fell back.

With a loud groan, he pulled one into his mouth and groped the other with his hand. Her breath stuttered deliciously as she panted. She kept tracing him with her hands and making hungry draws of his energy. It drove him wild.

He felt her energy ebb. She seemed to study him. Before he could determine why she'd slowed, she leaned and whispered in his ear. "I want to suck you. I want you in my mouth."

A low, desperate growl echoed from him as he fought the release that threatened to end everything.

"Em, baby." He shook his head. If she put her mouth on him, he wasn't certain that he wouldn't lose it instantly. Every ounce of the copious amount of erotic energy that permeated his entire body came from his dick. To give a Gifted guy a blowjob was even more incredible than it was for a Non-Gifted male.

She released him and began kissing down his chest.

He watched her every move. He couldn't take his eyes off of her as she laid her hand on his chest and pushed him back.

She kissed along his cut lines, and he gasped and moaned. With a deliciously naughty smirk, she dragged her tongue up him as a shuddering growl overtook him. He pulsed hot and heavy in her face, and she moaned out her approval.

Rainer used every ounce of concentration in his body to push away the imminent explosion as she pulled him in her mouth. As she sucked, she began drawing the erotic energy from him to fill the storehouse in her mouth. Their energies combined readily. Unable to help himself, he thrust his hips upward. He wanted her to take him deeper.

She moaned and slid more of him in her mouth. He grasped the quilt underneath him. He needed desperately to cling to something with all of his might, lest he explode in her mouth. Suddenly, his vision clouded. His muscles tensed. Everything in him drew tight, and he had to stop her.

"Em, baby, stop." He touched her cheek. "Please." She pouted deliciously as she released him with one last swirl of her tongue. "Did you set the cast?" he panted urgently. He wanted inside of her, and he wanted it now. She nodded as her eyes flashed in ardent desire.

"Then lay down and spread your legs for me."

"Yes," she panted as she did as she was told. "Take me." She made demands all her own. He didn't have to be told twice. He lifted her hips and buried all of his straining length deep into the silken heat between her legs. As she enveloped him, he groaned out his adulation.

Her body devoured his as her energy flooded the space around him. It joined his in dizzying spirals of ecstasy. He thrust harder as her moans became longer, louder, and more desperate. He ground against her.

"You feel so damn good." He kept his thrusts deep and rhythmic.

She lost control and screamed out his name. Her body flooded hot liquid sex around him, and he was done for. He exploded inside her and filled her with all of him. He reveled in the mingling of their energy as he felt their releases combine inside of her.

She shuddered in convulsive waves. He held her as it shattered through her. She stilled, and he withdrew but kept her as close as he possibly could. He never wanted to let her go.

"You are absolutely incredible," he vowed when he regained the ability to breathe. She grinned as she lay in his arms. She kissed his chest as they stared at their combined energies spinning wildly around them. Her breasts slid up and down against him as she continued to pant.

"I don't want to go to bed without you," she whispered. "I want to stay with you."

His heart ached. "We'll move out soon. Whenever you're ready."

She nodded but refused to let go of him. He made certain that all of her touched some part of him. They lay there for a long while and watched the energy of the enthralling love they'd created dissipate slightly in the humid evening air. Her need to be near him was palpable in her rhythms as she calmed.

Eventually she sat up and pulled his T-shirt back over her body as he pretended to pout. She giggled.

Once they'd redressed, they moved down the ladder quietly. They snuck around the swing set as they headed to the back of the wraparound porch. They stepped onto the landing and removed their flip-flops, but then Rainer heard someone whispering.

He put his index finger to his lips. She nodded and moved closer to him.

He held her hand and edged to where the back of the large decking met the side porch. They halted and began listening.

"I don't know." Governor Haydenshire was whispering, but he sounded disgruntled. Emily's parents were on the porch swing on the side of the house.

Panic washed through Rainer as he tried to determine if the Haydenshires had heard him and Emily in the hayloft. They didn't sound angry.

"If you don't, they'll move out sooner than they're ready. Especially Adeline. She needs a little more stability than to be living with the kids. They all do. You know perfectly well all of the rooms in my parents' house we did it in long before we were married, and they're going to do that as well," Mrs. Haydenshire huffed.

"Please don't remind me." The governor shuddered audibly. Emily bit her lip to keep from laughing.

"I just don't think it's appropriate to tell them we don't mind if Rainer moves out of Logan's room and Adeline moves in," the governor tried for an imperious tone, but Mrs. Haydenshire just laughed.

"I think you just don't want to think about Rainer moving into Emily's room."

"Look, you and I both know they're going to sneak around, just like all the rest of them. I think we should just leave it at that. They can sneak around like every other young, unmarried American couple. Just like we did, but there's a difference in knowing they're doing that and in condoning it."

Mrs. Haydenshire sighed audibly. "You're not listening to me. Adeline needs to stay here for a while with us, and we need to make sure she doesn't feel like she's disappointing us. That's only going to drive her further away. All of them are safer here than anywhere else."

"All right, but can we talk about it in the morning, please? I'm exhausted."

Rainer pulled Emily away from the back windows of the expansive kitchen.

"Thank you," Mrs. Haydenshire said. She seemed to feel she'd gained ground for her case.

The governor huffed, and then Rainer heard the swing give its customary creak as they stood. He held his breath and pulled Emily to him as he squeezed them against the white, plank wood between the kitchen window and the downspout for the gutters. He prayed her parents couldn't see them through the windows.

They waited awhile and then decided to chance it. They opened the back door. To Rainer's relief, the house was quiet, cloaked in reticent silence as they eased toward the stairs.

After kissing her outside her door, he watched her push it open silently and then furrow her brow. He peeked inside. Adeline wasn't in Emily's bed. Rainer slunk quietly to his bedroom door, which was closed with a bra hung on the knob. Logan was playing an extremely risky hand to have hung that there. Rainer pulled a note addressed to him off of the door.

Sleep in Em's room. I'll wake you up before Dad gets up tomorrow. -Logan.

As he weighed his options for a split second, Rainer hoped Governor Haydenshire meant what he'd just overheard him say.

He eased back to Emily's room and handed the note to her. She whisked to the window to read it in the moonlight. She gave him an excited nod.

Rainer pulled off his shorts and got under Emily's quilt.

"Your dad will kill me if he finds me in here." Rebellion swirled in his shield as Emily slid into bed beside him.

She shook her head and looked thoroughly delighted. "You heard him. He expects this, and you could always blame Logan."

"Yeah, 'cause I'd do that." Rainer was offended she'd even suggest that.

"I was kidding." Then, with a delicious giggle, she wiggled until her back was to his chest.

"If you stay with me, I'll let you play," she sassed as she took his hand and placed it on her right breast. He moaned quietly in her ear.

"When you put it like that."

CHAPTER 38
WHAT IT MEANS
GOVERNOR STEPHEN HAYDENSHIRE

The furor in Dan's shield reverberated around the office. Stephen tried to remain calm. He watched Dan pace as Mason Willow carried on a rather heated debate over the phone with the Non-Gifted District Attorney.

Stephen rubbed his temples and drew measured breaths. He couldn't bury another child any more than he could watch the magnitude of what was coming crush them. It was simply more than he could withstand. Something had to be done. Dominic Wretchkinsides could not be allowed to hunt the Haydenshires for sport.

Dan's jaw clenched with every armored step he paced.

Stephen had come up with excuse after excuse to keep the kids on the farm all week, but they were determined to go out into the world. It's what they were supposed to do, he reminded himself.

It was Friday evening, and Rainer had plans to take Emily out to try and get her mind off of her tryouts the next day.

Her tryouts—his lungs begged for air he couldn't seem to provide.

"I'm adding in extra security at the arena." Dan assured as if he'd read Stephen's very thoughts. "Other than that, as long as they stay in a relatively populated place they'll be fine. There will be dozens of people at Angels Arena tomorrow morning and at the gala here. I just need to find Cascavel."

"No, that won't do. You are ruining a perfectly innocent girl's life, and you don't even care." Mason tossed the phone down and squeezed the bridge of his nose between his thumb and forefinger.

Stephen stared down the men in his office. "So, let me get this straight. Wretchkinsides has flown Cascavel, a known rapist and kidnapper, and Alexi Pravus, the man who shot and killed my son at point-blank range, back into DC, and we can't find either of them. And Adeline Parker, the love of my son's life, is about to find herself in prison with criminal drug charges that we can't do anything about. Is that correct?"

In the slight nod he received from both men, Stephen's entire world slipped from its axis.

CHAPTER 39

THE ARLINGTON ANGELS

RAINER LAWSON

Saturday morning, Rainer awoke from another night of sleeping in Emily's room.

Connor was shaking his shoulder. "Stop feeling up my sister, and get up. Mom and Dad are already getting ready for the Gala today."

Rainer's eyes flew open, and he jerked his hand away, which had indeed been slung across Emily's right breast. Quickly deciding to pretend that Connor hadn't seen that, Rainer rolled over and sat up.

"'K, thanks." He yawned.

"No problem, but I expect payback if I ever get someone to sleep over with me."

"You got it." Rainer rubbed his eyes with the heels of his hands. The governor had unexpectedly asked Rainer and Emily to babysit the night before. He and Mrs. Haydenshire needed to be up at the Senate for some reason. The twins had worn them out. Then Emily had taken forever to get to sleep. She was a bundle of nerves about her tryouts. Rainer could still feel the nervous energy rolling off of her as she lay beside him.

"Em, baby." He kissed her cheek. Her eyes blinked open, and he smiled. "Hey there, we need to get ready." He braced for another round of nervous hysteria.

"I don't want to go. I'm gonna screw up the tryout, and they'll never let me be an Angel." She hid her face under her quilt.

"Baby, you're going to be phenomenal. You always are."

"I can't do it." She sat up and clutched her stomach.

"I'll be right there waiting for you. Just do the course, and then you get to get all dressed up for the Gala, and after that, we're going to Sam's." He knew perfectly well that he was much more excited about that than she was. She groaned and fell back on the bed. "You don't have to get anything tonight. I just want you to see some."

"I know, but I can't even think about a car until I get through this tryout."

Rainer heard the governor coughing from the room next door, and he quickly kissed her cheek.

"I gotta get out of here, baby, but you're gonna do great. I know it."

A little while later, he was holding Emily's hand as he cranked the Mustang. He willed calmness into her, but she was strung so tightly she was having a hard time receiving it.

That wasn't going to bode well for her tryouts, since the position she played was to quickly determine what kinds of energy were in the course, and then change them until they were able to be used however the team might need them.

"Em, you're gonna be fine. Just chill," Logan commanded from the back seat, which did nothing but infuriate Emily.

Rainer tried to distract her as he made the drive deep into Arlington right on the Alexandria line. Mrs. Haydenshire had made Emily's favorite breakfast, but she hadn't been able to eat more than two bites. Rainer tried plying her with tea, but she wouldn't drink that either.

"Deep breath, baby," he urged as they neared the large metal warehouses on the outskirts of Alexandria, that not only held Angels Arena but concealed it from the Non-Gifted population.

Logan and Adeline had come along for moral support, and Rainer hoped fervently that Emily could calm down enough to complete the tryout sequence.

After he pulled the Mustang into a parking space, Rainer gestured for Logan and Adeline to go on in. "Are you okay?"

She shook her head. She was as white as a ghost. "Sweetheart, you're an amazing Receiver. You're going to do great!"

"Let's just get this over with."

He opened her door and wrapped his arm around her, still hoping to soothe her as they made their way into the metal building that was the size of a football field.

They came to another set of doors, and Rainer cupped his hand. He summoned the energy from himself until it glowed green. The energy to protect was the easiest for him to summon because it was the energy that existed inside of him. The doors sprung open

If a Non-Gifted person should stumble into the warehouse and couldn't summon energy, the interior doors remained locked.

Rainer pushed them open and issued Emily through. Logan and Adeline were waiting on the other side.

"They haven't set the field aegis yet, so you can walk her down," Logan informed them. He looked truly worried about his little sister. "We'll be watching from the stands." He pointed to seats in the lower middle that were suspended over the energized field. "You've got this, sis."

Emily nodded and swallowed hard. Her complexion took on a greenish tinge.

"You're going to be amazing!" Adeline grasped Emily's hand and tried to give her peace just as Rainer had but didn't get any further.

Rainer guided Emily to the steps that led out onto the field. They joined a crowd of women who were moving around the arena. Rainer's mouth dropped slightly as none other than Fionna Styler, lead Receiver for the Arlington Angels, approached them. She gave them a broad grin. "Hi, I'm Fionna. I know we met at Venton and I've been out to the farmhouse with Garrett several times, but I wasn't sure you remembered me."

"Uh...yeah..." Emily was in awe. "I definitely remember you."

Fionna Styler was stunningly gorgeous. She had deep-olive skin set off by her long, thick, brunette hair. It cascaded down her back in loose waves. She also had a phenomenal body, with legs that went on for miles. She was certainly stacked in all the right places.

Rainer had seen her a few times. She was good friends with Garrett, but they didn't hang out on Haydenshire Farm very often. She was a tremendous Receiver, probably the best in the entire Realm.

"Don't be nervous," Fionna urged. She grasped Emily's hand and squeezed it. Emily relaxed immediately. "I have a really good feeling about you, but don't tell the other girls I said that, please."

This seemed to bring Emily a great deal of peace.

"Really?"

Fionna gave her another dazzling grin. She turned and extended her hand to Rainer.

"You're Rainer, right?"

Rainer nodded. "Lawson," he offered.

She laughed. "Well, I mean, who doesn't know that?" She wrinkled her nose. "That must be extremely annoying, actually."

Rainer nodded his adamant agreement.

"So, are you two actually engaged? I'm sure most of what they print about you two isn't true."

"Oh my gosh, I want to hug you," Emily gushed as Fionna and Rainer laughed.

"That won't get any better when you make the team, unfortunately."

Emily nodded, but Rainer wondered how the press's obsession could get any worse. He tried not to grin over Fionna's very obvious assurance that Emily was going to make the team.

"He asked me at the beach a couple of weeks ago." Emily showed Fionna her ring.

"It's beautiful! Congratulations!"

"Thank you." Emily smiled, and Rainer could feel her nerves subsiding rapidly.

"Okay, you can watch from the stands," Fionna instructed Rainer. "In a few minutes, Chloe will give the instructions and everyone trying out will have a trial run where we see how fast you can change the different forms of energy and make them passable. Like I said, I know you're going to be fantastic. There are two other girls trying out for the other Receiver position, but I just know it's going to be you."

"I really hope you're right." Emily couldn't seem to stop beaming.

Rainer squeezed her hand, then leaned in and kissed her cheek. "I'm gonna go, but I'm not even going to wish you luck because I know you don't need it."

"Aww." Fionna swooned. "What a sweetie."

Rainer joined Logan and Adeline in the stands, and he was pleased they were close enough to the field to not only be able to see Emily as she stood with Fionna and awaited the other hopefuls, but to hear them as well.

The Angels were also in need of a Junior Shield and Enforcer, and two other women were lined up near Fionna and Emily under the sign for those positions. Fionna walked away to talk to Chloe and a few other Angels.

A girl with dark brown hair and eyes, who towered over Emily, sported a sneering scowl and glared at Emily hatefully.

Rainer edged closer. He could still throw his cast. The energy-field aegis hadn't been set yet. Once set, the aegis kept any energy from the crowds or anywhere else from reaching the field.

Emily's brow furrowed as she glanced at the girl. She seemed to be wondering why the girl so obviously hated her. They weren't even trying out for the same position. Emily crossed her arms over her chest. Whatever she felt in the girl's energy, it wasn't nice.

Logan and Rainer shared a worried glance. As the two other hopefuls for the open Junior Receiver position took their place behind Emily, the girl edged closer.

"You're Emily Haydenshire, right?" the girl sneered.

"Yes."

Rainer recognized Emily's tone when she feigned bravery. He grimaced. He didn't want anything to distract her from her tryouts.

"Well, I guess if my daddy was a governor, and I was letting Rainer Lawson bone me, I'd have a guaranteed position on the Angels as well."

Rainer summoned instantly. She wasn't going to get away with that. Logan grabbed his hand and shook his head. Emily gave her a confident grin. "You know, acting like a bitch won't make dogs like you any more than they do now."

Rainer and Logan bit their lips to hold in their laughter as the girl glared furiously at Emily. Whatever vicious comeback she was going to make, she was unable to say. Chloe Sawyer was now giving the ladies directions.

Adeline laughed as well and then leaned against Logan. "Emily doesn't take a lot off of people even if she is a Receiver."

Rainer and Logan nodded their adamant agreement.

A few minutes later, Rainer's stomach churned as Chloe summoned a yellow iridescent light in her hand and touched several pads located along one wall of the stadium. They watched as a light-green haze covered the field as the aegis was set. Rainer kept his eyes trained on the course in front of Emily.

"Summon!" Chloe shouted and Emily began.

"Come on, Em!" Logan called. Rainer glanced at his watch as Emily began. It was a timed tryout.

Emily entered an area that contained a glass filled with a swirling white haze, along with a line of pistons from a motor.

Emily shattered the glass, summoned the heat energy, and spun her hand to convert it until she made the pistons fire. Rainer allowed himself to breathe as she continued.

A heat lamp was positioned right beside a lantern. In under a minute, Emily had converted the thermal heat into electricity and lit the lantern. The next was a large pool of water. Emily thought for a moment and then summoned energy from around her. She touched her hand to the pool and took a full minute to freeze the water so she could move across it.

Next was relatively easy. He watched Emily pull power from a light bulb and light a fireplace. The last room contained a dozen small windmills that weren't spinning as well as large turbine engine.

"Come on, Em, you don't need to turn them all!" Logan warned, though Emily certainly couldn't hear him. Rainer prayed as Emily began moving six of the windmills faster and faster, until she was able to summon the vast amount of energy. She shuddered suddenly. It was almost too much. Rainer was terrified as he watched her, but a moment later, the engine began to turn slowly and then with more force. Emily threw open the door to stop the clock and emerged. She was taking rapid breaths as she wiped the sweat from her brow.

"Wow!" Fionna beamed. "That was great, four minutes twenty-nine seconds!" she announced proudly. "As soon as Julie and Gwen finish, we'll know." Fionna winked at Emily, but she made certain neither of the other girls saw her. "You can go up and wait with Rainer, if you want."

"Thanks." Emily moved slowly out of the field and up the steps. Rainer sprinted to the top of the stairs. He couldn't descend onto the field, so he waited on her to emerge.

"You were amazing!" He pulled her to him. "Are you okay?"

"Just a little tired." They watched Julie Gordon try out. She'd been recruited to try out before, but she was having a difficult time with the pool of water. When she finally emerged, her time was over six minutes. Emily squeezed her eyes shut and clung to Rainer's arm.

"You got it, Em," Logan assured.

"Don't say that yet."

Gwen Jeffries, a girl Rainer had never seen before, stepped into the room next. They all watched closely. Their stomachs were on edge as they all glanced constantly from Gwen to Rainer's watch. Gwen struggled as she tried to spin all of the windmills, and Rainer watched the second hand on his watch circle for the fourth time. As it made it halfway around again, he held it up for Emily.

"Congratulations, sweetheart, you just made the Arlington Angels." He hugged her fiercely. "I'm so proud of you!"

Logan beamed and tousled her hair.

"Oh my gosh!" she whispered excitedly. She didn't want to celebrate with Gwen and Julie still in the arena.

"Congratulations!" Adeline hugged her next.

"Thank you." She seemed unable to believe she'd done it. Several minutes later, Chloe released the field aegis.

Fionna smiled up at Emily and mouthed, "I told you so."

Emily laughed and beamed down at her. Chloe moved to the middle of the field and summoned a glowing fuchsia light that she used to magnify her voice.

"Okay, the Angel who ran your tryout will talk to you before you leave to let you know whether or not you'll be challenging with us this year. If not, I wish you the best of luck, and we'll look forward to reviewing you again in the future."

Fionna quickly spoke to Julie and Gwen. She looked very sorry to tell them they hadn't made it, but then she rushed up the stairs to Emily.

"Congratulations!" she squealed.

"Thank you," Emily stammered.

"Okay, go get ready, because you and Rainer can sit at the Angels' table for the Gala," Fionna instructed. She looked just as thrilled as Emily.

Emily couldn't stop grinning as she nodded. Rainer, though certainly not a Receiver, had a feeling Emily and Fionna were going to be very good friends. They seemed to share an almost magnetic connection.

"It was nice to meet you." Fionna smiled sweetly at Rainer. "I'm sure we'll see a lot of each other for the next few years."

Rainer smiled and told Fionna they'd see her at the Gala. Emily bounced up and down as soon as Julie and Gwen made their way solemnly out of the arena.

"You know what I think we should do to celebrate?" Rainer wrapped his arms around Emily and picked her up in the exuberance of his embrace.

"What?"

"We should go buy you a car."

She rolled her eyes but then grinned.

"Hey, if she doesn't want one, I'm readily available," Logan teased.

"What?" Rainer quipped as they made their way to the exit. "You broke up with me last week, man."

They both cracked up as Emily and Adeline shook their heads.

CHAPTER 40
COLLISION OF TEMPERS

Rainer hadn't thought too much about the girl who'd insulted Emily at tryouts until he pulled the Mustang into the governors' parking deck of the Pentagon. He paused to admire the motorcycle parked in the space beside his car.

Logan emerged wide-eyed. "Damn! Is that a custom Brutale 575?" he asked reverently. Rainer opened his door carefully as he nodded and gazed with rapt adoration at the bike.

"I wonder who drives that?" Logan admired.

"That would be mine," came a deep, chuckling voice from behind them. "And," Vindico drawled, "if you'll slide that way two centimeters, I'd like to set a cast that will make a person melt if they touch my bike." He didn't sound like he was joking.

"Oh, right, sorry." Rainer moved away from the bike.

They watched in awe as Vindico cupped his hand, and a brilliant green glow emitted instantly from both of his bands. He turned his hand and released the protective cast. When he finished, he slung his helmet under his arm, dusted off his suit, and led everyone toward the Pentagon.

"Have fun at the beach?" he quizzed Rainer, with a hint of irritation in his voice. Rainer smiled and gave an uncomfortable laugh.

"Yeah, we had a nice time." He tried not to blush as Vindico shot him a cocky smirk.

"Had a feeling you might."

As they made their way to the elevator, they ran into the brutish girl who had been at Angel tryouts that morning. She was attending the Gala as well it seemed. Vindico's entire demeanor changed as he glared hatefully at the girl.

"Well, well, well," she drawled vindictively. "If it isn't Rainer Lawson's whore and her gang of groupies."

Rainer narrowed his eyes. "Look, I don't know who you are or what your problem is, but why don't you go fuck yourself sideways." To Rainer's horror the girl cupped her hand and summoned a furious red heat.

"My name is Marlisa Wretchkinsides," she spat, then turned quickly to Vindico to sneer. "Sound familiar?"

Before she could release the heat cast she'd summoned, Rainer threw a shield cast over Emily that knocked Marlisa into the wall behind her.

"No!" Vindico shouted, and Rainer dropped the cast. "Damn it! We're going to work on your temper…and on your cast control. You need to know who the hell you're messing with before you throw someone. You didn't have to send her into the next fucking state. Go inside and send out a medio."

Stunned at Vindico's reaction, since she'd only fallen to the ground where she'd been standing, Rainer argued. "Fine, but she was about to burn Emily."

Vindico drew a deep breath and glared at Rainer. "I was standing right here. Do you remember who I am? I wouldn't have let anything happen to Emily."

"I can make sure she's all right, sir," Adeline offered hesitantly. Vindico nodded but stayed very close to Adeline as she moved to Marlisa. After studying her and performing a quick energy scan, Adeline smiled.

"She's fine. It just knocked the breath out of her. She'll be up in a few minutes."

"Good. Leave her there," Vindico ordered as he spun quickly and cupped his hand to draw the elevator to the top floor. He rushed them all on.

Vindico scowled for the entire ride. "You do not mess with Marlisa Wretchkinsides. That's like signing a warrant for your own death."

Rainer gave a slight eye roll. He refused to apologize for protecting Emily, so he said nothing.

Tables dressed in white linen cloths were set around the vast entrance of the Realm level. The Senate Gala happened every year in June, to celebrate the graduates from Gifted academies who were going to work for the Senate, and to show off the new Summation teams along with the Gifted hospitals in Virginia.

The Haydenshires rushed to Emily.

"I made it!" she squealed as they embraced her heartily.

"Congratulations, baby girl," Governor Haydenshire gushed.

"I knew you would." Mrs. Haydenshire beamed. The governor moved away from Emily and her mother and cornered Rainer.

"Are you sure you want to buy her a car? I'm happy to do it. She's my baby girl, and you aren't married yet."

"I'd really like to if you don't mind." He knew easing Emily out of her father's grasp and into his arms needed to be handled with a great deal of finesse.

"If you change your mind…" Governor Haydenshire pressed.

"I won't."

The governor nodded his defeat.

"I hear my baby sister is the newest Arlington Angel," came from behind Rainer and Emily.

Emily spun and threw her arms around Garrett.

"Congrats." He kissed her cheek, which made Chloe and Fionna swoon as they stood beside him.

"Come sit with us, Emily," Fionna urged, but she didn't quite meet Emily's gaze.

Rainer followed her distant stare until his eyes landed on Dan Vindico. He was talking with his father.

"Oh, okay, but I think Rainer's supposed to sit at the Iodex table." Emily hesitated as she waited for further instructions.

"Oh." Fionna smiled. "Well, you could start out at our table and then move there for dessert, maybe. A lot of people move around."

Vindico was making his way back toward them. His father and several other men were following him.

"Lawson, Haydenshire, I wanted to introduce you to the other members of Elite Iodex," Vindico still sounded furious. "Gentlemen, these are our newest members, recruited straight out of the academy. I'm sure you know Rainer Lawson and Logan Haydenshire." He gestured to Rainer and Logan. "Guys, you already met Portwood and Ericcson. This is John Ramier and Ryan Tuttle. Hope you're ready to work." Vindico eyed Rainer speculatively.

Rainer and Logan shook the hands of the men and exchanged pleasantries.

"And you know my dad, Governor Arthur Vindico," Vindico offered with a pride-filled smile.

"Yes, sir." Rainer and Logan both shook the governor's hand. They knew him well. He often worked with Governor Haydenshire, and the Vindicos and Haydenshires were good friends. Governor Vindico and Rainer's father had been friends at the academy as well.

He had a very kind face. The governor didn't have the hard, determined air of his son. He congratulated Logan and Rainer on their appointments and wished them luck. After slapping his son on the back, he moved to talk to other people.

"Uh," Rainer cleared his throat. He didn't really want to piss his future boss off any more than he already had. "Emily made the Angels this morning. I wasn't certain where we should sit," he stammered and tried to gauge Vindico's reaction.

"Are you incapable of eating without her?" he drawled spitefully. "Does she have to feed you or something, Lawson?"

"No, I just wasn't sure where I should be." Rainer ground his teeth as Logan grimaced.

"How does Marlisa know Emily?" he asked suddenly. His tone lost some of its edge.

"I don't know. She was at the Angels tryouts this morning. She's got a mouth on her."

"I trust she didn't make it."

"No, her time was terrible."

Vindico nodded with an audible sigh. "Good, but that won't stop her. I'm certain," was his cryptic response.

Officer Tuttle offered them a kind smile. "Hey, if I could sit at the Angels' table, I sure as hell wouldn't sit with us." This made Dan shake his head and laugh as he rolled his eyes.

"Congratulations, Miss Haydenshire," Vindico offered Emily.

"Thank you." Emily still seemed unable to believe she'd made the team.

"You can sit wherever you want. I don't give a damn. I only come because I have to. I can't get any work done since my office is being used to hold the food." He looked annoyed he couldn't work even though it was Saturday.

"You're sure you don't mind?"

Vindico shook his head. "I may join you. I get to talk to these yahoos all the time."

"Oh, you're welcome to. We have extra seats," Fionna stammered suddenly as she cut into their conversation. Garrett rolled his eyes at her.

"Yeah man, come on. It's a table of beautiful women. There are worse places you could eat," Garrett pointed out.

Vindico chuckled. He seemed to decide to allow that. Logan and Adeline went to sit with the medios from Georgetown Hospital.

Rainer seated Emily beside Fionna as Vindico took the seat across the table near Garrett and Chloe.

Garrett and Dan talked endlessly about work and the stunts they'd pulled at the academy. Fionna and Chloe went over just a few of the courses they had worked over the last few seasons. Rainer tried to listen to both conversations. He wanted to learn everything he could before he began work.

After lunch, dessert was served, and Crown Governor Carrington made a speech. Governors Haydenshire, Willow, Sapman, and Vindico followed him. Afterwards, everyone began clearing the tables and stood to leave.

As he took Emily's arm, Rainer noted Marlisa once again. She was standing and talking to none other than Mitchell O'Ryan. Her scowl was still her predominant feature.

"Well, there's a matched set if I've ever seen one," Logan shook his head as he and Adeline made their way to Rainer and Emily.

With a concerned nod, Rainer suddenly wanted to get Emily out of the building. They bid all of the Angels who'd come to congratulate Emily goodbye and headed to the Mustang.

"Can we take a little nap before we go to Sam's?" Emily grinned. "I'm exhausted, and I want to make sure this isn't some fantastic dream."

"Sure." Rainer opened the door for her. He made a concerted effort not to drool over Vindico's motorcycle. He heard him chuckle from behind him once again. Rainer turned suddenly and wondered how his future boss kept appearing like that.

"Tell you what, Lawson, when I finish training you, and you pass my final tests, I'll let you take it for a spin."

Rainer's mouth hung open in shock. "Are you serious?"

"I sure as hell don't joke. So, yeah, you clearly know your way around a powerful machine." He gestured to Rainer's Mustang. "Maybe I'll trade you for a spin."

"Anytime."

"After you pass my tests." Vindico released the cast on the bike. Still in shock, Rainer sank into the Mustang and grinned.

"Did he seriously just tell you that you could drive his Agusta?" Logan demanded, wide-eyed. Rainer nodded, cranked the engine, and watched as Dan slid the bike with ease out of the parking deck.

"Okay, what is up with that motorcycle?" Emily demanded.

"That's a custom MV Agusta Brutale 575," Rainer stated. "As in there are only five hundred and seventy-five models of that bike in the entire world, and every single one of them is a little different. Different modifications according to what the owner wanted. It'll fly in around 300 mph unenhanced, and it costs more than most families make in about three years' time." He was still stunned by Vindico's offer.

Emily and Adeline shared an expression that said they thought boys were silly.

"Try not to drool on it when you get to drive it, baby," Emily goaded.

"I make you no promises."

CHAPTER 41

NOT A VOLVO...A CLASSIC

A few hours later, Rainer was in the living room with Logan. They were eating cheese puffs and watching the twins play.

"What do you think she'll want?" Logan quizzed for the fifth time. They were waiting on Emily to finish getting ready to go to Sam's.

"I don't know. She can have whatever she wants. I just want her to feel safe." Rainer grabbed a handful of puffs and inhaled them.

"Ugh, I cannot believe her. How could she not want a sports car?"

"I didn't say she wasn't getting a sports car."

"You should talk her into a Porsche."

"I'm not talking her into anything."

Logan shook his head. "She's going to pick something stupid. Just let me come with you."

"No, I don't want you trying to talk her into anything. No pressure. I want her to pick whatever she's comfortable in."

Logan threw more food into his mouth. "But you're going to get Sam to enhance it, right?"

"I'm going to get him to enhance the safety features, nothing else. If she wants an enhanced engine, we can do that once she's comfortable driving again." Rainer furrowed his brow as Keaton attempted to snatch a rubber ball out of Henry's hands.

"Keaton, come play with this ball." He offered him a similar ball he pulled out of the toy bin near the couch.

"No!" Keaton shouted defiantly. "Mine!" He stamped his feet.

Logan rolled his eyes. "I hope they don't ever want the same girl."

Henry proceeded to smack Keaton in the face with the current ball. Rainer and Logan moved in, each scooping up a twin, while both of them tried to wriggle away.

A few minutes later, Emily emerged. Her face held a mixture of excitement and terror.

"Are you ready?" Rainer took her hand after he handed Keaton to Adeline. She and Logan were babysitting so the Haydenshires could have dinner out. It was a little odd that the Haydenshires were going out so often, but Rainer was glad to help out when he could.

"I guess." Emily shrugged.

"Just don't pick anything stupid," Logan begged.

"Stay out of it," Rainer demanded through clenched teeth.

He followed Emily to the door and allowed himself a moment to admire her backside in the jeans she was wearing.

"Just don't get a Volvo," Logan shouted as they opened the side door to exit.

"Shut it!" Rainer called as followed Emily to the side barn. "You don't seem to be dreading this as much as I was afraid you were going to be."

"I guess I'm kind of excited."

"Do you know how much you're turning me on right now?"

They grabbed a quick bite from a drive-thru and then proceeded back toward Alexandria.

"I still can't believe I made the Angels," Emily squealed and took a sip of her Dr Pepper.

"I knew you were going to make it. You're amazing."

As they neared Sam's shop, she began to worry again.

"What if I don't like the cars and it hurts his feelings?" Being able to read emotions off of people meant that Receivers were generally extremely kind. Hurting someone's feelings was a tremendous fear, as they could feel the pain they'd caused.

"If you don't like them, he'll find something you do like. It might take a few tries, but that's okay."

His mind went back to Marlisa Wretchkinsides that morning at Emily's tryouts. For Emily to have made the comeback she'd made meant that the energy Emily felt from Marlisa was hateful, but it also must have also felt impenetrable. Emily sensed that Marlisa disliked her so much Emily's comment wouldn't hurt her feelings. She'd hoped it would just get her to back off. Marlisa was trying out as an Enforcer, which meant she was a Vis virres Predilect. Their energy did often feel impenetrable.

Rainer pulled into the small lot outside Sam's shop and smiled. Sam definitely had a flair for the dramatic. There were several cars, under sheets, parked in the open shop and out in the lot.

Sam was dressed in his usual coveralls. He was wiping his hands on a dirty rag as he sauntered to Rainer's car. Rainer emerged and gave Sam a grin as he moved quickly to open Emily's door. The scent of oil and Old Spice aftershave set Rainer's mind at ease. He'd missed that.

"Well, if it ain't the stud and Misses Stud." Sam winked at Emily. "Are you sure you want to marry this fool?" He teased as he pulled Rainer in for a hug. She nodded readily. "Well, don't say I didn't warn you, but I will say he's got a darn sight better taste in women than he does in cars." Sam gestured to the Mustang. "Is this why we had to have red, Rain Man?" He pointed to Emily's hair.

"You know it." Rainer laughed. "So what'd you find, old man?"

Sam feigned offense. "Old? Baby boy, I am not old. I'm a classic." He strutted momentarily before continuing. "And you know what that means?" Rainer raised his eyebrows. "Means I just have to be ridden low and slow." He winked at Emily as she continued to laugh.

Rainer shook his head and joined in Emily's laughter.

"All right, all right." Sam held up his hands. "I think you'll appreciate the fine craftsmanship which I have acquired for you and your lady."

"Let's see it then," Rainer continued to harass Sam.

"Is that how he talks to you, Emily?" Sam huffed as she continued to shake her head at Rainer. "If he doesn't treat you right, you know

I'll get after his skinny white butt with an iron." He picked up a tire iron threateningly as Emily continued to giggle.

Sam moved to one of the covered cars. "So, Rain Man says, put her in something real, real safe, Sam. So, I do as I'm told." Sam pulled the cover off of a brand-new tan Volvo XC-60 SUV. Emily studied the car, but Rainer studied her. He watched as she nodded.

"It's really safe?"

"Baby girl, this is as safe as they come, but don't worry. I have you lots to choose from." Emily smiled as Sam moved to the next car. Rainer could tell the Volvo didn't do much for her.

"So, I found something just as safe, maybe a little sportier, smoother ride, right, Mrs. Rain Man?" Emily smiled as Sam pulled the covers off of the next two cars, simultaneously.

He revealed a navy blue Audi A6 and a red Mercedes C-Class. Rainer chuckled. She liked the Mercedes. His heart swelled as he put his arm around her and kissed the side of her head. Sam moved on and laughed at Rainer.

"But, then, Rain Man says, if you find something we can't live without, we'll look at that too. So, I picked these up just for Rainer's girl to try out."

He pulled the cover off of a brand-new, loaded, cherry-red Hummer H3X. Rainer moaned as Emily laughed and rolled her eyes.

"And then," Sam strutted to the final car, with a goading smirk, "I struck gold." He pulled the cover off of a brand-new, bright white, Porsche Cayman. Rainer's mouth fell open as he moved magnetically toward the Porsche.

"Sam, man, if I wasn't already engaged, I'd propose to you right now."

"Hey…" Emily feigned offense.

Sam waggled his eyebrows and threw Rainer the keys.

"You are not buying me a Porsche," Emily informed him.

Rainer laughed as he opened the passenger side door. "Maybe not, but I sure as hell am taking you for a ride in it." She shook her head, but then seated herself in the car.

"You put a scratch on her, I'll shoot you, boy."

"If I put a scratch on her, Sam, I'll shoot myself."

Sam laughed as he watched Rainer push the button to start the car.

Rainer put the Porsche through its paces and moaned occasionally as he drove. Emily continued to shake her head.

"Uh, aren't I the one who's supposed to be picking out the car?"

"You wanna drive it, sweetheart?" Rainer offered, but she shook her head vehemently. "Do you like it?"

"About how much do these cost?"

Rainer grimaced. He glanced over at her and tried to decide exactly how honest he should be. Changing her tune seemed like his best option.

"If you like this, it's more than worth the money."

"Uh-huh, how much?"

"Well, I mean, none of them are cheap."

"Yes, I know that, but how much is this car that we are currently seated inside of, Rainer?"

He mumbled the answer.

"Uh, I didn't quite catch that."

"Around one hundred and twenty large, but it's more than worth the money."

"Absolutely not!"

"Aww, Em."

"No." She was adamant. With a sigh, Rainer drove the Porsche for another few minutes and then made his way back to the shop

"Just so you know, I may cry," he teased as Emily continued to shake her head. "You know Vindico's motorcycle cost almost twice that."

"I do not care how much Chief Vindico's motorcycle cost."

"And what did we think of that, stud?" Sam drawled as Rainer opened the door.

"Smooth, but no dice. She says it's too expensive."

"Smart girl." Sam winked at Emily as she emerged.

"It *is* too much."

Sam met Rainer's gaze. "Get her what she wants not what you want her to have."

"I know, I know," Rainer sighed. He gestured to the Mercedes. "Wanna drive it?"

She bit her lip, but he could see the excitement in her eyes as she gave a hesitant nod. Sam handed her the keys.

"What if I have a wreck?" she panicked.

"You won't. I'll be right there with you." Rainer forgot about the Porsche in light of her fear. She drew a steadying breath and nodded as Sam held the driver's side door open for her.

She drove the car painfully slowly for several miles. Rainer ordered himself not to comment as he watched her.

"Why don't you take it down a few exits and then bring it back."

"Is that okay?" Panic perforated her tone.

"He's got my Mustang. He knows we'll be back."

She pressed the pedal harder. "I can see everything really well," she commented. Rainer checked her mirrors and pointed out a few of the nicer features.

"Do you like it?" he asked.

"Yeah, but I like the red SUV with the H on the back too."

Rainer chuckled. "That's a Hummer, baby, very safe, very nice. You can drive it when we get back." He wondered if she might prefer the Hummer which offered her more visibility.

She turned back the direction they'd just come from. The longer she drove the more she seemed to relax.

"It's the next left," he soothed as she began frantically trying to remember how to get back to the shop. She pulled in, and Sam smiled.

"What'd we think?"

"I like it."

"Well, that's music to my ears then, Mrs. Rain Man. Any others you want to take for a spin?"

"I kind of like that one." She pointed to the Hummer and bit her lip.

"Now, I don't sell cars to pretty ladies and their sugar daddies, if they just kind of like them. I want you to love that car almost as much as you love Rain Man."

Rainer watched Emily laugh with Sam. His heart picked up pace.

"Here are the keys." Sam made a dramatic bow and held the keys out in his hand. Emily shook her head and took them from him with a wry grin. Rainer held the door open for her and watched her as she climbed up.

"Nice view," he teased. He watched her crimson blush work from her neck to her cheeks.

Emily rolled her eyes. "You mean the car?"

"Nope." He flirted shamelessly while he stared at her backside as he helped her up in the Hummer.

"Rain Man," Sam scolded as Rainer raised his eyebrows expectantly. "No trying out the back seat, until you butter Sam's bread, and for that,"—he gestured his head to the Hummer—"fry me some bacon."

Rainer laughed. "Hey, you've seen her." He threw his head back to Emily. "I make you no promises."

Sam shook his head and laughed outright.

Rainer climbed in the passenger side and pulled the door shut. He studied Emily as she turned the key. The huge motor under the hood revved to life, and she grinned. "There's my smile."

She put the car into drive and eased off the brake. The broad grin stayed on her face as she pulled the vehicle onto the highway.

Rainer quickly decided to up the ante. He pulled his phone from his pocket and attached it to the built-in docking system. He casted it and turned on the playlist of all of Emily's favorite songs. Utter delight lit her face as she beamed at him.

"Okay, so I love it, but why are you so far away from me?" She pulled onto the interstate and pushed the gas harder. The Hummer took off.

"Low center of gravity. They're a little bit wider so they're next to impossible to flip," Rainer pointed out. "Like I said, very safe."

"And how much is this one?" She looked terrified to hear the answer. Rainer slid his hand to her thigh.

"Substantially less than the Porsche. I take it you might like to purchase it, then?" She bit her lip hesitantly but was unable to hide her grin as she nodded.

Rainer moaned eagerly. "I've been in love with you since I was like two years old, but I don't think I've ever loved you as much as I do at this moment."

Emily laughed and slapped his chest playfully as he ducked away from her.

"Well," Rainer winked at her, "if you'll get off at the next exit and take it back to Sam's, we could buy it and then try out the back."

"I can take it home tonight?" She sounded thrilled. It made his heart swell.

"You can take it home tonight, baby. We can bring it back later this week. I'm going to have Sam enhance the safety features for you, but if you want it, it's yours." He listened to her squeal. She drew a deep breath, checked her mirrors, then moved to the lane to exit the interstate.

"I'm still scared to drive."

"I know, but you're doing great, and I will keep you safe, I swear."

"I know you will."

She made her way back to Sam's, singing along to her favorite songs. Rainer grinned at her. After she pulled it back into the garage, Rainer threw the door open.

"All right, Sam, how much bacon do I have to fry you?"

"Mm-hmm." Sam gave Emily a beaming grin. "I take it Mrs. Rain Man offered to let you sit in the back seat then?"

Rainer chuckled and ran his hands over the side of the Hummer. It was a sweet ride. Emily had picked well. As she was still seated in the driver's seat, Rainer grinned up at her.

"Will you pop the hood, baby?"

She fumbled with the pull for a few moments, but then the hood spring released.

Rainer pulled the hood up, secured it, and then looked over the engine as Sam joined him under the hood.

"So, what else can we do to make this thing as safe as it could possibly be?"

Sam nodded and got down to business. "We can enhance all the exterior, the roll cage, the brakes, and the air bag systems. We can fortify the windshield, and windows. Other than that, unless you want the engine upped so she can fly away, that's all I know to do."

"Let's do it all."

"Is somebody after her?" Sam looked concerned, but Emily got out of the car before Rainer could explain.

"How much does it cost?" she asked.

Rainer shook his head. "I don't care how much it costs, sweetheart. I will do anything in the world to keep you safe."

Sam bowed his head to Rainer in an obvious sign of pride.

"How 'bout we do it all for seventy-five?" Sam murmured, clearly not certain if Emily was supposed to hear the price. Rainer furrowed his brow, then shook his head.

"That's about ten short, isn't it? Especially if we deck it out."

Sam gave Rainer his kind smile. "I have a few friends at the dealers, and if she makes you that happy, then I want her safe too. So we'll call it an early wedding present."

"Sam." Rainer shook his head. "No, I don't want you to cut your price for me. This is the perfect car. She loves it. You worked your ass off." Rainer gestured back to all of the cars Emily hadn't chosen. "At least let me pay you for it."

Sam chuckled and shook his head. "Life isn't all about the money. There's a whole lot of things much more valuable than dollars. So, how about you and Miss Emily come see me more often? Let me work on the Hummer and the 'Stang, and maybe take me out to eat once in a while, and I'd say we're more than even."

Truly touched, Rainer swallowed down the emotion that settled in his throat. "You got it, anytime."

"So, you gonna let Rain Man drive you home in that jalopy he calls a sports car, Miss Emily? Or are you gonna pull up in this fine automobile?" He stroked his hand down the side of the Hummer. Emily giggled and bit her lip.

"We still don't know how much all of this is going to be. I don't want you to spend a fortune on me."

Rainer shook his head. "Already taken care of, sweetheart. She's all yours." He grinned as her mouth fell open.

"But, no, you couldn't have done that so fast. I was standing here, and you were there." She pointed to the hood with her mouth agape.

Sam and Rainer laughed. He pulled his wallet from his pocket and removed the check. Emily tried to see the amount as he filled it in, but he shook his head, wrote it quickly, and folded the check over. He handed it to Sam, who quickly stowed it in his coveralls.

"Rainer, tell me how much this was."

"Uh-oh, Rain Man. She's got the hands on the hips. You better run, boy." Sam laughed.

Rainer kissed Emily's cheek as he moved past her. "Are you ready to go? We're bringing it back Monday night to let him start the enhancements after we all go out for dinner."

"Fine," Emily quipped, "but you are telling me how much you paid for this when we get home."

Rainer had to work hard to hold in his laughter. He cocked his jaw to the side and pulled the keys from her hands. Her brow furrowed.

"You're driving the Mustang home so I can drive this, right?"

"No."

"Then start her up, baby. It's Saturday night. I'm surprised the women aren't beating down Sam's door for a date. He *is* a classic."

"Don't you know it, baby boy." Sam wiped the side view mirror of Emily's new Hummer with the rag he'd picked up.

"Thank you so much." Emily threw her arms around Rainer and then hugged Sam tight. Sam looked truly touched as he embraced her and patted her back.

"You hold on to her tight, Rain Man." Sam helped Emily back up onto the running board and into the Hummer. "Treasure each day, 'cause they go by way too fast."

"I will. I promise."

Rainer rolled his eyes as he answered his phone for the fourth time on his drive home.

"Just tell me. I'm dying here!" Logan demanded yet again.

"She's driving it home. We'll be there in ten minutes."

"Just tell me it's not stupid."

"Goodbye, Logan."

"Come on!"

"Go play with Adeline. We'll be home in a few."

"Ugh, fine." Logan ended the call. Rainer's phone rang again, and he smiled.

"Was that Logan again?" Emily giggled.

"Yes." Rainer glanced back at her in his rearview mirror. "You know, you look really hot driving that Hummer, Miss Haydenshire."

"Oh, yeah?"

"Oh, yeah, baby." Rainer signaled once they'd reached the exit for McLean, and he turned toward the farm.

"Just wait 'til you see what I can do in the back seat," she teased.

Rainer gave her a shuddering moan. "And when might I get to see that?"

"Today has been completely amazing, so I kind of feel like tonight should be as well. Any night I get to spend with you inside of me is pretty much my idea of amazing."

Rainer almost missed the exit. "Okay, you have to stop talking like that. I'm gonna wreck my car."

They pulled onto the Haydenshires' property and waited for the gates to open.

"I'm sure Logan and Connor are waiting in the yard, so I'll see you inside, baby."

"Rainer," Emily called quickly.

"Hmm?"

"Thank you for everything. But mostly just thank you for being you and always taking such good care of me. I can't wait to be your wife."

They'd made it to the barn before Rainer could respond. Logan was sprinting toward them, so Rainer rushed the words, "I love you, baby, so much."

Before he ended the call, he heard, "I love you too." Rainer emerged from the Mustang in time to see Logan flinging open the door to the Hummer.

"Oh my gosh! You are my favorite sister ever!" He lifted Emily out of the Hummer and then he spun her away so he could see the interior.

Adeline laughed as Emily whisked to Rainer. The Haydenshires emerged from the kitchen.

"Daddy, look!"

Governor Haydenshire smiled wistfully at Emily. "Very nice, baby girl. You just promise me you'll be careful."

"I promise."

"Will you take your old man for a ride? Just through the pasture."

Emily nodded.

"Oh, I'm coming too," Logan immediately invited himself. Before she could climb back up in the driver's seat, as Connor announced he was going along, Rainer grabbed her hand and pulled her to him.

"Em, I can't wait either, to be your husband and to make you my wife."

She smiled as he brushed a kiss across her forehead and released her.

"You wanna come?"

Rainer shook his head. "Take your dad, baby. I think he misses you." She blew him a kiss and climbed back into the driver's seat.

CHAPTER 42
THINGS TO COME

Rainer followed Mrs. Haydenshire and Adeline back into the house. He seated himself at the kitchen table as Mrs. Haydenshire plied him with blackberry cobbler, made from the berries she and the twins had picked that morning.

"You're spoiling her," Mrs. Haydenshire teased as she scooped vanilla ice cream on top of his cobbler.

"She's worth it and talk about being spoiled." He gestured to the bowl. She laughed and fixed Adeline an identical bowl.

"I think you're both worth it." Mrs. Haydenshire patted Adeline's shoulder.

Although Rainer knew the comment was mainly for Adeline's benefit, he gave Mrs. Haydenshire a kind smile.

"This is delicious. I don't know what I would've done without you all these years." He wished he could somehow formulate the words to make Mrs. Haydenshire understand what she and the governor meant to him.

She gazed at him with a wistful smile. "I would never have had it any other way, sweetheart, and I know Stephen has you scared to death, but we truly couldn't be happier about you and Emily. I'm so proud of you both." She squeezed his forearm before turning to Adeline.

"Well, my sweet Adeline, are you nervous about Monday?"

"I'm nervous about how I'm going to get there. I hate for Logan to drive me into DC every day and then come pick me up. It won't be so bad once he starts at the Pentagon."

Rainer furrowed his brow.

"Why don't you just take Logan's Accord? He can drive the Mustang if he needs to go somewhere. I'm assuming Em will let me ride in the Hummer occasionally."

Adeline and Mrs. Haydenshire laughed.

"Are you sure?" Adeline quizzed. "That's so nice of you."

"It's no problem."

"Thank you. I don't know what I'd do without all of you, either."

Mrs. Haydenshire took Adeline's hand. "You don't ever have to find out because we're not going anywhere." She studied Adeline closely.

Rainer watched her. He noted the depth of wisdom and knowledge that her face held. She seemed to know something that Rainer didn't understand, something outside of Adeline's conscious thought. She seemed to be seeing more in the situation playing out in her kitchen than anyone else seated at the table. Whatever it was that she knew, judging by the look on her face--it wasn't good.

"Thank you." Adeline managed a smile.

Emily and Logan burst into the kitchen. Governor Haydenshire and Connor followed behind them.

"I said I would think about it." The governor's jaw clenched in annoyance.

"Think about what?" Mrs. Haydenshire asked.

"The old guesthouse," Emily announced. This only further confused Rainer and her mother.

"What about it?" Mrs. Haydenshire asked.

"They want you to let them turn it into a love shack for the four of them." Connor laughed as he disappeared to the living room and flipped on the TV.

Everything about Emily's expression said she wasn't going to be dissuaded. She tugged on Rainer's hand. "We'll take Rainer and Adeline to see it, and you two can talk about what a great idea it is."

"Where is it?" Rainer had never even heard of a guesthouse. Logan rolled his eyes at Emily before pointing to the west.

"It's on the other end of the property. We've never done much with it. It needs a lot of work." He seemed to be trying to reason with Emily. Rainer knew that was a futile task when she was this determined.

"We could fix it up and then we'd still be on the farm. We wouldn't have to move away. If we do all the work then we do move, if you wanted, you could sell that end of the property and the house with it."

"We're not selling any part of our property, Emily Anne," Mrs. Haydenshire stated with a slight chuckle, "but that is an excellent idea."

As Rainer had never seen the house, he wasn't certain what an appropriate comment would be. If Emily was there, that's where he wanted to be. He didn't think that was what her father wanted to hear, however. "How big is it?"

"No one has agreed to this yet. I think it would be better for you all to stay here," Governor Haydenshire insisted.

"But you will agree to it." Emily pulled on Rainer's arm. "Come on, I'll show you." She turned to Logan. "If you'll be sweet, I'll let you drive."

"Deal," he immediately agreed. He took Adeline's hand and led her behind Rainer as he caught the keys Emily tossed to him.

"Do not get mud on my tires," Emily demanded as Rainer opened the door.

Logan scoffed, "It's a Hummer. It's supposed to have mud on it. And I'm driving through our pastures, so I'm not sure how I'm supposed to avoid that."

"Just be careful."

"I'll wash it for you tomorrow, baby." Rainer was extremely pleased that she was so taken with the car.

After rolling his eyes in disgust, Logan opened Adeline's door for her and then crawled into the driver's seat. "I'll wash it for you tomorrow, baby," Logan mocked Rainer in a high-pitched squeal. "Seriously, she cannot be that good in bed." He cranked the engine.

Adeline glared at him. Emily narrowed her eyes, but Rainer knew he had his number.

"She sure as hell rocks my world. You wanna hear about it?"

Logan convulsed. "Kidding. I was only kidding."

Emily and Adeline laughed as Logan continued to shudder and pretend to be sick.

"Tell me about this guesthouse." Rainer leaned forward and popped Logan on the back of the head for being crude.

"It's small." Logan rubbed his head.

"I'm not healing you. You deserved that," Adeline quipped as Emily and Rainer cracked up. Logan pretended to pout.

"How small?" Rainer tried to refocus everyone.

Emily shook her head. "It's not that small. I mean, it's smaller than the farmhouse obviously, but there are four of us not fourteen, so it's plenty adequate. It's a two-bedroom bungalow. I'm sure it needs some cosmetic work, but as far as I know, the plumbing and everything works. We don't have to even have the power hooked up, because no one would know we were living in it. We could just cast everything." She tried to strengthen her case.

Though Gifted people didn't necessarily need public utility electricity, most often they subscribed to it to keep the Non-Gifted from becoming too curious. It was also a great convenience. Every cast cost a Gifted person energy. Keeping multiple permanent casts in place would drain a person of their resources.

"It mainly just needs to be cleaned up," Emily commented.

"Your dad didn't seem too thrilled with the idea."

"Mom will talk him into it because she doesn't want us to move away."

Rainer had to agree with her reasoning.

"It would be kind of cool," Logan admitted. Rainer chuckled at his unwillingness to give his little sister any credit. "So, who are you thinking will get the master bedroom?"

Emily shrugged. "I don't see how it matters. They both have bathrooms, and they're about the same size."

Logan drove farther than Rainer had ever been on the

Haydenshires' land. He pulled up to a square abode. Bushes, weeds, and vines covered the outer walls. Rainer emerged from the back seat and helped Emily out.

"The porch is a little creaky," she lamented as they made their way to the front door.

"There's a garage in the back, but it's a mess," Logan explained.

Rainer smiled to himself. He would never have admitted it audibly, but he didn't want the Mustang out in the elements.

"This is more than a little creaky." Rainer picked Emily up and lifted her onto the porch as Logan did the same for Adeline. The porch steps were collapsed, and the porch itself was sunken in the middle.

"It needs work, but we could do it," Emily insisted.

Rainer chuckled. Though he and Logan had always worked the vast gardens and repairs around the barns and farmhouse growing up, he'd never seen Emily on the tractor or swinging a hammer.

Logan and Rainer grasped the only porch railing that appeared able to hold their weight and vaulted themselves over. Rainer braced himself, but the wooden slats proved sturdy as they landed.

Rainer summoned and lit the lights beside the front door and the two in the outdoor fans on either side of the porch that stretched along the front side of the bungalow. The pale yellow paint on the sides of the wooden home was peeling, and a feral cat screeched off the porch.

Emily shuddered as Rainer raised his eyebrows and wondered if she might be reconsidering. Logan turned the loosened knob on the door and threw all of his weight behind it as he forced it open. Some of the casing fell in as it creaked open. Logan batted away dust and insulation as it cascaded down in front of him. They coughed away the stale musty air that was thick with dust and mildew.

Logan cupped his hand and lit an old fixture that hung in the room. Adeline stepped in over the loosened doorsill.

"It does need some work, but I would love to fix this up for your parents. At least that's something I could do to help for all they've done for me."

Logan shook his head but then moved away so Emily and Rainer could enter. Rainer took in the room around him. It was a narrow entry hallway that led to a decent-sized living room. He edged forward and tested each of the slats of the hardwood floor before he would allow Emily or Adeline to cross.

They emerged in the living room. He took in the mildewed flooring with a grimace, but the room had a large working fireplace and built-in bookshelves. A bay window with a bench seat, that he knew Emily would love, was carved out of the back wall.

"All the flooring would have to come out," he commented as he studied Emily to see how she would take that news.

"Is that bad?"

Logan shrugged. "Not terrible if that's the worst of it, but it'll be quite a job."

With that, Logan pried a worn spot on the floor with his tennis shoe. His foot sank down a solid foot. "Yeah,"—he pulled it back out—"they all have to be redone." His eyes goggled. "Oh shit!" He spun quickly as he backed Adeline away from a snake uncoiling itself up out of the hole he'd just created.

Emily screamed and dug her nails into Rainer's biceps. He summoned and casted his shield over her. He pushed it out over Adeline as well.

Logan cupped his hand and harnessed the snake. He pulled the energy out of it, but he didn't want to it on himself, so he threw it off and let it dissipate into the air.

Rainer watched. He vividly remembered the dark, steely gray smoke that had come out of the copperhead he'd watched his father kill.

This snake keeled over quickly, and what Logan released into the air was only a faint, white heat. A second later, it was over.

Rainer contemplated as he watched Logan kick the snake's lifeless body back into the crawl space under the bungalow.

"I don't want to live here with snakes." Emily was shaking in her fear.

"We'll get rid of those when we rip out the floor," Rainer assured her.

"Are there more?"

"I don't know. Do you want to leave and come back tomorrow when it's light?"

"No, we have to give Mom time to talk Dad into it."

They continued to study the space but moved with extreme care as not to disturb any more of the rotted flooring. Off the living room was a decent-sized patio that needed to be completely rebuilt.

The living room opened into the kitchen with no wall between. The kitchen consisted of an island complete with bar seating.

The back wall of the kitchen held more counter space and a sink. A refrigerator that appeared to have last worked in the late 1960s stood in one corner. It was teal blue, with a freezer on the bottom. The brand name Kelvinator was scrawled across the top in peeling, silvered letters that stated that it was frost-free.

Logan scowled as he glanced through the hole into the cabinets below. There were windows above the sink and a place for a cooktop on the island. Part of the cabinetry was hollowed out to hold a double oven along the wall. A small breakfast nook was off the kitchen beside a set of stairs.

"I thought it was one story." Rainer pointed to the steps.

"Just attic space up there, I think. How 'bout we look up there tomorrow if we decide we're gonna do this," Logan said.

Past the stairs was a coat closet and a small laundry room that led to the garage. No one seemed to have the stomach to investigate the closet or the garage, so Rainer led Emily to one of the bedrooms.

"This is the smaller one," she hesitated. She was still concerned that the snake might have friends. She cupped her hand and lit the fixture in the room. It was relatively small but would hold a queen-sized bed. There was nothing in the room, but the flooring didn't appear to be as badly damaged as the common areas.

Emily headed to the closet and whispered, "Please, please don't let anything be living in here." Rainer moved to her as she edged the door open and promptly screamed. He casted her instantly but then released it and chuckled as he kissed her cheek.

"I don't think I need to protect you from hangers, baby." He lifted one of the swinging paper-covered hangers with advertising for Miss Daisy Mae's Dry Cleaners established in 1957.

"Sorry, little jumpy, I guess. I hate snakes," she admitted as if that were some kind of failing on her part.

"I know, sweetheart." He closed his eyes and willed calm into her which she took rapidly. The feeling made his heart hammer as he felt her calm under his soothing energy.

The room held another bay window with a bench seat and a bathroom on the opposite side of the door.

After guiding Emily to the bathroom, Rainer casted the light in there as well. There was baby-pink tile everywhere. The tub-shower combination was also pink. The counter did have a double sink, but they were shaped like seashells and made into the pink plastic countertop.

"Okay, so the flooring and the bathroom have to be redone." Rainer shuddered slightly as Emily giggled.

"What'd you scream for?" Logan demanded as they located them in the bathroom.

"Sorry, just a little jumpy."

"The other room's just like this. It's off the living room. The closet's a little bigger, and the bathroom is blue instead of pink."

Rainer could tell he was already figuring the square footage and the amount it would cost to replace the worn fixtures in the home.

"Hey," Rainer urged, "if we all want to do this, I would be delighted to foot the bill. I would love to be able to do something for your folks."

Logan gave him a genuine smile. "It'd be a lot of work."

"Yeah, no joke." Rainer looked around at all that needed to be done.

"I really, really want to." Adeline's plea shocked everyone in the room.

"You want to do this?" Logan quizzed disbelievingly.

Rainer wasn't sure if he was shocked she wanted to live there or that she'd actually asked for something.

"I want to do something for your parents, and I can't help out financially, but I can work. It would be nice to make it ours, I think." She looked nervous about making the request. Emily turned her pleading gaze on Rainer, the one he'd never been able to turn down.

"It'll take us weeks. Especially once we all start working."

Both girls nodded their acceptance.

"We could start tomorrow, and Adeline is only working half days next week," Emily pointed out hopefully.

"We have to get all new appliances, and we will need to get the electricity hooked up unless you want to hold a permanent cast on the refrigerator and water heater," Logan reminded her as Emily nodded her acceptance of that as well. "It'll be a lot of money, man. Are you sure?"

Rainer nodded. That was the one part he was most excited about. As he began considering turning this into a place that could actually be inhabited, he thought of a few other perks.

He knew, deep down, Emily didn't want to leave the farm. She loved it there. The gates surrounding all of the land kept the press at bay, and her parents didn't even want them to move out of the farmhouse. Moving on the same property had to be better than moving downtown or out into Alexandria. It was always safe there. *She* was always safe there, and that was all that mattered to him.

"I'm in if you are." Rainer grinned.

Logan nodded. "If that's what she wants, then I'm all in."

Adeline glowed over his pledge.

"And you'll get rid of all the snakes?" Emily shuddered.

Rainer pulled her to him, wrapped her up in his arms, and grinned.

"I promise. Can I make one request-slash-offer? If it's okay with Em, I thought maybe we could take the smaller bedroom if we could put the Mustang and the Hummer in the garage."

Logan chuckled and shrugged. "I don't care, but we could expand the garage. It's open on one side, so it wouldn't be hard."

Rainer nodded. He was perfectly willing to do whatever was necessary to keep his convertible out of the rain.

"All right, well, we have two weeks until we start at Iodex."

"Is it just me and you, or can we call in a few favors?"

"I'm sure all the Haydenshire brothers will help us out. We'll just be forever indebted to them, so remember that."

"What about furniture?" Adeline asked.

"Mom and Dad have a lot in the storage barn, and we could buy a few pieces once we all start getting paid," Emily suggested. Rainer immediately offered to fund that as well.

"No, we can all chip in on that." Logan's tone bordered on offense, so Rainer backed down.

CHAPTER 43

ROUGH TERRAIN

"Here." Logan threw Rainer the keys to the Hummer as they headed back outside. "I'm gonna call in a few favors on the way home." He winked at Adeline.

"Do you mind?" Rainer held the keys up and raised his eyebrows hopefully as Emily shook her head.

"I don't mind and," she drawled, "since my car isn't a stick, you can hold my hand while you drive us."

Rainer opened her door for her. Logan was already on the phone with Levi, or Rainer was certain he would've teased them for Emily's comment.

"Yeah, man, that'd be great. Are you sure you don't mind?" Levi was an architect at a firm in DC. He was currently designing a building that would change the skyline of the city. He was the ideal choice for their project. "No." Logan shook his head. "Em thinks Mom will be able to talk him into it."

Rainer eased the Hummer over the rolling hills back to the farmhouse. He smiled at how well it handled. After another round of thanks—and promises that Rainer and Logan would help Levi move Sarah in with him without letting the Haydenshires know they were living together—Logan hung up.

"We're gonna owe so many favors it's not even funny." He touched

Will's name on the contact list of his phone. Rainer chuckled as he pulled the Hummer into the barn beside his Mustang.

"Well, if she's sick," he heard Logan lament. "No, don't do that. It's okay." There was a long pause. "You sure?" Logan shrugged. "Yeah, I mean, that'd be great, but I don't want you to..." his concern was drowned out by Will. "Maybe see how she's feeling in the morning," Logan offered kindly. "I really appreciate it."

"We," Rainer corrected loudly.

"Okay, *we* really appreciate it," Logan amended. "Yeah, if you'll call Garrett and see if he and Chloe plan on surfacing anytime soon, then I can go listen in on Mom and Dad's conversation."

Emily and Adeline giggled as everyone exited the Hummer.

Logan placed his index finger over his lips and quieted everyone as they approached the side porch steps near the kitchen door. They could see the Haydenshires seated at the kitchen table absorbed in discussion. Logan cupped his hand and closed his eyes in concentration.

"You catch it. I'll amplify it," Rainer whispered. What they were about to do was rather difficult and also on the darker side of using Gifted energy, not that it had ever stopped them before.

Logan leaned in and placed his hand on the door. It took several minutes until he was able to catch the frequency of vibrating arcs of the sound energy of his parents' conversation.

After nodding to Rainer, Logan waited as Rainer cupped his hand until a faint glow appeared, and then he placed the back of his hand to the back of Logan's hand. He projected the conversation tentatively, and they all leaned in to listen.

"We could use Emily's room as a nursery for the twins, or as a guest bedroom," Mrs. Haydenshire sounded insistent. Emily's mouth fell open in shock.

Rainer shook his head at her. "Were you planning on leaving me and coming back home to live?" She shook her head and then leaned in. Her father was talking.

"Or, we could put the twins in Levi and Cal's room just like we'd been planning, and they can stay here where they are safe," Governor Haydenshire argued. He sounded weary. Mrs. Haydenshire sighed.

"They are going to move out, but if we let them do this they'll still be here. We can make certain they're safe. I'm scared too. I cannot lose another child. I need to know all of them are safe and sound. But they're not going to stay here in the house with us. I haven't slept in weeks just thinking about Logan and Rainer working for Icdex. Now, please."

Everyone sitting on the porch listening to the conversation felt like they'd been sucker punched. Tears sprang to Emily's eyes.

"They'll be fine. I truly believe that," Governor Haydenshire soothed. "Daniel will train Rainer and Logan. Emily will be fine, and we will take care of Adeline."

"You just keep telling yourself that. You keep convincing yourself that it couldn't happen to us again," Mrs. Haydenshire spat as Logan and Rainer shared a quick, uncomfortable glance.

"Fine," Governor Haydenshire conceded. "Can I please just have tonight to think it over? We can tell them in the morning. The house is in disrepair. If they want it, then they're going to have to work for it."

"That will be good for them, and when have Logan and Rainer ever not done whatever needed to be done? Give them a little credit."

Silence loomed, and Logan closed his eyes again to make certain he hadn't lost the frequency of the fluxing sound waves.

"Lillian,"—the governor's voice was pleading and haggard—"I know that, all right? All I'm asking for is a little time to consider. I know what fine young men they are, and I couldn't be more proud of either of them. I'm working on it, but every time I see him kiss her, or touch her, or I see that look in her eyes when she sees him, right now, what I see is the guy who took away my baby girl. The one who took away her innocence and who has her in his bed. And I don't care what an extraordinary young man he is, or what an extraordinary family he comes from, or how much he loves and adores her." Governor Haydenshire paused as Rainer reeled from the gut-wrenching confession. "And you know I love him like he was my very own, but this is difficult for me. Harder than with any of the boys. She's my little girl." Emotion strangled him.

The air squeezed forcefully from Rainer's lungs. He was unable to draw in renewed breath as tears spilled down Emily's face. He held her, not certain what else to do. Logan gave him a sorrowful gaze and slapped Rainer on the shoulder with the hand he wasn't using to channel his parents' conversation.

Mrs. Haydenshire urged, "I do know that. I know she's your baby girl, but she isn't a child anymore. You couldn't ask for a finer man than Rainer Lawson to be the one she gave that to, which was, by the way, entirely her choice. He didn't force her into his bed. She asked to go there." Her tone told everyone hearing it she wasn't to be argued with.

"And if you'll just give him an ounce of the credit he deserves, you'd realize he proposed to her the next day. He has only ever been with Emily, and will only ever be with her. That's the man we helped raise. He will be true, and good, and faithful to her for the rest of their lives. And you should really just get over her being your baby girl, and get down on your hands and knees and thank the Lord for him. Because as much as this hurts you, and as hard as I know this is…she isn't your baby anymore. She's his."

Mrs. Haydenshire's diatribe drowned out as they heard the infuriated click of her footsteps as she exited the kitchen.

Logan released the cast. No one spoke. No one knew what to say. Quiet tears leaked on Rainer's shoulder from Emily's eyes. He knew it wasn't a lamentation of what had happened. It was a release of what she was letting go.

Logan touched Adeline's shoulder. "Why don't we go get some milkshakes from Mae's? We'll bring you some back."

Rainer didn't respond. He tightened his grip on Emily, kissed her forehead, and wiped away her tears.

As Logan's Accord drove away, Rainer pulled Emily up to the porch swing.

"Are you okay?" He set his shield out over her.

She nodded, but he knew she wasn't, not really. He continued to wipe away her tears, not certain what he could say to take the pain away. It was just like the first night he'd ever been with her. He couldn't heal her, because then it would hurt the very same way the next time.

His heart ached that she had to go through the pain of growing up, of letting go, of leaving the security and certainty of her childhood, to step out in a world that was often cold and cruel, one that he knew all too well.

"I will always be there. You don't have to do this on your own." He held her tightly and soothed her with the gentle glide of the swing. She raised her head and gave him a forced smile.

She shook her head suddenly. "I'm not crying because I don't want to marry you or move out and be with you. I want all of that more than you'll ever know. I just hate that it hurts him so much. I can feel what it's doing to him. I can feel how hard this is for him, and it kills me."

He wrapped his arms around her tighter and let her cry. He consoled her with whispers of how much he loved her and how much her father loved her. He promised her that they wouldn't do anything until she was ready.

Though he meant every word he'd said, he knew she was ready. It was the governor who wasn't, and he knew how hard that must be for her to feel.

"Do you want me to take you to bed?" he finally offered. He hoped sleep would bring her solace and peace. She rubbed her eyes as she shook her head.

"No, Logan's bringing me a milkshake," she explained with a hesitant smile that made him chuckle. "But then I want you to, and I want you to hold me all night."

"Of course. There's nowhere else I'd be." His words seemed to bring her a modicum of peace.

By the time Logan and Adeline returned, she'd stopped crying and was cradled on Rainer's chest on the swing.

"Do we still wanna do this?" He handed Emily a vanilla shake and Rainer a chocolate one.

"Thanks, man."

With a begrudging chuckle, Logan sighed. "I guess I should really lay off and be thankful that it's your ring she's wearing and for how you take care of her."

"Thank you, Adeline." Rainer laughed. He knew where that must've come from. Adeline smiled sweetly.

"At least he listened," she pointed out.

"You got me extra cherries!" Emily rejoiced.

"And I'm not even gonna make a dirty comment about that." Logan smirked.

"Surely our moving on the farm is better than us moving to Alexandria or into the city." Emily sighed.

"After everything Mom said, I'm sure Dad's gonna go along with this, so maybe we should hit the sack," Logan said. "Garrett called me to ask me if I was crazy but then agreed to be here early tomorrow morning, so we have a crew." He seemed shocked by his brothers' willingness to help, but Rainer wasn't.

That's what the Haydenshires had always done, especially since Cal's death. If one of them needed something, they were there to help, no questions asked. They were a family, one Rainer would never feel worthy of joining.

"Come on, baby." Rainer helped Emily off the swing as she finished her milkshake.

"I'm sure Mom and Dad are already in bed, so are we...?" Logan hemmed.

"I'll see you tomorrow," was Rainer's reply as to where everyone was going to sleep.

A broad grin spread across Logan's face. "I guess once we finish the house, we won't have to ask that anymore."

"Yeah," Rainer nodded. "And I'll actually be able to sleep past five a.m."

Emily gave him an appreciative grin as she grasped his hand.

"You don't have to sleep in there with me if you don't want to. You could stay in Logan's room so you can sleep in."

"Yeah, but you're so much prettier than Logan, and he never lets me get to second base."

Everyone laughed quietly as they tried not to wake the Haydenshires.

"Night," Rainer whispered as Logan and Adeline turned to the left to proceed to Logan's room, and Rainer and Emily tiptoed into hers. After pulling off his shirt and shorts, Rainer studied Emily.

"Feeling any better?" he soothed, and she wound her arms around his chest and sighed contentedly.

"Now that I'm in here with you I'm perfect."

"You had a huge day." He began running his hands through her hair trying to soothe her.

"Do you honestly want to move into the guesthouse, or are you only going along with all of this for me?" She studied him intently.

"I think it's perfect as long as your parents don't pop in all the time. I want you to be safe, and this farm is pretty damn safe. I really do want to do something for your parents, and this seems like a great way to do that."

"Yeah, that's what I was thinking, and not paying rent will be good for Adeline until she starts getting a paycheck, anyway."

Rainer kissed her forehead tenderly and let his hands rub up and down her back. Occasionally, he dipped them lower.

"Let's go to bed, baby. I have a feeling tomorrow's going to be a long, hard day."

Emily giggled, and then with a deliciously naughty smirk she sassed, "I like it when you're long and hard."

He grabbed her backside, and kneaded it hungrily.

"Your parents are right on the other side of that wall." He pointed to the wall separating the Haydenshires' bedroom and Emily's.

"I know," she lamented.

"And like I said, you've had a hell of a day. So, why don't we go to sleep, and maybe we'll try out the back of the Hummer tomorrow night?" He listened to her sweet laugh.

She seemed to consider something as he brushed a kiss across her cheek. After whispering that he was going to brush his teeth, he promised he'd be right back.

CHAPTER 44

THE BEST-LAID PLANS

When he returned to Emily's bedroom a few minutes later, he found her laid out on the bed on her side. She was wearing an emerald-green, satin top with delicate black lace detailing and matching shorts that were so short they may as well just have been panties. Her breasts were only slightly obscured by low-cut black lace, and the sides and back of the shorts were nothing but lace as well.

As she was lying with her back to him, pretending to flip through a magazine, he took in the crisscrossing, black lace ribboning that wove from the perfect dip in her back to the center of her shoulder blades. He shuddered and tried to remember to close the door quietly.

"Wow," he groaned. When she turned over, her eyes were eager and inquisitive. "Do you plan on sleeping in that, baby?" He moved quickly to the bed.

She scooted away from him as his eyes flashed in heated desire. She shook her head and shot him a look that told him if he wanted her, he just needed to say the word but that he'd have to catch her first.

"You're gonna get me in so much trouble, Miss Haydenshire," he panted as her lips formed a naughty grin.

"I need you," she whispered in a heated plea. He slid into bed beside her.

"Baby, I want you so bad I ache, but you have to be quiet for me." He slipped his hand to her backside and massaged under the shorts, then he moved his fingers to the slick wet heat between her legs. "You have to be absolutely silent for me." He watched her eyes darken and her skin flush under his prodding touch. She shuddered and nodded as her eyes begged him.

He kissed her to keep from moaning himself and alerting the household to what he was about to do. As he slid the satin and lace crotch of the shorts aside, he slipped his fingers slowly inside of her. Her mouth fell open in a moan that he cut off quickly with his lips.

"Shhh, baby," he soothed as he plunged deeper, and she writhed. "Just feel it. Just feel me touching you." Her eyes flashed with untamed desire that drove him wild. "Does that feel good?" He used the hand that wasn't stroking her to lift up the top of the lingerie. He grasped her breasts as he began massaging her and easing her closer. Then he moved to cover one with his mouth.

"Rainer, please," she pled in a demanding whisper. "Take me. Make me feel you. I want it so bad," she begged as his body seized from her pleas. Unable to argue with her desires, he pulled his hand away. She was swollen and throbbing. She was dripping wet for him, her body already eager and ready.

He lifted the tiny top over her head and watched as her breasts spilled out of it. He didn't waste any time as he pulled the shorts off of her. He stifled a hungry groan as best as he could manage.

She was beautiful, and he wanted so badly to take her here in this bed. It was a fantasy he'd been adding to since he was fourteen years old.

He desperately wanted to live out his lurid dreams, but the reality of her begging him to give it to her, to give her release lying in the bed of her childhood, was so much better than anything he'd ever dreamed. He dispensed with his boxers quickly, and she wrapped her hand around his straining length.

Every muscle in his body pulled taut in an effort not to release the thundering growl building in his chest. He longed to pull her underneath him as he pounded into her. He couldn't wait. He wanted her too badly. He pushed his fingers back into her to make certain she could take him.

"Are you ready for me, baby?" He panted and prayed that she wanted him as badly as he wanted her.

"Please," she pled. "I'll be quiet. I set the cast while you were in the bathroom. Just take me."

He throbbed in her hand. Rainer clenched his jaw and tried not to lose it before he'd even begun. He grasped her upper thighs and massaged them apart.

Her breath quickened, and he could feel her heart race as he lay against her. Her energy arced feverishly. It matched the thrumming of her rapid heartbeat. He forced himself to remember where they were and who was very nearby. He drew a steadying breath.

"I'm gonna take it nice and slow, baby. Just feel it." He brushed his thumb over her lips to keep them both quiet.

He braced for half of a second and then gently prodded her lips with his cock. She panted, and he slipped inside of her, plunging her depths. He kissed her forcefully and matched the pulse of his slow rhythmic thrusts with his tongue to keep both of them quiet.

He hated to quiet her. He loved the sounds she made when they were together. The loud, all-encompassing moans that echoed from her every time he opened her drove him wild. He pulled his mouth away long enough to gasp for breath as he began grinding against her with more force.

"It's so good isn't it, baby? Feels so fucking good."

"Yes," hissed from her deliciously. She let her eyes close in the ecstasy of what he was doing to her. He felt her swell around him as he pounded into her.

Her release was just moments away, and he fought a war in his own mind. He wanted so badly to hear her come undone, to hear her call his name. He thrust harder, pushing and pulling in a rhythm that had her flying. Her swollen breasts melded into his hardened flesh as he pounded.

"God, you feel incredible." He was simply unable to remain silent. He needed her to know what she did to him.

Terror played in her eyes suddenly as they flashed open and pled with him. The climax began to consume her. Her rhythms arced in jagged, desperate quakes. She needed him. He kissed her again, capturing her cries in his mouth as he pounded into her. He buried himself deep as he exploded inside of her. He forced himself beyond his hilt, deeper than he'd ever been. She convulsed as she grasped the sheets in her fists.

Her energy spiraled wildly. She'd fought it and when he finally forced her surrender, it had been stronger than she'd ever felt it before. She couldn't catch her breath. The orgasm shattered through her in explosive waves of pent-up need and desire. He'd finally opened the floodgates.

They hadn't been together for over a week. They'd been terrified her parents would hear them. She'd needed it for some time, it appeared. She shook violently in his arms as he withdrew and held her tightly. He held her as she calmed, and her breath began to steady.

"Rainer," she managed in a stuttered whisper.

"What, baby?"

"We need to move soon." She sounded both shocked and embarrassed. He nodded and wanted her to know that she hadn't been the only one who had needed the soothing pulse of release.

"I'll work night and day until we finish it. We need our own place. We can't keep doing this." He gestured his hand out and then moved it to her back to continue to massage away what little tension remained after what they'd just shared.

"Go to sleep. We'll get started as soon as the sun is up." Rainer continued to caress her as she settled on his chest.

She nodded. She was exhausted from the power of the orgasm he'd drawn from her.

He never bothered to pull his boxers back on. He didn't want to let go of her long enough for even that. He wanted to hold her and never let go for the rest of their lives. That was all he'd ever wanted.

He watched her sleep in the light of the half-moon outside her window. As he brushed one last kiss on her forehead, he fell asleep in the haze of their energy still mingling, rolling, and combining together all around them.

CHAPTER 45

THERE IS NO WAY TO MAKE THIS BETTER

Rainer rubbed his eyes and yawned deeply. It took him a moment to determine what had awoken him. It was still pitch-black outside Emily's window. He turned his head and tried to see the clock without letting go of her. Three forty-five.

He eased the arm that was underneath Emily away as gently as he was able. As he extracted himself from the bed, he paused to make sure she wasn't going to awaken. He stood and tugged on his boxers. He pulled the covers back over her, but she wriggled in her sleep and slung her right leg over the quilt and sheets. He paused to take in the sight of her naked and on display.

"Come back," she fussed without opening her eyes.

"I'll be right back," he assured her.

She was adorable. She nodded but still refused to open her eyes as he kissed her cheek.

As he moved away, he studied the way the dip in her back formed the most gorgeous curve of her ass and then down her leg. With another yawn, he shook himself slightly. Rainer eased her bedroom door open. He continued to ogle her body as he stepped into the hallway. He turned and let everything he'd done to her a few hours before replay slowly in his mind as he walked…right into her father.

"Oh, shit," slipped from his mouth before he could stop it. This did nothing to help the situation. His eyes goggled as he took in the infuriated scowl on the governor's face.

"Uh…" Rainer tried desperately to think of some plausible reason that would explain why he was exiting Emily's bedroom at four in the morning in nothing but a pair of boxers.

"We weren't…" He shook his head fervently as he pointed back to Emily's bedroom. "I mean, we were sleeping." Panic seized his entire being. "We weren't…I mean earlier we did…no, wait, no…." he stammered stupidly as Governor Haydenshire's face glowed crimson in his fury.

"Your room is down there," he fumed in a lethal hiss. Rainer nodded but refused to say anything else. Every time he opened his mouth it just made it worse. "But, let me guess, Adeline is in Logan's room."

Rainer let his eyes close. He wasn't ratting out Logan and Adeline.

"I'll take that as a yes. Go sleep in Will and Garrett's old room, and we will discuss this in the morning," he snarled as he pointed to one of the other bedrooms. Then to rub vinegar in the gaping, oozing wound, Emily's door began opening.

"Are you okay? Come back to bed. I miss you," she fussed sweetly until she stepped around the doorway, completely naked, to meet her father's livid glare. Rainer turned away and shut his eyes tight as her father did the same.

"Would you please put some clothes on, young lady?" Governor Haydenshire demanded. His hissing fury was more volatile than if he'd been shouting.

"Sorry, Daddy." Emily shut the door, grabbed her robe, and then reopened it as soon as she was covered.

"Now!" Governor Haydenshire's voice broke, and his rage spilled from the wound as he shoved Rainer toward Will and Garrett's old room.

"Yes, sir." Rainer rushed down the hall.

"Do not go back in her room. Do you understand me?"

"Yes, sir."

"Daddy," Emily huffed. "We are engaged. He can come in my room, and he can see me naked. We're getting married," she defied hotly, which did nothing to quell her father's fury.

"Emily Anne Haydenshire," her father roared. "You will not speak to me that way, and you will act like a lady!"

Rainer heard one of the twins begin to cry. Mrs. Haydenshire carried Keaton into the hallway, bleary-eyed.

"Stephen, what are you shouting about?" she demanded. It took her half a second to determine just what had happened. She sighed dejectedly. "Rainer, Emily, go back to bed. We'll discuss this in the morning."

Rainer wasn't certain where he was supposed to go back to bed, but based on the look on Governor Haydenshire's face, he headed to Will and Garrett's room. Mrs. Haydenshire's brow pulled into a deep furrow.

"Did you tell him to sleep in there?"

"Yes, I did!" he shot furiously.

"Because that makes her have more clothes on and means that they weren't doing what you know perfectly well they were?" She paused briefly and rolled her eyes. "Go get your antacids, Stephen, and then come back to bed. You're being absolutely ridiculous. I told you this would happen." She bounced Keaton on her hip in an effort to soothe him back to sleep.

Rainer lay on top of the quilts on Will's bed unable to sleep. *There is no way to make this better* pulsed constantly through his mind like a hellish mantra he couldn't escape.

For the hundredth time, he reached for his phone to text Emily, but it was in the shorts he'd taken off in her room. He needed to talk to her to make certain she was okay. He'd heard her crying earlier, and it had nearly killed him to force himself to stay put and not go to her. His shield whirred constantly.

As the minutes ticked by, a plan began to formulate in his mind. He sat up and strengthened his resolve. He clenched his jaw and marched to the door. He needed to be wearing more than boxers for this.

As he slipped to Logan's room, he prayed that Logan and Adeline were asleep. He tapped lightly, but there was no answer. He eased the door open and leaned away to leave instantly if Adeline wasn't dressed. But she was in one of Logan's T-shirts and wrapped up around Logan, so he proceeded on.

He pulled a pair of shorts from one of his drawers and grabbed a T-shirt off of his bed. Not certain and not caring if it was either his or Logan's, he shrugged into it. He grabbed a pair of tennis shoes and socks before he marched back down the hallway.

He spun at the steps and issued down them quickly. He made coffee, seated himself at the table, and waited. It was just after five. The Haydenshires would be getting up soon.

He poured himself a cup of coffee as he rehearsed what he planned to say.

He met Governor Haydenshire's baleful glare as he entered with Mrs. Haydenshire right behind him at a quarter to six.

"Could I please talk to you?" Rainer requested calmly. He held Governor Haydenshire's eyes and refused to drop his gaze.

"Yes, certainly, and thank you for making the coffee," Mrs. Haydenshire soothed. She poured a mug for herself and one for her husband. She shot the governor a look that said he'd better not make this any harder than it was going to be. As he drew a deep breath, Rainer studied his future in-laws as they seated themselves near him.

"I'm sorry," he began.

Governor Haydenshire glared at him. "You're not sorry. You're sorry you got caught."

"Stephen, I swear," Mrs. Haydenshire erupted.

Rainer waited until they'd stopped. "I'm sorry that you saw what you saw last night." He completed his sentiment. "And, I'm sorry if you feel like I'm being disrespectful or defiant, but I'm not sorry for what happened and I never will be." He kept his voice low and smooth. "Governor Haydenshire, I cannot begin to tell you what you and this family mean to me or how much I respect you, sir. I love Emily more than life itself, and I cannot wait to marry her. She is everything to me," he went on, determined to make her father understand.

"I'm her Shield forever. She's my first thought when I wake up in the morning, and my very last thought as I drift off to sleep at night, holding on to her." He wasn't backing down. "And I understand that we're young, and we may not know everything about what our lives are going to hold. But I do know that's how I feel, and that the way I feel about her is never going to change. It certainly hasn't in the last twenty years." He edged closer to the governor. "I know she dared me to kiss her when I was eight, but I had a crush on her long before that, and I will do anything in my power to keep her safe and give her every single thing she needs if I have to die trying."

The Haydenshires shared a glance as Mrs. Haydenshire dared her husband to object.

"I will build her a house, because that's what she wants and because you taught me how to do that. Because everything that I know about how to love her and how to take care of her, sir, I learned watching you." Rainer's voice broke in the fervor of his plea.

"I have never been with anyone else, and I never will be. I left her, trying to keep her safe, but I will never leave her again. I love her, and I respect her. And if all of the hell that I've lived through,"—he didn't care that Governor Haydenshire had bristled at the word—"if all of that was leading up to my getting to be with her for the rest of my life, then, you know what, I think I'd do it all over again. She is all I've ever wanted. I would give everything I have to make certain she's happy and healthy, and that she knows every single day and every night when she falls asleep how much I love her." Rainer drew a deep breath before concluding.

"Now, if it's all right with you, I will build that house for her, and we'll move out because what happened last night was disrespectful, and that's not something I ever want to be again. You both mean too much to me, and I owe you everything that I am. So, if you don't want us to stay here on the farm, then I'll find us a place to live today. I can't choose between what you want and what she wants and still show you both the respect that you deserve."

He finished his diatribe with a feeling of accomplishment. The confession soothed his soul.

"We want you and Emily to stay, Rainer, and we know how much you love her, sweetheart," Mrs. Haydenshire assured. But it wasn't

Emily's mother he needed to hear that from so he waited. Governor Haydenshire and Rainer sat and stared at one another in prolonged silence.

"Stephen," Mrs. Haydenshire spat.

"I know I've been an overbearing ass," the governor finally admitted.

Rainer laughed and shook his head. The statement stunned him.

"I'm sorry." The words appeared to taste very bitter as they exited his lips. "I just couldn't get the image out of my head since the night you two left for the beach house. I don't, however, want to see what I saw last night ever again, so I think us getting you two set up here on the farm would be good for everyone involved. I still don't like what you're doing with my baby girl."

Rainer nodded his acceptance. "I know, sir." He knew that only too well, and he didn't really see the point in trying to make Emily's father feel any other way about it.

"What are you talking about?" Emily demanded. She marched to stand beside Rainer and leveled a glare at her father.

"You,"—Rainer smiled and kissed her forehead—"and the guesthouse."

Her eyes darted between Rainer and her father. The civilized conversation was clearly not what she was expecting to find when she awoke.

Her mother stood and supplied Emily with a cup of coffee. After drawing a restorative breath and smiling at Rainer and Emily, Mrs. Haydenshire began to soothe her family.

"Why don't Emily and Adeline and I go to the hardware store today and begin picking out all of the supplies for the guesthouse? I feel certain all of our boys will be coming by to help out, so we should get a good start on everything."

Emily grinned, but her eyes were red and swollen from her tears in the middle of the night. Rainer held tight to her hand.

"Where do you think we should start in the guesthouse, Rainer?" Governor Haydenshire quizzed, and Rainer knew it was a test. He wanted Rainer to prove that he knew his salt. He wanted to make sure

Rainer had been listening all the years Governor Haydenshire had been teaching him.

With a smile, he spoke. "We need to demo the back deck and the front porch. Rip out the bathrooms and all of the flooring. I think everything else can be salvaged," Rainer stated confidently. He had been listening, and he wouldn't let Emily or her father down.

"But," he added before he could be corrected, "we have to get everything out of the house and the shrubs cut back first."

With a wry smile and a nod, the governor couldn't quite hide the pride that colored his face.

A knock on the side door revealed Levi and Garrett as Logan and Adeline appeared in the kitchen. Mrs. Haydenshire determined that everyone needed a large breakfast before the work began, and the governor moved to help her.

"Are you okay?" Rainer pulled Emily to him and held her.

"What did you say to him?" she whispered.

"What I should've said on that walk by the lake."

CHAPTER 46
A FAMILY

Will and Brooke arrived a few minutes later as Connor and Patrick followed the scent of frying bacon into the kitchen. Will looked exhausted and was already covered in dust and dirt, but Emily's eyes lit excitedly as she took in Brooke. Rainer turned to study her.

Brooke was from Brazil. She'd been a transfer student at the academy during Will's senior year. She was definitely a knockout. She had a beautiful face and the body to go with it. Will occasionally commented, rather crudely, to all of his brothers that he'd follow her luscious ass anywhere, as long as he got to hold on to the balancing curves on top. Logan had drooled over her anytime she'd been on Haydenshire Farm the entire time she and Will had dated. This was long before Adeline had been in the picture.

Today, however, Brooke looked a little green and didn't seem to feel well at all.

"Will, I told you not to come if she's sick," Logan admonished his brother. But Mrs. Haydenshire looked thoroughly delighted as did Emily. Rainer furrowed his brow. He was completely lost as to what they knew that he didn't.

"Well,"—Will beamed as he took Brooke's hand and gazed at her adoringly—"she's been sick for several weeks now, and it's usually gone by about noon. So, she thought maybe she could keep the twins while we all work since she can't be down at the work site."

Governor Haydenshire instantly appeared to have understood what Will was saying. He pulled Will in for an all-encompassing hug.

Adeline looked thrilled as well. "Have you seen a medio?" she quizzed quietly.

Brooke nodded. "Yesterday," she announced with a broad smile on her face.

Garrett chuckled as he grinned at Will. "No way, man." He offered his hand.

"Oh," Mrs. Haydenshire rushed to Brooke. "I'm so excited. Here let me see if I have anything you can take."

"Okay, would someone tell me what the hell is going on?" Logan demanded.

"He knocked her up," Garrett quipped. Everyone grinned as they watched Will and Brooke gaze at each other.

"Yeah, I did," Will gloated.

"Well, then, this is a celebration," Governor Haydenshire vowed. In a gesture Rainer never expected, his future father-in-law put his arm around him. "This family has a great deal to be thankful for."

Emily threw her arms around him in a hug that seemed to soothe his soul.

Everyone moved to Brooke and Will to hug them and offer their congratulations. Mrs. Haydenshire began serving up plate after plate of bacon and eggs with cheesy grits and biscuits before she began fussing over Brooke.

"I'm not certain you're up to the twins when you're not feeling well. They're...a lot." She gestured to Henry and Keaton, who were devouring biscuits and then intermittently smearing jelly all over their highchair trays with their hands.

Brooke laughed. "We'll be fine. I teach kindergarteners all day."

Everyone seated themselves around the vast dining room table and listened to Mrs. Haydenshire retell the stories of her children's births.

"I had to push for almost three hours with Garrett. Do you remember that?" she quizzed the governor.

"Oh, I remember. You called me some awful names."

"And then Emily had colic and would scream if anyone but Stephen held her, and then I used to cry when he had to go to work," Mrs. Haydenshire lamented.

"That's because she has always been and will always be my baby girl," Governor Haydenshire dared either his wife or Rainer to disagree. Rainer smiled and winked at Emily. "But I suppose I might be willing to share her," the governor allowed hesitantly as Rainer bowed his head in appreciation.

Keaton declared that he was finished with his meal by dumping the remnants of his plate onto the floor.

"Keaton, no, sir," Mrs. Haydenshire scolded him as the governor cleaned up the eggs and biscuits.

"Keat-ton no sir," Keaton mocked repeatedly, until Mrs. Haydenshire cleaned him up and placed him in the playpen.

After Brooke sprinted from the table to the bathroom with Will following after her, Mrs. Haydenshire determined that perhaps only one of the twins would stay home.

Will settled Brooke on the sofa, wiped her face with a cold rag, and watched over her obsessively. His parents glowed with pride.

"I just don't understand how I can be so hungry and so sick?" Brooke fussed in her thick Brazilian accent. Will nodded and held her hand. He soothed her through his cast as he kissed her forehead.

"Maybe I should stay up here with you."

"No," she tsked. "Women have been doing this for millions of years. Your mother has done this nine times. I'll be fine."

"Oh, sweetheart, no." Mrs. Haydenshire handed Brooke some antacid tablets. "You just let him wait on you hand and foot until my precious grandbaby gets here. Just remember that it is entirely his fault you're sick."

In the end, Brooke stayed at the farmhouse with Henry while he napped. Mrs. Haydenshire, Emily, and Adeline took detailed notes from Logan and Rainer and then carried Keaton to the hardware store near the farm. The governor and all of his sons, along with Rainer, headed to the guesthouse.

"You're sure you want to live this close to Mom and Dad?" Garrett quizzed Rainer. "Okay, summon!" he called, and Rainer, Logan, and

Connor drew from the air around them. "Pull," Garrett huffed, and with the power they'd drawn, combined with Garrett's sheer strength, the rotted wood of the back deck collapsed at their feet.

Rainer brushed the dust off of his gloves before answering, "Em really loves the idea."

"How is it that my baby sister ended up with nine brothers who won't ever tell her no, and a father that sure as hell won't, and then marrying a guy who gives her everything she wants as well?"

"She's worth it," Rainer insisted.

"So." Will laughed as he came around the back of the house. He hoisted a stack of rotten lumber from the garage onto the large burn pile they'd begun. "Heard you and Dad had a meeting of the minds in the middle of the night." He gave Rainer a goading grin.

Rainer noted that he'd tossed a badly crumpled copy of a dated Playboy in the pile as well. Rainer furrowed his brow but decided not to ask.

"Something like that," Rainer huffed. He didn't really want all of Emily's brothers to know what had happened.

"Well, you're still alive, so I think that says something."

"I was actually concerned there for a minute."

Will and Garrett laughed.

After they'd added the wood from the back porch to the burn pile, they joined everyone else who was pulling trash and debris from the garage.

"Are we keeping the Kelvinator?" Logan chirped.

"Did the snake have any friends?" was Rainer's response to the ridiculous question.

"Not that I see," Logan assured.

"All right," Governor Haydenshire took command. "Garrett, you and Patrick, start dismantling the front porch. Everyone else, inside to pull up the flooring, then we'll start on the bathrooms." Everyone moved into the kitchen. "Were the girls real attached to these countertops, or are they going as well?" He pointed to the counters in the kitchen that were a horrible off-white color with tiny gray egg shapes in varying shades. The sides were covered in peeling aluminum sheeting.

Rainer laughed and shook his head. "Yeah, Em loved these almost as much as the pink seashells in the bathroom."

"I figured." Governor Haydenshire chuckled.

With that, he cupped his hand until a faint orange glow appeared. He placed it under one of the countertops, melted the residual glue, and hoisted it off of the cabinets below.

"Logan!" Levi shouted from the living room. "There's a squirrel's nest in the fireplace."

"That's probably bad, right?" Logan cringed.

"Only if the squirrels are home." Will chuckled. Most of the flooring in the living room was gone, and everyone walked along the floor joists to see the nest.

"There's nothing in it." Governor Haydenshire sounded relieved. "Just get it out. Wear your gloves."

Logan and Rainer nodded. They were universally voted upon to be the ones to remove the nest as they were the ones who would be living in the house, once it was free of small woodland wildlife.

"Ssshhhiiitttt," Logan drawled. He turned the one-syllable word into about four.

"Logan," Governor Haydenshire scolded.

"What? That's what's in it."

"Just get it out so we can get as much of those bathrooms removed before we all have to go back to work tomorrow."

There were several offers to help when everyone got off work over the next few days, but Rainer knew that he and Logan would be doing the majority of the construction work themselves. As he helped Logan lift the moldy nest into a large box to be burned, he was anxious to prove himself.

"How come being pregnant makes girls sick?" Logan asked as they pulled more of the nest out of the fireplace. Will chuckled as did the governor.

"It's a shock to their system, I suppose." The governor paused and then added, "One I'm hoping Adeline won't experience for some time now. At least until she's completed her residency at Georgetown."

Logan shuddered. "Uh, no worries there."

"It usually lasts the first couple of months. Your mother had it with most of you but not all. It used to make her feel better to drink seltzer water and when I rubbed her back." Rainer filed that informative lesson away for later use.

"So a medio can't fix it?" Logan asked.

"No, the baby is what causes it, so..." He waited for Logan to put everything together.

"So, they have to carry the baby, and get huge, and be sick, and then go through all of that pain just to have kids?"

"And because of that, and so, so many other reasons that you already know but don't need to be discussed, and for putting up with all of our crap, we should all worship the ground they walk on," Will explained as everyone in the room laughed and nodded their agreement.

"Yes, and your mother did that nine times. So, perhaps the next time you see her, you could give her a hug. Maybe offer to help her out with something," Governor Haydenshire urged.

CHAPTER 47

THANKS MOM

The ladies returned with lunch and dozens upon dozens of catalogs for everything from tile to sinks to countertops.

"We couldn't decide," Emily explained as Rainer kept her from entering the house.

"The floors are gone, baby, and can I please have those? I'm starving." He pointed to the stack of cheeseburgers in her hand and the large Dr Pepper she'd brought for him.

"Oh, sorry." She handed him the food.

After hearing the governor's lecture on all she'd done to bring them into the world and then care for them after she'd gotten them here, all of Mrs. Haydenshire's adult sons embraced her in a very sweaty seven-person hug.

She was shocked but seemed to enjoy the appreciation right up until Logan pledged his undying devotion by leaping on an overturned five-gallon paint bucket, placing one hand on his heart, and holding the other out to the woman who had given birth to him.

"Mom, I really appreciate the fact that even though you'd already given birth to so many complete losers before me, you decided to let Dad knock you up for the seventh time, in hopes that you would get a son as awesome as I am."

Emily rolled her eyes as all of Logan's brothers scowled, and

Rainer and Adeline guffawed. Mrs. Haydenshire shook her head as she ordered Logan to eat in an effort to shut him up.

They watched Keaton closely, all concerned over the snake that Logan had stumbled upon the night before.

Will glanced at his watch. "It's after noon, Mom. Brooke's probably feeling better by now. She really wanted to babysit the twins. I could take him back up to the house, and Rainer and Logan can show you what we've done."

"If you're sure she won't mind? Tell her I'll be up in just a little while."

Will scooped Keaton up and hoisted him onto his shoulders.

"It's fine. Take a look around." Will buckled Keaton back into his car seat and then drove Mrs. Haydenshire's Suburban to the farmhouse.

Rainer, Connor, and Levi quickly placed several large sheets of plywood from the Haydenshires' barn over the floor joists, so people could walk through the house. In a show of macho gallantry, Rainer hoisted Emily into his arms as she laughed and then wrinkled her nose.

"Eww, you stink but wow!" She took in all that had been dismantled while they were gone. "Are the horrible pink tub and sinks out?"

Governor Haydenshire shook his head. "Rainer was just saying how much you liked them. I thought we were leaving them in," he feigned confusion. Emily rolled her eyes at her Father.

"I want to help," Adeline volunteered.

Logan glanced around. "We're going to pull everything in both bathrooms and then that's probably about as much as we can do today. Hopefully, Rainer and I can take the old truck to the lumber yard tomorrow and get the deck and porch rebuilt."

CHAPTER 48

THE TRUTH MIGHT SET YOU FREE

Adeline insisted on helping pull the fixtures in the bathroom, and she did a tremendous job of it. Logan enjoyed showing off all of his knowledge and teaching her. She seemed content just being in his presence.

When Will returned, he threw open the door to the Suburban while he engaged the parking brake and turned off the motor, all in one smooth motion.

"Oh good, you're back. I need to go home and get dinner started. I have a feeling I'll have lots of hungry mouths to feed by sundown." Mrs. Haydenshire looked relieved that Will was back, but panic colored her features when Vindico exited the passenger seat of the Suburban.

Rainer and Logan dropped the sink they were carrying into the dumpster that had finally arrived.

"Hey, man!" Garrett leapt out of the house. He landed where the porch had been standing moments before. "Grab a sledgehammer. Have a go at the bathrooms. It's very therapeutic."

Vindico chuckled but shook his head. "Unfortunately, I need to talk to your parents and Adeline." Whatever he'd come to say, it didn't appear to be good news.

"I found him up at the house with Brooke. She wasn't sure how to tell him how to get down here. She was about to call when I pulled up," Will explained. He looked extremely concerned.

"Why do you need to talk to Adeline?" Logan asked.

Vindico glanced at the governor.

Governor Haydenshire's eyes closed for a long moment. "Why don't you go get Adeline, and I'll explain everything."

Will had already disappeared to find Adeline. She and Emily had been in one of the bathrooms discussing what they should purchase to put in there.

When she made her way back to the yard, she looked terrified. The air around them hung thick with tension, and Governor Haydenshire looked sick. She clung to Logan.

"Why don't we go back up to the house to discuss this?" The governor suggested, though it was more of an order. Rainer and Emily shared a quizzical glance. They weren't certain if they should follow.

"Come with us," Vindico instructed Rainer. "She's probably going to need you." After grabbing a nearby rag to wipe the sweat off of his brow, Rainer guided Emily to the Suburban.

Vindico was tight-lipped all the way back to the farmhouse. Tears leaked down Adeline's face as Logan tried to soothe her without much success.

"Is something wrong with my mom?" Adeline pled. She seemed desperate for Vindico to talk.

He shook his head. "Physically or mentally?"

After a few minutes, Governor Haydenshire pulled the Suburban up to the side door of the house, and everyone exited.

Mrs. Haydenshire began pouring large glasses of lemonade as Vindico gestured everyone to the kitchen table. After thanking Mrs. Haydenshire for the glass, he seated himself as everyone studied him.

Governor Haydenshire took the seat beside Adeline and patted her hand. "We will get you through this. I don't want you to worry."

"What is this about?" Logan demanded.

"First let me say how sorry I am to be telling you this." Vindico sighed. "As far as the Realm is concerned, you're fine. Your mother was to blame for everything that happened involving her arrest, but as you know, we have to play by the Gifted and Non-Gifted laws, and because your mother is not Gifted, she's causing a bit of trouble with the Non-Gifted court system."

Adeline nodded. Rainer willed Vindico to talk faster.

"You're not arresting her, Dan?" Governor Haydenshire vaulted suddenly.

"No." Vindico shook his head. "Not yet anyway."

"What!" Logan demanded. "Just tell me what the hell is going on."

"Logan," the governor warned, but Vindico didn't look like he minded Logan's language or his demand.

"Your mother's defense is that the men she was with were not paying her. That it was consensual sex and that all of the drugs in the apartment were yours," Vindico finally concluded morosely.

"My mother said that?" Adeline gasped. Logan tried to steady her. No one was able to believe someone would do that to her own child.

Vindico gave a hesitant nod. "The Non-Gifted legal system is different from ours in a lot of ways. We typically hold drug abusers in Felsink for the few days before their trial, and then we send them to mandatory Auxiliary rehab programs to treat the problem. The Non-Gifted Realm just puts them in jail."

Governor Haydenshire moved to his suit jacket that hung on the long pegged shelf in the kitchen. He pulled his cell phone from the pocket, and everyone watched as he began to pace.

"Jack, it's Stephen. You busy?" He closed the door to his office off of the living room.

Vindico turned back to the group at the table. "I'm sure that's Jack Stariff. He's the best attorney in the Realm."

"He's a family friend." Mrs. Haydenshire began rubbing Adeline's hand in the governor's absence.

"I've never, ever taken anything. I swear," Adeline pled. "I never wanted to. It's horrible, and it makes you do horrible things."

Vindico nodded. "Look, I'm here unofficially. Tomorrow, you're going to need to submit to a series of drug tests to try and clear your name. They'll be taking several hair samples and a blood and urine test."

He grimaced as Logan's shield pulsed.

"Hopefully, between the tests and all the power that Stariff wields, that will be the end of it. You're going to have to appear in court at a hearing and testify against your mother though. I'm certain Stariff will talk to your new employers at Georgetown. Just be extremely cautious. We can possibly get you out of this, but we're really going to need your cooperation." He turned to Mrs. Haydenshire. "Garrett's going to have to bow out of any dealings with her case until we get this settled. We can't have it looking like your family is covering for her."

Governor Haydenshire returned but still looked grim. "Jack's on his way. I've invited him for dinner, Lillian."

Mrs. Haydenshire gave a determined nod. She headed to the refrigerator and extracted two huge casserole dishes of pork chops.

"Can I go with her for the tests?" Logan asked.

Vindico considered thoughtfully. "Maybe for the ones tomorrow, but after that they'll be random. They can show up at her work, or when you're in town, or here at home, anytime, and you have to be prepared for that. Balking at even one of them could play into your mother and her attorney's hand."

"Who's paying for her mother's lawyer?" Rainer hoped Adeline wouldn't mind his intrusion, but Candy Parker never had any money. Someone had cooked all of this up for her. She hadn't come up with this on her own.

Vindico glanced at Logan who nodded for him to accept the question. With another deep breath, Vindico grimaced. "Paulo Ramirez. We've had run-ins with him before. He says he's your mom's boyfriend?"

Adeline shook her head. "He's her pimp," she fumed. Logan wrapped his arms around her tighter. He looked like he hoped if he held her tightly enough he might be able to shield her from everything crashing down around her.

"And her dealer," Logan confirmed what everyone had already assumed.

"Yeah, well, I'm more concerned with who Paulo works for," Vindico muttered almost inaudibly.

"Adeline, I'm so sorry. If I can do anything to help..." Emily swallowed back tears. Adeline didn't respond, and Rainer watched a concerned glance travel from Vindico's eyes to Governor Haydenshire's. Emily spun and laid her head on Rainer's chest.

"So, I take it you two are still an item?" Vindico quipped with a wry chuckle. He was clearly pleased to be able to change the subject.

Rainer's brow furrowed as Emily raised her head. She wiped the tears from her eyes. "I saw that while we were out."

"Saw what?" Rainer had no idea why anyone would think he and Emily were no longer together.

Emily rolled her eyes. "More stuff about you being with Samantha Peterson."

"They already did all of that after graduation. What could they possibly have to say about her now?"

Vindico shrugged. "It was nothing new. I've been working on trying to keep you out of the media. I have a long way to go, but like I told you, I will not have you photographed all the time. Part of working for Iodex is being discreet." This thrilled Rainer, though he tried not to show it in light of what was going on with Adeline. "I guess an old story was better than no story." Vindico rolled his eyes.

"Thank you," Rainer vowed. "You have no idea what that means to me."

"Rainer, why don't you and Emily head back to the guesthouse? We'll get Adeline all sorted out, and then we'll discuss everything with Jack tonight," Governor Haydenshire directed. "We'll take care of this, son. I'm certainly not going to let her serve time for her mother's doings." He looked disgusted by all that had happened.

With that, Adeline jerked away from Logan and sprinted up the stairs. Everyone stood stunned for a moment as Logan turned to go after her.

"No, let me talk to her. You can check on her in a few minutes." Emily followed after her.

Governor Haydenshire headed back to the refrigerator and handed Logan a beer and then offered Rainer and Vindico one. "Sometimes lemonade doesn't quite cut it."

"I really think with Stariff helping her, as long as she submits to all of the drug testing willingly, we can keep her from serving time. Our constitution demands that we play by the Non-Gifted rules here, so pleading her case will be condemning her mother. Do you think she's up to that?" Vindico gave Logan a concerned gaze.

"I don't know. She always refused to turn her mother in before she was attacked." Logan shook his head in disbelief. "That's what it took. I'd been begging her to move in here for years, and she refused. She's always protected her mom no matter what she'd done." He looked Vindico dead in the eye. "What happens if she doesn't testify against her?"

Governor Haydenshire put his hand on Logan's shoulder and braced him as Vindico's jaw clenched tightly.

"If she won't testify, and her mother's lawyer builds a good enough case against her, she could definitely end up doing time in the Non-Gifted system."

"Then we will see to it that she testifies," Governor Haydenshire vowed.

"Logan," Vindico urged uncomfortably, "does she have any idea who her father is? If she had another parent, it might make turning on her mother a little more palatable, not that Candy Parker is any kind of mother."

"All her *mother*"—Logan spat the word like poison from his mouth —"ever told her was that he had a British accent. She was mad Adeline wasn't born with one."

"Nice." Vindico clearly agreed with Logan's assessment.

"Daniel, you're staying for dinner, right?" Mrs. Haydenshire urged as she seasoned the pork chops and then began peeling potatoes.

Vindico shook his head. "I can't, Mrs. Haydenshire. Thanks, though. I have to get back to work, do a few more things, then I was gonna try to hit the gym before I head home."

"It's Sunday, Dan. Surely whatever it is can wait until tomorrow morning," Governor Haydenshire insisted. Rainer sensed it was a test.

"No, I need to get a little more done tonight, but hey, Will told me they're expecting. Congratulations," Vindico offered in an obvious attempt to halt the Haydenshires' efforts.

Mrs. Haydenshire smiled. "How about you? It's been a long time since you introduced us to anyone." She studied Vindico closely. He forced a chuckle, but the look in his eye bordered on fury.

"No, ma'am, I don't seem to have much luck with women lately." He stared right into Mrs. Haydenshire's deep blue eyes and told a lie that was visible to everyone watching.

"Logan, one more thing." He turned back to Logan and Rainer suddenly. "Paulo is trying to spring Ms. Parker in order to build the case against Adeline. Be careful where you go with her. Think about what you're doing and where you're seen. Anything they can use to make her look like a dysfunctional, rebellious child, they will. My recommendation would be to stay here on the farm as much as possible, and don't let her go off on her own." Rainer watched a conspiratorial glance that was shared between Vindico and the governor.

What little color had returned to Logan's face faded quickly. "I'm gonna go check on her." He rushed up the stairs.

"Rainer,"—Vindico extended his hand and Rainer shook it—"I'll see you in a few. If you both decide you want to start early, you could go ahead and get on the Senate payroll. I'll get you in whenever, but it looks like you've got quite a project going." He gestured in the general direction of the guesthouse.

"Yeah." Rainer nodded. "But thanks for the offer. I'm eager to get started. I really appreciate the appointment."

"I picked you and Logan because I think you know your stuff, and I think you'll make an excellent team. Don't prove me wrong," Vindico's tone turned threatening.

Rainer nodded and tried to appear vastly more confident than he felt at that moment.

Vindico offered everyone remaining in the kitchen a wave, then headed back out the side door. Rainer heard the Agusta roar to life as he sped away. Emily reappeared a minute later. She looked devastated.

"Is she okay?" Mrs. Haydenshire asked.

"No." Emily shook her head. "She feels abandoned, and unloved, and unwanted, and all the things she's always felt, but now she feels like she's burdening you and Dad with the lawsuit and everything."

"That's ridiculous," Governor Haydenshire fumed.

"I'm really worried about her. I think if she thought she had anywhere else to go, she'd leave." With that, Emily's chin trembled and tears began to fall.

Her father moved to her, but she turned to Rainer. He cradled her to him and wrapped her up tightly in his arms. He tried very hard not to see the heartbroken expression on her father's face.

CHAPTER 49

NOT EASILY SEVERED

Several hours later, Will and Brooke went home, and Levi left to pick up Sarah. Garrett stayed to make a few phone calls to friends from the police force and to talk to Jack Stariff. Rainer seated Emily at the dining room table and helped Keaton with his juice cup.

Jack grinned at Rainer and Emily. "I hear congratulations are in order. I swear most of the time when I think of you two I still see you out by the lake catching frogs."

Mrs. Haydenshire chuckled. "That was more than a day or two ago." She smiled sweetly and placed her arms on Adeline's shoulders.

Adeline was still distraught. Her eyes were swollen and red from crying most of the afternoon. Jack looked at her sorrowfully.

"Well," he began, but then halted as Garrett handed him the large casserole dish of scalloped potatoes. "Miss Parker, I really think we can deal with this little situation your mother has put you in." He tried to sound reassuring, but his disdain for Candy Parker was evident in his tone.

"You can call me Adeline, Mr. Stariff. I can't thank you enough for doing this. I feel terrible that I don't have any way to pay you." Her tears made a rapid reappearance.

"Stephen and I are more than happy..." Mrs. Haydenshire began, but was cut off by Mr. Stariff.

"No you won't, Lillian." He shook his head. "I just got off the phone with Dan, and we think the Realm owes you quite a bit for the life we've allowed one of our own to live. So, the Senate will be covering whatever I don't do pro bono, which won't be much."

Adeline was stunned.

Emily grinned. "See, so many people love you."

"Thank you." Adeline was visibly overwhelmed.

Mr. Stariff cut himself a hunk of the pork chop from his plate. "Stephen," he uttered with an admiring groan. "If the ten kids didn't seal the deal, then this meal should've." His vow elicited chuckles from around the table.

"Yeah, well, you just keep your eyes to yourself, Jack." Governor Haydenshire winked at Mrs. Haydenshire.

Jack laughed and nodded his acceptance of the threat.

"Let's get down to business." He began wiping his mouth on his napkin before sipping his tea. "I know Dan told you that you would need to be willing to undergo drug tests." Adeline nodded. "I'm sorry about that, but it really is the best way for me to build your defense."

"It's okay," Adeline offered hopefully. "I've never taken anything, so I guess it's no big deal."

"No, it is a big deal," Mr. Stariff insisted. "It's invasive, intrusive, and not something you should have to deal with on top of a medical residency. Unfortunately, I don't know any other way to deal with this." He shook his head. "I pulled all of the information on your mother's arrest, and her case file, as soon as Stephen called me. This isn't going to be easy. Her lawyer's done quite a bit of damage already. I hope I'm not being too forward," Mr. Stariff edged, "but, do you know anything about your father?"

Adeline shook her head. "Not really. My mom always said she thought he was British, but I don't think she really knows his name or anything. I'm sure it could be one of several people." She stared steadfastly into her lap. Logan's eyes closed for the length of one heartbeat before he wrapped his arm around her.

"That wasn't your doing," Mr. Stariff announced. Everyone at the table willed Adeline to stop taking responsibility for her mother's actions. Stariff shared an uncomfortable glance with Governor Haydenshire.

"Do you have any questions I can answer for you, or is there anything I can help you understand about this?" Mr. Stariff studied Adeline intently. She glanced uncomfortably at Logan, who gave her a reassuring nod.

"Do you think any of this will affect my job? I worked so hard for this position, and I need this job."

Mr. Stariff nodded as he began consuming a second helping of Mrs. Haydenshire's potatoes. "I've already spoken to Harrison Sawyer, the head of Georgetown, and he does understand the entire situation. Your job is not in jeopardy at this point. He would like you to be discreet with whom you discuss the trial and the testing. If your mother's lawyer gets a foothold with the claims that the illegal substances were yours, however, then it could compromise your position. I need you to exercise extreme caution."

"Is that Chloe Sawyer's father?" Emily quizzed. "Oh sorry. I didn't mean to interrupt."

Mr. Stariff didn't seem to mind. "Yep, Chloe and the Angels are his whole world. I'm sure you'll meet him soon. He's one of the team owners."

As Mrs. Haydenshire offered everyone dessert and coffee, Mr. Stariff concluded. "For now, we'll just take it a day at a time. We've fixed everything so that it appears in the Non-Gifted courts that you've already been arrested and released. Like Dan told you, staying here on the farm would really be the best thing for a while. It's extremely important that you don't step one toe out of line. That would be all it would take to land you in prison."

Adeline nodded. The pain and distress still resided in the depths of her eyes. She looked exhausted. Her rhythms were weighted with her terror.

"Mr. Stariff, sir," Adeline whispered. Stariff gave her a kind smile as he waited on her to continue. "Do you think it might help if I spoke to my mother? I haven't seen her or spoken to her since she was arrested."

"I really believe at this time, it would be best for you to sever any ties you have with her. I know that feels like a harsh thing right now, but from what I've seen, contacting your mother would only lead to more trouble."

Adeline's chin trembled as more tears leaked down her cheeks.

"Logan, son, why don't you two go sit on the swing or out on the dock? Take a little break," Governor Haydenshire gently suggested.

CHAPTER 50

BUILD YOUR LIFE THEN LIVE IT

The next morning, Rainer sighed. He was sleeping alone and cold in his bed in his old room. Logan was in the shower. The sound of the falling water had awoken Rainer.

He stretched and yawned and then stood to throw on a pair of cutoffs and a T-shirt. He headed downstairs to the kitchen. A smile formed on his face automatically as he passed by Emily's room. Her door was closed, but in his mind's eye he could see her wearing nothing but tangled bed sheets and wrapped up around him.

Logan was taking Adeline to Georgetown for her first day of training as a medio. Her drug tests were being performed after her shift was over. He'd decided to stay in Arlington for the day, so he would be there with her while she went through the many various drug screenings.

Adeline was already up, dressed, and pacing. Mrs. Haydenshire tried to ply her with food.

"I'm just too anxious to eat."

"You're going to do great," Mrs. Haydenshire assured her, "and we can't wait to hear about your first day."

Adeline nodded hesitantly and wrung her hands. Logan appeared a few minutes later.

"Oh good." Adeline rushed to him. "We should go."

He glanced at his watch. "Okay," he hesitated as he took in Adeline's mood, "but we have over an hour, sweetheart."

"I don't want to be late."

Logan decided not to fight a losing battle. He took the granola bars and banana his mother offered him on his way out the door.

"Stephen left the keys to the truck on the table by the door," she reminded Rainer.

"Thank you. As soon as Em's ready, we'll head to the hardware store."

"I'm taking the boys to the pediatrician for their check-ups. We'll be gone a while, I'm certain." Mrs. Haydenshire didn't sound too thrilled with her plans for the day. Rainer offered her a sympathetic smile. "The last time I took them Keaton kicked one of the nurses. So this time has to be better, right?"

Rainer tried not to laugh. "I think…there is a definite possibility that it…*could* be better."

Emily came down the stairs with a glum disposition. She was wearing one of Rainer's Ioses T-shirts, and her hair was in a tangled mass on her shoulders. Her bottom lip was protruded slightly.

Rainer grinned and tried not to think how adorable she was when she pouted. Her current expression was slightly less dramatic than the one she'd worn the night before, when Governor and Mrs. Haydenshire had sat down with Rainer, Emily, Logan, and Adeline. They'd informed them that since they would be moving into a home of their very own in a few weeks' time, they didn't feel it was appropriate that the couples be sharing bedrooms in the farmhouse, before they were married.

Logan and Emily had put up a fight, but Rainer and Adeline had kept quiet and listened to the verbal sparring match.

The governor triumphed with a final, "You're living in our house, and you'll follow our rules." So, save the indignant huffs from Logan and Emily, that had been the end of it.

A smirk crossed Mrs. Haydenshire's face as soon as she took in Emily's solemn glower. "Good morning, sunshine," she sang with more than a hint of sarcasm.

Emily rolled her eyes. Rainer bit his lip in an effort not to laugh.

Mrs. Haydenshire shook her head and forced a kiss on Emily's cheek as she scooted by her to get the boys ready for their appointments.

"Why don't you go get ready?" Rainer pulled Emily close to him. He let his hand slip under the T-shirt she was wearing and gave her a whispered growl as he discovered there was nothing underneath it.

She grinned and wiggled her hips for him. All thoughts of rushing to the hardware store evaporated from his mind.

"And," she drawled. Rainer tried to remember what he'd been planning to say before she'd thoroughly distracted him.

"I was gonna say why don't we get ready, and we'll get breakfast in town and then go pick up the lumber for the deck and porch. But now I'm thinking that in a very few minutes, we'll have the whole house to ourselves, Miss Haydenshire."

"Oh really?" She smirked.

He gave her a look that said there were many things he planned on doing that morning and most of them were to her.

"Well," Emily whispered, with her tone full of sass. "Why don't I go up and get in the shower, and"—she traced her hand over Rainer's zipper line. The motion made him ache for more—"as soon as Mom leaves, you can join me."

Her eyes beckoned him as she made plans all her own. Unable to contain the desire that had begun coursing through his veins as soon as she'd entered the room, Rainer wrapped his arms around her and devoured her mouth with his own. He let one hand trail back under her shirt. He hiked it up and began grasping and squeezing her backside. A needy aching hunger consumed him. He held her face with his other hand as he formed her lips around his own.

Mrs. Haydenshire cleared her throat loudly. They reeled apart. Emily quickly righted her shirt.

"Rainer, dear, I think you and Logan need to get the guesthouse finished quickly."

"Yes, ma'am," Rainer agreed as he lowered his clasped hands to try to hide the effect Emily had just caused.

"All right, you two, we're off." She was holding Keaton and had Henry's hand. Neither of the toddlers looked willing to leave peacefully. "Go to the hardware store and work on the house," she insisted as Rainer and Emily nodded their understanding. Once she'd exited the kitchen door, Rainer grimaced.

"I'm pretty sure your parents hate me."

"They do not, but she's right. We do need to move 'cause I want to be able to do you whenever I want." She took his hand and guided him out of the kitchen as Rainer growled heatedly.

CHAPTER 51

GUESTHOUSE AND HOME

"This thing is so slow," Emily complained. Rainer chuckled his agreement. The extremely satisfied smile she'd been wearing since their time in the shower had Rainer feeling like a king, but she was now frowning at the dash of the truck.

Her father's Ford F-100 circa 1965 was a classic. The bed was thoroughly rusted, and it topped out at around forty-five. It had belonged to Grandpa Haydenshire, and Governor Haydenshire used it around the farm to haul lumber or whatever needed to be moved from one point to another. Governor and Mrs. Haydenshire occasionally took it out for a drive when they went on a date or wanted a little time alone, but none of their children really understood this practice.

After their breakfast, Rainer drove the truck into the loading dock of the hardware store. They moved around the store relatively quickly, with Rainer pointing to all of the lumber and decking materials they would need. When he had everything, he helped the store employees load the wood into the truck.

An hour later, Rainer eased the truck down the fields toward what was to become their new home.

He kept what they'd done in the shower that morning and what he could do with her on a regular basis as soon as he built her the house planted firmly in the forefront of his mind and worked quickly.

Emily helped him unload the lumber. Then he glanced at the plans he and Logan had worked up the night before, after Logan had soothed Adeline to sleep in Emily's room.

Rainer decided that he needed to up his abilities before he started training with Vindico and Iodex, so he summoned and over-torqued all of the power tools.

He began cutting the lumber to the dimensions he needed. He felt the electricity flow through his body and knew that as long as a Gifted person worked carefully and pushed only a little at a time, he could gradually add to the amount of energy his body could withstand. He edged the amount of electricity pulsing through him slightly higher with each step as he worked.

"Damn it." He dropped the drill instantly as Emily rushed to him. He flipped his hand over to reveal angry, red, burn marks.

"Rainer," Emily panicked.

"I just forced too much through it without cooling it fast enough. I think I burned it out."

Emily shook her head, then held his hand in her own. She closed her eyes, and she was instantly moving her energy through him. She soothed and healed him.

Rainer was a natural-born protector. It was in his blood, and he was one of the more powerful Shields. This made his energy extremely hard to penetrate. The will to protect oneself was inborn and ultimately grew to become the Ioses shield.

His body didn't even fight her anymore. He no longer had to force himself to let her in. It was an automatic thing now, and he reveled in that knowledge. She moved her hand over his, and a few moments later he was healed.

"Thank you." He kissed her forehead as she grinned at him.

"Be careful, please. I love you, and I want to move out here, too, but I want you safe."

"I promise."

Logan and Adeline returned a little after two.

"Damn." Logan was stunned as he took in the completed back

deck. Rainer was cutting the wood for the front porch. "Somebody tells you that you can't get with my sister 'til something's done, you get it done."

Rainer laughed. "Yeah, well, tell me how today went and then pick up a saw and help me out."

"What can I do?" Adeline requested sweetly. She looked much calmer than Rainer had expected.

Logan kissed the side of her head. "You can help us place the boards for the porch if you want."

"I want," she assured him.

Emily returned from the farmhouse in the Hummer. She brought back more water and snacks. "Adeline, how'd it go?"

"Work was really great. I was assigned an obstetrics medio to train me, and I got to assist with a delivery because I'd been in the obstetrics training group that volunteered up there last year. So, that was really neat. I can't wait to do it on my own."

Rainer nodded. He wasn't certain he'd ever heard Adeline talk so much at one time.

"My Mentor's name is Brad, and he's been a medio for about two years now. He works under Medio Sawyer so he's a great person to train me. If Medio Sawyer likes my work, I could become a resident at Georgetown."

Rainer glanced at Logan. He knew Logan Haydenshire like the back of his own hand. He caught the slight scowl when Adeline mentioned Brad's name. He didn't want her training medio to be a guy.

"And after that...." She turned her head to the side and lifted a portion of her jet-black hair. She revealed two places where relatively small sections of hair had been cut very close to her scalp. Logan instantly wrapped his arm around her.

"Then they took blood. It was way more than I thought they were going to draw. Medio Sawyer said that Mr. Stariff had requested more than one vial. So, I guess it's to prove I'm not using. I healed that up as soon as they were done."

"I know you're glad that's over." Emily offered her a sweet grin.

"Oh!" Logan remembered suddenly with a teasing look in his eye.

"You won't believe who I ran into while I was hanging at that coffee shop across from the hospital."

"Who?" Rainer picked up the saw again and measured one last time before he made his cut.

"Fergus."

Rainer rolled his eyes. "I'm still irritated with him for throwing that party when we told him not to."

Logan helped Rainer edge the support beam between the ground and the porch roof, "Yeah, same, but he had a girl with him."

"One who's not related to him?"

Logan laughed. "Yeah, and she appeared to be there by choice."

"Maybe we're being too hard on him. He did help me catch O'Ryan when he keyed Em's Jeep, and he did get Connor out of trouble with Governess Martin when he plastic-wrapped the Auxiliary building."

"Maybe." Logan shrugged. "He apologized again when he saw me."

"Did you know the girl?"

Logan shook his head as he summoned and shoved hard to move the beam into place.

"Never seen her before. She's Gifted, but maybe she's not from around here."

Rainer summoned, and he and Logan lifted the next beam.

Emily rolled her eyes as Rainer walked her to her bedroom several hours later. "This is just so stupid. I don't know why Dad is being so stubborn. He's usually not quite this bad."

"Oh, I'd say it has a fair amount to do with the fact that his one and only daughter is moving out and is all grown up." Rainer winked at her.

He was exhausted from working on the house, and he'd been determined not to break his promise to her parents that he would only sleep in Logan's room and not with Emily.

He was too tired to have done anything but sleep anyway, but he didn't think that would make any difference to her father. As he kissed her good night, Rainer received a broad mischievous grin. He squeezed her backside when she turned.

"You know, if you come in here, I'll let you squeeze other things," she gestured to her breasts.

"Emily Anne, go to bed," Governor Haydenshire shouted from his bedroom. "Alone!"

With a grimace, Emily blushed, and Rainer blew her a kiss as he let his footsteps echo down the hallway. He wanted the governor to know he was headed to Logan's room.

CHAPTER 52
MOVING DAY

For the next two weeks, Adeline insisted on driving herself to the hospital every day so Logan could work on the house.

Adeline and Emily helped them do everything from laying hardwood flooring to installing countertops. All of the Haydenshires came by to help out when they were able, and the day before Rainer and Logan were to begin working for Iodex, the house was complete.

Every night, Logan and Rainer would fall exhaustedly into their beds at barely nine o'clock. They'd pushed their muscles and bodies further and further each day to speed the process along.

They were careful to always heed Governor Haydenshire's warnings. Pulling too much energy across your body could be dangerous. If a Gifted person took it too far, it could be deadly.

Rainer and Logan reveled in Governor Haydenshire's praise as they walked through the house. They pointed out all of the upgrades and improvements they'd made.

Things did get mildly uncomfortable as Rainer and Governor Haydenshire helped unload the new mattresses and box springs, along with the queen headboard and footboard that Emily had picked out. They carried it into what would soon be Rainer and Emily's room.

"I think I'll just let you and Logan set this up." Governor Haydenshire shuddered slightly as he exited the room.

Connor and Patrick drove down an old breakfast table from the storage barn, along with a love seat and a well-worn couch.

Emily and Adeline were in town with Mrs. Haydenshire. They were picking up trash cans, shower curtain rods, soap dispensers, and toothbrush cups for the new bathrooms. As he tried to will away his nerves over starting at Iodex the next day, Rainer smiled. He was pleased with everything they'd accomplished.

"Boys, I want to thank you," Governor Haydenshire commended. He stared at the wall and refused to look either of them in the eye as he spoke.

"I'm pretty sure we should be thanking you for letting us do this." Rainer gestured to the house.

Governor Haydenshire shook his head. "You're welcome for that, but I wanted to tell you I do remember being twenty-one, and I really appreciate your following the directive your mother and I gave you about the girls. That was very respectful, and I appreciate that."

Rainer stared at the floor as Logan nodded uncomfortably. The fact that they'd slept in their own beds had very little to do with Governor Haydenshire's request. It had much more to do with the fact that they were too exhausted to have sex after the way they'd forced their bodies to withstand more and more energy transformations with each passing day.

"No problem, Dad." Logan's face colored rapidly.

"All right, well,"—Governor Haydenshire looked relieved to be able to change the subject—"they're delivering your new furniture in a few minutes, right?" he asked Logan.

Adeline had been thrilled to purchase a bed frame and mattress set with her first paycheck from the hospital. She seemed to finally feel like she was contributing to their relationship.

"Uh, yeah," Logan choked.

"And you two can get them set up?"

The boys nodded their agreement. "All right then, I'm gonna get back up to the house. I may take your mother out to dinner if I can talk Patrick and Lucy into keeping the twins tonight. She's taking this kind of hard."

Guilt quickly took up residence in Rainer's gut. He was taking both Emily and Logan from their parents or at least that's how he felt.

The girls returned a little while later. Mrs. Haydenshire was trying hard to hold in her tears.

"Mom," Emily sighed. "We're still on the same farm."

"I know, but that doesn't mean I won't miss you."

Emily rolled her eyes. "You'll still see us all the time."

"You promise you'll still come up for dinner and to see the boys?"

"Of course," Logan assured her. He hated it when his mother cried.

A few hours later, Rainer sank onto the sofa and pulled Emily onto his lap. The shower curtains had been hung, the bathrooms arranged, and the beds assembled. Emily had put away all of their clothes and helped Adeline organize the kitchen.

"Let's order pizza," she urged.

"Sure, baby." Rainer handed her the phone. He let his head fall back on the sofa. He was exhausted.

"Are you too tired? Do you want to go on to bed?" Emily had been panicked over Rainer's exhaustion for over a week.

"Sorry." He rubbed his hands over his face. "I'm fine, baby."

"Geez, Em," Logan collapsed on the love seat with a beer, "He did all this for you. He's been working like a dog. Cut the guy some slack."

"I'm sorry. I didn't mean it like that. I know how hard you've been working. I'm just worried about you, and I miss you."

Rainer smiled and shook his head. "I'm fine, and I miss you too."

He moved to the new kitchen and pulled a Dr Pepper from the refrigerator. He was certain the caffeine and extra energy would help. Emily ordered several pizzas, and Rainer tried not to think about what the next day would hold.

Logan joined him in the kitchen as the girls flipped through bridal magazines.

"We're ready, right?" Logan asked.

"I hope."

"We've been working like hell. I've never been able to pull as much across me as I can now."

"Yeah, and your dad says Vindico is the best, and he's training us since we got appointed to the Elite Squadron." His reassurances dwindled as he willed himself to believe what he was saying.

"He can do some crazy shit," Logan admired reverently. Rainer chuckled. He was sure they hadn't seen even half of it.

Everyone sat on the living room floor as they inhaled pizza and reveled in their newfound freedom. Adeline stood to grab more Dr Pepper for everyone. Logan made quite a show of grabbing her backside. This seemed to thoroughly embarrass her.

Rainer rolled his eyes and huffed. "Man, you two have a bedroom. I do not need to see that unless you'd like us to put on a show as well."

Logan shuddered as he begrudgingly agreed to keep the public displays of affection to a minimum.

"Thank you." Adeline giggled. She stuck her tongue out at Logan as she thanked Rainer. He raised his glass to her in a toast.

An hour later, Emily was lying in Rainer's lap under a quilt on the couch. He was discreetly feeling her up under the cover the quilt provided. She bit her lip in an effort not to giggle.

"I'm kind of tired," she lied, and Rainer gave her a knowing grin.

"You ready to go to bed, baby?" His voice took on an excited thrum.

Logan scowled. "Yeah, just take the dirty talk on to bed with you. We all know what you're doing under that quilt." Everyone cracked up. Emily smirked as she stood, refolded the quilt, then grabbed Rainer's hand to pull him off the couch.

"Good night," she sassed to Logan and Adeline who were still laughing over Logan's comment.

"Yeah, and I do not want to hear how much fun you're having. So keep it down."

"Hey, if you're good, then you're good." Rainer shot him a pompous smirk.

Logan hurled one of the throw pillows toward Rainer's head.

CHAPTER 53
PAST SO GRIM, FUTURE SO BLEAK

DAN VINDICO

Dan gasped for breath. He shook the bed as he awoke violently from the same harrowing dream.

"Amelia," he panted as he tried to figure out where he was. "I'm sorry I left. We have to talk," he gasped before his eyes took in his surroundings.

Covered in salty sweat, he jerked upright in the bed. He let his face fall into his hands and tried desperately to catch his breath. Someone moved beside him. Dan leapt from the bed and reached for the pistol in his bedside table when he remembered why someone was in his room. His rapid, thundering heartbeat tried to steady as he forced air into his lungs.

He scrubbed his hands over his face as he futilely tried to rub away the relentless hell he lived each and every day.

What's her name? He tried to recall the bar the night before. After blinking several times, he studied her face as she lay in his bed.

Sarah? No...Samantha...maybe? Shelby? After landing on Sidney, he shook his head. That wasn't right either. He hadn't really cared enough to remember. He never did.

As he glanced at the clock, he debated. He decided that three-thirty wasn't too early to awaken her. He'd asked her not to stay, and she had anyway. He jostled her shoulder.

"Uh…honey?" That would do. She grunted and let her eyes open hesitantly.

"I have to go to work early. You need to go home," he ordered.

She sat up and rubbed her eyes. "It's not even four in the morning."

Dan headed to his bathroom. He didn't want to see her.

"I need to leave soon. Don't be here when I get out."

She scowled. "You're an asshole, you know that?"

"You're not wrong." Dan shut the door and locked it.

"Are you going to call me later?" she demanded through the door.

"Yeah, of course. Just have to get out of here today. I'll call you this weekend," he lied, and they both knew it.

"You can go straight to hell!" The deep offense was clear in her tone.

"Already there." Dan ran a cold washcloth over his face. He heard the front door slam, and he exited the bathroom.

After he pulled on his favorite running shorts and an Iodex T-shirt, he raced out his back door.

Desperation surged through him. He needed to drown the guilt and the heartache with every pounding thump of his shoes against the trail.

He ran faster. He passed the mile mark, and he pushed harder. Sweat pooled and burned as it ran into his eyes. He steadied his gasping breaths. He reveled in the pain. He deserved it.

Faster…just move faster…just fly away. He repeated the desperation with every steady throb of his heart. The miles passed with no reprieve. He circled and flew back to his house. He didn't bother showering. He certainly wasn't finished.

He refilled his water bottle and shoved a button-down shirt, khaki pants, and a tie into his bag and then slung his leg over the Agusta. He summoned and flew to the Senate. He made it there in less than five minutes. No one else was on the road.

He threw the bag onto the wooden gym floor and racked weight after weight on the bar before he allowed himself to feel the cold, hard bench under his back.

CHAPTER 54

THE ENDLESS CHASM

RAINER LAWSON

The next morning, Rainer and Logan tried to determine what Elite Iodex officers ate before work.

"I don't know. Vindico probably eats steel or something." Logan pulled the leftover pizza from the fridge.

"We'll go grocery shopping when we get home tonight," Emily determined. She looked absolutely terrified. Rainer was afraid if she didn't stop biting her lip she was going to draw blood.

"You're going to be amazing. You were great at tryouts," he reminded her.

"You wouldn't have made the Angels if you sucked," Logan reasoned.

"You wouldn't have been appointed to Elite Iodex if you sucked, and you're still nervous."

Logan inhaled a piece of cold pepperoni pizza in a few bites. "Whatever, let's just go."

He walked Adeline to the Accord and kissed her goodbye as Rainer performed the same move with Emily.

They both drew steadying breaths as Rainer engaged the clutch on the Mustang, and they all headed out. The beginning of their adult lives stood expectantly before them. It waited just a short drive from the safety and comfort of Haydenshire Farm.

They both glanced back as Rainer turned on to the two-lane road. They took in their refuge from the cold, cruel world, until it was only visible through the rearview mirror.

As Rainer signaled and exited off of the interstate headed to the Pentagon, he felt a piece of himself drift away. He shivered and felt empty for a long moment as he stood in the seemingly endless chasm between his childhood and his adult life.

He glanced over at Logan who looked just as lost and, quite frankly, just as scared. They'd been together since the very beginning. They'd even shared a crib together at times. There wasn't anyone else Rainer would want to be his partner at Iodex. He trusted Logan with every fiber of his being, and he would never let Logan down. Just like Logan would never let him down. He let those thoughts comfort him as he pulled the Mustang onto the parking deck.

Vindico looked annoyed as they entered the Iodex office. Rainer glanced nervously at his watch. They were early.

"You need badges, credentials, and guns," Vindico commanded.

Rainer and Logan followed him out of the Iodex office and into one of the Administration offices of the Senate.

They moved through the long processing line and spoke to several academy graduates who were beginning in various departments that day as well.

Rainer stood for his photo ID that was made into an Elite Iodex badge under Vindico's watch and then printed onto an ID to get into the Iodex parking deck.

Logan did the same thing, and then Vindico pointed out that the badges look very similar to the badges used by the Central Intelligence Agency.

"If you find yourself dealing with someone Non-Gifted, just flip the badge quickly. They'll never notice," Vindico assured them.

He directed them to the Iodex gun ranges. Both Rainer and Logan had been trained and qualified on various types of firearms during their last four years at the academy. They'd passed the Gifted Firearm Qualification Tests with perfect scores, and they'd out-shot every other Ioses Senior on the Urban Sniper courses they'd completed.

Vindico jerked two brand-new Glock 22s out of wooden cases and handed them to Rainer and Logan. They were told to target shoot from varying distances until they felt the gun was a part of them and then to return to Vindico's office.

"The gun is a part of me?" Logan quipped.

Rainer laughed. "At least he didn't say be one with the gun."

"Uh, yeah, I really only plan on being one with my girlfriend, no firearms involved."

Rainer casted the pistol, enhanced the potential energy in the hammer, and took aim. He fired a line from the head, straight down the center of the paper target that joggled on the line.

They returned to the Iodex wing, after they were cleared by the range master, to find Garrett standing and laughing with Vindico. They'd been shaking hands, and Garrett was holding a new badge that matched the ones Logan and Rainer had just received.

"What are you doing here?" Logan demanded. Rainer thought it odd that Logan seemed so irritated until he understood what was happening.

Garrett shared a knowing glance with Vindico. "You and Rainer went and got yourselves appointed to the Elite Squadron, and Dan's about to ask you to be on the task force, which we all know you'll agree to," he choked slightly. "I'm uh...I'm here to make sure you two don't fuck up too badly."

"What task force?" Logan turned to Vindico. Thrill lit in his eyes and his rhythms. The only task force Rainer was aware of in Iodex was the Interfeci task force, and only the very best were asked to be on the task force.

"We'll talk about it at lunch," Vindico brushed him off.

"So, you're here to check up on us?" Logan turned on his brother.

"That's pretty much it."

Rainer wondered if Garrett was lying, but he couldn't come up with any other reason why Garrett would suddenly want back on the Elite Squadron.

"Garrett's an outstanding officer. Damn near the best actually, and I'll take all the help I can get," Vindico vowed. Neither Rainer nor Logan could argue over Garrett's skills, but they were irritated everyone still thought they needed to be babysat.

"Come on in my office. You have to fill out your insurance forms and your Auxiliary forms for your service work," Vindico effectively let Garrett off the hook.

Before they could follow him, Governor Sapman entered from the governors' branch of the Pentagon. Vindico's face fell as he greeted him.

"Uh, Lawson, Haydenshire, you know George Sapman. He is, among other things, the governor over Summation teams."

Rainer and Logan offered the governor kind smiles. They'd certainly met before at Senate functions they'd attended with the Haydenshires.

"Rainer and I are good friends with Jeff Strenton." Logan gave Governor Sapman a kind smile. "He's dating Becca, right?"

Jeff Strenton was a great guy. He was a better friend with Logan than Rainer, but they were all in Ioses together. Jeff was a year younger. He'd been dating Governor Sapman's only daughter, Becca, for several years.

"Yes, he is," Governor Sapman agreed with more than a note of disdain.

Rainer couldn't fathom why the governor wouldn't like Jeff. He was polite, got excellent grades, and was a tech genius. He'd juiced an Xbox in Ioses house so that eight people could play at once. His mom didn't have much money, but Jeff worked hard and he adored Becca.

Governor Sapman turned back to Vindico. " I have the papers here. I couldn't stop him. He filed this morning." He shook his head as he handed Vindico a file folder of papers.

"I knew it was coming. No one could have stopped him, sir," Vindico huffed.

With that, he walked toward his office and began flipping through the file. Rainer and Logan followed.

Rainer was certain he was stepping onto hallowed ground as he began studying Vindico's office discreetly. Everything about the office seemed harsh. The substantial oak desk had two large computer monitors. There were numerous metal filing cabinets that lined two of the long walls. A few chairs were scattered in front of the desk.

Along the back wall of the office covering numerous floor-to-ceiling windows was a gigantic, pressed corkboard that blocked all natural light from breaching the room. Lined up along the board were pictures and rap sheets. Rainer swallowed as he noted different colored Xs that crossed out several faces arranged neatly along the wall.

Vindico was standing at one of the filing cabinets as he pulled out the paperwork he needed Rainer and Logan to fill out. His back was to them, so Rainer and Logan studied the wall closely.

The first picture was a mug shot of Dominic Wretchkinsides. His face was drawn in a simpering scowl. Beside his picture was Candor Pendergrath, the man Vindico had arrested at Mick's on Logan's birthday. Rainer's brow furrowed. A green X was drawn over Pendergrath's face. He noted that a few of the other men on the board had green Xs under the current black or red ones.

Rainer studied the sneer of the man he and Emily had seen on the boardwalk weeks before. The snake tattoos were visible in his mug shot. Rainer could just make out the man's first name, Tavio. Vindico had scribbled through the name with red marker and written the word "Cascavel" under the man's picture.

Alexi Pravus's picture was between Pendergrath's and Cascavel's. Logan's energy swam with hate and fury. Pravus was the man who'd killed Cal. Rainer offered Logan a sympathetic glance. He wished there was something he could do or say that could take away his best friend's pain.

Pravus's picture was one of numerous faces with no Xs. Rainer began to understand what drove Dan Vindico.

He moved to his desk but was focused on the monitors as he was printing something off his computer. Logan nudged Rainer and pointed to a mug shot on the lower end of the wall.

Rainer narrowed his eyes and tried to recall where he'd seen the man in the photo.

"Your uncle's," Logan reminded him.

Rainer nodded but then shrugged. He racked his brain as to why his Uncle Stan would have a member of the Interfeci Criminal Organization in his apartment. He assumed the man was probably his uncle's dealer. Stan had abused drugs off and on for years.

Rainer drew a deep breath. He took one of the chairs in front of Vindico's desk. After grabbing pens from a Senate mug that was crammed with writing utensils, Rainer and Logan got to work.

It was nearing lunch by the time they'd been assigned desks, and Governor Haydenshire and Governor Carrington made their way into the Iodex department.

"How do you think they'll shape up, Daniel?" Governor Haydenshire smiled.

Vindico smirked. "I figured I'd take them out for lunch before I start abusing them, but I'll make men out of them yet, don't worry." He seemed to enjoy the nervous glance Rainer and Logan shared.

"Don't go too hard on them, and give yourself a break occasionally as well," Governor Haydenshire urged.

"I promise I won't work them quite as hard as I push myself, just almost."

Governor Haydenshire slapped Vindico on the back as he shook his head and wished Logan and Rainer good luck.

CHAPTER 55
AMELIA

"All right, let's go grab some lunch and then we'll see what you're made of," Vindico challenged.

Determined not to look frightened in any way, Rainer and Logan stood up from their newly-minted desk chairs and smiled.

"Do you usually eat here in the cafeteria, or do you go out?" Rainer was impressed with his own nonchalance.

"Truthfully," Vindico sighed, "I eat almost every meal here, but I'd like to discuss something pretty important so why don't we head to Frye's? It's just a few blocks from here. Got great burgers, and if you agree with what I'm about to ask you, I'll buy you two steaks." Rainer and Logan shared another hopeful glance.

As they walked into Frye's, Logan nodded. "Oh yeah, we've eaten here with Dad before." They stood near the hostess and took in the dark wood moldings and hunter-green walls. The high-back leather booths were arranged around the large room, offering the guests quiet retreats from the workday.

The hostess gave Vindico a kind smile and gestured to a booth in the back corner.

"All of the governors eat up here quite a bit," Vindico commented.

They ordered burgers and baked potatoes, each matching Vindico's order, though he requested water, and they ordered soda.

He kept the conversation light until their food arrived. Then, with a smirk, he began, "Here, let's go ahead and have your first official Iodex training lesson, shall we?"

Logan and Rainer nodded. They were eager to learn something new.

"All right, Lawson, summon all of the sound energy you can from around our table."

Rainer wasn't entirely certain what he was supposed to do once he'd summoned it, but he followed orders. Sound energy was certainly easy enough to draw and contain. It didn't take much to pull and didn't tax his body to hold it, any more than listening to music did to a Non-Gifted person. Once he discreetly held the muted purple glow in his hand, Vindico looked pleased.

"Good, now listen." He leaned across the table. "I want you to take what you just summoned, and you may have to use a little of your own energy, but I want you to create a particle displacement around our table. You're basically creating a vacuum. Once you've set it, I want you to hold it so that no one else can hear the pressure and frequency of our voices. Essentially, no one will be able to hear what we're saying."

Rainer had no idea this could even be done, but he was excited to try to impress his new boss. Holding a complicated cast like that, however, was going to be rather draining.

He concentrated as he pushed the purple haze out from his hand into a circle that encapsulated their table. Logan, at least, looked impressed.

"Decent." Vindico smiled but then cupped his own hand and reinforced the barrier Rainer had created. Overwhelming awe washed through Rainer as he felt the sheer amount of power he could wield with so little effort.

"All right, now hold it while we talk," Vindico challenged. Rainer hoped he'd be able to carry on an intelligent conversation and hold the cast.

They all began eating. Rainer found the additional calories extremely helpful in holding the sound barrier. Vindico wiped his mouth and studied Rainer and Logan.

He cleared his throat. "This is kind of a hell of a conversation to have over a burger and Coke on your first day of work, but I've never been all that good at drawing things out, so..." He shrugged. After he let his eyes close for the length of one heartbeat, he drew a steadying breath. Rainer gathered that whatever he was going to share was particularly difficult for him to say.

"Logan, well, both of you really, let me say how sorry I am about Cal. He was an excellent Iodex officer, and I can't imagine the loss for your family. Please know that we miss him every day here as well."

Logan swallowed and nodded but was unable to respond verbally. Vindico smiled at him and then went on. "About ten years ago just before I graduated from the academy, I proposed to my lifelong girlfriend, Amelia."

Rainer's stomach clenched.

"Our families had lived next door to one another since we were both young, and we were inseparable until I went to Ventor." Vindico was certainly not married or engaged, so clearly something had happened. Rainer braced himself. "As you know, I was head of Ioses as well." He gestured his head in a bow to Rainer. "I went into special ops training my senior year and then was selected for Elite Iodex. I trained and studied under Gabe Caddick. He was one of the most powerful and disciplined men I've ever had the pleasure of working with. This was a few years after your father became Crown Governor, Rainer.

"We used to call Gabe 'Boomslang' because once he was after someone they always ended up in prison, no questions asked. He was relentless," Vindico stated admiringly. "So I trained hard and began working with Boomslang to try to catch one of the most vile men in the Gifted Realm. I was consumed. I spent every moment edging closer and closer, but Amelia, my fiancée, wasn't Gifted, and she didn't understand my obsession."

He downed a sip of his water. It appeared that he wished it would wash away whatever he was about to tell them somehow.

"But, like I said, I wouldn't give it up. So one night she asked me to stay home instead of going back into the office after dinner, but I was hot on the trail of one of the men working closest to the man I'm telling you about." Rainer's shield rejected what seemed like the inevitable end to the story. "Just like every night before that, I left our home and went back to the office." For a moment, Vindico seemed unable to go on. His voice choked, and he fought to control his emotions. "I left her alone and unprotected, and they took her." He stared at the table and was unable to look into either Rainer's or Logan's eyes.

"Dominic Wretchkinsides is the head of the Interfeci Criminal Organization, the organization that ordered Cal's death." He glanced back at Logan. Rainer and Logan didn't need any explanation of the Interfeci but neither of them spoke.

"He took Amelia because I had gotten too close, but even after I knew he had her, I never doubted that I'd be able to save her. My ego was so overblown it never even entered my mind that I couldn't save her. I was a cocky asshole, and I hunted him down. I had him cornered in a matter of hours in a warehouse outside of town. It never occurred to me to call for backup or even ask Boomslang to help me." He shook his head in utter disbelief.

"I took down his men, one after another after another. I still had no doubt. I could see her. I could almost reach her. She was unconscious and bleeding badly. I moved to take down Wretchkinsides and rescue her."

He shook his head. "Wretchkinsides doesn't fight. In a split second, he was in my head. He halted me instantly. I couldn't even throw a shield over her. He only had to control a small portion of the energy in my mind to make me unable to move or help Amelia in any way."

"I watched him kill her and then disappear. Boomslang followed me that night and got me out. I was obviously a disaster."

Rainer could hardly breathe. It took everything he had to maintain the sound barrier around the table, as he tried not to think of what it would be like to watch Emily be brutally murdered.

"I'm so sorry," Rainer managed as Vindico gave him a genuine smile and a slight nod.

"Yeah, me too," he choked. "Anyway," Vindico forced himself to go on, "this is the man who ordered Cal's death. He's murdered or had a hand in the murder of hundreds upon hundreds of people all over

Europe and North and South America. That list includes your mother, Rainer, and Governor Haydenshire didn't want you to know this, but he ordered the hit on your father as well. The man who killed your father didn't work for the Interfeci Organization, however. They needed someone less recognizable to carry out that hit."

Rainer swallowed down the bile that rose quickly in his throat.

"He plays evilly in the Non-Gifted world, always after a large score of cash. Adding to his massive bank accounts drives Wretchkinsides. Drugs, gambling rings, and illegal weaponry are his main sources of income, although he is branching out into human trafficking." Vindico sounded every bit as disgusted as Rainer felt. "As soon as I was able to even get out of bed after what happened to Amelia, which took quite a while, believe me, I turned what little evidence I had on Wretchkinsides over to the Russian government, and he was caught and imprisoned on tax evasion and fraud. But he's shattered his cage so to speak. Now that he's been released, he's moved here to wreak havoc in America and to piss me the hell off." Vindico drew another steadying breath.

"I've spent my entire career putting bad guys in Felsink and Coriolis, mainly members of Interfeci who worked under his partners and from his orders from prison, but I want the man. I want Wretchkinsides. I want to end the terror he's put on the Gifted and Non-Gifted alike."

Vindico grimaced as he studied Rainer intently for a long minute.

"Lawson, I know Governor Haydenshire spoke with you about Emily's safety." Rainer shivered slightly as the blood in his veins begin to run ice cold.

"She's of great interest to the Interfeci." Vindico said the words that had Rainer certain he was going to vomit. "Just listen," Vindico soothed in a tone calmer than Rainer had ever heard out of his boss's mouth. "I won't let you live what I've lived through. I will keep Emily safe, and I will teach you to keep Emily safe. But the only way for all of us to go on and live a remotely normal life, one where you don't have to be afraid to let her out of your sight, is to end him and take down the entire organization piece by piece. Wretchkinsides and Pendergrath, the man I arrested in Virginia Beach the night you were at Mick's," Vindico reminded Rainer and Logan. "They're both excelled mind-casters, which is, of course, illegal."

Both Rainer and Logan had studied mind-casting and ways to prevent it at the academy. To tap into the electronic synapsis and energy of a person's mind was extremely difficult. It was impossible to hold a mind-cast over more than one person at a time. The easiest task for the mind-caster would be to make the person they were casting halt any activity, to force them to shut down their brain slightly, which was precisely what Wretchkinsides had done to Vindico. It was also the only cast that could be performed on a Non-Gifted person. The Gifted could harness the electricity in a Non-Gifted person's mind almost as easily as a Gifted person.

If the mind-cast was held for any length of time, the caster could suggest repeatedly that the person being casted do any number of things. Generally, it couldn't be anything too outlandish, as something extreme tended to end the casted powers. Convincing someone to commit murder, for instance, would be next to impossible. Getting someone to change a will or insurance policy wouldn't be terribly difficult, however, if the caster convinced the person that it was in the best interest of himself or his family.

"Double-Predilects are mind-casted more easily," Vindico lamented. Rainer and Logan nodded as they both recalled that information from their studies. It was the fatal flaw in the exceptional power.

"Because your energy spins in double rhythms constantly," Rainer recalled.

Vindico looked pleased that Rainer knew the reasoning.

"Right, so if either one of my streams is taken over, my mind is casted." His jaw clenched. "Because I'm a rare Double-Pred of equal ability, my energy is much more potent, which makes it easier to be intercepted. And now,"—Vindico gestured his thumb back toward the Senate—"Wretchkinsides has purchased himself his own Summation team for his daughter, Marlisa. It's a front, of course. He has to launder the drug and gun money somehow, but I'll have to prove that before I can dismantle it. They'll force their way into the Angels schedule, mark my words, which puts Emily on a Summation field with Marlisa Wretchkinsides and copious amounts of energy available in the challenges." Vindico shuddered slightly. "I wanted to tell you all of this because I would like you to help me bring him down. I've seen your stuff, and you're both extremely talented, but there's a lot you need to learn."

Rainer understood the inherent risk in going after someone with as much money and power as Wretchkinsides clearly had. He and Logan shared a glance as they both instantly decided that men like Wretchkinsides needed to be done away with, and they both wanted to avenge Cal and ensure Emily's safety.

"We want to help," Logan urged as Rainer nodded.

Vindico nodded. "I had a feeling you would. You can release that barrier now, Lawson. Pretend you were distracted because that guy's been trying to ask you if you'd like a refill for several seconds now."

He gestured his head to the side. Rainer's eyes goggled as he released the cast and smiled.

"Sorry, off in my own world, I guess." Rainer lifted his glass so it could be refilled. He took a sip of the Coke in an effort to settle his stomach. He was unable to eat anymore after Vindico's disturbing story.

As they walked back to the Iodex office, Rainer was still distraught. He couldn't imagine how Vindico went on after something like that. It was too much to fathom.

Rainer's cell began playing "I Got You Babe," and he smiled automatically.

"Hey there, baby. How's the hottest Arlington Angel?" He reveled in Emily's delighted giggle.

Rainer noted Logan and Vindico's chuckle, but he didn't care.

"I'm good. I've already learned so much from Fionna. She's amazing. I'm just waiting on the joule meter guy to get me a new one," she explained how she'd had time to call.

"I thought those were on your uniforms?" Rainer followed Logan down the sidewalk.

"They are, but mine keeps messing up."

"Messing up, how?" As far as he knew, unless a meter was

tampered with, the joule meters used in professional Summation were virtually a perfect science.

"We were working with Piezoelectric disks, and Chloe wanted us to see how many disks we could transform and produce energy from before our meters were tapped. Anyway, mine would drop down to one bar and then all of a sudden, it would shoot back up completely full. It's so strange, because I'm kind of tired but it's still reading full. They had me put on a different practice uniform, but it just keeps happening."

"That is weird." Rainer climbed onto the elevator with Vindico and Logan. He casted his phone so it would keep the signal.

"Yeah, I hope they can fix it. I think that's why I'm still so nervous. My receptors are feeling weird," she admitted.

Rainer's heart seized. Emily's receptors being off generally meant something bad was going to happen. She had been awfully nervous about her first day of practice. That had probably thrown her.

"Oh, he's done," Emily chanted. "I'll see you tonight. I love you."

"Love you too," Rainer replied before the line went dead.

"Be careful casting your phone, Lawson," Vindico immediately instructed. "A casted cell phone can be cloned instantly and easily."

Rainer nodded as he followed his boss back into the office, still worried about Emily.

CHAPTER 56
WHAT ARE YOU MADE OF

"All right, let's do some training, shall we?" Vindico ordered.

Logan and Rainer followed Vindico, Portwood, Ericcson, Ramier, Tuttle, and Garrett into an impressive gym area just off of the Iodex offices.

"First of all," Vindico began, "you can pull a hell of a lot more energy across muscle than you can across your organs or across fat." He slapped Tuttle's stomach, which was by no means fat, but it wasn't as chiseled as Vindico's.

"Hey," Tuttle yelped as Vindico laughed.

"So, work out hard. The harder you work the easier everything else becomes."

Rainer and Logan nodded as they continued to watch.

"Lawson, throw a shield. Only summon from yourself, nothing around you. Give me all you've got." His eyes lit with challenge.

Rainer drew a deep breath and cast a green glow toward Vindico, who stepped back slightly. Rainer concentrated as he held the cast, while Vindico made several motions with his hand, cupping and forming several energy streams as he shaped them into a swirling orb.

In just under two minutes, Rainer's shield had dissolved, and Vindico was standing over Rainer, who'd collapsed on the mat.

"Are you okay?" Logan sounded just as shocked as Rainer felt. He helped him up off of the mat.

"Uh, I'm not sure," Rainer admitted as Vindico laughed.

"Don't worry. We'll make sure no one can get through your shield. Just give me a few days' time."

"All right, Haydenshire, same thing," Vindico ordered. After glancing at Rainer, Logan summoned and threw his shield. He held it several minutes longer than Rainer had been able, but still, in a relatively short amount of time, Vindico was standing over him as well.

"Now, why do you think you held it longer than Lawson? You're both of about equal skill and Predilect, correct?"

Rainer and Logan nodded and waited for the explanation. "Mr. Lawson held a relatively complicated sound barrier for our entire lunch and then tried to shield against me. Part of being a good Iodex officer is the ability to not only use and transfer energy but also to conserve it.

"Officer Tuttle will also be teaching you to suppress energy, both yours—which will make you unable to be identified by other Gifted people—but also to drain enemies to make them unable to fight against you," Vindico instructed as Tuttle gave them an expectant grin.

Vindico explained the rest of their training schedule and then led Logan and Rainer back into his office. He shut the door behind them.

"I want to thank both of you for agreeing to help us take down Wretchkinsides. I can't explain to you what it will mean to me to finally finish him. Tomorrow, I'm going to let you sit in on a questioning." He hesitated. "I believe you know Mitchell O'Ryan?" He seemed to already know the answer to that. Logan and Rainer nodded ominously.

"Yeah, well, his father's cut from the same cloth, trust me."

Rainer raised his eyebrows. The last he'd heard O'Ryan's father was serving time in Felsink for tax evasion to the Realm and forgery ties to insurance fraud.

"O'Ryan Senior's wife has a sister, Lucinda, and she happens to be married to Dominic Wretchkinsides."

"What?" Logan gasped as Rainer's mouth fell open.

"Yeah, so I was hoping if we pull O'Ryan Senior out of Felsink for a few hours, we might could work out a deal. I'll make his sentence a little friendlier if he provides us enough information on Wretchkinsides." He tapped a few file folders together and then slipped them back into one of the drawers. "Ever been to Felsink?" Vindico teased with a wry smile.

"No." Rainer shook his head. He tried not to sound frightened.

"I figured. You'll get to see it in the morning, and I'm certain you won't like it any more than O'Ryan does." Logan and Rainer shared a nervous glance.

All Gifted prisons were painful for the Gifted people. The harnessed energy from the earth's mantle and core affected their abilities in erratic ways.

"You can head back to Haydenshire Farm. Tomorrow, I'll teach you how we deliver and retrieve prisoners from Felsink. Then you can help me interrogate O'Ryan Senior. Do not get used to leaving early, and remember, I now own you."

As he moved back to his desk, Rainer noted that the sides of his and Logan's desks, which faced one another, were now occupied by Garrett's new desk.

Garrett would effectively become Vindico's partner, as he was the next highest-ranking officer. But Vindico worked alone. That much was obvious. Garrett was apparently taking it upon himself to personally train his little brother and Rainer.

"How about some burgers and a beer from Lesco's?" Garrett offered kindly. "That's a hell of a story. I was a pallbearer at the funeral, and I still can't wrap my head around what he lives with day in and day out." He gestured his head toward Vindico's office door.

Immensely thankful for the reprieve and for a little time to process everything they'd heard in their harrowing introduction to adult life, Rainer and Logan nodded their adamant agreement.

CHAPTER 57

THE BEGINNING OF THE END

They fell into their regular booth in the back of Lesco's. Rainer breathed in the soothing familiarity. The Haydenshires ate at Lesco's Pub regularly. Rainer's father used to bring him and Logan, and occasionally Emily, to eat at Lesco's every Friday night when he was alive.

Rainer and Logan had been given the facts of life talk in the very booth where they were currently seated. Rainer had woken up at Logan's one Saturday morning a few days before his thirteenth birthday, and his voice was significantly lower save for the words he'd squeaked out for the next few weeks, which had thoroughly embarrassed him.

Governor Lawson had arrived with a sentimental and pride-filled smile that morning, as soon as Governor Haydenshire had called him discreetly from his office.

Rainer's father and Governor Haydenshire had taken Rainer and Logan to breakfast at Lesco's. The talk had lasted through bacon, eggs, and pancakes, then into several milkshakes and ultimately burgers for lunch.

Les, who ran the burger joint, was a dear friend of the Haydenshires and the Lawsons, and he was perfectly willing to let them take up a booth for as long as they needed.

"Em keeping tabs, or are you okay?" Garrett quizzed Rainer with an eye roll. Rainer chuckled at Garrett's disdain over women wanting to know his whereabouts.

"The Angels are doing the photoshoot for the season's programs today, so she'll be in Alexandria for a little while."

"Adeline's working the late shift tonight." Logan sighed.

"Not too many years ago, you refused to sit anywhere near these two, Garrett," Les teased with a kind smile and a twinkle in his eye as he approached their table with his order pad.

"Yeah, but they've gotten way cooler in the last few years."

Rainer and Logan were both secretly pleased with the assessment.

Les chuckled. "What'll it be, boys? You want the usual?" When the Haydenshire boys and Rainer showed up together, Les typically loaded up the table with platters of cheeseburgers, onion rings, fries, and wings, along with milkshakes or pitchers of beer to be shared.

A few years before, Governor and Mrs. Haydenshire had purchased the building that housed Les's Pub. After upgrading Les's kitchen, the Haydenshires had worked a deal with him. In exchange for feeding their family a few times each month, Les didn't have to pay rent.

Governor Haydenshire deeply respected Les and his work ethic. He'd wanted to make certain Les didn't suffer from the economic downturns that often plagued the Non-Gifted Realm. Les was thrilled with the offer, of course, and always served the Haydenshires well.

"Sure, Les, load 'em up, but it's only three of us so don't put yourself out," Garrett instructed.

Les gave Garrett an appreciative smile. Neither side wanted to take advantage of the other in the deal they'd struck.

"You got it." Les returned to the kitchen quickly.

"So what'd Dan tell you, exactly?" Garrett probed. Rainer sensed he thought part of the story might have been left out.

Logan and Rainer shared a quizzical glance.

"That Wretchkinsides killed Amelia, and he couldn't stop him. He watched him do it," Logan managed, but his voice was strained and horrified.

Garrett nodded but didn't add anything else.

Les returned with the food, and they dug in.

Halfway through his second cheeseburger, Rainer's brow furrowed. All of the blood in Garrett's face drained quickly as he dropped his burger back on his plate.

"What the fuck?" He glanced nervously around the restaurant. "Unsnap your holsters, chamber, but don't pull," Garrett commanded quickly.

Stunned disbelief rocked through Rainer as he laid his right hand on his holster and unsnapped his brand-new Glock. He turned toward the door of the pub where Garrett was staring. His mouth fell open as Logan gasped.

They watched in cold-blooded terror as none other than Dominic Wretchkinsides headed their way. His hate-filled, malevolent glare was trained on Rainer.

Rainer's cell phone began playing "I Got You Babe."

"Turn it off," Garrett growled. Wretchkinsides was ten feet away.

"It's Emily," Rainer pled through his teeth.

"If you ever want to see her again, turn it off!"

Rainer sent the call to voice mail.

"Remember, you don't know who he is," was Garrett's last command before Wretchkinsides was upon them.

"Mr. Lawson, I believe..." he drawled in a distinctly foreboding Russian accent.

As he forced himself to breathe, Rainer kept his cool. "I'm sorry, have we met?"

"Well, not officially, of course, but doesn't everyone know who you are?"

Rainer forced a mirthless chuckle to escape his mouth before extending his hand. "And who might you be?"

"Dominic Wretchkinsides," he answered truthfully. "Most people call me Nic. I knew your father, and I believe you know my daughter." Rainer let a quizzical look cross his features.

"Marlisa," Wretchkinsides stated. "I believe you threw her at the Senate Gala a few weeks ago." The challenge was clear in Wretchkinsides's face.

"Ah, was that your daughter?" Rainer let Wretchkinsides know he wasn't going to play. Wretchkinsides simpered but waited on Rainer to continue. "I tend to get defensive when someone summons a heat cast near my fiancée." He let menace leak through every word.

Wretchkinsides gave an evil laugh. "Yes, well, Marlisa has always had a terrible temper. She gets that from me." With that, his face lost all traces of laughter.

Rainer glanced at Garrett, who was steadfastly holding Wretchkinsides's eyes with his own.

"How quaint a little family meal so near the farmstead," Wretchkinsides mocked Garrett. The threat was implicit. He knew everything about them, including where they'd been raised and the Haydenshires' favorite diner.

"Was there something you wanted, Nic?" Garrett asked coolly.

With another mirthless laugh, Wretchkinsides turned his glare back on Rainer.

"Just thought I'd stop in and say hello to Vindico's newest task force members. Tell Daniel I asked about him. Tell him I do hope life is treating him well these days," he drawled repugnantly.

Rainer clenched his jaw.

"Gentlemen." Wretchkinsides gave them a nod as he edged back toward the entrance. "And, Lawson..." he challenged as he tossed a vile grin back at Rainer. He narrowed his eyes. "It's interesting someone so ready to defend his fiancée lets her go off to Alexandria every day completely unprotected."

Rainer's blood suddenly ran cold as his head spun and his lungs begged for air. Wretchkinsides exited the pub.

Rainer stared up at Logan for one endless, horrifying moment.

"Emily," he gasped as they all moved at once.

"Call her and get in my car," Garrett commanded.

They raced out of the diner with Rainer calling Emily's cell and Garrett already on the phone with Dan.

"Call Dad!" Garrett ordered Logan.

They flew into Garrett's Highlander, and he took off.

"She's not answering." Rainer was certain he was being strangled.

He couldn't draw breath. His heart hammered out of rhythm. He couldn't see anything but the black hatred of Dominic Wretchkinsides's malignant glare. His shield flared in terror.

"Dan's on his way. He called out Elite." Garrett tried to sound reassuring, but terror riddled his words.

"Em, it's me… answer… or call me back," Rainer pled to Emily's voice mail.

Traffic was horrendous, and Garrett cursed as he maneuvered through the DC gridlock.

As they flew into the parking deck of Angels Arena, Rainer's heart stopped momentarily as he took in every member of Elite Iodex, all with guns drawn through the haze of blue flashing lights.

After sprinting through the assembled crowd, Rainer shoved two Gifted police officers out of his way. Emily was lying on the ground.

"Emily!" He fell to his knees. "Baby, what happened?"

Governor Haydenshire was standing over her. All of the Angels were gathered behind her and looked terrified. Fionna was seated beside Emily. She'd been casting her.

"Some guys were waiting near her car," she whispered. "There were two other guys trying to break into the arena, and all of the extra security was trying to deal with them. But she felt them, and then I don't know. It was amazing."

"What?" Rainer demanded as Emily fell into his arms sobbing.

"I tried to call you so many times," she convulsed.

Fionna touched her forearm again. She summoned and soothed Emily instantly. Rainer had never seen a more powerful Receiver's cast.

"She threw a shield cast. I've never seen one so strong from a Receiver. It shattered her phone and threw the guy backwards. Are you a Double-Predilect?" Chloe quizzed Emily.

She shook her head before burying her face in Rainer's shoulder.

"Are you okay?" Rainer studied her as he made certain no one had touched her. Vile, heartbreaking revulsion washed over him as the thoughts that had ricocheted in his mind for the past half hour began replaying in vivid detail. She nodded but didn't lift her head from his shoulder.

Vindico was pale and drawn. He looked sickly as he approached.

"Emily, I'm so sorry, but would you mind telling me if you can remember what any of the men looked like?"

Emily leaned away from Rainer as she allowed him to wipe away her tears.

"It was that guy we saw on the boardwalk that day," she informed Rainer through her terror-ridden tears. "The guy with all the snake tattoos."

What little color was in Vindico's face disappeared instantly. He shuddered. "Cascavel," came out in a choked whisper.

Incensed fury lit Governor Haydenshire's features. "Damn it, Daniel," the governor spat. "This will not happen."

"I know, but the only way to stop it is to end them." He squatted down near Emily. "Was he the only one?" His voice sounded distant and frightened.

Emily shook her head. "No, there was one other. He had a suit on and brown hair, but that's all I remember." She shuddered. Rainer pulled her back against him and shook his head at Vindico. He wouldn't allow her to be questioned anymore.

"I, uh,"—Vindico drew a deep breath—"I need you to come back to the office before you go home. We need to talk about how she threw that shield," he whispered so that no one else could hear him.

"I am taking her home," Rainer demanded.

"No, it's okay," Emily immediately placated, but Rainer saw the desperation in her eyes.

"Look, Lawson, I understand, believe me, but we need to talk about this. I can come out to the farm if you'd rather, but we need to talk now."

Rainer studied Emily as he thanked God that she was all right. He nodded his begrudged agreement to Vindico's request.

"Why don't you come out to our new house? I want her at home where she's safe."

"Oh, I'd say she's pretty damn safe wherever she goes, but that's fine," was Vindico's cryptic response.

"He sent the snake," Emily whispered. She was still in visible shock. "What, baby?"

"Just before I threw the shield, he said, 'Lawson isn't here to save you like when you were a little girl.'"

The copperhead. Rainer shook his head, unable to sort through the endless sea of emotions.

The evil, black smoke of the copperhead was from Cascavel. He'd casted the snake. It was his own black energy. That was why the snake that Logan had stumbled upon in the guesthouse hadn't felt evil in any way and had only emitted a white heat. Rainer shuddered and forced himself to focus on Emily alone.

He could hear the conversation he'd had with his father on the way home that night with acrid clarity.

"Your shield wouldn't have reacted that way if it had been me."

"But I love you so much. You're my whole family."

"I know, son. And I love you more than life itself, but...your Shield works on instinct. And your instincts are to protect Emily at all cost."

CHAPTER 58
WITH THIS RING

little while later, Rainer handed Emily a mug of tea and sat beside her on their couch as he cradled her to him again. The time it had taken him to make the tea was the longest he'd gone without having his arms around her since he'd arrived at Angels Arena.

The Governor and Mrs. Haydenshires were standing in the living room, as were Garrett, Logan, Adeline, Connor, and Patrick. The twins were playing on the floor as Vindico paced.

"I really didn't believe it was true," he kept stating in disbelief.

"You didn't believe what was true?" Rainer asked.

"There was a rumor." He shook his head. "It's a legend actually, that the ring you're wearing, Emily, the Lawson family ring, was imbued with promethium. It's inside the rather large diamond there. It's an extremely rare element from deep within the earth's crust," Vindico explained. "The way the ring is formed completes the transference between the wearer and the extreme amount of untapped energy the ring holds," he elaborated as he studied Emily's hand. "When the wearer needs to draw on the energy, it supplies it in ready doses."

"You mean promethium, as in...?" Rainer quizzed in stunned disbelief.

"Nuclear energy." Vindico nodded. "When your mother was killed, people discounted the ring. They said the legend wasn't true or that she would've been able to defend herself. Your dad locked the ring up after her death and it wasn't discussed anymore."

"Okay." Rainer tried to take in everything Vindico was saying. "So if the ring holds all this energy, how did my mother get killed?"

"My best guess is that your mother wasn't a Receiver. She couldn't feel them coming for her the way Emily can. She didn't have time to stop them, but with Emily's extremely strong capabilities to feel black energy, combined with the energy in the ring, I'd say she's about as safe as she could possibly be. But," Vindico shook his head, "you certainly can't play in Summation challenges wearing that ring."

"That's what happened at practice today," Emily gasped. "When my meter kept messing up." Rainer nodded but was still shocked by all he'd just heard.

"But I also don't want to give any credence to the legend," Vindico went on. "Like I said, most people don't believe it's true, and we don't want that ring to become any more valuable to the press or to Wretchkinsides."

Rainer took his hands off of Emily, just long enough to rub his eyes with the heels of his hands before pushing them through his hair.

"So, is she safer with it on or off?"

"Definitely with it on. We just need to have a duplicate made that she could wear for challenges. That way no one will know what we've learned. The ring needs to be with one of you at all times. I think Wretchkinsides may believe the legend, and that's why Pendergrath complimented the ring at Mick's that night."

Rainer's mind reeled. He had almost forgotten Pendergrath's words that night at the restaurant.

Governor Haydenshire had been quietly listening the entire time, but finally he drew a deep breath. "What is the extent of this energy, Dan? What does it do for her exactly?"

"The fact that Emily is a Receiver who can detect dark castings and can transfer all kinds of energy so easily, means that with the sheer amount of energy inside that ring, and her own body's ability to close the transference loop—I really don't believe anyone could touch her, as long as she's wearing it. But she also may not be able to hold that level of energy for any length of time. Obviously, just throwing a shield with it was good enough though."

"My brother, Tad, could duplicate the ring for her," Mrs. Haydenshire finally spoke. Those were the first words she'd uttered since she'd met everyone at the guesthouse and had clung to Emily for several long minutes. She'd forced her from Rainer's grasp.

Tad Anderson was Mrs. Haydenshire's younger brother. Emily and Logan's Uncle Tad was an extremely talented jeweler. He was an Occamy Predilect just like Mrs. Haydenshire. He was, however, one of the only Gifted individuals alive who could lock on to the energy in the atoms of carbon and turn them into diamonds. It was an extraordinary thing to watch.

Rainer had known Tad all of his life. Whenever Tad and his husband Nathan came to the farm, he'd always enjoyed hanging out with them.

Tad and Nathan spent most of their time in New York where they owned a jewelry shop on the Upper East Side. Emily adored her uncles and the jewelry they made. Tad had crafted her several pieces for different occasions.

"But, Lawson," Vindico shook Rainer from his distraction. "Like I told you this afternoon when you agreed to help me with Wretchkinsides, I won't let you live my regrets. If you want to bring her with you to the office when she's not at practice, I have no issue with that. If you want an officer to pick her up after practice, I'll make that happen as well. If you'd like to hire her a private security team, I'll make certain everyone on it is highly skilled and ready for anything." Rainer considered the offer as he locked eyes with Emily for a long moment.

"I, uh," Rainer breathed, "I think we just need a little time to process all of this." Emily nodded her agreement.

"The Sirens, that's the team Wretchkinsides formed today," Vindico reminded Rainer of their discussion at lunch. "They are going to force the Angels to add them to their schedule, probably as the first challenge. This weekend will be the best time to make the trip to New

York. That will be before the Northeast Exhibition and before Summation season challenges begin.

"We'll go Saturday," Rainer assured him.

"I'll keep her safe, Lawson. I swear to you," Vindico vowed. Rainer nodded solemnly as he watched the governor walk Vindico out of the guesthouse.

CHAPTER 59

SUPERGIRL VS. WONDER WOMAN

L ater that evening, Rainer cradled Emily to his chest and wrapped her up in his shield. He pushed away all of the horrible thoughts of what might have happened and focused on feeling her energy as she lay beside him.

"Are you sure you're okay?" he whispered.

"I don't know," she admitted. "I'm trying not to think about it, but I can't seem to stop."

Rainer breathed in the scent of her hair and willed his energy to calm her. She felt him soothe her rhythms, and she closed her eyes and allowed him in. She rapidly consumed everything he passed to her.

When Rainer no longer felt her energy coming in sharp jagged arcs, he posed his idea, "Would you like to spend Saturday night in New York, sweetheart?" He was certain a change of scenery might be the perfect thing for her, and Emily loved New York.

She shrugged. "Maybe. That might be fun." Her sweet smile sealed the deal for Rainer. He mentally planned out a romantic weekend that would get her mind off of the horrors of their day.

"Do you want to come to work with me tomorrow? You could stay with your dad while we're at Felsink." He shuddered. He didn't want to think about visiting the prison with everything that had already happened.

"No," Emily whispered. "I want to go stay at the farmhouse with Mom." Rainer reminded himself that the farm was very safe, and that with the ring on, she was virtually invincible. He didn't argue, but he did intend to immediately find her a security team. Emily trembled slightly as another memory haunted her.

"I've got you, baby. Try to get some sleep."

"Do you promise to hold me?"

"Of course. I won't let you go. I'm right here. I won't let anything happen to you."

After pulling the quilts and blankets around them, Rainer made certain as much of his flesh was pressed to hers as he could. He was then able to push more of his energy through to her. After a little while, he'd finally gotten her to sleep.

She jerked awake a little after midnight with a frantic cry.

"Em." Rainer's heart thundered. "It's okay. I've got you."

Logan burst into the room having heard her terrified scream.

As he clutched his chest and panted for breath, he started to apologize as he realized what was happening.

"It's fine," Rainer assured him. "Emily!" he called louder as he shook her slightly until she was finally free of the nightmare. She clung to him and sobbed as he held her and rocked her.

"I'll make her some tea," Logan offered. He looked devastated as he gazed at his little sister.

"Shh, baby," Rainer soothed. "I'm right here. It was just a nightmare."

As she trembled in his arms, guilt and terror took up residence in his gut. She calmed slightly when Logan handed her the tea. He hesitated, but Rainer gestured to the end of the bed, and he seated himself near Emily's feet.

"Em, baby, I'm just gonna quit. I can't do this to you. This is all my fault."

"Rainer, no." She shuddered as he helped her sip the tea. "You heard Chief Vindico. They can't touch me. It was just a stupid dream," she fumed, but terror swirled in her eyes and fractured Rainer's heart.

Logan shook his head. "I don't think you quitting Iodex would change anything. If it weren't your money they were after, it would be Dad's influence they'd want. They've been after her since she was a kid, remember? Plus, if you quit, you'll have to live off of your inheritance. You'd hate that." He knew Rainer far too well. "And if you get rid of the money, then you'd need a job."

"You're not quitting. I'll be fine," Emily insisted.

"Is everything okay?" Adeline knocked timidly, though the door was open. Logan grinned and beckoned her in.

"Yes, I'm just a weirdo," Emily announced dejectedly.

"That is true, but shockingly enough, he still wants to marry you. So, now you have the...ring of power," Logan announced in his best superhero movie voice. Emily's laughter soothed Rainer's heart. "See, all of those times we made you play superheroes with us growing up, we were really just preparing you for your engagement," Logan continued to harass her.

"Oh, you mean like the time you tried to push me out of the barn loft to see if I could fly?" Emily suddenly sounded much more like herself. The combination of the memory and of Emily's feeling better had Rainer laughing along with her and Logan.

"You tried to push your little sister out of the barn loft?" Adeline shook her head at Logan.

"I was five, and Will caught her before she took flight." Logan smirked. "Hey, we should try that now with the ring. See if you can go all Supergirl."

Everyone laughed as Rainer rolled his eyes. "If you all don't mind, I think I'll try to get Supergirl back to sleep."

"I didn't want to be Supergirl. I wanted to be Wonder Woman," Emily reminded her brother as he began leading Adeline out of their bedroom.

Logan snickered. "Oh, yeah, well, I bet Rainer wishes you were Triplicate Girl."

"Would you get out?" Rainer tried not to laugh but cracked up anyway.

He turned back to Emily and kissed her cheek. "All right, my little Amazon Warrior Princess, why don't we try to get some more sleep before we have to get up and I have to go to work? Then, this weekend, I'm taking you to New York."

She settled down on Rainer's chest, and he folded her up in his arms.

"If you're good, then when we're in New York I might let you take off my magic belt," she teased.

Rainer was delighted she was joking with him again.

"Yum! And think of what we could do with that lasso." He reveled in her sweet laughter.

After falling silent for a few minutes, Rainer wrapped his energy around her and felt her calm as his shield enveloped her.

"I love you so much, and I'm so sorry for everything that happened."

"It wasn't your fault," she reminded him yet again, "and Wonder Woman only had bracelets. I have a ring. I would like a tiara, though." She yawned.

Rainer laughed again. "If you get the tiara, it seems like you should have the whole suit."

She smirked. "Do you think so?"

"It only seems right. What's the crown without the skintight suit? Where would you keep your lasso?" he growled in her ear.

"I'm not sure my rack is up to Wonder Woman's."

Rainer slid his hands over her breasts. "Oh, I heartily disagree."

"Oh really?"

"I do, and I would know because I had a huge crush on Wonder Woman right up until this really smoking hot seven-year-old dared me to kiss her." He cradled Emily closer and brushed a kiss across her cheek in the approximate location of the kiss he'd given her in her parents' backyard when he was eight.

"Aww, you broke up with Wonder Woman for me?"

"Well," he feigned heartbreak. "What Wonder Woman and I had was great and all, and I'm sure she was devastated, but when perfection comes along, you have to go after it."

She gazed up at him with all of the adoration he felt for her. Her added giggle delighted him.

"Plus, you told me when you were five I had to be your boyfriend," he reminded her.

Emily laughed as they both recalled the afternoon in her room when she'd informed Rainer that he was her boyfriend because she said so.

Rainer clung to her and tucked the quilts around them as he soothed her back to sleep.

He had to keep her safe, no matter what that meant. He had to end Wretchkinsides. He would not allow Emily to go on living in terrorizing fear. He shuddered and tried not to recall the hollow, empty, hellish abyss he'd existed in during the endless moments when he hadn't known where she was. He now understood what Dan Vindico lived with each and every day.

The fervent drive took hold of Rainer as he held Emily on his chest.

They would end the Interfeci and protect what his father had fought so hard to establish. He would overcome the impossible odds, live up to the Lawson crest, and he would do it all for her.

ABOUT THE AUTHOR

J.E. Neal (aka Jillian) vastly prefers coffee to tea, guac to salsa, the beach over anywhere else, and the world inside her head over the one outside her front door. She also loves not having to choose.

Driven by the question 'what if,' J.E. Neal's world began to manifest. What if there were people with powers the rest of us couldn't see? What if the energy of our world could be summoned and used at their will? Characters with these amazing abilities took shape in her mind. She created—and continues to create—an endless number of stories full of delicious escape from our reality where emotions are visible, desire is palpable, and danger is universal.

Learn more about J.E. Neal at JillianNeal.com

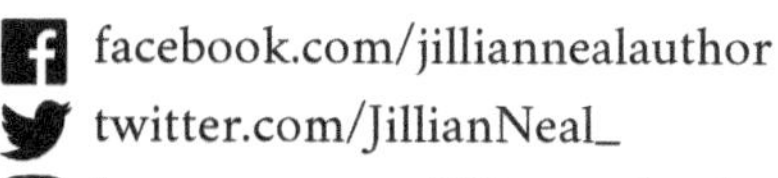

facebook.com/jilliannealauthor

twitter.com/JillianNeal_

instagram.com/jilliannealauthor

ALSO BY J.E. NEAL

ENERGY OF MAGIC

Shield and Shattered Cages (Book 1)

Shield and Faltered Steps (Book 2)

Shield and Splintered Oaths (Book 3)

Shield and Humbled Crown (Book 4)

Shield and Vile Serpents (Book 5)

Shield and Coveted Splendor (Book 6)

Shield and Guarded Shadow (Book 7)

Shield and Worthy Sinner (Book 8)

Shield and Sacrificial Heirs (Book 9)